FROM THE C.
STEVE ROCKFISH - 4

THE BALLAD OF THE GREAT VALUE BOYS

KEN HARRIS

Black Rose Writing | Texas

The author grants the final approval for this literary material.

First printing

This is a work of fiction. Names, characters, businesses, places, events, and incidents are either the products of the author's imagination or used in a fictitious manner. Any resemblance to actual persons, living or dead, or actual events is purely coincidental.

ISBN: 978-1-68513-553-9
PUBLISHED BY BLACK ROSE WRITING
www.blackrosewriting.com

Printed in the United States of America
Suggested Retail Price (SRP) $24.95

The Ballad of the Great Value Boys is printed in font

*As a planet-friendly publisher, Black Rose Writing does its best to eliminate unnecessary waste to reduce paper usage and energy costs, while never compromising the reading experience. As a result, the final word count vs. page count may not meet common expectations.

PRAISE FOR THE BALLAD OF THE GREAT VALUE BOYS

"Prepare for twists, turns, and more than a few laugh-out loud moments in this rollercoaster of a thriller that pits wise-cracking private investigator Steve Rockfish and his band of unlikely cohorts against a right-wing extremist militia group with a dangerous agenda."
–Patti Liszkay, author of *The Equal and Opposite Reactions Trilogy*

"Steve Rockfish is back and kicking militia ass. In fact, the whole crew is back, busting balls as they solve crimes and track down the bad guys. The wisecracks fly fast and furious. So do the twists and turns. The bad guys are badder, the danger more dangerous, and every character as endearing as they are dysfunctional. I couldn't turn the pages fast enough."
–Haris Orkin, award-winning author of *The James Flynn Escapades*

"Great gobs of serious yet hilarious crime-solving by Steve and Jawnie, along with their cast of friends ranging from dependable to what-the-hell-now crazy. Absolutely a fun ride! But I warn you, you'll want to read the entire series tonight."
–Val Conrad, author of *The Julie Madigan Thriller Series*

"This fourth novel in the Rockfish series is the best yet! Harris has written another fast-paced story with hard-hitting action, mounting suspense and delightful, biting humor. Outnumbered and outgunned, Rockfish, McGee and Raffi take on the Great Value Boys, revolutionaries with a violent agenda. With signature bravado fueled by intrepid hearts, they serve up their own distinct brand of justice."
–Rebecca Warner, Amazon Bestselling Author

"If my good friend was missing, I would have gone, too. Rockfish & McGee are up to their elbows in a pseudo-patriotic conspiracy that is a cover for greed, glory hounding, and kidnapping a former police captain. Getting in wasn't easy. Getting out? The only way to do it is Rockfish style. Loud, large, and with friends. I couldn't stop turning the pages and, yes, I want to strangle Raffi."
–TG Wolff, Mysteries to Die For podcast co-creator

For Peter Straub (1943 – 2022)
The author who made the largest impact on my reading
and writing career.
From reading Shadowland as a teen to the multiple re-reads of
The Blue Rose Trilogy – Your words, stories, advice and
occasional reply to my Tweets are greatly missed.

Thanks for the support! - kah

THE BALLAD OF THE GREAT VALUE BOYS

Connie, Thanks for the support & enjoy the Ride

PROLOGUE

The icy January wind cut through Daniel's knock off North Face jacket and the night as if they neither existed. Snow flurries had begun falling a few minutes earlier, and the temperature followed suit. One and two-story brick buildings lining the street of this desolate coal mining town. The storefronts did little to protect Daniel from the elements.

His ride was late. Daniel stood on the corner of Bedford and Ocala as instructed, in front of Scott's Pharmacy and across from Cambria Woodworking. Bedford Street was dark, working streetlamps were few, and the sidewalks had rolled up hours ago. Daniel tried hiding from the cold by squeezing into the pharmacy's small front alcove, but it was only a few seconds before the howling wind found him again.

Daniel had flown into Pittsburgh earlier that afternoon and taken an Uber two hours east. He had contemplated renting a car, but assumed the ride share would leave less of a paper trail if anyone tried to trace his route. He created a fictitious Uber account with a throwaway e-mail address and a debit card purchased from the dark web. These actions would provide Daniel with the cover or eventual head start he might need.

Daniel had no plans to spend the night in Grindsville after the exchange and only carried with him a small backpack. He had booked a return flight to Boston for first thing in the morning and the prior Uber driver was on standby for a cash-heavy and profitable ride back to the airport. The profits from this evening's deal, along with the backpack, would not make the return flight. The cash filled carry-on would remain behind, stuffed in an airport locker for safekeeping. He had no reason to give TSA any opportunity to confiscate it under the Government's current draconian asset forfeiture laws. A black man carrying a large amount of cash? No matter how well rehearsed Daniel's story, the money would never make it past security. At an unidentified point in the future, when any potential law enforcement interest had died down, he would drive back to Pittsburgh and retrieve the funds that would usher his foray into Bitcoin and Forex trading.

A snowy ten minutes later, a pair of headlights lit the street from two blocks away. Daniel's mind rushed back to the matter at hand. The hair on the back of his neck and his extremities stood tall as he moved out from the pharmacy's doorway and down onto the curb. He swallowed hard and for a moment had trouble believing all the internet forum posts, email, and secure messaging had finally led to this moment. He stood and watched a jacked-up Dodge Ram 1500 Crew Cab creep down the opposite side of the street. Daniel raised his hand, and headlights flashed in return. As it drew closer, the noise from the diesel engine almost drowned out the wind. It slowed to a stop on the opposite side of the street. The drivers-side window lowered and a man with XXL jowls and a dark cavalry hat pointed at Daniel. The man ordered him into the idling truck.

Daniel nodded and glanced both ways--despite the hour--before looping around the front of the truck. The wind held the right rear suicide door open. Daniel stepped onto the running board and climbed inside. His eyes cased the inside of the cab, now at full capacity. The two other men, aside from the driver, wore neck gaiters and orange knit caps. Daniel was the only one whose outfit did not contain any type of camouflage pattern.

"Hands up," the man sitting to his left said.

Daniel placed his palms flat against the cab's roof. The man unzipped Daniel's jacket and patted him down.

"Clean." With that word, Cavalry Hat took his foot off the brake, and the truck lurched forward. Despite the vehicle rolling down the street, the driver turned around and glared at Daniel.

"Let's see it," Cavalry Hat said before pivoting back. His eyes returned to the road ahead.

Daniel looked to the truck's rearview mirror, from where Cavalry Hat now stared at him. Then down to the backpack on the floor at his feet. He reached for the zipper and pulled it halfway open before yanking it back shut.

"The money first," Daniel said. His voice was unnaturally deep, not wanting to appear weak. "We had an agreement." He needed to see the cash. *Don't let them play you. This cash will set right so much shit that's gone wrong in your life. Out of debt and never looking back.*

The condensation from Daniel's breath hung in the air. Tiny clouds lingered a few inches in front of his face before dissipating. The sound of a handgun racking followed Daniel's refusal. The noise from the front passenger seat echoed throughout the small, confined space. He had failed in his one attempt to hold his ground. He was outgunned and outmanned. Bravado moved aside, made room, and anxiety arrived front and center.

Daniel's hands shook as he reached down and fully unzipped the backpack. His fingers wrapped around a small, yellow Pelican case, not much larger than an iPhone. He lifted it out and held up for all to see.

"Open it," the man to Daniel's left said.

Cavalry Hat's eyes nodded in agreement from the rearview.

"Can't. Won't," Daniel said. His voice cracked, and he audibly swallowed hard. His mind raced to form a coherent sentence the men would understand and not think was some sort of stall tactic. "The road. Potholes. One of these vials falls out or, worse, breaks open. We all might be in serious shit. You know what this is and know what it's capable of. Not to mention you'd be out of product. We've gone over the potential dangers."

"Alrighty then. A smoother surface at a full stop it is." The agreement from the driver's seat relaxed the tension in the cab, but did nothing for Daniel's increasing anxiety. He bought himself a couple of minutes, at the most, and his hands tightened around the small plastic box. *Shit, I'm too naïve to think I could have made the exchange back on the corner and been waiting on the return ride to the airport.*

Silence filled the inside of the truck until the sound of a turn signal pulsed. The truck turned into a residential shopping center. A sole lit sign, at this late hour, was for a Giant Eagle Supermarket. The truck continued down the row of storefronts and hung another left after the grocery store. Cavalry Hat steered the truck along the lane that ran behind the stores. They inched past dumpsters and loading docks. In this spot, the truck would not draw suspicion from anyone on a late-night grocery run.

Brakes squeaked, and the truck slowed to a stop somewhere behind the Hallmark or Five Below, if Daniel's estimation was correct. Before he realized they had in fact reached their destination, the driver threw the gearshift into park, and the man to Daniel's left pried the pelican case from his hands. Daniel should have expected the man's forced fumble, but his attention had found and focused on a greater threat. The barrel of the racked handgun now pointed out from between the front seats. The firearm's entry into the meeting emphasized a point that Daniel needed to understand. *Come on, get through this. The sooner the better. Don't try anything stupid and no more delay tactics.*

The man to his left flipped the latches on the case and opened the lid. "Looks like it's all here, but we won't know until Clyde can test it." He then closed and secured the small container.

"Well, what are you waiting for?" Cavalry Hat said. "Get."

The drivers-side suicide door swung open, and the man disappeared into the dark. A second later it slammed shut with an assist from the wind.

Daniel's ears caught the sound of all four doors locking over his rapid heartbeat. His sphincter clenched. He understood what little leverage he had on the deal was now exhausted. Long gone and to someone named Clyde. The cab's dome light flickered to life and Daniel continued involuntarily practicing the world's longest kegel exercise. Cavalry Hat twisted and joined the man in the passenger seat, the one holding the gun, staring down Daniel.

"Mr. Sparks, you do not know how glad I am you made it and upheld your end of the bargain."

Daniel stared back. He had a feeling his previously expected outcome, the one that would enable him to corner a small portion of the Bitcoin market, would not come to fruition. He immediately realized all the little things around him. Cavalry Hat's distended belly pushed hard against the steering column. The light from above illuminated off the metal on the front of his hat. Five gold stars stitched into the front in the shape of a cross.

The man in the passenger seat kept silent, with the gun trained between Daniel's eyes. He played Stan Laurel to the driver's Oliver Hardy. A long, wild gray beard stuck out from and through his thin neck gaiter. Clothes hung off his thin frame as if the man had purchased each piece of the outfit sixty or seventy pounds ago.

"We had a deal," Daniel said. He wanted to, needed to, make this work. "You provide me with what's mine and I beat feet back to Pittsburgh. I won't remember a thing about you or this meeting, Mister, er..."

"Names aren't important," Cavalry Hat said. "What you'll want to do here in the next few minutes is convince me those vials are enough to make a boatload of folks violently ill, not kill 'em, right? I need 'em sick and contagious. Not dead and piled like cordwood. Ain't no good to me then."

"That was our agreement," Daniel said. "The vial's contents are as advertised and I've held up my end." He continued to try to hold his composure against the rising fear. "Once introduced into the body, the individual comes within an inch of the line. They may see a bright light, but in the end, they'll recover with little to no lasting side effects. But if the person is elderly, I can't make promises." He shrugged his shoulders with a slight tilt of his head.

"If we lose a few to the cause, so be it," the thin man said. He spoke more to the driver than Daniel. "Martyrs ain't such a bad thing to have and run out from time to time."

"Shut up, Amos," Cavalry Hat said. Daniel watched the man in the passenger seat sink back a few inches. "I didn't ask for comments, but if you feel that way, perhaps we'll test 'em out on your well first."

Daniel's eyes grew wide. The man who had only a few minutes ago said names weren't important, called out his associate. By name. Daniel knew this small bit of identifying information signified bad news. In the matter of three words, the odds of him stepping out of this truck under his own power plummeted. Daniel's right arm shot out and tried the locked door, already knowing the outcome.

Amos wagged an index finger in front of Daniel's face. "Nuh-uh."

BAM

The gunshot echoed through the small cabin. Two sets of ears went numb and the third now lay in chunks across the seat and rear window.

"Ah shit. Colonel, I swear it was an accident. This trigger's always been touchy as shit."

"No excuses. Why the fuck'd you do that?" Cavalry Hat's right arm shot out and smacked Amos upside the head.

"He was trying to run," Amos said. "And I slipped. Told ya, I need to get one of the men to clean this and give it a good once-over."

Cavalry Hat sighed and pinched the bridge of his nose. "The door was locked. Dumbass. He wasn't leaving and now neither one of us is headed home any damn time soon."

"Best drive us deep into the woods and then over to the open-air car wash on Bedford. How many quarters you got?"

CHAPTER ONE

The first month of 2023 for the investigative partners at Rockfish
& McGee was uneventful, compared to the latter half of 2022,
which found them battling mob families from two separate cities.
While Rockfish and Jawnie enjoyed the quiet month of January,
Annetta Provolone, the first female head of the South Jersey
Provolone crime family, killed time making grilled cheese
sandwiches on a radiator at the Federal Correctional Institute in
Brockton Mills, West Virginia. Angelo Marini, the Boss of Baltimore,
remained in federal custody awaiting the start of his RICO trial. His
high-priced   lawyers   had   successfully   lobbied   for   one
postponement after another.

   Steve Rockfish, senior partner in the firm and age, was for the
first time, in which he could remember, enjoying the lull in clients
and cases. His usual demand for hard-hitting investigations
lessened with each sudden, aching change in the weather. Cold,
rain, and dampness. Each caused his left arm to throb a little more
from where the bullet, fired by a Provolone soldier months earlier,
had passed through. His bones and muscles didn't bounce back like
they once did, and Rockfish slowly understood time off did a body
good. Not to mention it was Raven's playoff time, and he was damn
sure Lamar was going to lead the boys to their third Lombardi
Trophy.

   Jawnie McGee, fresh off testimony in one trial, stared at her
calendar and reluctantly counted the days until the prosecution
called upon her for the second round of judicial proceedings. It

didn't matter if it was the one on her desk, refrigerator or trusty iPhone. To her, the lull had the complete opposite effect than on her partner. Free time enabled those far away in prison to reach dark crevices in the back of her mind to run wild. The anxiety intermixed with words Rockfish had passed on after the first case they had worked together. *It never ends, kid. There's always someone who feels the need for retribution in order to impress. Doesn't matter if it's IBM, Jim's Corner Deli or Cosa Nostra. Someone wants, no, needs, to climb the company ladder.* She hoped the pink Glock 19 and recently gained concealed carry permit would prevent her from relying on kicks to the groin and roundhouse rights to hold those potential climbers at bay.

Lynn Hurricane-Tesla, the firm's only other employee, excelled at running the office's day-to-day administrative duties. She continued to emerge slowly from the PTSD-shell she had retreated to, via the abuse suffered from the Earl Porbeagle case. She had found it therapeutic to work through these same issues with filming the second season of Rockfish and Jawnie's NikolaTV docuseries, which covered that investigation. Lynn had even volunteered for minor tasks outside the confines of the office, and it thrilled the partners to have her back lending a helping hand in the field, no matter how small or far between.

Raphael "Raffi" Pérez, Rockfish's long-time friend, part-time confidential informant, and full-time scam artist was more than willing to recount, to anyone who wanted to hear and some that didn't, the epic show down off the coast of New Jersey with a handful of mafioso. He and Rockfish had come out on top, but to hear him tell it, it was Raffi that single-handedly laid the smack down. He prayed for the partners and their producer to green light a third season. One where he would have a more prominent role, unlike the second where his work had mostly ended up on the cutting room floor and Lynn had received a good portion of screen time.

Their show was the highest rated quasi-reality show on Elon Musk's NikolaTV, and their producer, Angel Davenport, couldn't be happier. The second season focused on Earl Porbeagle and the Church of the Universal Nurturing II investigation. The network had scheduled the premier for the first week of February. Rockfish remained sort of angry over the network's veto of his suggestion to title the eight-episode run, *See You Next Tuesday*.

Mack Rockfish, Steve's father, continued to be the rock that kept his son grounded, and the entire crew well fed. Age hadn't stopped Mack from offering nuggets of advice, most of which came from police procedural docuseries on DiscoveryID, which took up most of his afternoon and evenings. Television and caring for his eighteen-month-old black Labrador, Zippy wasn't a bad way to do retirement.

Steve's baby, affectionately known as Lana, continued to wake the neighbors when he used the remote start. The Dodge Challenger Hellcat and its 717 horsepower sounded better but looked as sweet as the original. The previous Challenger now sat in the backyard, crushed into a block measuring three-and-a-half-feet high, two-feet wide and four-feet long. On many nights, Steve would drag a chair down off the deck in order to fill her in on all she's missed.

Little did anyone know that Raffi's latest get rich scheme would soon bring an end to the peace and quiet.

* * * * * * * * *

You've reached Rockfish & McGee, Investigative Specialists. At the tone, leave your name and message. Someone will get back to you at our earliest convenience. [Beep]

"Steve, why don't you ever answer your cell? I'm in deep shit here and you are my one call. Grindsville. Somewhere in Pennsylvania, heading west. The locals have me locked up on a trumped-up charge. You gotta believe me, Steve. I didn't do a damn thing..."

The partners stood around Lynn's desk and listened to the voicemail, left the previous evening. Their administrative assistant had heard Raffi's plea for help first, and immediately reached out to Rockfish and Jawnie to advise of a friend of the office's predicament.

"I'm guessing you didn't pick up his call yesterday?" Jawnie said, with a perturbed look on her face.

"Would you want to talk to Raffi every time he calls?" Rockfish said, raising his own eyebrows. "Plus, I didn't know it was him. The notification came up, Unknown Caller, and I forwarded it to the office line. I assumed it was spam, figured we'd listen and handle it on Monday. And well, here we are. Plus, I didn't want to mute the television. It was that new Marvel movie, *Hawkgirl Takes Topeka*."

"DC Universe, but I totally get where you're coming from," Jawnie said with a grin. "Too bad it wasn't a scammer halfway around the world calling regarding our Medicare benefits."

"If I was his only call, then he's expecting me to come up there and bail him out. Where the hell is Grindsville, anyway?"

"Central Pennsylvania, Boss," Lynn said. She glanced up from her computer at Jawnie and Rockfish, standing on the other side. "Two hours east of Pittsburgh. What do you think he did?"

"You heard as much of that rambling message as I did. Lord knows what type of scheme he had in mind and was trying to run on the rural bumpkins," Rockfish said. He stepped back into the office's bullpen area before slumping into his favorite recliner. *This is the last damn thing I need today. The Andrist case keeps raising its ugly head and I don't have the time to handle two problem children at once. Where is my morning coffee?*

"Steve, you know as well as I do Raffi's outgoing voicemail message changes with each money-making opportunity," Jawnie said. He hadn't noticed she followed him and had taken up her normal seat on the couch, laptop open and at the ready. "Might as well dial and listen. It might give you a leg up on what you're facing in Grindsville. Assuming you're going and someone powered down his phone. It's probably in an evidence storage locker. The call should go straight to voicemail. If you're considering following up on this."

"You know as well as I do, I can't leave him hanging," Rockfish said. "Google says it's anywhere between three and four hours to get there as the Lana flies. If I can get out of here before noon, I might have him sprung by dinner." He shifted his body in the chair and turned toward Lynn's desk. "Lynn, let's hear it."

"Speed dial four on speaker. Gimme a sec."

Rockfish and Jawnie got up and stood around Lynn's desk. They both leaned across and listened as the number rang once and rolled over to voicemail.

"Hello, you've reached the desk of Raphael Pérez, President of Patriot Meals on American Made Wheels. Please visit our website, www.Q-Rations.biz for orders and to view our FAQ. Please leave a message and a true patriot will get back to you shortly. God Bless."

"He's catering to the insurrectionists, isn't he?" Jawnie said. The concern in her face was clear, and Rockfish wasn't sure how to answer. He chose his words carefully. Raffi was a friend.

What am I going to tell her she already doesn't know? The guy will do practically anything to make a buck, no matter the gray area involved. Social, political or moral issue be damned. That's Raffi.

"Jawnie, we've all got parts of us that aren't the most desirable. Hell, look at me. Who the fuck in their right mind would want to be associated with me?"

"Are you implying I'm not in my right mind?"

"Yeah, me too," Lynn said. "Shots fired, Steve."

Rockfish walked back to his chair and stood behind it, elbows resting on the back. "That's damn well not what I meant, and you both know it."

Both women cracked smiles, and Rockfish relaxed for a minute before continuing.

"We all know he straddles that line, but I've known him longer than either of you two. The man's in it for the money. Nothing more, nothing less. Let me go figure out what kind of mess he's gotten himself into and we can revisit adjusting his moral compass when I get back."

Rockfish poured himself a cup of coffee. *I'll need more than this tonight after I sweet-talk his ass out of jail. Might as well stop at the liquor store before making the drive. Hotel bar drinks are on the expensive side. Shop for a happy ending and will it into existence.*

"I'm headed back to my office. Try to figure out my next couple of moves and exactly what he was doing up in the middle of nowhere." He turned and walked down the short hallway to his private office.

Once out of the sight of prying eyes, Rockfish finished constructing his homemade Irish coffee and turned on his monitor. *I need to figure this mess out. The sooner the better. Patriot Meals on American Wheels and something about rations.* Since the Porbeagle case, Raffi usually focused his semi-legitimate business opportunities on the bumpkins he felt he could run circles around intelligence-wise. Especially should any part of his half-assed plans go sideways. *Only makes sense he zeroed on those who continue to celebrate January 6th. Best to start researching with his website and gather what I can.*

Rockfish picked up his desk phone and dialed Raffi's cell again. He jotted down the URL on a pink Post-it and stuck it to the bottom of his monitor. *I need to talk to Lynn. We need good old-fashioned yellow ones. At least for me.*

His fingers tapped out the web address and Rockfish paused as his pinky hovered over the return key. *Do I really want to know? Can't I drive up there with a credit card and pay the fine or whatever percentage of his bail the bondsman requires? You should know this already. The less you know about the man's shenanigans, the better. No chance of being sucked into the Raffi vortex.*

Curiosity won out and the Q-Rations.biz website filled the screen.

In the years since Jawnie had arrived on scene, Rockfish now had more experience with the Information Super Highway. While he wasn't on her level, even he had to question the design of Raffi's cracker-jack website. *Looks like a site a middle school kid made in 1998. I can almost hear the dial-up modem noise.*

The top of the page read *Q-Rations* against a black background, the letters alternating between red, white, and blue. The image flickered every couple of seconds. *How many patriots had visited the site with full intentions to buy this shit but suffered a seizure before navigating to their shopping cart?* Under the image was the slogan from the voicemail, *Patriot Meals on American Made Wheels.* What really caught Rockfish's attention was the picture directly to the right of the bit of jingoism. Raffi stood at attention, dressed in what Rockfish thought was George C. Scott's uniform from the opening scene in *Patton.* His right hand cocked and saluting.

The set of balls on this guy, but give him credit, he knows his audience. Pander to them until they open their wallets and then turn the grift up a few more notches.

The rest of the site's front page laid out a story full of fear mongering and catered to the benefits of hoarding Q-Rations. Each meal would be priceless once Hillary Clinton, the newly appointed Biden Gun-Czar, came a knocking on your door. Think the supply chain is fucked six ways to Sunday now? Wait until George Soros declares martial law. *Repackaged MREs? How did he come up with this idea?* Rockfish imagined the interest and rising demand. He wondered where Raffi would or had gotten his supply from. *He ain't cooking and packaging this shit in the basement of his townhome.*

The rest of the page detailed the different options of Q-Rations available for purchase, but Rockfish had seen and read enough. He moved his mouse over to the top of the browser and printed the page, before hollering down the hallway to where Lynn and Jawnie continued to talk.

"Lynn, can you use that webcrawly thing and download me a copy of Raffi's entire website?" Rockfish said. "Chuck it on a USB along with the prison voicemail, and I'll take it with me. I'm not sure what kind of internet I'll have out in the mountains of West Central Pennsylvania."

"Gotcha, Boss. I'm on it," Lynn said.

"You're a lifesaver." Rockfish smiled to himself and heard a light knock. He glanced up to see Jawnie standing in the open doorway.

"You're going this alone? There's something to be said about going lone wolf in that area of the country, if you know what I mean. Plus, I don't have the time to find a good-looking shot for when the milk container people call for your missing person picture."

"I get it, but he's my friend, and occasional support to this office," Rockfish said with a shrug. "Listen, I'll run up there, grab a hotel, pay his fine and come back with him riding shotgun in the morning. Worst case, it's bail money instead of a fine, but at least he'll be back on the street and owe me one."

Jawnie shifted her weight from one leg to the other and leaned against the door frame with her arms crossed. Rockfish understood his reasoning, hadn't fully sold his partner on the trip. In fact, Rockfish had lost count of exactly how many favors Raffi currently owed him.

"I can see you still don't think it's a grand plan. But if you come, who's going to stay here and handle Andrist? I mean, I love he keeps hiring us, but that man is a handful and I can't, in good faith, ask Lynn to deal with him on an almost daily basis." Rockfish saw this line of reasoning was an easier sell by Jawnie's nod and expression.

"He is our best client at the moment," Jawnie said. "Best paying, too."

"Coddle him. Hold his meetings at arm's length. Do whatever you need. I'll be back before noon tomorrow and be on my phone at all times," Rockfish said. He stood up and grabbed his messenger bag and laptop.

"You're leaving right this instant?"

"Yeah, I need to swing by Bass Pro Shops and pick up a few camo shirts, knit hat and a jacket. It'll be pretty cold up there and I'll blend in better. In small towns like this, the natives are restless. Just tryin' to prevent any kind of run-in."

"Better grab one of Mack's old trucker hats and by all means, don't shave," Jawnie said and stepped back out of the doorway.

Rockfish paused and held out his fist and Jawnie bumped it. He picked up the USB from Lynn on his way out the door and auto-started Lana before stepping out into the February cold.

* * * * * * * * *

The snow had fallen steadily throughout Rockfish's trip up the mountain range and down the other side. The further he drove into central Pennsylvania, the heavier it fell. He had always prided himself on using the right tool for the job, but in this case, Lana's rear-wheel drive was far from optimal. *I can't believe I didn't check the damn weather app before hauling ass onto the highway. Jawnie's Subaru wouldn't have me running almost two hours behind schedule.*

By the time Lana literally slid across Grindsville city limits, the sun had set. The late hour had Rockfish debating calling an audible on his plans. He headed straight for the police station instead of checking into the hotel. He could check in anytime, but the visiting hours at the police department would end soon, if they hadn't already. Seeing Raffi and getting his side of the story was an absolute must. If not, he would most likely have to wait until Monday. He wouldn't let that kind of delay happen and had a contingency plan to cut through the bureaucratic red tape. Afterwards, he'd check-in at the Holiday Inn and find a place to eat.

The town of Grindsville had seen better times. Set in a valley that curved along the Penrod River, the city once served as the bustling center of commerce for the steel and coal industries. Except the previous five decades had hit the city hard. A double whammy of mill closures and children growing up with dreams of escaping a dying town immediately after graduation had caused a severe economic downturn. All that was left? A declining population of blue-hairs and not much of a tax base to keep Main Street from boarded-up storefronts and vagrants.

Rockfish street-parked in front of the Grindsville Police Department. The brick building appeared more like a bank, and he double checked the sign over the door. *Right place. Probably moved here after a city inspector declared their previous building unsafe.* He jumped out of the car and, despite the slippery conditions, jogged up the steps to the front door. Rockfish stepped inside and brushed the snow from his hair and shoulders before glancing around.

The inside of the building resembled a small local bank branch. The lone officer sat behind the glass as if he was the sole teller on duty. A handful of chairs sat to Rockfish's left, where the public would sit and wait for a banker to introduce himself and then beg for a loan, but in this case an officer would take a report of stolen power tools. *I betcha meth is an enormous problem up here. Can't be much other in the way of crime. And what there is can all be traced back to Billy-Bob. Too dumb to use a free public education to escape and make a better life. What little smarts he and his cronies had were put toward a failed bathtub meth business.*

Rockfish approached the window and the officer on duty never picked his eyes up off the newspaper spread across the countertop. He cleared his throat, and the man raised his head.

"Can I help you, Sir? If you have a crime to report, please have a seat over there. Someone will be out to speak with you shortly. If this is an emergency, please call 9-1-1."

Rockfish shook his head at the man's words. *Sounds more like a script. A call center of one. Either he ain't the brightest or it's the end of shift. Whichever, I'm thanking my lucky stars.*

"Officer Sobotka, is it?" Rockfish said, reading the man's name tag. "I'm here regarding one Raphael Pérez. I understand he's in your jail and I'd like to speak with him if possible." He went with the forward, truthful approach and kept his ace in the hole close.

Sobotka stared back from behind the glass. His posture wasn't good, and he bent forward despite taking his eyes off the newspaper and rolling his chair back. Rockfish noticed the man's beady, little blue eyes. They gave him the creeps. Rockfish guessed with the tiresome look, lack of customer service and large bags under his eyes. The man was possibly on the tail end of a double shift. *A little more in my favor.* Rockfish smiled on the inside.

"I'm sorry. Visiting hours ended forty minutes ago," Sobotka said. His eyes shifted back to the paper.

Rockfish dug into his breast pocket and pulled out a pre-printed business card he snagged before leaving the office. He had different versions printed for every occasion. He slid the card under the glass before beginning his own well-rehearsed spiel. One that had opened many a door in the past.

"Officer, I'm James Taggert, Attorney at Law and I represent Mr. Pérez. I'd appreciate it if you'd give me a few minutes with my client. I understand it is late on a Friday afternoon and the Cracker Barrel is calling. But the weather delayed me and I owe the man the best defense money can buy. By the way, can I get a copy of the arrest report? You understand, for my records. If not discovery purposes." Rockfish's smile was wide as his eyes.

Sobotka glanced up and moved his attention to the computer on his left. He swiveled his chair and half-a-dozen key strokes later, Rockfish heard the printer fire up. Sobotka handed him a single sheet of paper.

"That's all I have access to at the moment, Mr. Taggert. Like I said before, visiting hours are long over, but if you're his attorney,

I can give you ten minutes. After that, you'll need to leave as we'll be in the middle of shift change. You can come back Monday morning before his arraignment."

"Understood," Rockfish said, thanking his lucky stars.

"I'll buzz you through the door over there." Sobotka pointed to a door on the far side of the room.

Rockfish folded the printout without reading it. He slid it into his jacket pocket and headed toward the door.

"Once I buzz you through, second door on your right. Grab a seat and I'll have one of the deputies bring the prisoner around."

Rockfish pulled on the door handle when he heard the lock disengage, and stepped into a short hallway.

* * * * * * * * * *

The small visitor room was painted an off-white. Paint chips littered the floor and cracked under Rockfish's shoes. Two chairs faced each other, separated by glass and a corresponding doorway directly across from the one Rockfish had entered through. He sat down and waited. Ten minutes later, another buzz filled the room. The opposite door swung open, and Raffi shuffled in. Rockfish took in his friend, hands cuffed in front. Raffi raised his eyebrows at Rockfish, and he nodded in return. The officer exited and left the two men alone.

Raffi wore a pink jumpsuit with "Grindsville Jail" stitched across the front like a baseball jersey. His hair, usually worn in a wild afro that would make the patrons at Studio 54 jealous, was flat and matted against his head. The bags under his eyes rivaled Sobotka's in terms of dark color and size. This was the first time in a long while Rockfish had seen his friend not dressed to the nines in his signature three-piece suit. The look of defeat weighed heavily on Raffi's face.

Rockfish gazed to his left and then right for the standard telephone receiver. He came up empty and noticed that the glass partition did not extend all the way to the ceiling. It ended after roughly six feet. Their voices would drift over the partition and bounce off the walls. *I guess it's easier to eavesdrop on what we said instead of spending money to tap the hard line.*

Raffi tapped on the glass to catch Rockfish's attention and placed his palm flat against it. The sound brought Rockfish's attention back to the matter at hand. He looked at Raffi's gesture and shook his head.

"Cut the shit, Raffi," Rockfish said. "You called, and I got here as fast as I could. The guy at the front desk said we'd only have a few minutes and then I need to go, because of a shift change or some bullshit. Speaking of, if anyone asks, I'm your lawyer." *Yup, let's hope no one's listening in after that slip up.*

"Steve, you gotta get me out of here. There's a big score waiting for me a few hours further west and if I don't get a hold of my contact soon, I'll lose it all." Raffi's face appeared as if a dozen different emotions battled for control. Sadness, anger and desperation appeared to have the inside track. "I stand the chance of losing a serious payday the longer I stay locked up on this bullshit charge." He slammed both hands down on the small shelf at the bottom of the glass.

"Listen, Raffi, I didn't battle snowmageddon and almost bite it a few times coming down this side of the mountain to listen to you whine about your latest money-making venture. I heard your outgoing message. I think I know all I need to," Rockfish said and folded his arms. "Plenty of time for that later. I need to understand why you're in here. Your version, I have theirs right here." He pulled the paper from his jacket pocket.

"Man, I got set up."

"Oh, really?"

"I'm not bullshitting you, Steve," Raffi said. His eyes were wide as saucers. "I was only trying to drive through this podunk town. Nothing more. The truck started sputtering, and she finally gave out on this crappy two lane road as soon as I passed the *Welcome to Grindsville* sign. I sat there, no heat, no cell service and freezing my ass off."

"You have a truck?"

"Had. An old white box truck. I know, not exactly trying to fly under the radar, but I swear I'm legitimate here. You got to believe me. I borrowed it from Marvin and may have dropped your name."

Rockfish shook his head. Marvin Trotter was an old friend and owner of Baltimore Pike Motors. Marvin had gone through a not so messy divorce, thanks to Rockfish's investigative prowess. Trotter was always happy to lend a nondescript vehicle out for a day or two when the case called for wheels less flashy than a Challenger Hellcat.

"We'll deal with that line stepping later," Rockfish said. "You broke down. Big deal. You had to do something to draw the attention of Grindsville's finest?"

"What did I do? I'm DWL. Driving While Latino. I'm here in the middle of what looks like Appalachia with a broken down old white box truck. Three guesses on what I seem to be to them."

"A Mexican cartel dude."

"Exactly. I'm standing on the bumper, shivering with the hood open and staring at the engine like I had a clue what I was doing," Raffi said. His voice cracked as if he was pleading for Rockfish to believe him. "Next thing I know, this cruiser rolls up, and the cop asks a lot of questions. Not one was if I needed a tow. You know the deal. This young, 'roided up kid, fresh off a dishonorable discharge and academy graduation, was dying to get the drug-sniffing dog on the scene. He hoped for any excuse to slide the back door open and start rifling through my shit."

"You're Q-Rations, I'm assuming?"

"Yup. You listened. Did you check out the website? This one is going to be THE one, Steve."

Rockfish saw the twinkle reappear in Raffi's eye, even if it was for a moment. He was happiest when a plan came together. As quickly as it appeared, it faded out, and he continued.

"Another clown arrived and led the dog around the truck. Of course, the mutt sat down right next to the rear bumper. Indication, my ass. The cop takes the key from me, rolls up the door and immediately thinks I'm transporting a thousand kilos to muscle in on the local drug market."

"No drugs?" Rockfish raised his eyebrows and tilted his head. He needed the truth from his friend in case this MRE deal was a front for something larger. Dirtier. Rockfish didn't believe so, based on what he heard so far and with Raffi's body language, but he had to ask.

"Not even a roach in the ashtray. That's how old this damn truck was. I should have thrown Marvin a few bucks when I dropped your name for a newer model, and I wouldn't be in this damn mess. But when the cop's field test failed, they still couldn't look past their picture on the front of the newspaper. Next thing you know, I'm in the back of the cruiser and a tow truck arrives to cart my inventory back for further investigation and more detailed testing." Raffi lowered his head into his hands and kept speaking. "You gotta help me, buddy. I can almost see them dumping leftovers from the back of the evidence vault into the bed of my truck. Snap a few new pictures and some goober is going to win Cop of the Year."

"First of all, head up," Rockfish said. "If you're clean, you have nothing to worry about. Even if this place is like a bizzarro Mayberry. Come Monday, someone will realize they don't have shit. You'll be let go and we can get out of here. Speaking of, I'm about to get kicked out." Rockfish said, glancing at the gigantic clock on the wall. He leaned in closer toward the glass. "Remember James Taggert, Esquire, if anyone asks. I'll be here on Monday. I've got a credit card to cover any towing or other expenses they try to dump on you. Check that. Not try, but will. This smells like a moneymaking venture for a dying town. Sit tight and I'll see you Monday. Trust me."

Rockfish stood up, and the buzzers for both doors rang. He opened his and turned to watch Raffi be escorted back to his cell. His friend peered over his shoulder. Raffi didn't mouth a word, but his eyes said it all.

I gotcha buddy. We'll head south come Monday. You can bet on it. Might have to sacrifice the truck and those shitty MREs, but I can sweet talk Marvin out of charging Raffi over a broken-down engine. And I could give a fuck about the survival meals. Not my scheme, not my problem. I'm here to get you back home in one piece.

The storm had grown more intense during his short time inside, and no one had bothered to shovel the front of the building. Rockfish inched down the snow-covered steps. The last thing he wanted was to fall ass over elbows and end up in the hospital. *Probably have to life flight me to Pittsburgh.*

Snow covered the car and the most recent plowing had thrown eight inches of compacted ice and snow around Lana's exterior. Rockfish made the command decision to leave her street parked and instead walk the three blocks to the Holiday Inn. *I'll come back for you in the morning, girl. Don't worry.*

Rockfish grabbed his bags from the trunk. He locked the doors and trudged off toward the large green neon sign.

CHAPTER TWO

Rockfish woke early on Saturday morning to the sun's early rays shining through the window. He cursed his surroundings and stupidity. If he had a dollar for every time drunk Rockfish forgot to close the blinds before collapsing into bed, he wouldn't need this job, or the reality docuseries. He squinted and glanced at the circa 1992 clock radio on the nightstand. The red LED numbers stared back. Seven thirty-two, a.m. Breakfast started an hour ago and cups of serious coffee were on his agenda. But first, he needed to close the blinds. *Better late than never. On second thought, throw on clean clothes, grab a jacket and go check on your girl. Make sure she wasn't taken out by a drunk Mr. Plow.*

Rockfish walked over to the window and closed the blinds. He picked up yesterday's clothes off the floor and dressed. He exited the room, and the elevator took him down to the lobby. He glanced over at the small restaurant area where twelve hours previously, he had befriended Larry the bartender. Despite stopping at the liquor store on the drive in to save a buck over high priced hotel drinks, Rockfish wanted genuine conversation after dealing with Raffi and a local dinner of pierogies and cabbage.

The space off to the side of the lobby had flipped an hour ago into a continental breakfast bar with a waffle station. Danish, fruit and small cereal boxes lined the table. A stale coffee smell wafted out into the lobby. Rockfish's head ached from Larry's heavy pours. With each drink, Rockfish had complained more about the town and how he felt the local police were railroading his friend. It wasn't until he had bought Larry the third shot of the night that the man on the other side of the bar opened up. He all but confirmed Rockfish's assumptions. Chatty Larry had spoken of a dying city, yearly budget deficits and a police force that was more than willing to flex its muscle to help make up for a declining tax base. Rockfish had thought aloud that anyone, at some point, would have reported this to the Attorney General's office or even the Feds. Larry lowered his voice and confirmed the FBI had been out a couple of years ago to investigate accusations of corruption and shake downs, but as far as he knew, nothing ever came of it. His opinion was the locals had probably cut the FBI in on the grift.

The morning wind whipped straight through Rockfish as the sliding glass doors closed behind him. The snow had stopped in the early morning hours, but the temperature seemed to have continued to drop. *At least someone got up and shoveled the sidewalks. The streets, too, by the looks of things.* He turned right at the corner and retraced his steps from the previous evening. Fresh snow mixed with red brick and the filthy concrete of the city's skyline. The sun's rays ricocheted off all that was white, causing Rockfish to curse that he had forgotten his sunglasses in the car. He squinted in the general direction of the police station but couldn't make out the shape of his car parked out front. *She should stand out against all this white. I'm coming girl. Don't tell me a city employee towed her to make a buck. Shit, did I overlook a no parking sign?* He picked up the pace and a few minutes later, made out an enormous pile of snow where he had left Lana.

Rockfish crossed the street. He took an ungloved hand and dug through the eight inches until he hit the passenger side window. The maintenance workers had earned their overtime last night and completely plowed her in. And made a few extra passes for shits and giggles. *Fuck. The street's clear, but how the hell am I going to get her out? Is there a mom-and-pop hardware store anywhere around? Maybe I can borrow a shovel from the hotel. No fucking way I'm doing this with my bare hands. And I'm not walking up those stairs to inquire on a loaner shovel.* Rockfish pulled out his phone and checked the weather app. The day's temperature would stay well below freezing for the foreseeable future. *Oh goodie, another storm coming Monday afternoon. There goes the idea of sitting back and waiting for the sun to do its job.*

Ten minutes of consternation later, Rockfish gave up and walked back to the Holiday Inn. Once in the lobby, he stomped the snow from his shoes. He moved across the floor to where breakfast was in full swing. He filled a coffee cup and took up the same stool from last night. *I'll need food too before I go see about finding a shovel. But caffeine and warmth above all else in the meantime.*

Rockfish reflected on yesterday's meeting with Raffi for the tenth time since he had exited the police station. He didn't share his friend's paranoia over the entire situation, even with Larry's allegations. *If Raffi says the truck's clean, then why shouldn't I believe him? Because he's ridden that line between truth and fiction way too many times with you? As long as I've known him, he's never dabbled in dope. Not even counterfeit baby aspirin. No reason to start now when it appears he's got a good thing going with the prepper food scam. No law against hauling near expired MREs across state lines. He needs to pay, or should I say, I need to pay whatever fine they levy on him and run back to Baltimore without looking back. I'm sure no one on that force is trying to plant evidence. Larry spoke of ticky-tack fines, but no major frame jobs. Get over it, Raffi, and keep your mouth shut come Monday with the judge.* Rockfish hoped they wouldn't impound the truck over a minor violation. Then he would have to deal with Marvin as well. He had a feeling Raffi would be hard to locate when it came time to explain to Marvin what exactly happened on the trip and where exactly the truck was now parked.

Rockfish sipped his coffee and ignored the waffle maker for the time being. The station appeared to be a few breakfast rushes past due for a cleaning. Too many remnants from waffles long gone by were stuck to the sides and base. He chose a different route of a banana and oatmeal, followed by a second, then a third cup of coffee. At that point, he felt energized enough to ask the man behind the front desk about borrowing a shovel.

The front desk clerk led Rockfish over to a small closet and handed him a red plastic snow shovel with a wooden handle.

Rockfish thanked him and handed the man a fiver. He then zipped up his jacket, cursed himself again for only talking a good game regarding a stop at the Bass Pro Shops on the drive up. He shook his head and waded back into the cold.

He was less than a block from the hotel when the chirp of a siren spun him around. A police cruiser had pulled up alongside and came to a stop. Rockfish glanced over his left shoulder as the passenger side window lowered. He turned and crouched down. *Those crappy pinhole eyes again. Sobotka. Why am I not surprised? What the fuck does he want? Maybe something happened to Raffi? Nah, they would have called. Dude has my card.*

"Officer Sobotka, to what do I owe the honor? I need a hand digging out my car. You look like you got muscles."

Sobotka leaned across the passenger seat and locked eyes. Rockfish did not like the man's nonverbal response. Nor that he wasn't in uniform.

"Good morning, Mr. Rockfish. I'd like to ask you a few questions."

"Jig's up, huh?" Rockfish said. He felt his face flush and the pit of his stomach flop. *Gets no easier when you're found out. I thought it would take them at least until Monday.*

"Yeah, why don't you jump in here with me and get out of the cold? We need to get a few things straight. Don't worry about your car. It's been dug out and transported down to the impound yard."

FUCK!

Rockfish slid the hotel's shovel across the backseat and then got into the cruiser's passenger seat.

* * * * * * * * *

Saturday night found Jawnie fully enjoying her day off with her friends Lynn, Kara, and Pilar. Rockfish, potential office problems, and Monday morning emails were the furthest thing from her mind as she ordered another Cucumber Gin Martini.

The friends, a coworker and two former clients, had agreed to meet up out by BWI Airport at what was once Rockfish's favorite gentlemen's club. The Bounce House had rebranded six months ago as Hibbleton's Hideaway, the hottest ladies only club in Anne Arundel County. It quickly became their go-to spot, no longer having to drive all the way to downtown Baltimore. While it wasn't exactly Lynn's scene, the combination of food, drinks, music and close friends made her a willing fourth wheel and Jawnie wouldn't have it any other way.

Despite the sun setting on a chilly February afternoon, the foursome sat outdoors on Hibbleton's well heated patio. Encased in plastic with LED patio lights that pulsed and changed color with the music, the outdoor space was private because most patrons remained inside. The ladies were carefree, happy hour drinks in hand and appetizers on order. The small patio dance floor called Jawnie's name as the DJ hit all the right notes, but the strength of her previous martini gave her cause to sit this one out. She remained seated and watched the other three cut a rug and a half.

Life is good. The business is booming. I love these girls and love that Lynn's comfortable hanging out with us now. Especially with the energy she brings to the group and the dance floor. All the above played a major role in the lessening of her anxiety, and how she handled it when certain situations caused it to rear its ugly head.

When the song ended, the others moved back to their seats. At the same time, a table full of appetizers arrived. Jawnie reached for a piece of naan and dipped it into the slow roasted tomato hummus. The conversation picked up right where it left off before the dance floor had called. Pilar lifted her glass.

"Ladies, a toast."

"What's the occasion?" Lynn said and picked up her pint glass.

"Girls' night out?" Kara said.

"Obviously! And us finally finding a trustworthy assistant manager for Guardian Angels," Pilar said. "We can get out and enjoy weekends again!"

"Let us not forget last week's back-to-back episodes premiere," Jawnie said. "The VP over at NikolaTV said the second season's initial ratings are higher than the first. Porbeagle's a hit. People seem to love white trash biker types." She raised her glass for a second toast but noticed Lynn's half-hearted effort to reciprocate.

"I'm sorry to bring him up, Lynn. One too many of these," Jawnie said and gave her near empty glass a shake. "Not to sound like Steve, but those network checks have to make it somewhat easier to deal with?"

Lynn pursed her lips and gave a slight nod.

There are times I hate Buzzed Me. I should have known better. Change the subject and make a note for sober Jawnie to apologize in the morning. She turned her head and mouthed *I'm sorry* to Lynn. Lynn returned a slight smile and moved her gaze to the food on the table. *Let's go. Switch gears and get this party back on track.*

Jawnie put on her biggest smile, tried to forget the past two minutes, and raised the martini glass again. "And speaking of Steve, I'm giving thanks he's two hundred and twenty miles away, driving someone else up a wall."

"Don't jinx yourself, J," Lynn said. "The night is still young."

Jawnie and her friends laughed and clinked glasses. Lynn's response took a little weight off Jawnie's shoulders and her faux pas. She took a deep breath, knowing it was far from over as the man who ran the anxiety machine in her head would make a point of replaying the embarrassing scene multiple times. Her deep breath turned into a bigger sigh.

Half an hour and three cleared plates of appetizers later, Lynn's phone vibrated across the table. She reached out and picked it up.

"The forwarded business line. It's Andrist. Again."

"You've got to be kidding me," Jawnie said. Her disappointment was apparent.

"I wish I was."

"Let it go to voicemail. Nothing we can't address Monday," Jawnie said. Her quip caused the group to crack up again. "Worst case, I'll listen to it in the morning and make sure it's not an emergency on his part." She raised her glass and joined in the laughter.

The evening continued without pause past a late dinner and well into one too many dance hours. They ordered another round of drinks, and all agreed that they would have to retrieve their cars in the morning, or more like afternoon, the following day. No one wanted to stop the party. Ride shares were made for evenings like this.

That was until the opening notes of Tool's *Eulogy* caught Jawnie's attention and she glanced down at her own cellphone.

Cheese and crackers. No. Not now.

It was Rockfish, and she knew there was no way she'd get away with letting his call go to voicemail or listening to the message come Sunday morning. Reluctantly, she picked it up and tried to mask her disappointment.

"Hey Steve, you're going to have to shout over all the noise here. You find Raffi?"

"Jawnie. Just listen. I've run into trouble up here. I need you in Grindsville. Monday at nine a.m., sharp. Or a little earlier. Check the weather. Bring a Hollywood-sized briefcase full of money. They only take cash here. No cards or check. I got railroaded on a trumped-up charge of obstruction. My fault. I totally thought I'd dance circles around these rubes. You are officially my one call."

Click

Jawnie stared at the phone in her hand. *Had Rockfish hung up? Or had the provider dropped the call? No time to worry about which. Crisis mode activated.* Only six months ago, Jawnie would have sat frozen unable to agree on the next move without outside help.

Jawnie peered across the table at Lynn. "One, I definitely jinxed myself. Two, do you want to listen to Andrist's message in the car on a drive to central Pennsylvania with me at the crack of dawn on Monday?"

* * * * * * * * * *

Sunlight streamed through the window and Rockfish awoke again, cursing the drunken version of himself from the night before. *One of these days, you'll learn.* He shut his eyes and rolled onto his side, away from the brightness. The pain in his back was instantaneous, and his body shifted again. He squinted at the night stand to check the time. The red LED lights did not return his gaze. Nothing did. There was no clock, no night stand. His eyes took in the room. Not a solitary piece of Holiday Inn furniture in sight. Gray painted cement block walls and a stainless-steel sink-toilet combo filled the small six-by-eight space. Only then did the terrible memories come flooding back.

Saturday's ride-along to the police department with Officer Sobotka had not gone as planned. The man had promised they wouldn't keep him long. Only a couple of questions to straighten a few things out. All they needed was a better understanding of the situation and Rockfish's involvement. Sobotka said all the right things, but it was his facial expressions that led Rockfish to believe the hotel would soon tack a late fee onto his bill for not returning the shovel in a timely manner.

Sobotka had gone back and watched the video from one of the department's outdoor surveillance cameras, not long after Rockfish had left on Friday. *He had to have listened in on our conversation or had a gut feeling something was off. Rewatched me pull up and then turned to his little computer and ran the plate. It didn't help that Raffi called me Steve half a dozen times in the visitors' room.* The jig was up. No turning back. *Not to mention there's only one hotel downtown, and I was dumb enough to check in under my real name. Couldn't be any stupider if you tried.*

Rockfish knew everything Sobotka threw at him regarding his role in Raffi's organization had no proof or evidence behind it. Those few questions soon turned to sitting alone in an interrogation room with the occasional blue uniform coming in to repeat the same accusations over and over. *Where are the drugs hidden? It's only a matter of time before we find them. Better for you if you come clean and turn on your partner. Only one of you is getting a deal and he's ready to talk.* When Rockfish would shrug, the officer would leave the room, and another would try again an hour later.

Rockfish entertained their little fishing game until the late afternoon, when he had grown tired and began pushing back. Hard. When the officers met force with stubbornness, he had enough. When he asked to leave, the charges of obstruction of justice and lack of candor to a sworn officer of the court were first floated. Then chiseled in stone. Sobotka's parting words were of the judge's unavailability until Monday. *Enjoy your weekend with us and if you've got a real lawyer, they can wait until Monday, too.*

The police then moved Rockfish to yet another small, nondescript room where he waited to be booked and processed through the Grindsville system. The sun had long set by the time they pushed him into a cell. He collapsed on the bed with mental exhaustion and wished nothing but erectile disfunction with a side of prostate cancer on each of the officers he had the pleasure of meeting today.

Not a damn thing in that van. There was nothing ever in the van. Well, nothing that the Chief could hang his hat on and call for a press conference. Which is all this podunk department wants. Good press and asset forfeiture.

The police were desperate to uncover something. Anything before court convened on Monday when the Judge would let Raffi off with a random fine levied to make the initial stop appear legit. And as for Rockfish? Nothing they threw against the wall would stick; he was sure of it. But he was also positive he wouldn't leave Grindsville before being separated from a good-sized portion of his hard-earned money, too. *You wanna leave? Pay.*

Rockfish swung his legs over the side of the steel bed and gazed down at his pink jumpsuit. He felt the blood churn faster through his veins and move closer to the boiling point.

"Goddamn mother fucking pieces of dog shit!" He directed the rant and those choice words that followed to no one in particular. The words bounced off the block walls and down the short hallway. "I lied to get in and see my friend. Sue me. All we did was talk. I know a reporter! The Baltimore Sun!"

"Steve, is that you?" A familiar voice echoed back from the cell to his left. Rockfish stood up and approached the bars where a shared wall separated the two cells.

"Raffi?"

A hand holding a small mirror, shot out from between the other cell's bars. Rockfish saw his friend's reflection.

"You were the guy they shoved in here last night? Didn't hear a peep out of you until now."

"You've been in here two days. Where did you find a mirror?"

"As you like to say, not my first rodeo."

Rockfish grinned and saw Raffi's smile in the mirror.

"Well, I'm in here for obstruction and lack of candor. Once they knew I wasn't Taggert, they assumed I was some cartel muscle or brains sent up to get you out before one of them uncovered the mother lode."

"Steve, there ain't no hidden compartments. Just a broken-down truck full of expiring MREs, repackaged and sold to a bunch of grown men who like to play dress up in the Allegheny National Forrest. Their stupidity or willingness to be conned does not constitute a crime on my part. I'm only taking advantage of an opportunity presented. Free market and such."

"Where did you even get a truckload of expiring MREs? Wait, I don't want to know. Maybe six months from now when we're out on the bay tossing back a few cold ones, but not now. I need to concentrate for the next couple of days." Rockfish took a step back into his cell so Raffi couldn't see his expression. *You were cocky.*

Thought you'd pull one over on Barney Fife and get your friend out of Dodge, no worse for wear. Let it be a lesson. A costly one.

Rockfish returned to the bars and looked down the hallway in both directions. The jail area was as small as the one he encountered back at the start of the pandemic in Elk Township when he first met Jawnie. This hoosegow comprised four cells. His, Raffi's, and two empties directly across. The hallway ended a few feet after Raffi's cell and the entry door was to Rockfish's right. A small black and white television monitor, airing Tom & Jerry cartoons, hung mounted above the doorway.

"Raffi, sit tight," Rockfish said. "Jawnie's on her way up here with the cash. We'll need to leave this shit town in our respective rear views. I'm not sitting here singing woe is me. Wheels are in motion."

Rockfish didn't wait for an answer and turned back toward the bed bolted to the wall. He sat down and hoped to get lost in his thoughts.

BEEP BEEP BEEP

The sound startled Rockfish. He did not know how long he had been out. Contemplation had turned to sleep and he, at some point, had laid back down. Now he stood up and followed the noise. It was coming from the direction of the hallway and Rockfish stared up at the monitor. The cartoons were gone, and the words Breaking News scrolled underneath two news anchors, seated behind a large desk.

"...coming out of Warren County, where Federal officials are reporting the arrests of several high-ranking members of the Janus Sixth Nationalist Militia. Officials have released few details but we are waiting on an 11 a.m. press conference from the US Attorney's Office for the Western District of Pennsylvania."

"Hey Raffi, up and at 'em. What was the name of the idiot group you were supposed to sell the Q-Rations to?" *No way in hell this is the same group. Can't be.*

"The Janus Something or Others. Why?"

"Wait, that name alone didn't give you pause? Come over here and check out the TV." Rockfish watched as the reporters continued. *What were the odds? If the truck doesn't break down, maybe Raffi's caught in the middle of a whole 'nother shit show. A federal one. One we can't pay his way out of.*

Raffi pressed his face against the bars, and without the mirror, Rockfish strained. He glimpsed absolute disappointment in his friend's eyes.

"Those are my buyers. Truth be told, Steve, I'd care less if they were the Rip Taylor Dancers. Cash is cash, and it's not like I was selling them AR-15s or stars and bars branded tiki torches."

"Were. Your. Buyers. What are you going to do when Jawnie gets us out of this, with a truck full of Q-Rations? You might have the supply, but demand seems to have landed in Federal lockup. I got news for ya, pal. The Supermax doesn't allow deliveries."

"I don't know. There's gotta be a group of army LARPers between here and home I can unload 'em on. I'm staying positive, Steve. I got a lot of cash wrapped up in that truck. Imma have to do a few Google searches when we get out. Maybe take the scenic route south and luck out. Find someplace on the way home."

Both men continued to focus on the monitor as the reporters continued.

"... sources have told WPVI that an undercover FBI agent infiltrated the group six months ago to assist with an ongoing ATF investigation into illegal gun running. As officials make more information available, we will bring it to you..."

The monitor flashed, and the screen reverted to a Three Stooges episode already in progress.

"That's a pretty damn violent show to air here in prison." Raffi said.

"Raffi, it's only the two of us. You plan on poking me in the eyes out in the yard?"

Come on Jawnie. I hope you're already on your way.

* * * * * * * * *

Moonlight shone down on parts of the parking lot outside of the Rockfish & McGee office. Two cars were parked out front. One engine idled and the second cut out as the drivers-side door swung open. The office blinds parted, and Lynn watched as a woman got out. She approached the idling car and paced in front.

"She's here, J. Let's roll," Lynn said as she retreated from the window.

Sunrise wasn't scheduled for two more hours, but Jawnie wanted to get an early start. Grindsville was three hours away, and the courthouse opened at nine a.m. Her plan was to beat the early traffic on the Baltimore Beltway and head west on I-70 before things got too crowded and the weather worsened.

Jawnie grabbed her messenger bag and a smaller case filled with cash pulled from the office safe the previous day. She shut the door behind her and set the alarm. *If all goes right, we'll be back by late afternoon, and I can pretend to be enthralled by Steve and Raffi's recounting of their adventures. With any luck, I can hope a client conveniently calls and I can cut out. Sorry, gentlemen, duties call. There's a first time for everything.*

Jawnie walked over to where Lynn and Susan Giacchino stood next to the idling Subaru. She had started the car ten minutes ago, so the inside would be toasty by the time they departed. Jawnie also came up with the idea for Susan to join the team for the day. Susan was Kara and Debra's lawyer and had been a great help in her and Rockfish's previous investigation against Fulsome Commercial Realty Group. Susan was a smart call to the bullpen as the firm's latest lawyer, held on retainer, Rockfish had fired a week earlier. *You never know when things might go sideways and get all squirrelly. Better to be safe than sorry. Sorry Steve, not flying by the seat of my pants with this one.*

Susan Giacchino was close to AARP eligible if not older. She wore her hair in a short silver bob with cat-eye glasses. The cerulean frames with bedazzled points rode high on her nose and gave off more of an elementary school teacher vibe than a senior partner in her own law firm. Susan had jumped at the chance to tag along to the middle of Pennsylvania when Jawnie made a desperate call late Saturday night.

"Susan, thank you again for coming along on this adventure," Jawnie said as she approached the idling car. She greeted Susan with a hug.

"My pleasure. After all, it's the least I can do after all you and Steve did for Kara and Pilar."

Pleasantries exchanged, the three women opened their respective doors and slid into the Subaru with Susan taking the backseat.

Jawnie's early morning departure call was dead on, and the Subaru rocketed around the city before hitting I-70. She slalomed around commuters still trying to wake up, and long-haul rigs getting an early start to the day. The women made small talk from time to time over the noise from the speakers. Lynn connected her phone to the radio via Bluetooth and Jawnie tasked her with picking the tunes. Jawnie waited until she felt Lynn was in a good head space before addressing the elephant in the car.

"So, Lynn, how are you feeling about being back in the field, so to speak? Anxiety level, one to ten?"

"Come on, J, it's not like we're doing actual work," Lynn said with a solid punch to Jawnie's thigh. "I've done field work for you, lived to tell about it, too. This is more like a road trip to bail a couple of nincompoops out of trouble. Pay a fine and reverse course. I'm good. Don't worry."

"Well, it is a rescue mission of sorts," Jawnie said with a laugh. "I'm glad you're up for it and honestly thrilled to have you riding shotgun again. Steve can be a handful. Maybe you can ride back with him."

All three ladies busted up over Jawnie's comment.

"But seriously, Lynn, if anything sneaks up on you, please let me know." Jawnie turned and caught Lynn's attention. "If you need to bail, for any reason, I'll use the company card to get you a rental. Drive it back at your leisure. We can't afford to have you relapse into a dark space of your mind. And I'm speaking for Steve, too. You've made amazing strides since the whole Porbeagle mess." Jawnie held out her fist and Lynn bumped it. *She's gonna be fine.*

Jawnie kept her eyes on the road and leaned over. She raised the volume on the radio and lowered her voice.

"I'm sorry, Lynn, for bringing all that up in front of Susan. I totally blanked on her sitting in the back seat."

"Please. I'm proud of the progress I've made in the past year," Lynn said with a tight-lipped smile. "Not to mention as our lawyer for this case, isn't she sworn to secrecy?"

"Attorney-client privilege came into play the minute Jawnie called me on Saturday." Susan shouted over the music from the back seat. "And if you really wanted me not to listen in, you needed to turn up the speakers back here, not in the front."

All three enjoyed a hearty laugh at Susan's comment. Lynn reached over and lowered the volume. The rest of the ride was uneventful. As their ETA ticked under thirty minutes, Jawnie laid out her thoughts on the to-do list once they crossed the Grindsville city limits.

"We're making good time," Jawnie said. She glanced at the clock on the dashboard. "What I'd like to do is swing by the Holiday Inn, where Steve stayed and settle his bill and pick up his things. Then head over to the county building. One less thing we'll have to do on the way out. This way he can get Lana out of impound and take off."

"What about Raffi and his truck of goodies?" Lynn said. The sarcasm dripped off each word. "I hope you don't expect me to keep him company on the drive back. That's a fate worse than riding with Steve."

The ridicule with a dash of venom didn't escape Jawnie's ears. It had been well over a year since Raffi had convinced Lynn to go along with his harebrained scheme against Rockfish's direct orders. It set off the first of a handful of falling dominos, resulting in Lynn at the bidding of a deranged psychopath. *Earl Porbeagle. I'd never wish that against my greatest enemy.*

"Not unless you want to. I get there is a history there. More like a chasm never to be traversed again," Jawnie said with a wink and playfully returned Lynn's punch to the thigh from earlier.

"Thank you, J," Lynn said. "Truly, for everything you and Steve have done for me since then. Both professionally and socially. To include letting me hang out with Kara and Pilar. It's been a long while since I've had a solid group of people to hang with."

"Friends. Way better than a bunch of randos," Jawnie said.

At exactly the three-hour mark, the Subaru passed the *Welcome to Grindsville, Home of the 1978 High School State Baseball Champions* sign. The road sloped downhill for as far as Jawnie could see. What appeared to be the downtown area was off in the distance, and she made a point of changing into her game face.

"Better lay off the gas pedal. You don't want to join the other two," Susan said, leaning forward between the two front bucket seats. "I wouldn't put it past a town like this to have speed traps on the downside of the mountain, no matter the conditions."

Jawnie lifted her foot off the gas pedal and rested it on the brake. It wasn't a minute later when she spotted a patrol car parked off the side of the road, partially obscured by bushes.

Almost got me, Steve, but we're coming.

CHAPTER THREE

Jawnie pulled into the municipal parking lot with fifteen minutes
to spare, after dealing with the manager on duty at the Holiday Inn.
She had learned a lot from Rockfish over the past two years, but
she still lacked the all-important skill of verbal manipulation. The
manager stonewalled her request to gather Rockfish's belongings
from his room but was more than happy to rip the corporate credit
card from her hand and settle his bill, to include one missing snow
shovel. Susan nudged Jawnie to the side as the folio, marked paid
in full, was handed across the desk. Susan put on her litigator hat
and spun logic circles, one after another, around the manager until
he gave in and had a member of the cleaning staff escort them up.

Once at the courthouse, Jawnie and Susan moved through the
metal detectors and continued down the hallway in the direction
the security guard had pointed. They moved in single file, with
Jawnie in the lead. For a reason Jawnie couldn't quite put her finger
on, she was eager to see Steve. She quickened her pace and
squinted back over her shoulder to see how far Susan had fallen
behind. *The man said there was only one courtroom on this floor, let
alone the entire building. If I lose her, she 'll be okay and I 'm sure she
understands.* Jawnie put her hand up and waved Susan on before
shifting into overdrive.

As Susan fell further behind Jawnie in the race toward the
courtroom, their third wheel had stayed on the outside, not looking
in. Lynn wished to remain on the public side of the metal detectors
and found a seat on a bench a short way inside the entrance. Jawnie

had tried to convince her to come along. After all, it wasn't only Raffi in there and Rockfish would appreciate her support, too. But Lynn shook her head. *No reason to get her spun up if she felt that way. Susan and I have the situation well in hand. Pay the fine and head back up the mountain. Well, under the speed limit, of course.*

When Jawnie strode through the doors into the courtroom, the first thing she noticed was how small the room was. Even for a backcountry town in decline. The gallery comprised two rows of five folding chairs. An empty jury box, a table for the prosecution and defense, and of course, the judge's bench with accompanying witness stand filled the rest of the room. The great seal of the Commonwealth of Pennsylvania hung crooked on the wall behind the judge. Jawnie's OCD ticked up a notch.

She spotted Rockfish and Raffi at the defendant's table, to her right. The pink jumpsuits were a dead giveaway, as were the men's slouches. She stepped into the first row of seats, directly behind them, and coughed into her hand. Rockfish turned around and smiled. Jawnie let out a slight chuckle and reached her fist across the space between them. Rockfish bumped it.

Susan eventually caught up and walked into the courtroom. She approached the bailiff, leaned in, and whispered. With a nod, he opened the swinging door which separated the gallery from the official court space. She approached the defendant's table and sat down in the empty seat next to Rockfish. A minute later, before she even conferred with her clients, the hearing was called to order. The Commonwealth's Attorney opened the proceedings.

His ill-fitting brown suit and Ben Franklin glasses resting on the end of his nose caught Jawnie's attention. *Isn't he too young for the job? An undergrad at most?* She then looked up at the judge. *Now he seems more age-appropriate.* The elderly man had a salt-and-pepper buzz cut and his robe hung open as he stared down over the courtroom.

The first order of business discussed during the hearing was the amending of Raffi's charges. In a surprise to no one, the prosecutor dismissed the indictment for trafficking with intent to distribute a Schedule One narcotic. Raffi had faced a felony conviction and prison time from five to forty years, including a fine up to $500,000. The relief felt by all was short-lived as the amended charges now included driving with an expired license and without proper registration. The Commonwealth's Attorney recommended a fine of $3,500 and the judge raised it to an even $4,000.

Rockfish's head swiveled to Raffi, and Jawnie leaned in to eavesdrop on their conversation.

"How the hell do you not have a valid license?" Rockfish said.

"There's a pandemic out there. Or was. I'm not sitting at the DMV in those long lines. People hacking and coughing through their dollar store chin-diapers. I never got around to it, even when things calmed down. I'll move it up the priority list. But the expired registration? That's on fucking Marvin, man. Who lets a rental roll off the lot with bad paper? If I have to pay that to get outta here, he's going to owe me. With interest."

"He's going to pay me back. Unless you've got a cash machine shoved down in that jumper of yours. Thank your lucky stars something didn't suddenly show up during their third or fourth search of the truck."

Susan stood, and without consulting her client, entered a guilty plea.

"Objection!" Raffi said and stood up. He hadn't gotten the third syllable out when Rockfish yanked him back down by the seat of his jumper.

"The bailiff will escort you out at hearing's end to the cashier's window," the judge said. "Next case. Mr. Rockfish. I assume, Ms. Giacchino, you are representing the defendant in this matter?"

"Yes, your honor."

"Mr. Rockfish is charged with knowingly providing false information to a sworn law enforcement officer," the Commonwealth's Attorney said.

Rockfish turned to his left. He glanced past Susan to the prosecutor's table. Beady-eyed Sobotka sat to the left of the Commonwealth's Attorney. The cop returned a sideways glance. Jawnie had followed Rockfish's eyes and seen the same expression on her partner's face too many times. The furrowed brow, the flushed cheeks and quick shakes of his head from side to side. She knew exactly, or damn close, what he was thinking regarding the man that had done him wrong.

Congratulations on ripping off honest, hard-working members of society so your department of six can finally afford the upkeep on the fifteen-person armor personnel carrier courtesy of Homeland Security. Should be hell on wheels when you execute those shoplifting and jaywalking warrants.

Rockfish put his hand on Susan's forearm and then stood up. He addressed the judge. "Your honor, what will it cost me for a guilty plea?"

"Same as your partner, $4,000. Cash."

He turned around and Jawnie nodded, patting the bag on her lap.

"Sold. Jawnie, pay the man. Let's get home before the coal dust in the air brings us all down with a serious case of the mesotheliomas."

An hour later, Jawnie's bag was eighty percent lighter. The three ladies shivered and waited in the parking lot by the jail's exit door. When it finally swung open, Rockfish and Raffi appeared. Jawnie tried to keep her composure, but it was for naught, and she ran to embrace Rockfish. Hugs and handshakes were had by all, with Rockfish surprised to see Lynn had made the trip. Their embrace was longer than the others and Jawnie noticed he whispered in her ear as they separated and held hands. What she also noticed was Lynn's three steps backwards when Raffi took a single step in her direction. *Some wounds may never heal, no matter how often Steve and I continue and try to mend that fence.*

"Where to now, Steve?" Jawnie said.

"How much you got left?" Rockfish said.

"Roughly two thousand," Jawnie said. "I emptied the emergency safe since this adventure of yours occurred during non-banking hours."

"Good call. I don't know how much the impound fees will be to get Lana out, but I'm betting they're negotiable. Especially after the amount we just dropped into the city coffers."

"What about my truck?" Raffi said. He stepped over to where Jawnie and Rockfish spoke.

"What about it?" Rockfish said. "Are we going to pay to get it released and then a cop in the next township or town over stop you again? It's not like you'll magically have a good license or registration the minute you slip back behind the wheel. Hell, wasn't that truck broken down on the side of the road when the cop came across you?"

"It was, but wherever they towed it to, they ordered the mechanic to get it up and running ASAP," Raffi said. "That one with the eyes--"

"Sobotka," Rockfish said.

"Yeah, him. I overheard him talking about a cop auction next week. If they found all the dope they had hoped for, asset forfeiture would come into play. They would then auction the box truck for a quick couple of thousand."

Rockfish glanced at Raffi with unconvinced eyes.

Raffi cleared his throat and swallowed. "I'm sure it runs, or so I hope. I can't leave the merchandise here. You don't know how much I've got invested in these Q-Rations. Initial purchase, re-packaging and labels ain't cheap."

"Listen Raffi, Steve's only trying to help you not go further in debt to us than you currently are," Jawnie said. "What Steve can do is make a call over to Baltimore Pike Motors and get Marvin to straighten out the registration. Email us a copy of the new form and one of us can drive the truck for you."

The last sentence hadn't left her mouth and Jawnie knew she would be the driver of the box truck. Rockfish had Lana and there was no way Lynn was stepping up with her sworn enemy riding shotgun. Not to mention Susan was on retainer, but not as a delivery driver.

"Really?" Raffi said. "You'd do that for me?"

"Yeah, of course I would. Lynn and Susan can head back in the Subaru."

Rockfish patted Jawnie on the shoulder. She took it as his attaboy for dissolving a potentially volatile situation. Her solution worked for all parties.

"I'll reach out to Marvin now," Rockfish said. "Let's get these vehicles out of impound and grab something to eat on the way out. I'm starving and took a hard pass on the jail's morning bowl of gruel."

"I saw a little hole-in-the-wall diner on the way in," Lynn said. "It was packed with pickup trucks for the breakfast rush. I'm betting the food is good and cheap."

"I hope so," Jawnie said. "We don't have a lot of cash left. You think they take cards?"

"Look around," Rockfish said. "Your guess is as good as mine."

Laughter filled the parking lot, and they all squeezed into the Subaru. Lynn and Jawnie in the front and Susan, along with the jailbirds, wedged into the back.

* * * * * * * * * *

Two hours later, only after showing proof of registration, the caravan pulled into the gravel driveway of the Hog Sweat Diner. Most of the small parking lot was clear of snow, but large mounds from a plow covered half a dozen potential free spots. Lana and the Subaru could find spots alongside the two rows of Chevy Silverados, Ford F-150s, and Dodge Rams. But Jawnie and the bulky white box truck had to make three laps around to find a spot big enough and one she would feel comfortable backing out of.

Rockfish, Lynn, and Susan waited outside the front door for Jawnie and Raffi. Rockfish gave the outside of the dive the once over. The concrete block building was whitewashed on the sides with a black and red sign mounted on the roof. It faced the four-lane road heading down into town and appeared to be outlined in non-working neon lights, but Rockfish couldn't be sure without grabbing a ladder and climbing up for a better take.

This place has seen better days, and the outside needs a solid power washing, or maybe it's part of the charm. Rockfish laughed to himself. *I bet the seats are well enforced, the food out of this world and Jawnie will order a dish she'll push around her plate but never bring close to her mouth.* Vegan options would be nonexistent. Rockfish hung back and let the others walk inside. He tugged on Jawnie's arm so she didn't follow Raffi directly in. Their procession came to a stop in front of the *Please Wait to be Seated sign.*

"By the looks of it, captaining that damn boat doesn't seem to be going all that well. I thought for a second, I was going to have to call my favorite Grindsville police officer and report an accident. Or worse yet, a hit and run."

"I can drive it," Jawnie said and frowned. She was direct, and Rockfish heard the tension in her voice. "It's dealing with my copilot and his passenger seat driving. Does he ever shut up?"

"You wanna switch places. I've trusted you with Lana before."

"Not the new gal, you haven't."

Rockfish didn't answer but tilted his head in thought. *Hadn't I? First time for everything, I guess. At least I know she has a valid license and my girl's registered and insured.*

"I can do this. Consider it a test. But how about he goes with you?" Jawnie said. "Passenger seat, backseat, or trunk. After the last ten minutes, I really don't care which. Just pick one."

"Good one," Rockfish said and slapped Jawnie on the back as they followed the others deeper into the diner.

Rockfish was last in line as they snaked their way across the main dining area. *The outside isn't the only thing that needs a solid cleaning.* The inside was dark. Small square tables littered the floor, in a pattern that Rockfish couldn't figure out. Most dining parties were hunched over brunch plates of bacon, eggs, and home fries. Separate plates stacked high with pancakes waited for their turn in the rotation. The smell of bacon grease, fresh paint, and three pack-a-day smokers filled his nostrils.

The hostess led the party of five to a singular square table where a bus boy had added a fifth plastic folding chair before disappearing back into the kitchen. Rockfish cleared his throat and snagged the attention of their waitress. He gave her his best WTF face.

"Last table available, sweeties," the waitress said while simultaneously cracking her bubble gum. "You'll squeeze in just fine. If not, I'll personally find this hunk a seat." She gave Rockfish a smack on the ass as she walked away to grab menus and water.

To Rockfish, she appeared to be a dead-ringer for Flo, a waitress from the old 1970s sitcom, *Alice. Yeah, if Flo had a grandmother who needed to keep working in order to afford food for sixteen cats and Depends, which were obvious to all under her hot pink rayon uniform.* Not that he was scoping it out. *I mean, it's just there. Can't miss it.* Rockfish pulled out the added chair. Raffi and Jawnie shared one side, Lynn and Susan on the other side, with the other pushed against the wall.

"Ladies, and Raffi, despite the accommodations, I checked out some plates on the walk over and I gotta tell ya, I have a good feeling about the food." Rockfish pulled a napkin from the dispenser on the table and laid it across his lap.

After Flo dropped off waters and a carafe of coffee for the table, she promised to return shortly to take their orders. Rockfish raised his white porcelain coffee mug in the air.

"To the entire rescue committee. If it were not for the cash and Susan's keen eye to make sure the Commonwealth Attorney didn't drop any shenanigans on us last minute, Raffi and I would still be eating shit on a shingle off an aluminum tray. I'll spare you the stories of the green bologna."

Glasses and mugs clinked at the center of the table. Everyone took a drink and the other diners looked over, puzzled.

"Steve, it was the least I could do after all you did for Pilar and Kara," Susan said. "When Jawnie called and said she needed a last-minute lawyer to help, I packed an overnight bag. In case things got crazy."

"Always good to know I've got a lifeline the next time Raffi drags me into trouble and I'm no longer on speaking terms with my previous representation."

The group made small talk while they ordered and waited. Rockfish noticed Lynn and Jawnie had the expression of wanting to get back on the road five minutes ago on their faces. *I get it. This isn't the hottest new gastropub they're used to. But it's not like we're coming back. I need to fuel up before hitting the road. Take one for the team, I say.*

Rockfish spent most of the meal people-watching. Not only those at his own table. He overheard the loud conversations all around. The couple to Rockfish's right. There was trouble in paradise and the two small kids in the booster seats had front row seats to their parents' impending break-up. Directly behind, the monthly meeting of the Grindsville Senior Citizen Klan meeting was underway. There were no punches pulled, sideways glances or code words used in Ma and Pa Kettle's discussion of the much better and whiter days gone by. *Thanks Obama* seemed to be a standing reply to any of the off the wall statements. To the left was the director of the local Meals on Wheels affiliate. The man helped those eligible in the area sign up for every Federal assistance program available under the sun, while over breakfast railing against those latched onto the Gub'ment tit at every opportunity.

Fucking hypocrite—

Raffi interrupted Rockfish's thoughts. His friend stood up and excused himself. He headed off toward the restroom sign. Rockfish wondered if he had imagined the tremendous sigh of relief from the rest of the table. "Okay, let's spread out and enjoy the extra leg room until he gets back." Rockfish said with a grin.

"Can you go with him and make sure he washes his hands?" Jawnie said. For the life of him, he couldn't tell if she was kidding.

"He's a big boy," Rockfish said. "I got faith."

Raffi hadn't returned when Flo reappeared with their orders, and everyone dug in. Even Jawnie, Rockfish noticed. She nibbled at the edges of the two over easy eggs on her plate. The table conversation slowed to a crawl as everyone ate and it wasn't long before they pushed empty plates toward the center of the table while Raffi's remained untouched.

"What about this one?" Flo said, pointing toward Raffi's plate of untouched creamy grits over biscuits and two well-buttered English muffins, as she bussed the rest.

"Do you think he fell in?" Lynn said. The sarcasm was heavy.

"If I leave now, then he has to ride back with you, Steve," Jawnie said. "If you can find him and he's not back in that same cell we rescued him from."

"Okay, I'll go search for him. Jawnie, you have the corporate card. They take 'em. I saw the sticker on the front door. Don't embarrass me with the tip. I'll be back in a few." Rockfish stood up and retraced Raffi's steps.

He used his elbow to push open the men's room door and immediately came up empty. A sink, urinal and stall with an open door stared back. *Strike one.* Rockfish backed out and took a quick lap around the inside of the diner. He hoped to find Raffi on a stool at the small lunch counter, talking off someone's ear. All four stools were occupied, but he wasn't there. *Strike two. Only one other place to go check out, but what the hell would he be doing outside in the cold, his jacket draped over his chair?*

Rockfish pushed open the front door, and the cold hit his lungs. His eyes scanned left to right and came up empty. There was only one other place he'd be, and that was sitting in the box truck. Or standing on the other side of it.

Rockfish approached where Jawnie had parked the truck and heard a few voices on the far side. He picked up his pace, turned the back corner and spotted Raffi in what appeared by hand gestures, an animated conversation with two men in matching flannel. He stepped forward and drug his foot on the gravel to announce his arrival.

"Raffi, everything good here?"

"Things are great, Steve," Raffi said. He didn't turn around. His hands stopped moving and one reached out toward the two men in front of him. Raffi shook hands with each before they turned and walked away.

"What did you do now?" Rockfish said. "I had thoughts of you beaten, head stuck in the toilet, and your wallet on its way to the closest meth dealer's trailer."

"All good, buddy. A few days ago, I rolled in dog shit. But today? Smelling like a rose." He smiled wide and gave a chef's kiss in Rockfish's direction.

"I don't know what you're talking about. We need to grab our shit and head back to civilization. Stat."

"My Q-Rations," Raffi said. "I've got a deal in place. Well, a handshake deal with those two guys. They like to play dress-up in the woods too. One door closes and you know the rest."

"Who would have thought?" Rockfish said.

"I'm getting seventy-five cents more per Q-Ration than those January 6th clowns. Fuck 'em for trying to low ball me. I hope they enjoy their time in Federal pound-me-in-the-ass prison."

Rockfish crossed his arms and stared at his friend. "How much of that is being set aside in order to see to paying me back?"

"Not a clue. I'm an ideas man. Deal maker wheeler dealer. Calculator's in the glove box. But I need to hang around Grindsville for a couple of days. I can't believe the luck. They came up to me! We started talking and WHAM. I'm driving a truck filled with money home instead."

"You still don't have a valid license. And stick around here for a few more days?" Rockfish said. He turned down the sarcasm and increased the concern modulator. "You're asking for trouble. All this means is I'm stuck here too. Easier to bail you out again without having to make the drive a second time."

"Jawnie actually did, but I get where you're coming from. You're a good man, Charlie Brown."

Rockfish shook his head and hoped Jawnie and Susan hadn't burned his bridges at the Holiday Inn.

* * * * * * * * * *

"Hey, you two. You abandoned us inside for some reindeer games?" Jawnie shouted as she walked across the Hog Sweat parking lot, carrying Raffi's jacket. The steam from each word floated in front of her face as she stepped through the vapors, hell-bent on figuring out what was going on. She didn't have a good feeling about the shit-eating grin on Raffi's face and the dumbfounded look on Steve's. "So, what did I miss? That one appears to have swallowed the canary."

Jawnie had left Lynn and Susan alongside the Subaru. She stopped inches from the two men and threw Raffi his jacket. Her hands landed on her hips. She waited for the cockamamie explanation she knew was coming.

"Good news," Raffi said. "You and I are no longer playing BJ and the Bear."

She didn't even try to figure out what that reference was regarding. She turned her attention to Rockfish and hoped he would be less cryptic.

"I know, another dated reference you don't get," Rockfish said. "What he's trying to say is that he's already made friends up here who will pay him cash for his truck-load of expiring MREs."

"Q-Rations," Raffi said. "Always be branding."

"Yes, sorry for being all generic regarding your one-of-a-kind product. But what it means is that he's going to pay us back quicker than either of us ever thought. Hell, I had wondered if it would ever happen at all. That being said, I'm going to stick around and make sure the deal, as soon as I figure out exactly what it is, goes down with no monkey business. Make sure he gets paid, and we get our money. Then I'll drive the truck back home."

"Why don't I stay up here with you?" Jawnie said. "Lynn can go back and FedEx a cashier's check to the Holiday Inn. This way, I can cash it at the local bank to bail you out again." Her tone wasn't lost on her audience of two.

"Point taken, McGee," Rockfish said. "But I've learned my lesson with the locals. Not gonna happen again. But you need to get Susan home before this next wave of lake effect snow hits and, hey Lynn..." He waved her over and tossed Lana's key fob as she moved closer. "Take it easy on my girl but get over that mountain before the weather changes. Leave her at my house."

"Huh? What?" Lynn said. The confusion on her face was clear.

"I'll explain in a second," Jawnie said. "Give me and Steve another couple of minutes here and we'll head out."

Lynn nodded and stepped back to where Susan stood.

Jawnie and Rockfish part argued, part discussed Raffi's new deal and what it meant for Rockfish & McGee - Investigative Specialists. Jawnie brought up the potential problems with staying behind in Grindsville and Rockfish used his senior status power of veto. They were fifty-fifty partners but from time to time the old man pulled the *I built this company from nothing* card and Rockfish would guilt Jawnie into agreeing with the harebrained scheme of the day. She was far from agreeing this time, but would only be three hours away if Steve, or more likely, Raffi got them behind the eight ball again.

Jawnie reluctantly agreed, and they said their goodbyes. She continued to shake her head to emphasize her disagreement but would play the part of the good and loyal soldier. She trudged back to where Lynn and Susan waited.

"What's the deal? Why the sudden change of plans?" Lynn said. She held up the key fob. "And he wants me to drive his baby back?"

"I know, I know. We can talk here in a few. Let's get on the road before the snow comes. I'll take the lead. Plug in your phone and call me hands free when you're settled and comfortable behind the wheel. I'll try to make this make sense. Sort of."

Lynn nodded. She chirped the key fob and unlocked Lana. Jawnie and Susan climbed into the Subaru and the two-car convoy pulled out of the gravel driveway and onto the street. Ten minutes later, as the cars started their ascent up the western side of the mountain, her phone rang. Jawnie reached over and tapped the car's touch screen.

"J, you're driving like a grandma. Something about this car makes me want to go fast and you're in the way," Lynn said. Her laugh echoed through the Subaru.

"Easy does it Danica Patrick," Jawnie said. "Sorry if I'm short with ya. Those two back there really got on my last nerve."

"Understood, but what's going on?"

"A couple of local militia-types approached Raffi back at the diner. They got to talking and offered to take the Q-Rations off his hands. He sees dollar signs and Steve sees potential trouble. Then he immediately switches into the savior role. But he won't let anyone else help. I think it's an ego thing with him."

"And it ticks you off?" Lynn said.

"Of course, it does. Raffi leads Steve down the wrong path nine out of ten times and instead of standing his ground and saying adios, Steve goes along thinking he'll play the part of the older brother. Keep Raffi from screwing up, or, even worse, dead."

"J, they're big boys. You can't resort to their level and play mom. Nothing's going to stop them from doing what they want."

"I get it, but I have an aching suspicion that I'll be headed back down this side of the mountain before I know it and Lord help either of them when I turn off the engine."

"Here's a thought. Why don't you put on those big girl pants you talk to me so much about?"

"Lynn, now you sound like Raffi. Non sequiturs that make no sense to me when I'm in this mood."

"Equal partner, at least in your eyes, correct?"

"Mine? Yes," Jawnie said. "His? Depends on the situation and the time of day."

"What's stopping you from pulling over, leaving Susan on the side of the road and surprising those two at the Holiday Inn? Stand your ground."

U-turn? Not Wrong Turn. There isn't a thing wrong with what she's saying. And that's why I love her to death. Go back. Stand your ground. Make sure this deal goes down exactly as promised and get both of them back to Baltimore, no worse for wear. Carpe diem!

Jawnie turned to Susan before giving Lynn an answer. "You okay with switching cars and driving back at what could approach light speed?"

"I'll wear my seatbelt and lean into the airbag," Susan said. "You go take care of business."

Jawnie had put on her blinker and angled for the shoulder before Susan even finished. Once the passenger exchange was complete, Jawnie swung a U-turn, laid rubber on the pre-treated asphalt and headed back down the mountain.

"Drive safe, Lynn, and don't get a ticket. He'll never let you live it down."

"Same goes for you," Lynn said. "Don't follow them into trouble. I'll never let you live it down."

"Deal."

CHAPTER FOUR

Rockfish awoke Tuesday morning to a continuing blizzard and the sound of snowplows outside his window. The first flakes had appeared yesterday, late afternoon, and continued at a more fervent pace throughout the night. The weatherman on the WJAC broadcast predicted the snow would continue until the early evening. *So much for walking around to see if there was a decent local spot to grab breakfast nearby.*

Rockfish dressed and took the elevator down to the bar-turned-breakfast-nook. He alternated his glances out the front door at the hotel employee attempting to keep the walkway clear and then down at his rapidly cooling waffle. While his breakfast lost heat, Rockfish continued to be red hot. He and Raffi had not been seated at the bar for over ten minutes yesterday when he spotted Jawnie stride in and walk up to the front desk. A few minutes later, key in hand, she had spun around and spotted them. She waved before stepping into the elevator. Rockfish had rolled his eyes and felt his stomach tighten.

Come yesterday evening, the partners then had tried talking circles around the other, on why Jawnie should or shouldn't have returned. They had finally agreed to disagree on her actions as they walked back through the blustery snow from the Lettuce Eat. The small mom-and-pop soup and salad establishment was closer to the police department than the hotel and Rockfish had bad thoughts about the beady-eyed cop rolling up behind him again. The memory had made him pick up his pace on the way. *That guy reminds me of the type that doesn't like to lose. And when they do, figure out a way to get payback. If I can get through Raffi's deal tomorrow night and check out the following morning without running into him, I'll consider myself damn lucky. Leave Grindsville way behind.*

Now, Rockfish glanced down at the waffle. He drained his orange juice, cursed the lack of champagne, and tried to keep his mind off of Jawnie's return or the eventual run-in with Sobotka. *It's only a matter of time. I've got that kind of luck.* He now had two other people to worry about and that was more than his comfort zone of one.

A blur to his right caught his attention, and he glanced over. Jawnie, carrying a full plate of fruit and a glass of water, sat down across from him. *If I didn't know her diet better, I would think the other guests had devoured all the pre-packaged muffins, small boxes of applejacks and stale cheese Danishes.* Jawnie didn't say a word, but smiled and stabbed a piece of mystery melon.

Rockfish picked up the napkin on his lap. "Well, aren't you bright eyed and bushy tailed this morning?"

"Have you taken a gander outside?" Jawnie said. "It's so beautiful. Peaceful looking."

"Funny, I don't see it. We're trapped in this one and three-quarter star hotel for the time being. That damn box truck won't be able to maneuver on these streets, no matter how many plow trucks drive by my window. At all hours of the night."

"My car is all wheel drive. It can get us anywhere we need to be."

Rockfish pursed his lips and threw the napkin back in his lap. "It's not even supposed to be here, so it doesn't play in any part of my equation. Much like the owner." Rockfish said. His face was stoic and lacked emotion. But his words contained venom.

"Glad to see you're a man of your word on moving past this issue. We had an agreement yesterday."

"Yeah, that was yesterday, and I was hustling back to the hotel before I caught pneumonia. We didn't shake on it."

"Good to know."

"It's a case-by-case basis. Let's get through tomorrow night and get on the road. Then we can forget about it like it never happened until you don't listen to me again. It's a reoccurring theme, if you've been paying attention to these past couple of years." Rockfish flashed a shit-eating grin and pushed his plate away. *My anger towards her dumb decision will dissipate. She should know that by now. Gimme a couple of days and we'll be back to normal.*

Jawnie plucked a strawberry from her plate and then stabbed a piece of pineapple. She washed it down with a long swig of water. The smile never left her face.

"Where's Raffi? It surprised me he didn't want to battle the elements and walk to dinner last night."

"No idea, I'm not his keeper," Rockfish said.

"You could've fooled me. You practically jumped at the chance to hold his hand tomorrow night," Jawnie said. The sarcasm was thick, and Rockfish felt its impact. "He might be in trouble for all we know. Right this instant."

"Oh, he's in trouble alright," Rockfish said. "He was in rough shape when we closed down the bar last night. I followed him up to his room to make sure he didn't pass out in the hallway. With the amount he drank, he's sleeping it off. Or choked to death on his own vomit. Either way, we'll hear about it relatively soon, Mom."

Jawnie didn't reply, but Rockfish wondered what thought stopped on the tip of her tongue. She lowered her head and poked at the remaining pieces of fruit on her plate. *Does she not understand I'm now responsible for her? Granted, we're not in any real danger. Have to watch a bunch of fake army dudes unload the truck and then drive away with Raffi's cash. My cash. Our cash. But*

I'm proud of you, kid. Doing the right thing and knowing I'd be mad.
"Anyway, here we are. My bitch moaning about it ain't helping."

Jawnie picked up her head and nodded.

"Do as I say tomorrow night, not as I do, and we'll be fine. We're good, right?"

"Of course," Jawnie said. "But the one sticking point is you haven't told me how any of this is going down."

"Simple exchange, really." Rockfish said. "We're meeting the buyers in the parking lot of the Giant Eagle Supermarket. I think Raffi said around 8pm. Park at the far end and the fake army guys will unload the truck into whatever vehicles they've brought. Raffi gets payment and then immediately turns the cash over to me."

"Why at night? Why not during business hours, if this is so legit?"

Rockfish didn't need to squint to see the wheels turning in his partner's head. *Don't overthink this one, kid. It will only get us into trouble. A simple exchange. That's it.*

"Don't approach it with common sense. I try not to with him. Raffi's made a career of weird shit like this. He's done it since we were in high school and rarely does it go sideways."

"The odds have caught up since I met him."

Rockfish ignored Jawnie's solid point and continued. "He and the buyers agreed to it. Maybe they all work and need to get home, have dinner and then head back out before they can play delivery. A truck has to be unloaded and a second loaded. You do it when the physical labor is available."

Jawnie stopped asking questions, and Rockfish concentrated on his coffee. He'd enjoy the silence for the rest of breakfast. It did not surprise him that she lasted less than three minutes.

"How does one come across a truck-sized load of expiring Government issued MREs?"

Rockfish put his ceramic mug down. He dropped his head into his hands and rubbed his temples. Truth was, he didn't even know. With Raffi, a lot of questions were best un-asked. *Co-conspirator isn't high on my list of future job titles.*

The loud chime from the elevator caused Rockfish to look up. A very hungover Raffi stumbled out of the elevator.

"Speak of the devil. You can ask him."

* * * * * * * * *

Raffi gently made his way across the lobby floor and moved in the general direction of where Rockfish had told him the coffee station would be. *Get some caffeine and grease in me and I'll be right as rain. Fuck me for thinking I'd keep up with Steve. I should have known better. What's that definition? Insanity is doing the same thing repeatedly, expecting different results. Well, I'm certifiable.*

The tattered Holiday Inn robe kept him warm over his previous day's clothes. Socks enabled him to slide across the floor as each traditional step caused a minor earthquake to go off inside his head. Raffi squinted and scanned his fellow breakfasteers. He failed to recognize a face or the back of any heads. He zeroed in on the coffee station. Raffi shuffled over and filled two cups. He turned and gave the crowd the once over again, hoping this time to find an empty table away from other guests. Instead, he spotted his drinking buddy holding up two fingers. *Ah, there they are. How did I miss them? Be careful. Don't spill. Glide.*

"How the hell do you look so good?" Raffi said as he sat down. "I feel like Porbeagle did after Mack zeroed in on his skull with that thirty-ought-six. Also, no donuts, huh? Some hotel this is."

"You wandered down close to closing time," Rockfish said. He shook his head in disbelief. "You think they're paying the donut man to replenish the supply in this storm? No way, Jose."

"There might be an Aunt Ester bran muffin next to the green bananas," Jawnie said. "You want me to go check? You seem like it might be a major undertaking for you to get up."

"Thanks, Jawnie. I'll appreciate whatever you bring back."

Raffi reached for one of the coffee mugs and took a sip. "Ahh. Luke warm, didn't see that coming."

Rockfish laughed. "Your timing is perfect. Jawnie asked how you came up with this endeavor. MREs aren't exactly the thing one comes across in day-to-day life. Not to mention a damn truck full. Hell, I don't even know the back story."

"Q-Rations. Gotta stay on brand. You never know who might be listening in." Raffi said and tapped the side of his head with his index finger.

Raffi waited for Jawnie to return with a small plate of food before continuing. The bran muffin, tangelo and single serving box of generic Sugar Smacks wasn't the hangover cure he wanted, but it would get him through story time. He poured the cereal into a bowl and leaned in. He lowered his voice and began the story of how he planned to dominate the doomsday prepper meal market.

"There I was, sitting in my recliner, down to my last handle of Tito's. Watching the stock market tank and the constant reruns of the President's hand-picked supporters storming the Capitol. And I thought to myself, how can I capitalize on this grift? I mean, everyone else was making money on the poorly educated. His words, not mine. Why not Raffi?"

"Why not, indeed," Jawnie said.

"She gets it," Raffi said. He tried his other cup. "Is hot coffee not a thing in Central Pennsylvania? Any way, you read about how his base gave money to those promising to run the Democrats out of the swamp, only to realize their single contribution turned into biweekly automatic withdraws from their checking accounts? There's an angle for me with this type of consumer. I knew it."

Rockfish raised his coffee mug in a solidarity toast and Raffi continued.

"It doesn't take a rocket scientist to see there is money to be made here. Hand over fist. Shit, if that televangelist Kinard Backer can sell his own brand of post-apocalyptic meal kits, why can't Raffi?"

"Isn't that the lizard-looking old creep?" Rockfish said. "Tried to fart COVID away?"

Jawnie nodded.

"So, one night I met a guy drowning his sorrows at McHebe's. Stool right next to me. Come to find, we're in the same boat. Drunk and whining to anyone who would listen. He was a weekend warrior stationed in Chambersburg, PA, at the Letterkenny Army Depot."

"Isn't that a Canadian comedy show?" Jawnie said.

"I dunno. My free NikolaTV subscription ran out," Rockfish said with a shrug. "You'd think with our ratings, it would be a lifetime subscription."

This time, it was Raffi's turn to shake his head. *These two. Wait, is this what it's like when someone tries to tell Steve and me something? Nah. Can't be.* "Anyway, the weekend warrior fashioned himself a modern-day Radar O'Reilly."

Jawnie glanced at Rockfish for a little help.

"Way before your time, kid," Rockfish said. "Go on, Raffi, I get you. A wheeler dealer."

"Bingo. But he recently had one pulled over on him, hence his two-fisted drinking that evening. He's stuck with a military ten-wheeler filled to the brim with expiring MREs. Fresh off a plane from Afghanistan. Apparently, we left all kinds of weapons and technology behind, but brought the MREs home. Turns out he can't move them to save his life through internal channels. That's where my ingenuity and marketing skills came in."

Raffi paused for dramatic effect. He checked to make sure he had his captive audience's attention. Jawnie had leaned in, but Rockfish had heard this story a million times before about a million other "business ventures" from Raffi.

"I remember. I've got another guy who owes me a favor. This one works in a print shop. Can make me stickers in bulk on the overnight shift, without prying eyes. And wham, bam, thank you ma'am, the Q-Ration is now a thing. I buy them for pennies on the dollar and start posting on the survivalist and doomsday message boards. Doesn't take long before I have a deal in place to make a nice profit on my initial investment. That was with those Janus Sixth chuckleheads."

"Your opinion of your customer base notwithstanding, you were involved with some pretty dangerous nut jobs," Jawnie said. "Especially since they ended up on the FBI's radar and an undercover infiltrated them."

"She's right," Rockfish said. "You're damn lucky that truck shit the bed when it did. You could've been caught up in that take down and no bag of money from my rainy-day fund would have gotten you out."

Oh, don't I know it? A couple of days in Grindsville jail sure as hell beat twenty to life in Federal lockup. But don't let them catch on.

"I'm sure I would have talked my way out of it, but in the end, I made a better deal here and saved gas money. A win-win for old Raffi. Goodbye Janus Sixth Nationalists and hello Penn Forest Patriots." Raffi wiped his hands in the air. "I gotta tell ya, Steve, this state is overflowing with insurrectionists."

"It's really not surprising," Rockfish said. "But back to sales. Can I walk up to you and buy a single, if I'm like homeless and hungry? That might be an emerging market you might want to think about. Hit up the tent cities popping up in all the big metropolises."

Raffi shook his head and laughed. "Always with the jokes, Steve. I sell in bulk. A four-week supply, two-thousand calories a day, meal packs for two-hundred and fifty dollars. You can't shop cheaper than that in the frozen food aisle of the Dollar General."

Raffi picked up his coffee and moved his eyes from the soggy cereal to the two across the table. He admired his audience as they nodded in agreement. *Captured. Hanging on every word. But I gotta wrap this up.* The coffee, despite the lack of heat, had run its course, and he needed to head back upstairs. Something totally different was percolating.

"That's the backstory in all its glory. Thank you both for sticking around and having my six, as the militia-types like to say, tomorrow night. Should be a piece of cake. In and out. Back here and count the money."

"Not the first time we've heard that from you," Jawnie said.

Rockfish leaned in over the table. "Listen, bud. Pull this off without a hitch and then you pay us back," Rockfish said. "In real time."

Raffi felt all the air go out of his balloon. *Jawnie's busting my balls and Steve is all about getting paid back. Like I'm not good for it. I'll have to show them who's running things and how successful this endeavor can be. Not to mention, I've got expenses to cover. He'll get his once I'm made whole. Maybe on the next deal?*

"Of course, Steve. As soon as I get my hands on it, you'll get yours back in spades. Maybe a little extra for your troubles. I never want to be indebted to either of you for any extended period. Now, if you'll excuse me, I need to see a man about a horse."

Raffi didn't wait for goodbyes. He stood up and duck walked toward the elevator. For a second, he contemplated the public restroom around the corner, but preferred to watch TikToks in private with the volume up.

* * * * * * * * *

Jawnie awoke on the morning of the big deal and walked over to the window to let the sunshine in. Her Apple Watch let her know she had slept in until after ten a.m. She pulled the curtains to the side and noticed the snow had finally stopped. The view of downtown wasn't much, but the foot of fresh powder gave it an almost postcard-like appearance. *Appears the plows spent the night trying to stay one step ahead. That bodes well for us this evening. But would it be so bad if Raffi had asked to make his exchange in the Holiday Inn parking lot? I could watch from my window and look forward to our exit the following morning.*

She leaned forward and pressed her nose against the glass. Shop keepers from what few businesses operated downtown were out in force shoveling the sidewalks. *I don't see anyone driving downtown today, no matter how good the roads were, for an insurance quote or that fine piece of vintage 70s furniture. Definitely not for a Subway sandwich.*

Jawnie showered and then got dressed. The need to leave this small room, and in fact, the hotel, for even a few daylight hours, was at the top of her agenda. *I'm not sure if it's all the snow or being confined to this narrow rectangle of a room the past couple of days. I need a dose of sunlight, fresh air and not have to see these same lobby zombies each time I get off the elevator. Not to mention the bad thoughts creep back into my head.*

She didn't count Raffi's business transaction in the evening as any kind of hotel escape. *Anytime I don't feel I've got the entire story from Steve or Raffi, I've got concerns. Plus I haven't seen another African-American around, unless you count the court bailiff. Wear a hat, pull it down over your face. How hard will it be to sit in a truck while it's unloaded and drive off? I'm sure it will all go off according to plan. It always does with those two.* Jawnie rolled her eyes and picked up her phone off the nightstand.

"You up?" She texted Rockfish, knowing the answer before hitting send.

"Coffee in my room, they ran out right quick downstairs. Supposed to be a resupply truck coming over the mountain this afternoon. Fingers crossed." Came the reply.

"I need to get out and stretch. Anywhere but this hotel. Thinking of seeing if the Steel Mill Museum is open. The lobby's full of pamphlets for the place."

"If it's not the lobby or these four walls, I'm in. You have to love the idea of a museum honoring the memory of a crumbling industry. One that drove the town to the brink of bankruptcy," Rockfish texted back.

"Like you said, it's something to do."

"I'll let Raffi know."

With those four words, Jawnie heard the air escaping from her balloon. Her fingers danced across the screen's keyboard. "Really? Can't this be a partner's only excursion? We've already had plans with him tonight and they have a no-cancellation policy."

A flood of thumbs up emojis danced across her screen, and the leak was temporarily plugged.

Half an hour later, the partners were in the Subaru and Jawnie pulled out of the Holiday Inn parking lot. The sun's glare off the blanket of white was immediate. She took her foot off the gas and reached for her sunglasses.

"Good call on leaving the Q-Ration King back at the hotel," Rockfish said as the car straightened out and crept down Washington Street. "On the way back, I'd like to check out this Giant Eagle parking lot for myself, without him yapping in my ear. Also, your car is all-wheel-drive. No need to blue-hair it."

"No backseat or passenger seat driving, please. We can swing by it on the return trip," Jawnie said. "It's only a few blocks past the museum on the edge of downtown. And in between steel mill factoids, I'd like to get your opinion on this whole Raffi deal, without him playing point counter-point."

"Not much to it, but yeah, I'll get you up to speed. At least as far as I am. And speaking of my shadow, have you heard from yours?"

"Lynn?" Jawnie said.

"Yeah, I haven't. I'm assuming we've not missed anything exciting back at the office."

"Do you mean professionally, or me trying to talk her down off a ledge after she almost took out a support beam in your garage with Lana's front fender?"

"Don't remind me," Rockfish said with a shake of his head. "Mack filled me in. Kind of his fault. He's not the best at guiding someone into a tight space. Old people and depth perception don't go hand-in-hand. Also, he apparently forgot about the promise he made to her, not to tell me."

"Well, that makes two of us, because I took the same sworn oath," Jawnie said with a wide grin.

After a handful of turns, Jawnie spotted the museum's small parking lot and put on her blinker. The asphalt here, as opposed to the roads and other portions of the city, was clear and dry. Black from corner to corner. It was also barren of any other cars.

"Whoa," Rockfish said as he took in the museum's outside. "This ain't made of steel. Crappy beige bricks and nice stonework around the foundation. They have lied to us. THE steel museum should be made of good old American forged steel."

Jawnie smiled, and they walked around to the front steps. Rockfish held the door open. She entered and felt Rockfish grab her coat and yank her back out onto the small landing.

"What, you change your mind?" She said as he let the door close in front of her. "It's ice cold out here, if you didn't notice."

"It's WHAT I noticed. The old man, the ticket taker, I assume, was talking to the security guard. Again, why this place needs one, I'll never know. But the guard? The cop that tried to fuck me. Figuratively, of course. I'm not that easy."

"Of course. What you did in the privacy of your own cell is none of my business," Jawnie said with a smirk. It felt good getting a zinger in.

"Serious. This is a bad omen. The uniform is a different dull color, but I'd recognize those eyes anywhere."

"Nonsense. I paid your fine. The museum is free. You're free." Jawnie said, threw open the door and walked inside. Rockfish might not have liked her viewpoint, but Jawnie felt him follow a few steps behind her.

The hallway opened into a well-lit cavernous room. Standing structures of twisted steel filled the left side, while photos and small displays lined the walls to her right. An old man, sitting at a small desk, separated the two display sides. *Is he playing dress up? An example of a mid-70s steel worker when the industry thrived?* He wore filthy coveralls, two sizes too big for his thin frame, a red hard-hat and goggles that rested atop. *Seriously though, I wonder if he actually retired from a mill before times got bad, or are those only props?* His long gray beard gave Jawnie another pause. *That thing must be a real pain when he's assigned to work around the blast furnace.*

She approached the desk and made eye contact with the man.

"Good morning. Two, please."

"That's fifteen dollars. We don't take credit cards."

"I'm sorry," Jawnie said. "This pamphlet I picked up at the Holiday Inn stated the museum tour is free?"

"Those were printed back when the Democrats were in charge. Everything was a handout back then. Our newly elected city council understands how economics work. But it would be too much of a pain to gather up all the old pamphlets."

Jawnie tilted her head and stared at the man. His contempt was apparent. *Is it my skin color or the Pride sweatshirt?*

"Ah, gotcha. I don't have any Confederate currency on me," Rockfish said, stepping out from behind Jawnie. "Used my last fiver at the Stars & Bars rest stop down the road."

The old man didn't say a word. Instead, he reached under the desk and the security guard strolled over a few seconds later, confirming Rockfish's earlier presumption. He had exchanged the police blues for the dull brown of a rent-a-cop.

"Do we have a problem over here, Amos?"

The old man lifted his head. He looked from Jawnie to Rockfish and simply nodded.

"Ah, Mr. Rockfish. I'm shocked that you stuck around our...how did you put it to me...one horse town, if the horse had chlamydia and was shot in one leg. Not to mention the reference to Mr. Hands. Hadn't heard that one before, had to Google it."

Sobotka hadn't finished speaking when Jawnie already regretted not listening to Rockfish outside. The cop's eyes were creepy. Small compared to the rest of his enormous face and the brightest blue she had ever seen. She also knew Rockfish was never one to step away from a verbal pissing match. Instead, she cringed and hoped what came out of her partner's mouth next wouldn't land them both in custody.

"Sobotka, I'm shocked you need this side gig. Shouldn't you be out separating a poor lost motorist from their wallet? A little off the top for yourself would prevent having to moonlight, or in this case, daylight. Screwing hard-working people out of their savings not getting your dick hard anymore? Then I'm glad I recommend the Mr. Hands documentary." Sobotka gave the twosome the evil eye.

Another Rockfish reference I need to research later. But I need to cut this off before it escalates. Jawnie pulled a twenty from her wallet and handed it to the man at the desk. "Keep the change." She didn't wait for a reply and moved toward the large exhibits. Her interest in the process used to create ultra-high-strength maraging steel had grown a hundredfold in the past three seconds.

"Please follow the arrows on the floor," Amos finally said. "It's a self-guided tour."

Jawnie peeked over her shoulder. She assumed Rockfish had failed to follow her, and she wasn't wrong. They were locked into a staring contest. They might have continued to exchange insults under their breath, but she was too far away to make out what they said.

"Steve," Jawnie said, as stern as she possible could without raising her voice. She watched as his head turned and then swung right back to Sobotka. His lips moved, but she didn't make out the parting shot before he stepped over to where she patiently waited.

"Can't help it, can you?" Jawnie said with a slight shake of her head. She hoped he got the disgust in her voice.

"Mom, he started it. I only made sure I had the last word. Trust me, if he wasn't here, I'd be waiting in the car. But I don't trust either of those two clowns."

The self-guided tour kept Jawnie and Rockfish occupied for the next half an hour, although she noticed and assumed Rockfish had too, that Sobotka seemed to lurk around every corner. The men exchanged more dirty looks than words and they were back in the Subaru before Jawnie let out a tremendous sigh of relief.

"Not that bad, was it?" Rockfish said.

"The tension in that place. Thick is an understatement. I would have put a couple of dollars on the fact you two would have been rolling around on the floor before we left."

"Well, here's to having to never run across those eyes again," Rockfish said, slipping a small flask out of his jacket before taking a swig. "Now let's see what kind of shape this supermarket parking lot is in. I want to have a clue what we're driving into tonight."

Jawnie blinked and bit her bottom lip before shifting the car into reverse. "The Giant Eagle isn't too far from here and since when did you start carrying?"

"Since I've been snowed in and had to deal with power hungry jerks like that."

Jawnie thought about it for a second and decided not to follow up. *Get through today and by noon tomorrow, life will be normal.* Sleeping in her own bed never sounded so good.

The supermarket was down the street. Duplexes surrounded the medium-sized shopping plaza. Most of the dwellings appeared to be waiting on a bureaucrat to condemn the lot. Jawnie noticed a sole figure walking down the street away from the shops. The woman dressed in rags, with a worn comforter across her shoulders. She pushed a wobbly shopping card filled with cans, bottles, and cardboard.

As the plaza came into view, both partners came to the same conclusion. Raffi's truck wasn't getting into, much less out of the unplowed lot. They watched customers exit the store, groceries in hand, and walk to a line of cars parked along the street.

"I'm guessing half those lights in the parking lot are shot out, too. Not ideal," Rockfish said. "I'll text him and tell him it ain't gonna work. The guys he's dealing with probably have jacked-up four-wheel-drive vehicles, but the Marvin Trotter Special won't make it off the street."

"Agreed. Wonder if the men he's in contact with expected the parking lot would have been plowed, based on prior storms. People need supplies. Is there another storm moving through? This isn't ideal."

"Get us back to the hotel before Raffi makes alternate plans that I won't have any say in," Rockfish said. "This deal needs to go down in the very well-lit and public hotel parking lot."

* * * * * * * * * *

The Wednesday afternoon sun had long disappeared from view and the box truck's headlights illuminated each snowflake as it fluttered down from the darkness. More lake effect snow fall was called for, but the local WJAC weatherman swore live on air, it would not bring any additional accumulation. Rockfish didn't believe a word. He reached across Jawnie and raised the heat on the truck's front defrost. Almost as if on cue, the wipers moved across the windshield.

They sat three across the cab's bench seat, Rockfish driving and Jawnie squeezed in the middle. He wasn't too keen on the new Raffi-only negotiated plan and his own lack of trust in weathermen. It only increased his anxiety. Murphy's law was bound to catch up with them. *Christ, if I'm feeling this way, I'm surprised Jawnie could pull herself together and climb up into the cab.*

"Steve, my guy didn't stutter. Eight-thirty, p.m.," Raffi said. "The place is twenty minutes, give or take, outside of town.

Listening to you will have us there half an hour early. I don't want to upset 'em by showing up while they're in setup mode."

Rockfish heard the contempt in Raffi's voice. *Little bird is trying to fly on his own and isn't thrilled big brother is trying to have his say. Well, I got news for you, pal. I don't trust a damn thing about this evening. The simplest of exchanges always go sideways and one of us needs to be on alert. Mr. Murphy is always at the ready. Especially since I had no say in the change of venue. It's good to have the element of surprise.*

Rockfish choose to raise his concern. "Seriously? I texted you half a dozen times to not reach out to these--"

"Penn Forest Patriots," Raffi said. His head rested against the passenger side window. "Please don't disparage them to their faces. You'll put this whole deal in jeopardy."

Rockfish sighed. *Raffi didn't get it. He was already back in Baltimore, counting his profits and thanking his lucky stars for finding a second buyer for his load. Fuck him, it's not my job to make sure he makes it back in one piece, but somehow, I always volunteer. Little Stevie Saves the World, his dad had once called him.*

"You ignored my plea to wait before coming up with another plan of action. Now you're stuck with me and my input regarding this shit show. You don't think your pretend army buddies will be early? Waiting on us? I want them to be, at a minimum, shocked as hell when we roll up. Surprise, surprise. On their heels."

Rockfish glanced over, but Raffi continued to gaze out the window. "I know you think this will go off swimmingly, but I got bad vibes. Another reason this one should have to stay back in the hotel." Rockfish jerked a thumb at Jawnie.

"Not on your life. I'm on site to help, not show up to bail you out later."

"I do not know what's up with you two. They transfer the load and then give me a big bag of money. I've done this a million times." Raffi said. His breath fogging the glass with each word.

"If it was that easy, they'd have met us in a spot well-lit and meticulously traversed," Rockfish said. He begged for his friend to see the issues from his point of view, but the rest of the drive was quiet. From all parties.

The new rendezvous spot was the Grindsville water treatment plant. It lay on the outskirts of town and down a hundred-yard-long gravel road. The satellite image Jawnie pulled off the internet showed a small two-story building surrounded by a chain-link fence. A cell tower sat on the grounds behind the building but outside the fence line. As the truck approached the turnoff for the entranceway, Rockfish noticed the lack of signage for a proper city-run facility.

The only sign on the side of the road read *City of Grindsville Private Property - Trespassers Will Be Prosecuted.*

"I'm gonna slow to a crawl here," Rockfish said. "Once we turn off the main road, you don't know what or who might jump out of the woods. Not to mention the condition of the road. The shocks on this thing might bust."

Rockfish took his foot off the gas and the box truck slowed down. The slower pace would give him an extra couple of minutes to think. *That damn sign. City property. Why pick here? Out of the way, or the peace of mind knowing that no one would come up this lane, uninvited?*

Raffi straightened up and reached for the door handle. "Alright Steve, you got us here. Now it's time to switch. My deal. They're expecting to see me behind the wheel when we pull up. If they see a strange face, all bets might be off."

I can argue with him or let him have his minute in the sun. Plus, I might observe better, if I'm not driving.

"I agree. Don't want to spook 'em," Rockfish said. The men opened their doors and crisscrossed in front of the truck.

Rockfish didn't click his seatbelt after climbing back in and reached over to undo Jawnie's. "In case we need to make a fast exit." She nodded in agreement. *No room for you Mr. Murphy, cab's full.*

The truck rolled forward again. The cab rocked with each dip in the gravel. *Gravel. Someone plowed this and not too long ago. A coincidence? City property and part of the critical internal infrastructure, so it makes sense. Come on now, you're getting way too paranoid.*

The brakes squeaked, and Raffi brought the truck to a stop. Rockfish leaned forward and peered across the hood. The headlights shone on two men standing before a chain-link gate. One held his hand up, as if using the force to stop their progress. They were exactly how he had pictured the other half of this exchange. Both dressed almost identical, as if camouflaged jackets from an Army Navy surplus store were indistinguishable. Matching knit hats and gaiters covered most of the surface area of their heads. AR-15s hung across their chests. Fingers at the ready. *Look at the trigger discipline on these yahoos.*

"Recognize 'em?" Rockfish said.

"Yeah, that's them. Penn Forest Patriots. See that patch on their jackets?"

"I can't see shit, but they seem more like Great Value Boys to me."

"Huh?" Jawnie said, not following the conversation.

"Great Value is the pride of the Walmart brand," Rockfish said. "These guys are more like Proud Boys wannabes, but with knock-off Carhartt and cheaper equipment."

"You two and your damn pop culture references," Jawnie said. "I'm shocked you didn't go the Y'all Qaeda route."

"We are north of the Mason-Dixon Line."

Jawnie softly chuckled. "Says who? I've gotten the banjo-vibes up here since day one."

The levity eased the tension inside the truck. While the first Great Value Boy kept his hand raised, the second walked over to the drivers side and climbed onto the running board. He didn't speak and his eyes gave no instruction. He lifted a flashlight and swept the inside of the cab. Without saying a word, he nodded to his compatriot on the ground. He held onto the side mirror as the gate opened inward.

Someone appears to have a key to the city's gate. I'm positive they didn't bring a set of bolt cutters and a replacement lock. Rockfish's spidey-sense intensified. His eyes shot across the 'compound' from left to right as Raffi took his foot off the brake. The truck jerked forward and entered a paved area in front of the brick municipal building. Once the back end of the truck cleared the gate, their stowaway jumped down to the ground.

Rockfish watched both side mirrors to see if the gate slid shut behind them. If it did, he knew they'd be in for a heap of trouble. But it didn't budge. *Interesting. Maybe they'll back up a truck for us to unload from one to the other. Might Raffi be right? First time for everything.*

His eyes moved back to the front end of the truck. Four more Great Value Boys had emerged from the shadows as he had checked on the gate. Six armed men now stood in a semi-circle around the front of the truck. At first glance, the men seemed identical. Neck gaiters and camouflage from top to bottom. Rockfish noticed that those without AR-15s slung across their chest had side holsters. *No lack of firepower with this group. LARPing in the woods, but I'm betting that ain't pretend ammo.* The concealed handguns he and Jawnie carried would be no match if things went south.

"Steve, I'm feeling uncomfortable," Jawnie said and twisted in her seat. "Outnumbered and obviously out-gunned."

"Don't worry, little lady, I've got everything under control," Raffi said with an assuring grin. "Everything's gonna be all right."

Rockfish tapped his hand against Jawnie's knee and gave a reassuring glance. "Take a deep breath. They'll hate you the minute you walk into the light. Can't do a damn thing about that. We need to see where this goes and not jump the gun. Worse comes to worst, they take his merchandise and send us home without his money. If getting ripped off is as bad as it gets, then we can count our lucky stars. No way these wannabe weekend warriors are killers."

"Come on, Steve, lighten up. I'm running the show," Raffi said. "I got the goods. Don't believe me? Just sit back and learn a thing or two."

Raffi opened the drivers-side door and jumped out of the truck. His feet hadn't hit the ground before two Great Value Boys broke the semi-circle. Rockfish could only watch as Raffi was thrown to the ground, face first, and a red laser-sight danced across the back of his head.

* * * * * * * * * *

The spectators in the truck's cab could only watch. Their respective minds ran through possible exit strategies. Each came up empty when considering they were heavily outgunned and lifelong hunters tended to be good shots. Eyes darted from the weapons to the action on the ground and then to each other. Ass cheeks remained rooted to the bench seat. Not frozen in fear, but not moving to save the day, either. Rockfish's mind raced. *Suicide or a traumatic brain injury if I leap out and try to pull him to safety. Or should I try? You just told her they aren't killers.*

Raffi remained on the ground, face in the dirt. His arms stretched out and legs crossed at the ankles. Rockfish heard the frostbite creeping across the side of Raffi's face as it fused with the ice-cold pavement. *You need to help him before he literally hangs himself with that mouth. Won't be lucky enough to have it freeze shut before then.* Rockfish saw Raffi's head, but it was what he didn't see and hear that worried the fuck out of him. Raffi's lips. *I can only assume he's speaking a million miles-an-hour and who knows what excuses or promises he's making.*

"Jawnie, can you call 9-1-1?" Rockfish whispered out of the side of his mouth. "Nonchalant-like."

"I can try," Jawnie said. Her hand crept up from her lap towards the inside pocket of her jacket.

"Hey!" The shout came from the ground and two men swung their rifles towards the cab. "You! Keep dem hands up."

Rockfish and Jawnie barely heard the man clearly, with the windows up and the heat blowing. Yet the command was explicit and obeyed. Their hands touched the roof of the cab and Rockfish understood choices needed to be made. *This instant. If Raffi hasn't realized it by now, he never was running this show. I gotta do something before he says the wrong thing and one of those greasy chicken fingers slip.*

Rockfish glanced at Jawnie. He pursed his lips and gave his head a tilt to his right. His arm shot out for the door release, but Jawnie was quicker.

"No," she said. "What are you planning? Think about the weapons and numbers alone. I won't be able to bail the both of you out this time. Be smart, Steve."

"Hey! I said..." The man outside shouted.

"I will. No one's beat on him yet," Rockfish said. He pushed open the passenger door and landed feet first. He moved slowly, deliberately, around the front of the truck and kept his hands up. Barrels across the parking lot moved from Raffi to his approaching savior. *Or idiot.* Rockfish wasn't even sure which one he was.

"Whoa, gentlemen. I'm not trying to do anything other than save my friend from having to cash the checks his mouth is writing." Rockfish took another couple of steps forward and the only other words in the night air came from Raffi.

"...we had a deal, man. Where the fuck is your boss? Lemme..."

Rockfish tuned his friend out and concentrated on the armed men. One of which appeared to have heard enough and moved closer to Raffi and raised a leg.

"Hold it right there!" Rockfish said. "Don't you dare pee on him." He hoped the levity would give the man pause and Rockfish another second to actually prevent the boot from coming down on Raffi's head.

Raffi outguessed both men and didn't wait to see how things played out. He rolled away from the raised boot, sat up, and braced for another type of blow.

"Enough of that, Wilson. Get our guest to his feet." The words boomed from the far corner of the municipal building. Rockfish quickly spotted the man behind the voice as he emerged from the shadows. "That's no way to treat our prospective business partners."

The first thing Rockfish noticed was the man's gut. It entered the dimly lit parking lot before the rest of his torso. He dressed in camouflage coveralls and a dark blue cavalry hat. A design was stitched across the front of the hat, but Rockfish couldn't make it out. His eyes, instead, locked on the giant side arm, hanging half out of a coverall pocket. The Great Value Boys guarding Raffi and Rockfish parted like the Red Sea as the man, clearly their leader, approached.

Fifty cal, Desert Eagle? At the least. Speaking of, seems like General Fat Patton's in charge. How is this going to play out, especially if Raffi doesn't shut the fuck up? And what's up with the niceties? Rockfish continued to weigh his options as the leader continued past Raffi, ignoring the outstretched hand. Instead, Fat Patton stepped in Rockfish's direction.

"Mr. Rockfish, I presume. Sorry, our exchange diverted off course. The name's Colonel Jesus Earnhardt Jr., Penn Forrest Patriots." Earnhardt held his hand out until Rockfish finally took it.

Rockfish glanced over and even in the dimly lit parking lot, the red in Raffi's face stood out. He was supposed to be the star of this show. At least in his mind.

"What? The? Fuck?" Raffi said. He took a step toward where Rockfish and Earnhardt Jr. stood. Two Great Value Boys stepped in front, blocking him from moving any closer. Rockfish knew that wouldn't go over well. *Hold on, here we go.*

"Goddamn it. These are my MREs," Raffi said.

"Q-Rations." Rockfish couldn't resist.

"Steve, please. This is my deal. Work with me or walk the fuck away. I've got militias clamoring for this shit all up and down the east coast..."

Rockfish saw the steam beginning to emerge from Raffi's ears. *He's ready to blow.*

"... and none of those damn groups would have the gall to point assault rifles at me. They'd welcome me. I'm part of the movement. A fellow patriot. I'm in--"

Earnhardt Jr. gave a slight nod, and one of his men flinched. The butt-end of his rifle found Raffi's jaw, and he was out before his own butt hit the pavement. Rockfish reached for the small of his back and Earnhardt Jr. turned and faced Rockfish. He slid the Desert Eagle out and dangled it along his thigh. Rockfish's arm slowly returned to his side. He measured his response and bit the inside of his lip. He wanted to turn and give Jawnie reassurance, but a second sudden movement was no longer in the cards. *Change of plans. Drag Raffi back to the cab and get out of here before any further damage is done. Fuck his Q-Rations. Fuck the cash we were probably never ever gonna get.*

"If we're done with amateur hour," Earnhardt Jr. said. "And we both understand exactly who's in charge and what's at stake. I'm going to let you know how the rest of this meeting is going to go."

Rockfish bit down harder on the inside of his lip. He gave a short, quick nod.

"Good. First, don't think me and my men haven't noticed the obvious handgun in the small of your back. I'm going to ask you to remove it. Slowly, and heave it into the woods. You can retrieve it later, after we're gone. I really don't give a shit."

Rockfish did as instructed and heard his gun land somewhere in the darkness. He kissed any chance of gaining the upper hand, no matter how minuscule, goodbye.

Earnhardt's snarl shifted to a twisted smile. "Second, I've been instructed to not pay for these goods, but to rather convince you, this donation will serve a greater good. How you convince your accountant of the write-off is not my concern."

"But you're Fat Pat--err, I mean the Colonel." Rockfish said. "THE Colonel Jesus Earnhardt. I can't see a man of your stature taking orders from anyone. Surely there is room for negotiation?"

Earnhardt Jr. spitted a wad of tobacco juice at Rockfish's feet. "We all have bosses, Mr. Rockfish. The orders from mine are not up for interpretation. This exchange will not go the way you planned, but..."

Rockfish knew how this rodeo was going to end. No need to listen to the rest of Earnhardt Jr.'s spiel. Instead, his eyes darted around the parking lot to see if there was anything he missed which he could grab hold of and take advantage of. His glance was met with six other pairs. A few even shook their heads. *Don't think about it? Time to put the hands up and live to get home in one piece. I owe that to myself, if not to Jawnie and Rip Van Winkle over there on the ground.*

"Leave us the truck at least?" Rockfish was hopeful despite the evening's general direction.

"Not gonna happen. Jerome, go get that nappy-haired broad out of the cab and check her too. Then set her down next to Mr. Pérez. And Mr. Rockfish, I expect you not to get on your phone until we're at least twenty-minutes out. But if you feel the need to tempt fate, and I will assure you, whoever answers the emergency line will be of no help. None. Whatsoever."

CHAPTER FIVE

A month had passed since the Q-Rations sales team had returned to home base. The unpleasant taste of the Great Value Boys lingered, ever so lightly, on the back of everyone's tongues. Back in the office, safe and with only Raffi's jaw seeing any action that night, Rockfish couldn't complain about the outcome. Especially since it wasn't his pocket that was turned inside out. But an exciting story to tell didn't stop Marvin Trotter from blowing up his phone over the missing truck after Raffi stopped taking the man's calls.

But for Raffi, the other wannabe musketeer, the past was not easily forgotten. From the minute he regained consciousness to his latest set of tirades, whether in Rockfish's office or on the back deck, Raffi was centered on a revenge tour. Fortunately, he'd been unable to raise a crew for his expedition. An outcome Rockfish was also grateful for. He knew if Raffi returned to Grindsville, even with a rag-tag army of mercenaries in tow there would be no retribution. No matter what Raffi had promised his band of freelancers leading up to the trip.

This particular Thursday morning found Rockfish pulling into the office parking lot a few minutes after nine a.m. The long line at the McDonald's drive-thru had set the tone for his morning. And seeing Raffi's orange Taurus parked directly in front of the office door sealed his mood. *Not first thing in the morning. Let me at least get through this McGriddle before I have to listen to you.* Rockfish chirped Lana's key fob and bounded across the sidewalk, breakfast sandwich and coffee in hand. He reached for the door and said a silent prayer.

"Morning, Boss," Lynn said. "He's in your office, but you probably know that. Waiting. Not patiently either. I tried telling him I didn't know when you'd be back, but he said he'd wait. I can only deal with him so much." Lynn frowned and shrugged.

"No problem, Lynn, I understand. He won't be staying long. And Andy Andrist should be here at ten. Jawnie says that's a meeting neither of us can push or skip. Not that I know what it's about, but it has to be better than what's waiting on me right this minute."

"I can help you there," Lynn said and pushed back her chair. "Jawnie's had the lead on Andrist but with her down in Washington until this evening... anyway, with the new marijuana laws taking effect a few months back, Andrist trying to vet employees for his planned extensive grow and retail operation."

"But the law says adults, and I quote, may grow up to two cannabis plants in their homes for personal use." *Who the fuck would he need to vet?*

Lynn shrugged. "You know Andy. Second in skirting the law, only to your waiting appointment."

"Speaking of which, expect him to storm out of her momentarily. I don't have the time or the patience this morning for his shit."

"I'll drink to that," Lynn said and raised her coffee mug. "I'll make myself scarce."

"I'll join you in a few," Rockfish said. He turned away from Lynn, headed through the bullpen area, and down the short hallway to his office. A shadow emerged at the end of the carpet and the yapping began.

"Steve, I've been waiting," Raffi said.

"But not in the normal waiting area, nor are you on my calendar. I don't care what obstacles you and Lynn can't work though, but I cannot have you bullying your way into my office," Rockfish said, stepping around his friend. He sat down behind the desk and Raffi was in the visitor chair across. "I don't plan on shutting and locking the front door, so you're the one needing to curb the behavior."

Raffi pulled the visitor chair closer to the desk. Close enough Rockfish saw the pores on his friend's face. Raffi had something to say and there would not be any stopping him. But Rockfish held up his palm, anyway.

"Gimme a second to get situated before you start," Rockfish said. He picked up the remote and turned the television on. The screen flickered to life with SportsCenter, but the volume muted. He dumped the McGriddle and hash brown out of the grease-soaked bag and took a sip of coffee. Rockfish pursed his lips, nodded and prepared to shut down whatever harebrained revenge scheme was about to spill forth.

"Now hear me out. If you can--"

"I can't do a thing," Rockfish said. "Especially if you're still obsessed with getting back at these hillbillies."

"Hear me out, Steve. I don't need much from your end."

"Good, because you ain't getting shit." Rockfish shook his head for emphasis and picked up the McGriddle. "I don't have the time or resources. I can't afford to deviate from the firm's current caseload. That includes personnel, money or tools of the trade." Rockfish took a bite and shook his head again. "Be happy we all walked away. Marvin lost a truck and you're down a few thousand. It might have been so much worse, and I don't see how you can keep side stepping those points."

"But, Steve, you don't even know what I want or what my plan is," Raffi said.

Rockfish looked across the desk and saw his friend's eyes were wide. Pleading almost. As if the last month of shooting down idea after idea on how he'd get even, or at the very least, his merchandise back.

"That's the first right thing you've said since we returned last month," Rockfish said. "And I don't want to know. Do you know how far that set me, this company, back? I'm talking about potential and current clients. The cash was one thing, but my future and major income stream have taken a hit."

"You know I'm good for it." Raffi's right hand massaged the back of his neck and then moved to his temples.

"Yes, I do, but I also know that it might be my grandchildren that collect. I need to be here and working. Referrals are a huge part of our business plan."

"Don't give me that bullshit, Steve," Raffi said. He pounded the desk with an open palm. "You've got all that Hollywood streaming cash coming in hand over fist. I see that boat sitting behind your house. You ain't bouncing no checks."

Rockfish glared at Raffi. He had lost count of the number of times this conversation had happened over the past thirty days, but the pleading eyes, the pounding on the desk, showed him that the volume knob was turned up to eleven.

"I'm not complaining, Raffi. Just stating facts. Yeah, the network has been good to me, but it's not like I haven't worked for it. Shit, your work on the Porbeagle case alone got you a pretty payday from that same Hollywood account, if I recall."

"I was there. I was shot. At. Almost."

Rockfish rolled his eyes and glanced at the clock in the corner of his monitor. *Ten more minutes, max.*

"I know. I was there. But again, don't play this *you can afford it game.*" Rockfish pushed his chair away from the desk and sat up straight. It was a subtle hint, and he was prepared to show Raffi the door if his friend didn't catch on. Quickly. "My finances are no concern to you. You're a friend, not my accountant. And I wasn't crying poor. Simply stated, there was money I expected, and I can no longer count on. All because I went up to bail you out and my current, I mean former clients, didn't think too much of my prioritization skills. But I'm a loyal guy, you know that."

"I do, which is why if you'd only listen. This is pretty much fool proof. All I'm going to need is--"

"Nothing." Rockfish inched his chair forward, leaned forward, and rested his elbows on the desk. "Not a thing. From me. Can't do it. Won't do it. And I'd prefer you don't go either. Stick around here. I'll toss some work your way. Nothing exciting, but it'll help recoup a portion of your losses. Next time, it might be the other end of the rifle that comes for your chin. Think about that." He sat back and folded his arms.

"Okay, I can take a hint," Raffi said. "Especially when you have repeatedly emphasized it. But I'm not giving up. I don't need your handout. I'm going to fix this and you'll see."

The men's hands met across the desk, and they agreed to disagree. Rockfish sensed his friend's disappointment and threw out a pool noodle to keep the piece. *Not exactly a life preserver, but it'll do.*

"Whatever you do, do it safely. And shit, before you leave. Mack's making Chicken Taco Pie tonight," Rockfish said. He knew Raffi's penchant for his dad's home cooking. "Jawnie and I will be there around 6 p.m., after swinging by Decker's. With the Grindsville shenanigans, I'm late dropping off his retirement gifts. If I wait any longer, he'll get pissed and I'll end up drinking one of his gifts alone on my deck. Plus, I'm itching to hear how his hunt for a second career is coming along. Not well, if my sources are correct."

Baltimore Police Captain Dan Decker was a friend of Rockfish's who had recently retired. By the time word reached Rockfish, retired wasn't exactly how he had heard it. *More like pushed out. Here's your gold watch and don't let the door hit you on the ass.* He was curious to hear his friend's version of events later that afternoon over drinks. *Not sure which I feel worse about. Him losing the job he lived for, or me missing his damn retirement party.*

"Thanks, Steve. I appreciate it," Raffi said. "I'll text ya later if I'm able to swing by. Give Decker my best. I should stop by and see him soon."

Rockfish watched his friend walk out of the office. *He didn't appear too bad, did he? I don't have time to worry about his feelings now. He's safe on that back burner.* Rockfish glanced at the clock on his monitor and sat down. *Five to ten, right on time for Andrist, the self-described South Baltimore Weedfather-to-be.*

Knock

Rockfish looked up to find Lynn standing in his doorway.

"You okay, Boss? By the expression on Raffi's face as he sped past my desk, you must have run over his dog, flipped him the bird, and kept driving."

Now that I'd feel bad about. Turning down the opportunity to ride shotgun to Grindsville for the Deliverance reboot? Not so much.

"He's disappointed. He'll get over it. Kind of like me and this next meeting. Send him back."

* * * * * * * * * *

Not long after the conversation with Raffi faded from Rockfish's memory, the sun disappeared behind the rolling clouds. By the time he and Jawnie left for Dan Decker's house, a light rain had started, and the wind picked up.

"Any idea if this is going to continue or get worse?" Rockfish said. "It's a good thing we picked up his gifts in advance and don't have to make mad dashes across various parking lots."

"It's supposed to rain well after dinner," Jawnie said. "Honestly, after Grindsville, no matter how beautiful, I'm thrilled about not seeing another snowflake for a while."

"You and me both." The partner's fist bumped across Lana's center console.

Soon, Rockfish turned into Decker's development and stopped at the front gate. He entered the visitor code and Lana moved slowly across the speed bump. Rockfish knew it was coming, but Jawnie held off until the gate closed behind them.

"Quite the upscale neighborhood," she said from the passenger seat. "I wouldn't place Dan living here."

"And you'd be right. This is all Rosie, his wife. I'm betting Dan's not a big fan of carrying this mortgage and HOA payment into retirement. Good thing he married rich." Rockfish smirked and caught Jawnie shaking her head out of his peripheral. Four additional speed bumps and three four-way stops later, Lana pulled into the white brick driveway.

Former Captain Dan Decker and Rockfish's friendship--and working relationship--went back over a decade. Mutual respect allowed each man to willingly bend the rules in help of the other's work. The collaboration always ended the same. The good guys victorious, their friendship on the temporary outs, and Decker in hot water with his superiors.

The partners exited the car bearing their respective retirement gifts and hustled between the raindrops. Jawnie struggled with a flower arrangement larger than her torso and Rockfish cradled a bottle of Yamazaki 12-Year-Old Single Malt Whisky. His card also included a gift certificate for three one-hour sessions at the mall massage chair kiosk. One thoughtful present and one ball busting. It was the Rockfish way.

They moved along the matching white brick walkway and veered right before stepping onto the porch.

"Said he'd be around back," Rockfish said and led the way across the grass.

"I'm not sitting out in this storm under a fancy pergola."

"You saw the houses on the way in," Rockfish said. "I think you'll be pleasantly surprised. And dry."

Rockfish turned the corner and unlatched the gate to the backyard. Decker waved them in from his seat in the Florida room. It ran the length of the house and, aside from the standard table and swivel chairs, a large flat screen hung above a well-stocked bar.

Rockfish raised his eyebrows and held the back door open for Jawnie. She nodded her approval.

"Come on in, you two, get out of that rain. It's only supposed to get worse."

Decker didn't move from his chair and motioned towards the table. The door closed behind him, and Decker's appearance surprised Rockfish. He was barefoot and dressed in a plain colored T-shirt and shorts. *Heating bill be damned.* He felt the change in temperature. The heat was cranked, and he wondered if Decker's new beard kept his face toasty. But it was the semi-automatic on the table to Decker's right that gave Rockfish more cause for concern. *Jesus. From outward appearances, he looks like Tom Hanks in Castaway, if a SIG Sauer P365 washed up on shore instead of the damn volleyball. Happy with all the free-time-beard, or crazy Howard Hughes? I'll find out here in a sec.*

Decker reached for the remote on the table and shut off the television. The gigantic head of Detective Joe Kenda and the DiscoveryID logo faded to dark.

Decker smiled wide and turned his head. "Hey Jawnie, that Hollywood buddy of yours. Angel Davenport. The producer of y'alls show. You pitch him one of these Kenda-type murder shows for me? One where I stare at the camera and talk about old cases? I could use some of that NikolaTV money you and grumpy here are so fond of."

"By the shape of this place, you aren't exactly hurting," Jawnie said. She placed the large arrangement down on the table and leaned in for a hug. "Congratulations on a distinguished career. Well deserved."

"Thank you. Rosie will love these. Let me move them off to the side." Decker slid the large vase to his right and blocked the view of Rockfish. "There, perfect."

All three laughed, and Rockfish sighed a little in relief. *At least he's still got a sense of humor. Maybe he only appears homeless.* He stepped around the corner of the table and handed Decker the bottle of single malt and the gift certificates.

"Japanese, huh?" Decker said as he held and spun the bottle over. "I'm betting its expensive."

"You have no idea. Not to mention, Mack saw it and dove for an imaginary foxhole in the front yard. I had to hide it in the garage until today. Enjoy it Dan and don't be stingy with the invites. I like the dress code here. If I can have the Wi-Fi password, the work from home possibilities are endless."

Decker put down the bottle and held out his hand. The friends shook, and Decker pulled Rockfish in uncomfortably close.

Small talk filled the first part of the visit once Rockfish and Jawnie pulled up chairs. Decker relayed the story of how a newly appointed Commandant and he banged heads on every aspect of the job.

"The guy was a blue flamer. For whatever reason, the brass loved him and saw me as an obstacle. Things got to where the Chief signed off on an early retirement package and implied it was in the best interest of all parties." His face emotionless, but there was a hint of quiet desperation in his eyes.

"Blue flamer?" Jawnie said, a quizzical appearance on her face.

"A fast riser. But dumb as a box of rocks when it came to actual police work. Guy had it out for me from day one. No reason. But I wasn't ready to stop, no matter how close I was to actual mandatory retirement age."

"There's no fighting bureaucracy," Jawnie added. "The worker drone never wins."

"Yeah, but there's gas left in the tank, if you know what I mean," Decker said. "Anyway, let's break open this bottle before Steve starts drooling." Decker walked over to the bar area and returned with three rocks glasses and poured one, two and three fingers.

"One for the lady, two for Steve and since I've got nowhere to be..." Three glasses met in the center of the table and kissed.

As the conversation progressed, Rockfish had a feeling his friend had a hidden agenda he was setting the table for. *Nothing*

concrete, for sure, but damn if he doesn't seem to dance around
something. Trying to make us very at ease.

"I can't believe you two missed my party. Rosie spent a good
portion of the ride home berating me with the *I told you so's.*"

"Hey Dan, don't drag me into this. This guy never told me there
was a party." Jawnie said, giving Rockfish the side eye across the
table. "I didn't know until we were back in town exactly what we
had missed."

"All of this is long past. Move on people," Rockfish said. "Unlike
Rosie. I know she's not my biggest fan."

Jawnie glanced at Rockfish and gave her head a slight tilt.

"Story for another time, kid," Rockfish said with a quick head
shake. "But, Dan, I had a ton of extra stuff to take care of last month.
We were out of town with our hands full, and because of my
allegiance to a friend, the firm lost a few clients due to my
prioritization. Or lack thereof. The jury remains out on that one."

"Raffi?" Decker said, knowing full well the answer. "That's one
relationship of yours I never quite understood. From my
experience he's caused you nothing but grief."

Rockfish smirked. "Ah yes, the one and only. I'm loyal to a fault.
We've done a ton for each other over the years, even if his side of
the ledger is always in the red. I can never explain it clearly when
I'm sober." Rockfish winked and picked up his glass. "But anyway,
thanks to him we had to run out to East Bumfuck, Pennsylvania.
Thought I was only bailing him out of jail and ended up getting
sucked up into one of his schemes. By the time Jawnie and I got
back here, I had three different clients tell me to pound sand.
They'd find a firm more attentive to their needs."

"Sounds like the BPD," Decker said. "I've had my resume out on
LinkedIn, but not even a nibble. No response from any of those I
worked with in the past, now set in their cushy private sector jobs.
Busted my ass for these people. All those years." Decker drained
his rocks glass and another heavy pour followed.

As if on cue, both partners turned and looked outside. The sky had grown considerably dark, and the wind picked up enough to rattle the porch windows. Rockfish polished off his glass as the rain increased.

"Another?" Decker said.

"You know me well, but today, I'm going to pass. Seems pretty bad out there and your business card won't get me out of my next traffic stop."

"You could always call it a day and hang here. At least until Rosie comes home."

Both men laughed and Rockfish turned the conversation towards Decker's newly found spare time. He warned against becoming addicted to soap operas and pointed toward the nice set of retirement golf clubs gathering dust in the corner.

"... of course you'll have to shave and change before the country club will accept you."

"And on that note," Jawnie said. "I apologize, Dan, can you point me toward the closest bathroom?"

"Sure thing. Through the door, head past the kitchen island to the hallway and it's the second door."

Jawnie stood up and stepped through the Florida room door and into the kitchen. Rockfish turned to his left and braced himself for what he somewhat felt was coming. Once again, Decker drained his glass and held it with two hands in front of him on the table.

"Steve, now that we're alone, this is the part of my presentation where I have to ask. Do you have anything for me? I gotta keep these particular skills sharp. Listen, I don't need you to add my name to the marque. Also not in search of Raffi-type work, but probably wouldn't turn it down either."

Bingo. He was angling for an in. But why not bring it up before both of us? It's been a few years since I had the helm solo. A PI thruple? Me thinks, and I bet Jawnie would agree, too many cooks for the size of the pantry at the moment.

"Maybe I will take that second drink," Rockfish said and shook his empty glass for emphasis. He waited until Decker re-corked the bottle and swallowed a sip before continuing. He needed to let Decker down, gently, but kid gloves were never a Rockfish thing.

"I gotta be honest with you, Dan--"

"Wouldn't have it another way, friend."

"I don't see it happening," Rockfish said. "At the moment, I mean." He placed the glass down, and like clockwork, thunder and lightning followed. *Right on time. Someone up there doesn't like me.*

"God knows you're holding back," Decker said with a shit-eating-grin.

"Dan, I have a partner. She's got her say, and she's indisposed at the moment. I mean, if we get backed into a corner, or happen upon a case where we can use your experience as a force-multiplier, you are my first call. But until then, don't bank on us and why are we even discussing this? I'm sure a private company is going to throw a boatload of cash your way. After all, it's only been a month, right? Enjoy the downtime. Don't be so eager to jump back into the game. It ain't going anywhere. Like me at the moment. Leave it to Jawnie to blow up the bathroom at a time like this," Rockfish said, adding a dash of levity.

Decker stared back. There was no joy in Mudville. The mighty Rockfish had struck out. He turned his attention away from the glaring eyes to the corner of the table with the SIG Sauer.

"It's not the end of the world, Dan. I know a lot of cops have trouble adjusting to civilian life. Not having anything for you in the near term doesn't mean we can't come to some sort of arrangement when things pick up. Shit, by then, I'll come begging for your help and you'll have a highfalutin corporate gig. Your turn to tell me to pound sand. Kinda like the old days. The more things change..."

Decker grinned. He leaned forward, resting his elbows on the table and his chin firmly atop his hands. Rockfish practically saw the wheels turning.

"Steve, you know me better than that. Old habits die hard. But if my job hunt experience tells me anything, I might be desperate enough. Soon."

The door to the house slammed shut, and both men glanced up as Jawnie reentered the patio.

"What's so funny?" Jawnie said. "It appears I missed a good one."

"Nothing. Couple of old friends bullshitting," Decker said.

"What he said." Rockfish leaned back and watched Decker's phone vibrate within the chair's cup holder. *Third time in the last five minutes. You think he'd check it or at least glance down at the screen? Rosie's probably checking to see if it's safe to come home yet.*

"You need to take that?"

"Nah, it can wait till you guys leave. Matter of fact, Jawnie, Steve said he was running late for something or other." Decker stood up and slid the offending phone into his pants pocket. "I'll take you through the house. What kind of host would I be making you walk around the house in this storm?"

Rockfish read the confusion on Jawnie's face as to the sudden end of the visit. He managed a slight shrug and followed Decker through the doorway and into the kitchen.

* * * * * * * * *

Raffi pulled his car over to the shoulder of the road and shifted into park. He'd need to wait out the rest of the fast-moving storm on the narrow residential side street. The aging Taurus' wipers had failed to keep up, and he was getting too close to Rockfish's ritzy neighborhood. The more imminent his destination, the odds increased of houses having outward facing security cameras. His chances of a successful hit-and-run plummeted. *Better safe than sorry. Especially with correcting all the driver's license fakakta, I forgot to renew my insurance. One step forward, two backwards. Same shit, different day.*

Raffi removed the cellphone from the gizmo securing it to the dash and unlocked the home screen. *Not one notification. You gotta be kidding me.* He shook his head and pretended to gaze out the windshield. The perfect storm stared back. *Give it time. The guy's not exactly your biggest fan. Let the offer sink in and follow up in a day or two if needed. The high pressure sell ain't gonna work with this dude. You know that.*

A teeny-tiny flash of smoke appeared on his right shoulder. Raffi turned, knowing full well what it was. A miniature version of himself, dressed in red and holding a pitchfork, smiled back.

Desperate times call for desperate measures, bucko. Why not just go over and knock on Decker's door? What's the worst he'll do? Slam it in your face? Not exactly like he's returning your emails or texts. He lost his badge. He can threaten you, but in all actuality, he can't do shit. Citizen's arrest ain't a real thing.

"I know, but do you know how much easier this would be if Steve did the right thing? Man, we go way the fuck back. Obviously, the ledger of life shows that I owe him a few more than vice versa, but damn it. I need a little help here!" Raffi punched the steering wheel. The horn sounded. His ass lifted a few inches off the seat, and he dropped the phone. It landed on the floor mat between his legs.

"Damn motherfucker!" He leaned forward to retrieve it and stopped short. "Ah, you fucking bitch." He reached down and released the seatbelt. Middle age had been good to his gut. Raffi grabbed the phone and dropped it into the cup holder before removing the dash attachment from the vent. Over his shoulder it flew and into the backseat.

Hey, back over here. The small devil grinned widely. *Who better to have your back than a washed up cop? Sure beats a washed up, Hollywood-infused private eye. You've always had his back. Time to turn yours. Think about it.*

Raffi checked the time. Seven minutes after six. And then glanced outside. The monsoon had let up enough, and he felt safe enough to continue the drive. *I've always said never call me late for dinner, but Mack started serving at six sharp. The only problem now is, which direction am I headed in?*

ARE YOU NOT LISTENING? The devil jabbed Raffi's neck with the tiny pitchfork.

Raffi turned the wipers back on. His left hand then continued across his body and backhanded the devil off his shoulder. The little man splattered against the passenger window and slid down the door frame. Eventually settling on the front seat.

"Yeah, the problem is, I am." He reached over and raised the radio's volume. The Santana and Rob Thomas collaboration *Smooth* drowned out the imaginary whimpers emanating from the passenger scat. Raffi shifted the car into drive and checked his mirrors before pulling out into traffic. The wipers now kept pace with the droplets and a few minutes later, he clicked the blinker for Rockfish's street.

As the house came into view, a sliver of doubt crept back into Raffi's mind. He glanced right. His imaginary passenger remained quiet. This was all on him.

This is the right thing. Don't badger Decker. He don't have the best opinion of ya in the first place. If he's desperate for work, he'll see this for what it is. A great opportunity to get his name out there. Shit, maybe even he can come work full time for Steve and me. My name will be next on the big sign, so he better play nice. And if he doesn't? Steve will come round sooner. Gotta keep the faith. Plus, who doesn't love a successful revenge story?

The garage door was open on la casa de Rockfish, and Raffi spotted his friend standing inside as he maneuvered down the driveway. A mad dash, dodging raindrops, would be shorter toward the garage than up the walkway to the front door. *That Steve, always thinking and looking out for me. Maybe he's right about not going back to Grindsville? Nah.*

"I've had this open and freezing my ass off since five to six. You're never late for one of Mack's free meals."

"I know, first time for everything," Raffi said. "Ended up having to pull over. I'm horrible at carrying on a business conversation and dealing with the heavy rain at the same time. I can only concentrate on one thing at a time."

"Stop right there. I don't want to hear another word. No work talk. Food and drink. Heavy on the drink and my plate growing cold. Now walk around the far side of the door. I don't need any of that dirty rainwater getting on Lana."

Raffi watched as Steve slid between the Hellcat Challenger and Mack's Ram 1500. *Was that a hint of disgust on his face?* He couldn't tell. At this point, what did it matter?

Raffi made his way around the back of Mack's truck, and his breast pocket vibrated. He stopped alongside the passenger door and read the notification: *New message from D.Decker@Hotmail.com Re Opportunity.*

At least he didn't ghost me. That's a good thing. Raffi's index finger slipped twice with excitement before he tapped the notification. The email opened, and it was everything he had ever hoped for, and more.

Yes, still looking and intrigued. Stop by the house tomorrow around 2 p.m.

Raffi returned the phone to his pocket and pumped his fist. He stepped in front of the truck's front right wheel and saw Steve standing in the doorway. Watching. Eyebrows raised.

"Hey Steve, I'll take a Jack and Coke if you're pouring. On second thought, make it a double and since I asked for mixer, I'm betting you still keep the skirts next to the ice?"

CHAPTER SIX

Sunday's pre-Easter service for the faithful of Calvary United's Covenant of King Solomon was ablaze. The fire and brimstone that Elder Erwin Archibald shouted from the rafters had parishioners moving in their chairs and the sweat running down the small of their backs. A standing room only crowd of rural families was wedged into the converted elementary school cafeteria, along with antiquated broadcasting equipment. Plastic folding chairs, shipped in from Party Supply, filled every square foot. Many of the worshipers were elderly, who constantly requested the thermostat raised.

Jesus Earnhardt Jr. and his two lieutenants, Clyde and Amos, occupied three sweat-soaked seats in the far-right corner. Leadership of the Penn Forest Patriots had turned out this morning in their Sunday best coveralls. But it wasn't so much for the gospel, albeit the money from today's grift would eventually trickle down to help supply the militia with the equipment necessary for the upcoming civil war. Instead, the Elder had summoned them.

Earnhardt Jr. pulled a bandana from his pocket and drug it across his forehead. The already saturated cloth did little to ease the increasing moisture problem. He had shoved the damp do-rag back into his pocket when Clyde leaned over.

"Couldn't we have met him outback? Afterwards like."

"You never know how long the man will go, when the Lord speaks through him," Earnhardt Jr. said. "Pay attention. You might be worth saving. Of course, depending on how much cash you brought." The men shared a laugh until the woman next to Earnhardt elbowed his ribs. They returned their fake attention to the man at the pulpit.

"... and the Lord Jehovah said to Mahershalalhashbaz..."

Elder Erwin Archibald fully subscribed to the old adage, *play the part, be the part*. The popular local televangelist had dressed this morning in a white suit, a crimson red shirt and short white tie. Sweat matted the chin-length long, frazzled gray hair on the sides of his face. His complexion and the venom he spewed matched the color of his shirt.

Archibald dreamed of being called up to the big leagues. Playing to a bigger audience with larger tithing aspirations. *Disposable income makes the dreams work*, he said, around his inner circle. Dreams of the lifestyles of the rich and famous. The Highchurches, Olsteens and Swaggarts of the world. Leaving the snow-filled UHF dial far behind.

"... and so I leave you with the gospel according to Christ's enemies..."

Once the sermon died down to a dull roar, Archibald's men safely secured the collection baskets from prying eyes, and most worshipers meandered out into the parking lot. Thoughts of Cracker Barrel danced in their heads. The Penn Forest contingent made their way against traffic towards the front of the cafeteria. To the left of the makeshift stage from where Archibald had homilized, two men in three-piece suits stood before an open doorway. The arch led to the kitchen area, where lunch ladies toiled during the week making square pizza and Sloppy Joes.

Earnhardt Jr. was three strides away, with his men flanking either side, when one suit held his palm up. He glanced not at the approaching men, but at a smartphone held in the other hand.

"He's not ready for you."

Earnhardt Jr. nodded and stepped to the side. His boys followed suit but were not as content as their leader. Clyde immediately got into his ear.

"I took time out of my day to be here. Not like I ain't got a shit ton of chores that need to be done. Send me to hell, but working on the sabbath is the only way I'm keeping my head above water. And now, his Highness says wait?"

"I get it, Clyde," Earnhardt Jr. said. "You're not the only one whose wife is ready to nag the fuck out of him over how the repairs to the chicken coop are months behind schedule. We all don't have enough hours in the day. But when the money man says wait, the only correct answer is, *how long?*"

Clyde frowned and Amos shook his head, each finding an empty chair to wait in. Earnhardt Jr. stood, arms folded and resting upon his massive gut. *I know they're pissed, but everything we have is because of Archibald. I'm not cutting off the golden goose to appease them. One day they'll get it.*

He didn't have to wait long. Five minutes later the same suit stepped to the side and allowed Earnhardt Jr. and his men to pass.

Archibald sat on a wooden bench behind a prep table and appeared to be holding court with his inner circle. Spotless, stainless-steel bowls and appliances littered nearly every available surface. When he noticed Earnhardt Jr.'s cavalry hat behind the others, Archibald waved his warriors in with welcoming arms. Those that previously stood around him took a step back. The preacher remained in his sweat-soaked suit but had taken the time to comb his hair. His face remained a deep crimson.

"Jesus, I hope you enjoyed the sermon this morning. Perhaps a key point to bring home to the rest of your family that failed to get out of bed to thank our lord and savior Jesus Christ for his bounty."

Earnhardt Jr. gave a slight nod and pulled his stool as close to the table as his belly would allow. Clyde and Amos mimicked the Colonel. He second guessed not removing his hat after seeing Archibald had loosened his tie. Amos stood back up and pushed a large mix master to the side for an unobstructed view of all parties.

"I'll pass your words of encouragement to the deaf ears, Elder. You have to understand. With Jenny's disability, these teens are trying my patience, and it's easier not to fight back. For my sanity."

"Anyway, enough about your problems. I am happy you and your men made it," Archibald said. He then turned his head. "Paul, if you'll take Otis and the others out front. Make sure they clean the entrance way and parking lot. I don't need another call from the school board about the slobbery of our parishioners."

A minute later, the population of the cafeteria reduced to four. From the Lord's view, it appeared like a three on one chess match with various silver utensils as pieces. Archibald ignored the opening with e4 (the King's Spatula), but launched into a less politically correct version of his earlier sermon.

"Wokeness. It's all around. Creeping in. No matter how small the crack in our foundation. Satan will lead the way. The liberal indoctrination of our impressionable children escalates while we do nothing. Think outside the box? Hell, if I had the nerve to do that while I was growing up, a switch would find my backside before I even tried to get in damn the box." Archibald quickly made the sign of the cross. "Speaking of boxes, I hear litter boxes are now available in first-grade classrooms. Right down the hall from where we sit in this very..."

"Even NewsMax reported that's all made up," Amos said under his breath.

"Quiet, he's on a roll," Earnhardt Jr. said.

"... We did as told and questioned nothing. The Lord speaks to me. Do you think I question one word? We must stop making our children stress and worry over a past they played no part in. A return to simpler times. We once considered this area God's country."

Archibald paused and picked up a bottle of water. He ran the cool plastic across his forehead before taking a long swig. He offered the bottle to the men across the table and all three declined.

"First it was the Chinese restaurant downtown and then the Italian bakery. Soon after, the Patels snuck across the county line, in the dead of the night, mind you, and bought the old WinGate Motel. And this, gentleman, is where you boys come in."

Earnhardt Jr. wiggled on the stool. His ass was too large for the small wooden circle, and he had already spent too much time precariously balancing. His ass cheeks were going numb.

"I understand you're hoping for an update on our efforts, but there is no change since we last spoke." Earnhardt Jr. gritted his teeth and waited for the other side of the table to explode. The men on either side mimicked Earnhardt Jr.'s body language. They gnashed their teeth and winced at what was to come.

"You've had the vials for almost two months now. No one has confirmed the contents or done a thing with them. Meanwhile, the woke continues to creep across this land I love." He shook his head. "Unacceptable."

"But, Elder, my tools," Clyde said. "The ones you graciously donated to the cause are not up to the task and I--"

Archibald held up a finger. "Unacceptable. Try it. Sample size. I don't care if you dump a sample in old man Richard's irrigation pond. Then see how many of his prize swine remain. Test and move on. We can't sit here and wait for an obviously lacking chemistry set to verify the contents. Spring is almost upon us, and I need to put fear into these people. They need to do the right thing with the incoming federal and state tax refunds. Cannot give them a chance to spend it on frivolous shit and further breathe life into the woke wagon."

Amos held his hand up and interjected. "My error with the seller set us back, and the authorities sniffed around here way too long before calling off their dogs. Mistakes are to be--"

Archibald raised his index finger and waved it. "Unacceptable. What happened to that boy is of no concern to me. We have a plan. A timetable. You need to position yourself better to stay on track. There will be no second chance to save this country."

Earnhardt Jr. had had enough. *Tread lightly bud, you don't want the financial spigot to shut off.* He stood up and attempted to lean forward, but his belly prevented his arms from reaching the desk. With a wiggle, he flopped a good portion of it up over the edge and rested his weight on his hands. *I need to put an end to this berating. These are my men. They answer to me. I take them to the woodshed, not the man behind the curtain.*

"Elder, these are my men. They work as hard as you or I for the cause. Don't doubt their work ethic or faith." Earnhardt Jr. paused and adjusted his arms. Pins and needles flowed down the right forearm. "We're running short-handed now. Like most employers. Recruiting is not what we expected, especially after the latest Trump indictment. They should be lined up out the door, ready to sign on the dotted line. But I've gotten sideways in the conversation. We're talking about the here and now. I've got a handful of men on the sideline after last week's training exercise out in Cambria Park Forest. It appears those MREs we highjacked, are causing an outbreak of dysentery through the ranks."

"Unacceptable!" Archibald said again. "Perhaps we should dump them in the water supply, then. Problem solved. At least we know they'll accomplish our intended endgame."

"Look. We're taking this slow but attempting to make progress," Earnhardt Jr. said. By this time, his left hand had gone numb, and he leaned back on the stool. "Everyone at this table is aware of the plan. Verify what is in those vials. Infect the Grindsville water supply. Watch while much of the population gets sick. Not dead. Exactly the reason we need to verify the contents."

"My brother in Jesus, with that, we are in full agreement," Archibald said. It was his turn to stand up and drive a point home. "After all, we are not murderers. We are Calvary United's Covenant of King Solomon. I wish to only bring attention to the filthy, rotten migrant caravans invading our country daily. Thus, rally the sheep to the cause, increase membership in the Penn Forest Patriots and fill all our coffers with the real difference maker." Archibald took a deep breath and sat back down.

Months before, the foursome had accomplished that pact, but they still agreed on the overall plan. Timelines and turning tragedy to an advantage remained the sticking points.

"To further that," Earnhardt Jr. said. "My man at The Grindsville Tribune-Exponent, is ready to run a conspiracy story to rally the populace. It shouldn't take long to get the genuine patriots to pick up tiki torches and pitchforks."

"No tiki torches," Clyde said.

"Yeah, they represent an utter failure," Amos added.

"Correct, gentlemen. I need something to put the fear of our Almighty Christ into the migrants as they flee," Archibald said. "The next step is to get our slate of candidates elected to the local board of supervisors, not only in Grindsville but neighboring areas. Create our own piece of paradise sandwiched between liberal Philadelphia and fake-news-conservative Pittsburgh. The model others will want to replicate across the country. In time, January 6th will seem like a failed liquor store holdup." A wide grin spread across his face.

In my mind, it already does. Earnhardt Jr. stood up again and his men followed suit. *We won't be part of a two-bit sequel.*

Archibald stood and ushered the men back towards the doorway.

"Jesus and his disciples. Go in peace, but I want to make this abundantly clear: We need to move forward. The sooner the better. Yet, I don't want any advanced notice as to spoil my realistic surprise when I step before the media and point the blame firmly where it belongs."

* * * * * * * * *

At the same moment Earnhardt Jr. and his men climbed back into their pickups and drove toward the Hog Sweat Diner, one hundred and eighty miles to the southeast, Rockfish and Jawnie drew their own unexpected Sunday meeting to a close. Jawnie walked the newly signed client, Faith Fairbrace, out to the parking lot and crossed paths with the UPS man while Rockfish rummaged through the bar for the makings of a half-assed Bloody Mary.

The previous evening, Fairbrace had left a panicked and lengthy message on the office answering machine. Lynn, ever faithful in her managerial duties, had listened to the voicemail on the drive over for a girls' night at Hibbleton's Hideaway. After the second play through, she thought it important enough to talk with Jawnie upon arrival. And she only needed one listen before making a brief trip out to the parking lot. A few minutes later, she set up the Sunday emergency client meeting. If Steve wasn't able to make it, she'd handle the intake on her own. But Rockfish surprised her. He not only showed up but arrived with a kind of positive mindset.

Fairbrace had left the original message after an unsuccessful three-hour stint at the Ann Arundel Sheriff's Office. Saturday afternoon's duty officer couldn't have rolled his eyes more as she retold the story of her missing daughter. Constance Fairbrace was legally an adult, albeit holding steady with level-one autism, and very familiar to Rockfish and Jawnie. A little over a year ago, the mother had hired them to locate Constance when she tried to flex her independence and disappeared with a man she met online after her closing shift ended at a local Arby's.

Faith Fairbrace was in full momma-bear mode on the voicemail and even more so the following morning. Constance now worked at a Long John Silvers, but the modus operandi was the same. Last seen getting into a black Dodge Challenger with a man who held the door open for her. The car piqued Rockfish's interest, not to mention it was apparent to all around the table, except one, that Constance entered the car willingly. The partners were in silent agreement and understood the reasoning behind the Sheriff's Office asking Faith to return in forty-eight-hours and fill out a missing person form.

By the time Jawnie had walked back inside, Rockfish had given up trying to locate tomato juice and moved on to the true hair of the dog.

"No mimosas?" She said.

"We gotta get Lynn to restock back here. I know it's not exactly in her job description, but a simple trip to Costco to pick up a handful of mixers isn't too much to ask."

"Well, since she's not here at the moment, open this for me, will you?" Jawnie said and tossed the small package the UPS driver had handed her outside.

"What did you order now?"

"A new batch of AirTags, but not really AirTags," Jawnie said. She sat down on the couch as Rockfish looked confused and pulled out a pocketknife. The blade sliced through the tape on the top of the cardboard box.

"Huh?"

"I'm moving us away from the Apple product and implementing these new trackers from a company called MirageTrax. AirTags rely on additional Apple devices in the immediate vicinity to function, but MirageTrax works off of current GPS satellites."

"Sounds expensive," Rockfish said.

"Totally, but we shouldn't cut corners with our equipment. In the past, if anyone took your precious drone and drove off to a desolate area, we'd be out of luck. Now? We'd know exactly where to go in order to get your toy back."

"I rarely question our cash flow, but maybe stick with the Apple ones until we get a full client load again or the next residual check arrives?" Rockfish said. He stepped out from behind the bar and handed the now open box to Jawnie.

"Look, Steve. We're spending serious cash on the new high-tech tools you love to operate. Shouldn't we keep track of them? Lost, stolen or misplaced, these little beauties can only help us in the long run. Save us money, too. You watch."

"Is there anything you don't put them on?"

"I associated them with anything valued at five hundred and above, you know the deal. Heck, Steve, you signed off on the inventory control policy. And I emailed you a copy."

"Yeah, I gotta say, I don't remember any of that. Now, back to this Fairbrace boondoggle."

Here it comes. He'll lay into me for calling him in on one of our few days off, all over a teenager out on the town sowing her oats.

"Nothing so urgent as to pull me out of bed on the Lord's day. And don't you roll your eyes at me. You deserve time off as much as me, maybe more. But I should be home eating a Mack McMuffin or three while getting ready to watch the Orioles' final spring training game."

I really should play the lottery more. But I can tell he's not done lecturing.

Rockfish leaned in and continued. "We did all the legwork for this case last time. Reach out, again, to our contact who knows someone over in the security department at RealSwipe.com and see if they'll provide us with the guy's info. Sure as shit, we'll find her hiding in the closet at the guy's house exactly like last time, not wanting to go home. The girl has an itch and momma ain't having any of it."

"And doesn't know how to deal with it," Jawnie said. "I can reach out, but there's one minor problem I can see."

"Only one? Out with it, McGee," Rockfish said and took a sip from his rocks glass. "Rain on my parade. Rainy day Sundays are my favorite."

Jawnie took a sip of her own water and paused. She wanted to frame her reply without coming off too much of a Debbie Downer or class know-it-all.

"I hate to say it, Steve, but the last time Constance went all horndog on her mom, Decker was the one who had the inside source with the online dating site."

"Goddamnit."

"Yup. Not sure he's able to do that now," Jawnie said. She watched as Rockfish pursed his lips and shook his head. "Or even make the call on our behalf. Maybe this is his first contract job for us?"

"Toss him a bone," Rockfish said. "See if we didn't totally piss him off that day at his house. I like it."

Jawnie nodded softly, began rifling through the contents of the box. Rockfish sat down to her left in his recliner and leaned forward in the chair.

"I seriously doubt he's even interested after how our last visit abruptly ended. He wasn't thrilled when I shot him down."

"I think you read too much into it. I've had the occasional social text with him since then. Seems okay. And I check his LinkedIn profile from time to time. No change, no new listing for a high paying private sector employer. He'll make the call for us, with the hope it leads to more and higher profile contract jobs."

Jawnie put the box down on the coffee table and opened her laptop. She pulled up Constance's Facebook profile, having friended the young woman after last year's walk of shame. The screen scrolled, and she searched for any type of post to follow up on in case Decker no longer had a legitimate contact at RealSwipe.com. Jawnie continued the conversation with Steve, her senses multitasked. Eyes glued to the screen, mouth handling the words, and her brain juggled it all.

"It might be nice to farm a portion of our work out as business necessitates, and not have to worry about one of us getting bogged down and dropping the ball," Jawnie said. "Speaking of lackluster performance and people not exactly thrilled with us, you hear from Raffi lately? Not that I'm complaining, mind you."

"Was that a shot across my bow? Raffi's? Or both?"

"Poor choice of words. I'm half paying attention to Constance's Facebook wall, seeing if anything jumps out. Sorry about that."

"To answer your question, I haven't," Rockfish said. "And to tell you the truth, I mean, he is my friend, but I sure don't miss the stress."

"I am surprised he's gone quiet and stopped trying to get you onboard for Operation Q-Ration Recovery."

Rockfish cracked a small smile. "Me too. Very unlike the man. But I'm sure if history tells me anything, it's only a matter of time before he's back here, pressing full court with a new cockamamie scheme. But we'll deal with it then. Tell me your thoughts on our missing batch of hormones."

Jawnie gazed up from the screen. No matter how long she and Steve had worked together, now going on three years, his request for her input always caught her by surprise. She closed the laptop, returned it to the coffee table, and picked up her glass.

"We found her with ease last time. No need to reinvent the wheel. You reach out to Decker instead and I'll scrape all her social media accounts and see if we meet in the middle. Get her back to mom's house before Faith has an aneurysm. Deposit the check and onward."

"Agreed. I'll call him. Get his thoughts, pick his brain. Make him feel helpful, so to speak. See if he continues to keep that pistol within arm's reach. If having you around has taught me anything, it's the importance of mental health." Rockfish stood and moved around to the back of the recliner. He rested his elbows on the backrest.

"Ummm, Steve, you still shove everything down inside and don't talk about it."

"Other people's mental health, McGee. You didn't let me finish. Now, if you'll excuse me, I'm headed back to my office and give him a buzz. Holler if you find anything."

Rockfish retreated to his office, but not before refilling his glass with a couple fingers of Tullamore Dew. There he left the first of four unreturned messages on Decker's home and cell phones.

* * * * * * * * * *

Monday morning found Lana at a dead stop in the middle lane, northbound on the Baltimore Beltway. In today's age, metropolitan rush hour traffic shouldn't be a surprise, but there Rockfish sat. His eyes were on the pushing empty gas gauge as Lana's Hemi engine idled.

A parking lot and an empty tank. Think much, asshole?

He headed to Timonium, north of the city, to follow up on the only lead Jawnie had gleaned from Constance's social media accounts. With Decker not returning any type of message, including smoke signals, and the security team at RealSwipe.com not caring what name Rockfish dropped, the drive was his only morning option. Besides crawling back in what he left of yesterday's Tullamore Dew bottle. And it wasn't like he didn't heavily debate the options before pulling out of the driveway. *At least this one pays.*

Constance had spent much of her online time the past two weeks liking or commenting on every post made by one Cre'Von LeBones, across many social media platforms. Cre'Von's responses were sparse and short, but their lack of substance didn't seem to deter Constance. She waxed poetically about dreaming of a transfer to Long John Silvers in Timonium. With that nugget of information, Jawnie's collection of online people finder resources disclosed Cre'Von LeBones had lived in apartment X-1 at Magooby's Village Apartments in Timonium since 2019.

Jawnie stayed behind to work the phone and computer lines. She exhausted her Rolodex trying to sweet talk any of her cultivated law enforcement sources with help regarding RealSwipe.com. One, a previous paramour, came through as a check of DMV records revealed Cre'Von did not own a black Dodge Challenger. Or at least didn't have one registered in his name, Rockfish reminded her. It also didn't mean he wasn't in the drivers seat when Constance went missing. Rockfish planned on circling

Magooby's parking lot a handful of times, on the lookout for Lana's second cousin.

With a little luck, I sit in the car, and the happy couple walks out. Casually meander over. Hope she doesn't recognize me after a year and have a simple conversation about our mutual love of muscle cars. Can't force her to come, but at least I can report back to Mommy Dearest that her daughter was in no immediate danger. Honey, those apron strings only stretch so far. If he failed there, he'd try to sweet talk the apartment complex rental office into providing some information on Cre'Von which he or Jawnie would follow up with.

The fuel gauge warning light on the dashboard dinged and turned yellow. *Estimated forty miles to empty and I haven't moved in twenty minutes.* Rockfish's thoughts turned to the double bird he'd eventually give the accident victims when he crawled past. *I'm not one for wishing harm, but this morning, I'm hoping for a few dumbasses strapped to a gurney. May their recoveries be successful yet painful.*

After finishing with the morning's tour of Timonium, Rockfish had an idea on how to get an answer out of Decker. *Who said sitting in traffic is unproductive? I've got a plan and wished death upon a couple of different crappy drivers this morning.*

The plan was genius in its simplicity. He'd pound on the front door and hope Rosie didn't answer. If no one answered, Rockfish planned on walking around to the backyard and would let himself into the Florida room. Pour a couple of fingers of that Yamazaki 12-Year-Old Single Malt and put on ESPN until Decker came outside. *The man never ignored a good confrontation. A win-win all around, if I say so.* Rockfish didn't pat himself too hard on the back and followed the Toyota Tundra directly in front as they crept forward a few feet. The FJB and Ultra MAGA bumper stickers seemed out of place on an import, but who was he to judge?

Ten minutes and approximately a quarter of a mile later, an orange Taurus caught Rockfish's attention. The car was in the left lane, five cars ahead and despite the size of the Baltimore metropolitan area... *No fucking way, there are two of those orange shitboxes. Raffi. I'd bet my last two gallons on it.*

Rockfish laid on the horn. He hoped to get his friend's attention, knowing it was mostly a long shot. The person behind the Taurus' steering wheel stared at the traffic jam ahead. Instead, vehicles on both sides and behind Lana replied with non-verbal salutes. *Strike one. What's next?*

Rockfish picked up his phone from the cup holder and instinctively let up on the brake to creep forward. *Damn it. Screw you, Flo, and Progressive with your Snapshot bullshit.* He knew it had registered the use of his phone while the car moved forward, no matter how slow. Another increase to his insurance premium was inevitable.

The cell phone went back into the cup holder. Rockfish reached for Lana's display screen and tapped the Messages icon, then Raffi's name.

"What do you want to say to Raffi?" Siri said.

Rockfish paused and tapped cancel. *I will not break first. I didn't do a damn thing wrong by not jumping on his harebrained revenge scheme. Chalk Grindsville up to the Raffi learning experience I should have made him sit through years ago.*

A car horn exploded behind, and Rockfish shook his head. His turn to salute. He slid his foot off the brake and pulled up ten yards before coming to a complete stop. Again. The urge to punch anything flowed through his body.

Lana, you are damn lucky I love you. What I need to do is try to get across one lane and aim for the next exit. Fill 'er up. No desire to blow the morning on the shoulder waiting for the roadside assistance truck.

Rockfish put on his blinker and inched to the right. *Come on! Let me in!*

* * * * * * * * *

The sun had worked its way down the horizon by the time Lana rolled up to the small wooden booth. Rockfish waved at the guard, punched the code and drove through the wrought iron. *Can't be that bad. If he doesn't have me on the don't let in by any means list.*

He pushed down on the gas and cursed the approach of the first of many speed bumps. The turn onto Decker's street came with a different type of bump. Rockfish's stomach turned sour, and a little bile crept into the back of his throat. There was no reason for the worry, at least none that Rockfish came up with. But he listened to his body and kept his foot off the brake. Lana crept past the driveway at low speed.

Rockfish couldn't remember a time when his nerves weren't dead on about a situation. Rockfish turned around at the next cul-de-sac and put her in park. He focused on the front of Decker's house, hoping for another sign that anything was amiss, other than indigestion. *Not a brick out of place. No pile of newspapers on the front stoop. Maybe it was the gas station sushi that came free with the fill up? Had to be.* Rockfish wasn't one to pass up a deal with his ExxonMobil loyalty card. Who knew Long John Silvers would be closed for renovations?

And in the words of Borat Sagdiyev, the day's earlier assignment, was a great success. He'd wait to fill in Jawnie on his earlier text. She had immediately replied, asking for details, but he didn't answer. First, he needed to clear the air with Decker. There would be plenty of time later, after hours, to recount the picturesque ending of the second annual Constance Fairbrace Recovery Case.

For the second time today, Rockfish found himself at a standstill. Not moving. This time by choice. No hope of seeing a severed limb or twisted steel as a reward for his patience. He wouldn't, couldn't, believe it was the awkwardness that had grown and settled in the time since he and Jawnie had left a little over two weeks ago. *Blame the sushi. It's the perfect out and you get to keep that stone cold exterior in place, and no one is the wiser.* Emotions firmly pushed down inside, he slid Lana's gearshift down into drive.

She came to a stop directly across the street from Decker's house. Rockfish slid his phone into his breast pocket and hustled across, slightly ahead of a speeding Amazon delivery van. He pushed through a thin veil of fear when his feet hit the brick walkway. He had his hand on the storm door handle before he thought about turning around. The door didn't budge. *Locked. Are you surprised? Don't bang on it like you're the local authorities ready to serve a warrant.*

Rockfish noticed the video doorbell to his left, mounted on the door frame. Archibald shook his head and knocked on the frame, six inches above the camera. No answer. He waited another minute before knocking again. Harder. Louder. Silence answered the knock. He glanced around to see what neighbors had moved their curtains to see what all the fuss was about.

Last option it is, before packing it in. Or maybe I'll walk around back? Don't. An idiot will call the cops on you. He's not sitting there, waiting on you like last time. Press it, will ya?

Ding-Dong

"Not interested. No solicitation. Can't you read?"

He glanced at the No Solicitation sign that was stuck in the frame of the storm door. *Definitely not in the mood for this.* It had been a while, but Rockfish recognized the voice. The venom and sarcasm were classic Rosie Decker with his previous history of interactions. With him, that was. Rosie stood or sat somewhere inside, staring at the live stream on her device and was content to screw with him. *Come on, deal with her and move past it. Civility will win out. Don't play her game and give Dan one more reason to be pissed at you.*

"Always great to see you too, Rosie, although, at the moment, I can only hear the resentment. Can I come in?"

"You can leave the package on the porch. Thank you. I'll rate the delivery on the app."

This is going about as well as expected. Can you even remember when or how the bad blood started? Shit, has Dan ever mentioned aloud why she hates your guts? Probably something I said or did. Probably? More like which time. No use not returning fire.

"My condolences on Aunt Flo's visit. Can you at least send Dan down? Or I can meet him out back. I'm good with either option. I promise you won't have to see me. Put in your AirPods and it's like I never knocked. It's a win for both sides."

"Lo siento no entiendo ingles."

Rockfish stepped back from the video feed. His heels hovering on the brick's edge and blood pressure beginning to climb. He wasn't happy to play the fool with half the neighborhood watching. This was far from how he expected the visit to go. He pictured Rosie making a post on *NextDoor* warning of a strange man, soliciting who-knows-what objectionable items. *All the while, are you inside, Dan? Laughing alongside the Mrs?*

"Tell ya what, Rosie. I'm going to open the gate and go around back. Dan can come out to play when he's ready to talk like an adult. I know where he keeps the whiskey and remote. There's gotta be a game on I can watch to kill time."

He waited for the next zinger. Patiently. And then another minute passed. It never came. After a period of awkward silence, he tried again.

"Rosie?" More silence. He tapped two knuckles against the video doorbell's plastic shell.

"Dan's not here, Steve."

Barely audible. Rockfish swallowed and chalked another one up for his indigestion, reading the room better than he did. Rosie's words lacked all the sting of her previous comments. *Don't sound alarmed. Say anything to not make her put up the shield again.*

"Well, when's he coming back? Like I said, I can wait out back. You won't even know I'm here. Scout's honor." Rockfish held up his index, middle and ring fingers, side-by-side before the camera lens. He waited and was rewarded. The sound of cylinders turning hit his ears first, followed by the door's weather stripping sweeping across the wood floor.

Rosie stood on the other side of the storm door. The baseball cap pulled down did little to hide the bags below her eyes. The oversized sweatshirt and matching pants hung off her limbs. *Was she always this thin?* It had been a long while since they could take a serious look at the other. *Dan would want me to be worried and over helpful.* Rockfish reached for the storm door's handle and Rosie grasped the handle from the other side. She shook her head and Rockfish retreated. *He'd also want me to listen and not push her over the edge.*

"That spiral you saw him in. I know you saw it. Recognized it. The gun nearby. The rants against those taking his resume and then not returning his calls. All of it gone as quickly as it came. A few days after you left, he suddenly had pep in his step and spoke about someone finally reaching out. Not the other way around." Rose ran her sleeve across her eyes. Those first few tears weren't absorbed and slid down her cheeks.

"Wait, I didn't hear about him getting on with a company," Rockfish said. "Good for him. Sounds like a reason to celebrate. Dan deserves a cushy private sector paycheck more than anyone. Excluding yours truly." The crack at the end didn't land, and Rosie continued to stare through him without emotion.

"There was no job offer. It's a one-off deal. That's all he told me. Left on the sixteenth. Wouldn't say where, but that he'd be in touch. He's been gone a week, and I haven't heard a thing. Steve, I'm scared." Rosie opened the screen door and stepped into Rockfish's arms.

CHAPTER SEVEN

It was a little after six o'clock, the reversible open/closed sign on the office door had been flipped, and the shades drawn. Rockfish had taken up residence in the bullpen area, his feet extended on the recliner, with Lynn directly across from him in the other chair. He recounted his investigative prowess from the late morning, which resulted in the location of Constance Fairbrace while they waited on a tardy Jawnie. She had drawn the short straw and left earlier to tell Momma Bear Fairbrace the good-news-bad-news update on her daughter.

Good news is that our diligent investigative work has not only located your daughter in record time, but we've also spoken with Constance. The bad news is that she's found a job, a boy, and said she'd reach out to you when she's good and ready. No, we cannot go into specifics. She's over eighteen and entitled to a life of her own. Here's our bill. Payment is due by the first of the month.

Each caught the other staring at the empty couch where Jawnie and her laptop usually camped.

"She should have been back by now," Lynn said. A furrowed brow exclaimed to Rockfish exactly how she felt.

"You would think, but you also haven't met the mother. Calling her a piece of work is an understatement. Remember Claudia Coyne?"

"How could I forget? Her husband was one victim swindled by Hightower and Porbeagle."

"That's her. Except Faith Fairbrace is ten times worse." Rockfish smiled. He watched as Lynn tried to wrap her head around a higher level of Karen than Claudia Coyne.

"That's damn near impossible. Coyne was one of a kind. Bat shit crazy, as my daddy used to say."

"You'd be surprised. I'll tell you what. Next client meeting with Faith Fairbrace, and there will be one. Mark my words, you're riding shotgun with whichever of us draws that damn short straw."

"Can't wait," Lynn said, returning the smile. "I can only hope it's a tad more exciting than my time in Grindsville."

"I can't promise ya shit. You've worked here long enough to know that," Rockfish said. He shared a hearty laugh with Lynn.

It was another twenty minutes before Jawnie blew through the door. Each looked up from their respective loungers and saw the exhaustion on her face. Mental exhaustion.

"Sorry I'm late. I texted, but neither of you replied," Jawnie said. She threw her coat over the back of the couch and sat down, the only one without an adult beverage in hand.

"No worries. I was filling in Lynn about all things Fairbrace, aka next level Claudia Coyne."

"And then some. That woman is an ass-whopping. You have no idea. Well, you do, but Lynn doesn't. You should come next time. And to quote a song that gramps over there might recognize, *I don't like Mondays.*"

"Steve's already mailed the invite," Lynn said. "And everyone knows the Boomtown Rats." Lynn held out her fist and Rockfish pretended to bump it from across the room.

"Nice. You listen to the History Channel on Sirius XM too," Jawnie said with a grin. "As for Fairbrace, stay tuned for Episode Three. It already sounds like you three have a date. There's no scheduled broadcast for that episode, but I guarantee it's coming."

"How'd she take it?" Rockfish said, getting up to pour another drink. "Where's my manners? Who needs a refill?"

Lynn held up her glass and Jawnie dug into her bag for her ever-present bottle of water. When Rockfish had returned to recline mode, Jawnie recounted the specifics of her late afternoon client meeting.

She had met Faith Fairbrace at a small coffee shop, hoping the public location would prevent the meltdown everyone involved knew was coming. The crowd at Jamocha Jubblies did little to stop Fairbrace's tone or volume. To say the other patrons hung on every word was an understatement. Fairbrace was shot out of a cannon before Jawnie even opened her notebook and flagged down the waitress for a lemon ginger kombucha. The cannon morphed into a Howitzer at the mere mention of Constance enjoying adult life out from under mom's thumb. That her daughter was an adult and venturing out on her own, changing jobs, finding love, did nothing to ease the stretch but never break strength of mom's apron strings.

"... and at the end, we agreed to disagree on why we shouldn't move forward. I told her we had fulfilled the contract she signed. Did exactly as she requested. If you need anything else, please reach out, but we consider the case closed. I nodded, paid the bill and told her we'd be on the lookout for her check."

"Sounds like we had comparable afternoons, but you got closure," Rockfish said. "And technically, she did too. Whether she likes it or not."

"Why, you and Dan not hit it off? After you finally filled me in on your Constance findings when you had left Decker's house. I never heard a peep about the visit."

"I never saw him. I ended up speaking with his wife. Via the video doorbell and then I progressed to talking through the storm door."

"Wait, she didn't even invite you in to see him?" Lynn said. "Why would Dan need a person to run interference for him? Not that I couldn't use a person like her in my life." She laughed and

Jawnie smiled, but Rockfish stayed stoic. He took a decent draw from his glass, swirled the ice and then answered.

"Yeah, through the glass. Like it was a prison visit. Whatever's going on with Dan, she's concerned, but still hates me enough to not take down the sneeze guard."

"Vampires can't enter unless invited," Lynn said. The girls laughed and Jawnie followed up with her own zinger.

"You need to wait till spring and try to fly in an open window. Or hide behind a bush in the backyard. That Florida room is too sweet for Decker not to use it daily."

Rockfish glanced from Jawnie to Lynn and raised his eyebrows. "Have you two got everything out of your systems? Can I continue? She didn't block me from anything. Well, maybe, but he wasn't home. Or so she claimed. Her story was he took off a little while ago for a job. He didn't tell her much, but only that it's a short time gig. Nothing permanent. But I can tell she's worried. No matter how hard she tried to hide it. And she failed miserably at that."

"Strange. On both parts. Him picking up and disappearing over a mercenary job and her making a conscious decision to hold a grudge for how many years now?" Jawnie's smile faded, and her facial expression aligned with Rockfish's. Filled with concern.

"Too freakin' long. I tried to get information out of her, before saying the wrong thing and watching the door shut in my face. I exited gracefully and hope to recount the entire conversation with Dan over a beer in the very near future. He'd probably knight us both for being civil." Truth be told, Rockfish anticipated that beer more than anything he had in a very long time.

"Rosie doesn't have a clue? Nothing she said, or he said before taking off, stood out to either of you?" Lynn said. She put her glass down on the coffee table and leaned forward.

"The only thing she recalled was him cursing under his breath as he packed a small bag. Mumbled something about having to spend St. Patrick's Day with a bunch of Polacks."

"Polacks?" Jawnie said. "First. Polish American. Second, you know exactly where he's at. And with who. This isn't rocket science. Think about everything you've bitched about the last couple of weeks. It'll come."

"How Bud Light, with one ad campaign, might have solved the battered wife and child problem in rural America?"

"Close." Lynn said. Her smile told Rockfish she had already figured Jawnie's riddle out.

"Then I give up," Rockfish said and threw up his hands. Whiskey sloshed over the rim of his glass and ran down his wrist.

"So-Bot-Ka. Earn-hardt and Raf-Fi," Jawnie said slowly, with emphasis. "You didn't notice the Lech Wałęsa statue in the center of town? We drove by it half a dozen times. Heck, Steve, we became one-seventieth Polish by spending a few nights within the city limits."

"Decker's in Grindsville? Providing a helping hand to his so-called arch-nemesis, Raffi? Do you think that cop is aligned with or one of the Great Value Boys?" Rockfish had fired off his questions as he stood up and moved behind the bar for a paper towel or a pile of napkins to clean up his mess.

"Slow down, Machine Gun Kelly. I'm only saying his name is Polish," Jawnie said. "That whole town was pierogies and cabbage. Not to mention, there were quite a few sets of beady eyes sticking out from between hat brims and neck gaiters that evening. Even with bad lighting, I'll err on the side of an old white, possibly racist cop, being an insurrectionist." Jawnie flipped her laptop around and showed a picture of the statue from the Grindsville Chamber of Commerce website.

"That's seen better days," Rockfish said as he reclaimed his seat. "No one has a power sprayer in that town? And you are dead on. That part of West Central Pennsylvania is home to a shit ton of Polacks."

Jawnie cleared her throat loud enough for the storefronts on either side of the office to have heard. Rockfish nodded over his slight. *Not like I'm not trying. It ain't easy trying to change forty-odd-years of saying dumb shit. They'd cancel me each day over something else. At this rate, I'm never gonna catch up.*

"The two guys, each who I thought were pissed at me, giving the silent treatment, have actually teamed up? Decker took the revenge job I never considered? But I'm damn near sure I saw Raffi on 695 this morning. Had to be him. No one else drives a shitbox orange Taurus around here."

"The clues point that way," Lynn said. "And I'm not even licensed for this type of work."

"That might have been him. Maybe only Dan is up there, or they're both here, doing some pre-planning," Jawnie said. "Either way, I'm not saying Raffi is or isn't in Grindsville with Dan. Remember, he's a known entity there and one who always finds it hard to keep his head down."

"I follow the logic, but I can't buy it. No way Dan's getting in over his head regarding mildewy MREs. I won't believe he's made an unholy union with Raffi. The odds are more along the line that a super creepy outfit like BlackWater hired him, and he can't say anything. Forced him to sign an NDA prior to being hired. That's my story and I'm sticking to it." Rockfish folded his arms across his chest to make his point.

"She's not saying you're wrong, Steve," Lynn said and nodded at Jawnie.

"Right. But there's a chance they came together and are headed for trouble. Just throwing it out there."

"And I'm shooting it down. Senior partner privilege," Rockfish said. He got up again and walked around to the back of the recliner. He stood for a second before leaning his weight onto his forearms. Rockfish paused until both women stared back. Only then did he continued.

"And if we consider your theory... they ripped off Raffi for free food so they can play in the woods for longer periods of time. I get it. And despite the bruise on Raffi's jaw and the weapons we saw,

I'm betting those guys are absolutely harmless. Rosie has nothing to fret about." Rockfish hadn't finished speaking and he already didn't believe his own words.

* * * * * * * * * *

Saturday, April 1st, found Jesus Earnhardt Jr. and his two top men, Clyde and Amos, deep in the Penn Forest. Each occupied a rocking chair on the half-rotted porch of an old hunting cabin, which now served as the Penn Forest Patriots' base of operations. The monthly meeting of the militia had concluded half an hour previously, and the three men watched as the last set of taillights disappeared in the darkness.

From the view of a lost hiker, the cabin was straight out of the *Evil Dead*. Blow on it and the walls would come tumbling down. Most of the renovation work by the group had benefited the inside. Earnhardt Jr. appreciated the creepy outside vibe and assumed if anyone had the gall to ignore the no trespassing signs, the haunted cabin exterior would keep them moving. Exactly how he wanted it.

"Well, should we call the executive board meeting to order?" Amos said. "I got shit to do at home and need a couple of hours of sleep if you're expecting us to show up and listen to Archibald rant again tomorrow."

"Gimme another one of those Iron City Lights before you bang that gavel," Clyde said. He looked at Earnhardt Jr. and agreed with Amos' statement.

Amos lifted his feet off the Coleman cooler and grabbed three cans. His Great Value Boots landed with a thud on the closed lid as he passed the beers around.

"I get it, Amos. We'd all like to sleep in and send the rest of the family to pay our respects. But with today's world and the advancing liberal agenda, a show of force is more than a show. The larger that crowd, the better. Archibald will reciprocate our show of support. Fivefold. The more popular his sermons, the larger the skim off the top of the offering baskets for us. And if I recall, Clyde, our coffers didn't exactly overflow after your wife's bake sale."

Not a word more was uttered regarding Sunday's mandatory hymns and instead, the sound of three pull-tabs officially called the meeting to order.

"Clyde, I need a full report on the test run out at Albert Scott's Alpaca Farm," Earnhardt Jr. said. "Operation Shot Heard 'Round won't get an ounce of traction if we can't get the damn serum ratio correct. Too much and the Feds descend on our town and turn everything upside down. The perfect amount? Our unknowing martyrs get sick as dogs, and we can run the narrative. Control the story. Gimme a status report on the latest."

"Before he goes into that, Colonel, quick question," Amos said. He stared Earnhardt Jr. in the eyes and took a long swig from his beer before continuing. "I understand our discussion tonight, but at what point do the rank and file become aware? Each one of them will have to be onboard with the consequences, even for perhaps their loved ones, before starting the Operation."

Earnhardt Jr. shook his head. "You leave the recruits to me. I say jump, they reply how high. They believe in the mission or else they wouldn't be here. One hundred percent commitment is required of all our men. You know that."

"And Clyde and I would follow you through whatever shit-storm is thrown our way. But what if someone's at ninety-nine point nine-nine-nine? With a monkey wrench at their side? Do we take the chance? Especially on the new ones?" Amos said. He balanced the beer can on his knee and didn't take his eyes off it as he spoke. "I say we keep it at this level. No dissemination outside of us three. Let's allow the men to be as outraged as John Q. Public when shit goes down. Easier to herd the sheep that way."

"I agree," Clyde added. "Once it is done, they'll be desperate for leadership and revenge. That's where us, the Elder and our man at the newspaper, comes in. If all goes well, NewsMax and Tucker will be here doing live remote broadcasts. Everyone will want to say they were at the new Lexington and Concord when the shot heard 'round the world was fired."

"And that, gentlemen, is why you're on the board with me."

"To the end," both Clyde and Amos said in unison. Three more pull-tabs signaled the motioned passed.

"Next order of business," Earnhardt Jr. said. "Circling back to my first question. Are we satisfied with the results of the test run?"

Clyde dug deep into the front pocket of his coveralls and pulled out a thrice-folded piece of lined paper. "Memory's not what it used to be, so I made notes."

"Only means you'll have to eat the paper before we adjourn," Amos said. Looking for confirmation, he turned to Earnhardt Jr. who winked in response.

"Okay, if you didn't already know, the average alpaca weighs between one hundred ten pounds and one ninety. Great test subjects. I only wish I had figured that out earlier. Might have saved us time and Ted Johnson a swine or two." Clyde paused and glanced down at his paper. "From running into Scott, down at the feed store, it doesn't seem like him or the vet figured out what the alpacas had gotten into."

"Sounds like a win-win for us," Amos said. "We've got a close to correct dose and still flying under the--"

Earnhardt Jr. pushed back his chair. The rockers scraped across the old wood and cut off Amos. He stood and turned to face the other men. He precariously perched his ass on the railing. *Bend but don't break, baby. We can sit here all night and pat ourselves on the back. But that won't move the ball forward one inch.* He held his palms out.

"Outcome?"

Clyde shuffled his feet under the chair and glanced up. "Sick for a couple of days, but with the right antibiotic, they came around. Right in time for shearing season."

"What antibiotic?" Earnhardt Jr. said.

"Not a clue," Clyde said. "And Dean didn't know either. Many people around here are too trusting of doctors."

"Store bought or administered by the vet on scene?" Earnhardt Jr.'s questions continued. Faster and with more angst.

Clyde shrugged, and Amos picked up the ball. "We've got plans to run into Dean at the Squiggly Wiggly Tavern tomorrow night. Buy him a few beers and play the part of concerned neighbors. I'll get every drop of information out of him."

Earnhardt Jr. gritted his teeth and sucked the night air between the enamel. "Figure that shit out. We need to know exactly what it will take for the affected to recover. I don't want them rising on the third day, but something short of a two-week COVID stint would be optimal. How do we know we'll get the same results with a human?"

"Wanna try it, Colonel?"

"I'll have to trust you on this one, Clyde. But, hear me out here, I'm spitballing. What if we slip it past one of those new recruits? Give them a few of those fucked up MREs too. Then we've got a scapegoat and keep suspicion under wraps. See how sick they get and dial back accordingly if needed?" Earnhardt Jr. stared down at the two men before him. He tugged at his beard with his free hand. He waited. *Their expressions and words will tell me all I need to know. Wit me or agin me.*

"One last test run before green lighting? A recruit who might wash out in the end, anyway? I like the way you think, Sir," Clyde said and drained the last of his can.

"I agree," Amos said. He dropped his empty on the porch and motioned for Clyde to get another from the cooler. "I suggest we use the same new recruit for the actual Op. Use them to taint the water treatment tank or at least leak information that they did. That way, if anything goes wrong, we can disavow any knowledge and let them take the blame. Plausible Deniability."

Earnhardt Jr. and Clyde turned to Amos. Their heads cocked to the side.

"Learned it on Jeopardy the other night. Don't blame me for educating myself. It means if they catch our guinea pig, we can't be tied to the conspiracy."

"I get it," Clyde said. "And then a few days later, Elder Archibald is leading a protest on the steps of city hall, pointing the finger straight at the immigrants and the paper is ready to lead with 'Our own 9/11' lead story. Give us time to ramp up the disinformation and get the entire Conemaugh Valley behind us." Clyde jumped out of his chair and joined Earnhardt Jr. leaning against the railing.

"Now who's sounding like Archibald?" Earnhardt Jr. said with a laugh and put his arm around Clyde's shoulders.

"If they ain't here for the love of our country, to save it from the CRT indoctrination--"

"Don't forget Obama and his minions," Amos said.

"You always interrupt me when I'm on a roll," Clyde said. "We need to provide our children with a place to grow up where piss water Bud Light, drag queens and feelings are never spoken of again, let alone taught. Keep that radical indoctrination agenda as far away from God's country as possible."

"All about government by the people for the common man," Amos said. He, too, pushed his chair back and joined the others standing. "This is going to be a recruitment boom for us. Huge."

Earnhardt took in the men on either side. *There is no doubting their devotion to the cause and, more importantly, to me.* He took a long celebratory swig from his can. And then a second before ending the executive meeting on a high note.

"Speaking of which, I might have just the fucking new guy we need. Let's go ring him up."

* * * * * * * * * *

Jawnie and Lynn stood outside the office door, deep in thought. The sun had crept up over the horizon the Monday following April

Fool's Day. Lynn glanced at the familiar car in the parking lot, steam rising from her hood, and then to Jawnie.

"A little early for the big guy, don't you think?" Lynn said. "I betcha Lana's hood is hot to the touch."

"My thought, exactly," Jawnie said. "Careful with that door handle. He's probably got a joy buzzer contraption hooked up to it. The man never was good with dates."

Jawnie pulled a piece of cloth, previously used to clean her sunglasses, from her messenger bag and draped it over the door handle. She locked eyes with Lynn and opened it. Silence met both women as they walked across the threshold and past Lynn's desk.

"Steve?" Jawnie called out.

"I'll ring his office, maybe he's back there guzzling down a McDonald's number three extra early breakfast meal," Lynn said.

"No need, ladies," Rockfish said as he stood up from behind the bar. "After seeing Angel's text messages last night, I assumed a celebration is in order. Or at least a tiny one this morning, followed by quite the bender this evening." He held up the bottle of Freixenet Cordon Negro Brut and placed it next to the three flutes already atop the bar.

"I thought you had your phone on do-not-disturb after 8pm?" Jawnie said.

"Old man bladder. Had to pee and instinct had me check the screen for notifications."

The three shared a laugh over Rockfish's incontinence before moving on to their producer's texts and what appeared to be a successful season conclusion of From the Case Files of Rockfish & McGee. The eight-episode season had wrapped to a larger viewership than expected. Ratings were up almost ten percent over the first year and the executives at NikolaTV, not to mention the show's producer, Angel Davenport, were more than happy with the show's continued performance.

"We're here this morning because of text messages too," Lynn said.

"Yeah, Steve, we'll have to pass on the Monday morning mimosas. Duty calls," Jawnie said.

"Yeah, Boss. Jawnie's taking me out for some light field work," Lynn added. Her enthusiasm was unmistakable.

Jawnie immediately saw the concern in Steve's face as he put the bottle back in the fridge and moved around to the bullpen area.

"Osborne's headed out on the prowl, I assume," Rockfish said. "And Lynn, you're good at doing a little eavesdropping slash surveillance work?"

"I'm good. Trust me. I'm only sitting in a quaint brunch place listening in on a piece of crap cheating husband. Nothing to push my PTSD buttons."

"Simple and safe, Steve," Jawnie said. She walked over and stood behind her spot on the couch. "Kitty Osborne reached out a little after six this morning. She heard Troy call in sick to work yet again."

"He and his bimbo-of-the-day are grabbing brunch before retiring to the Salem Motor Lodge for a long afternoon," Rockfish said and smiled.

"Seems that way," Jawnie said. "He doesn't deviate from the routine, no matter who's on his arm. He'll dress for work as if Kitty's clueless to the whole charade and return home as she's setting the table for dinner."

"And for that repetition, we're thankful. Makes it easier for us. Yet, despite the routine, don't let your guard down. Either of you. Be careful, get the evidence Kitty needs to actually move forward on this divorce--"

"Not like we haven't given her enough already," Lynn said.

"I know that. You know that, and one day, Kitty will come to grips with it also," Rockfish said. "But as long as she's cutting that check on the first of every month, we'll do as instructed. Kitty's good people. She's no Faith Fairbrace." Rockfish paused and waited for the smirks. "Once you get back, put away the tools of the trade and get your asses over to the house. Mack's whipping up an early celebratory dinner and I'll already be there knee-deep into an early happy hour. It's not too often we get to celebrate in this job."

"What about Raffi?" Lynn said.

"Nowhere to be found and not returning messages. So, no. Despite a limited role this season, he won't be there raising a glass. Maybe another place, on his own." Rockfish shrugged, and the trio of collective sighs surprised everyone.

Two hours later, Jawnie and Lynn sat at The Lunchbox Tavern. Each at separate tables, both within earshot of Romeo as he laid on the charm. A few bills, folded and slipped to the hostess, made sure each woman garnered a table on either side of the date in question.

The restaurant, known to locals as LBTeets, was a Linthicum Heights staple going back to the 1970s, and little had changed since the Bicentennial grand opening. Unfortunately, over the course of the past couple of years, its Yelp rating had declined in direct ratio to influencer reservations. But for those needing a dark interior, mixed with booths and small square tables, with patrons that minded their own business, it was the perfect place for a pre-horizontal mambo protein and carbo-load.

The surveillance team had arrived in separate cars, leaving nothing to chance, should Osborne and his lady friend split up. They communicated via text while seated, as the act from two young women wouldn't draw any concern from their target, his paramour, or other patrons.

Half an hour into the uneventful and less informative early lunch, Jawnie continued to push her salad around the plate. Fifteen feet away, Lynn was finishing the last of her crab omelet and steak fries. *She dove right in, as if she's been working off an expense account her whole life. Should I take this salad home? What's Mack got planned for tonight? How much longer do I have to listen to this lovey dovey crap? Yup, McGee, it's been a while, hasn't it?*

Jawnie fired off a frustrated text to Lynn: *Schmoopy this, love you more. You're so f'ing hot. Gag me with a spoon!*

Lynn's audible giggle caused a few heads to turn in her direction. Jawnie kept her's inside as Lynn frantically turned her phone over on the table but not before firing off a quick reply: *Yeah, been a while for me too.*

Ten minutes after the bright red color faded from Lynn's face, Jawnie overheard what she had expected. They had planned to hold the afternoon's cardio session at the Salem Motor Lodge. *Now we wait. Probably should send Lynn there in advance and get arrival photos. Does he have a punch card for that place? Ten visits and the eleventh hump is on the house? Yes, my dear, it has been far too long.*

"Hey Chief, gimme two champagne coolies. One for here and one in a to-go cup... I get it, you don't have them. Here's a little something extra to help fix that problem."

The voice brought Jawnie's posture to attention and her head on a swivel. *Raffi!* Or his doppelgänger had grabbed a seat at the bar, his back to Jawnie's table. She glanced over at Lynn, but her partner's eyes were focused on the small screen in her hands. *Meet me in the bathroom NOW.* Text sent.

"What's up?" Lynn said as the door swung shut behind her. "You want to strategize about the motor lodge? Head over there and slip the cleaning woman a few dollars?"

Jawnie shook her head. "Raffi's here. At the bar."

"Not my circus, not my monkey."

Jawnie's head moved side to side again, with pursed lips this time.

"You sure it's him?" Lynn said. "Steve thought he saw him the other day, too."

"Positive. Listen, we don't have much time..."

Jawnie swapped car keys with Lynn, as Raffi would easily spot the Subaru. Lynn would drive to the motel and get pictures of the happy couple's arrival and then sweet talk the front desk clerk or cleaning staff out of any information they might use to further their report. The plan was to meet back at the office later that afternoon and exchange notes. The two casually walked out of the bathroom, paid their respective tabs, and went their separate ways.

Jawnie hunched down in the drivers seat of Lynn's car and watched her partner pull out of the parking lot. This would be Lynn's first solo work since the Porbeagle case, and Jawnie said a silent prayer. *Back in the saddle and be safe out there. I know you can do it.*

Raffi's orange Taurus sat two rows over, backed into its spot, and confirmed Jawnie's suspicions. She reached up and pulled the visor down to help camouflage her with the car's interior. She waited until the front door opened and Raffi bounded down the front steps, white Styrofoam cup in hand. *One for the road, huh? Where the hell have you been and where are you headed? Rockfish might seem to act like he doesn't care, but he'll give me an attaboy when I fill him in later today.*

The Taurus pulled out of the parking lot and turned right onto the boulevard. Jawnie followed suit and kept her distance. She hadn't worked with Raffi much. That was Steve's deal and wasn't sure how observant or sharp his counter surveillance skills were. *If he even had them at all in his toolbox.*

The two-car caravan soon left the boulevard and exited onto the northbound lanes of I-695. *Exactly where Rockfish spotted him the other day. But where the heck is he headed today?* The where became clear when Raffi put on his blinker and took the exit for I-70 West. The large green sign over the road said Frederick, but Jawnie thought about what lay beyond. Breezewood, Pennsylvania and the Turnpike. *He's headed back to Grindsville.*

Two things came to mind. She had been right regarding Decker's off-the-cuff remark to his wife and second, there was no way in hell she was following Raffi for the next six hours, round trip. She glanced ahead and then checked her rearview for any lurking State Troopers. Seeing none, Jawnie slowed until Raffi's car sped out of sight and only then made a hard left across the gravel median and onto the eastbound lanes.

"Hey Siri, call Rockfish."

* * * * * * * * * *

The orange Taurus turned off of Scalp Avenue and into the WinGate Motel parking lot. A paper bag filled with groceries shifted in the passenger seat. A few days had passed since Raffi thought he had spotted Lynn at LBTeets. One minute she was there, and the next gone. Had he spooked her? Wouldn't be the first time. *One day she'll get over her problem with me, but it was exactly that. Her problem. I moved on a long time ago.* He was sure she had seen him. Lynn hadn't bothered to tell Rockfish. Or he didn't care. The voicemails and text messages from that side of the argument had stopped long before he had run into the man's secretary.

Raffi parked on the far side of the parking lot. He walked around to the passenger side and grabbed the paper bag before heading towards the motel office. He passed the frosted glass door and instead climbed the cement stairwell. On the second level, he walked the length of the building and headed back down a second stairwell. Here, he turned left into a small hallway. When he was sure no one had followed, he stopped in front of Room 109. Raffi knocked before pulling the keycard from his jacket pocket and let himself in.

"Dan?" His voice echoed off the bare walls.

Speaking of decades of shenanigans, what if Steve saw me now? Overseeing my recovery operation with the help of his good buddy. Get my shit back here and Steve's gonna see old Raffi in a new light. To be honest, desperate times called for desperate alliances. Each man held a thing the other was jonesing for. Raffi needed someone to infiltrate this bunch of idiots and determine where his stolen Q-Rations were being held. Decker needed an opportunity to show that his initiative and drive didn't retire with his badge. A successful stint that he'd market to the snobs of LinkedIn and transform into what he hoped would be a lofty private sector salary.

"Anyone home?" Raffi called out again.

At first glance, the small room was empty. One of the two queen beds looked as if someone had wrestled with the comforter and lost. The armoire was closed, but Decker wouldn't be hiding within. The chair and small table nearest the door were piled high with dirty clothes. Raffi placed the grocery bag on the floor next to the table. On the other side of the room, behind another door within a small alcove, a toilet flushed. And then again.

He's still belly sick. Glad I haven't caught it. Yet. Praise be I'm at the Comfort Inn.

A third flush and then, Dan Decker, former Captain with the Baltimore Police Department and now hired mercenary for Patriot Meals on American Made Wheels, exited the bathroom.

It had been a few days since Raffi had gotten back to town and checked in on his employee, but the man seemed paler. Sweat plastered his hair to the sides of his face. *He wore a wife beater and boxers. Probably the best uniform for the circumstances.*

"Raffi, sorry, man, I didn't hear you come in. This bug is killing me. Can't shake it."

"Figure out where you caught it yet?" Raffi said, standing against the door. "No one at my hotel is complaining about anything. Well, those people I overhear at the continental breakfast bitch moan about everything, but whatever you got doesn't seem to be taking the town by storm."

"No, hob-knobbed with the Great Value Boys on Sunday morning at a goofy tent revival and then at a picnic afterwards. I gotta tell ya, Steve might not be the smartest man I ever met, but he's straight-money with nicknames. After the picnic, I've been in contact with a few of 'em and no one else is reporting the nuclear shits but me. I've bought the Giant Eagle out of grape Pedialyte three days running now. Not to mention trying every over-the-counter option available. Might have to give in and find the closest Urgent Care."

"Don't be out and about too much. Anything could blow your cover. Especially if you use a Blue Cross Blue Shield card with your real name on it. Can't risk it. The woman taking your information is probably married to one of these yahoos. The mission is too important."

"To you, maybe. And spoken like a true amateur," Decker said. He opened a dresser drawer and pulled out a clean T-shirt and sweatpants. "But my diarrhea ain't why I asked for this meeting. Two-fold, actually. One you might be interested in."

"I'm all ears. Got nothing but time," Raffi said as he pushed the piles of clothes off the chair and sat down.

Decker rolled his eyes. "Sure, make yourself at home."

Raffi waited on the news until Decker finished dressing and found a seat of his own on the edge of the untouched bed.

"There's something afoot with these guys. I'm betting big. Sooner rather than later, I'm feeling. Not sure exactly what it is, but here's what I know--"

Raffi loudly cleared his throat and crossed his arms. "Dan-o, you're doing a hell of a lot of talking, but I'm hearing nothing about locating my Q-Rations. That is what you're being paid to do, if I recall."

"Fuck that shit. This is light years beyond your stolen MREs," Decker said. His voice strained and face crimson. He punched the mattress repeatedly. "Listen to me. For once. Something big is about to go down with this group. Except I don't know quite what it is. All I got is a name. At least I think it's a name. Haybarn, Hayward, Hayseed. Close to one of those. Bad, I'm telling you." Decker's voice rose and sounded more strained.

"Tell anyone, but I hate to tell ya, I'm not that person," Raffi said. He shrugged and wanted to desperately wash his hand of this entire venture.

"I would, but I don't have a drop of evidence to go to the authorities with. Something's coming down the pike. I know, I'm repeating myself. But I'm not in any position to sound a warning siren. I need a few more days. Figure out what this Hay person is all about. But if you really want to know where your precious cargo is, I can draw you a map." Decker stood up from the edge of the bed and paced toward the bathroom door.

"Where?"

"Grindsville Municipal Landfill."

"Cut the shit, Dan."

"Oh, it's too liquidy to cut. Seems a bunch of the Patriots got the runs. Not as bad as me right now, mind you. From eating your product. They were deep in the woods doing 'maneuvers' and ended up wiping with what turned out to be poison ivy. These guys ain't the smartest."

Raffi threw his head back and roared. He stood up and walked between the beds and dresser, intent on meeting Decker halfway. The man he hired had stopped at the alcove and turned to face Raffi. Decker shook his head. "Anyway, serves 'em right. But I'm out a shit ton of money," Raffi said. "Sadly, if I can't get 'em back and unload 'em on another unsuspecting group of LARPers, I'm going to be late with payment. Your end of our bargain."

"I don't give a fuck about your money. This was never about getting paid." The spittle flew from Decker's mouth as his palm backhanded the bathroom door.

Raffi watched as the door hinges shook from the blow. A second would pull the already loose screws away from the frame. An expense he couldn't afford as the room was on his credit card. One rapidly approaching its limit. A partnership that had been held together by half-rotted string and a worn Velcro strip was unraveling.

"You don't get it. Never will. I knew I should have broken down and talked to Steve before agreeing to this. Listen. To. Me. This is no longer about you. I don't give a shit if you pay me or not. The cop in me never retired." Decker slammed his right fist into his heart. And then again. "It courses through my veins despite the badge mounted in a shadowbox on my mantel. I came here for your dumb shit, but I'm staying on because people are going to get hurt. Who? I don't know. Where? Somewhere. I need to get a better handle on their plans and then alert the authorities. Before we end up with another Rosewood Massacre or Charlottesville TikiTorchPalooza. You haven't heard their private rhetoric. I have."

Raffi stepped back towards the chair, no longer wanting to close the gap between the two men. Decker appeared a second or two shy of erupting again. *What if I pick up the groceries, since he's no longer on the clock for me, and silently back out of here? Regroup at the Comfort Inn. Lose my shit over lost profits and the missed opportunity to impress Steve. No marquee for me.*

"Listen, Dan, I get where you're coming from, but forgive old Raffi. Saving the world ain't my thing. I've got more than I can handle covering my own ass. You say my shit's in the dump, then it's game over for me." Raffi took another step backwards and felt behind him for the door handle.

"Jives with your bio," Decker said, inching forward. "Scamming. Snitching. Looking out for number one. That's why you made such a good informant for half a dozen of our squads."

"Well, you--"

"Me? To Protect and Serve. You don't get it. I lived it, but it's not about me. It's about helping those who can't for themselves. My gut, years of experience, tells me something bad is brewing. Beyond a rally and simple assault on counter-protesters. More sinister. You wanna run? I'll be more than happy to fire the starter's pistol."

"Go to the damn cops if you feel shit's gonna get weird." Raffi said and turned the door handle.

"The cops? The same ones that tried to railroad you and Steve? Whose members are more than likely active Penn Forest Patriots members or recruits?"

"Fuck, I dunno. The state police. The county mounties. Whatever."

"What exactly would I take to them, Raffi? The tingling in my loins? The mystery gnawing at my stomach walls? I need facts, not hearsay, that they may or may not follow up on. And on the slight chance they do, how long would it take them to build that shit into actual investigable facts? Been there, done that. It's not microwaveable."

Raffi shook his head, swung open the door, and turned his back to Decker. He picked up his grocery bag from the floor.

"... that's right. Run. Head home with your tail between your legs, mourning the loss of your expired Hello Fresh bullshit."

Raffi didn't dignify the man with an answer and picked up the pace. The door slammed behind him, and Raffi made a line for his car.

* * * * * * * * *

Wilbur John Lyczek pushed the motel's cleaning cart along the cement walkway towards the broken ice machine. He focused his attention on the perpendicular row of rooms, ahead, at his one o'clock and Room 109. He squatted behind the cart, half hiding and half keeping an eye on the prize. Lyczek watched as the man carried out the same Giant Eagle paper bag he had entered with. But this time, the man walked directly across the parking lot.

Lyczek was a lanky, high school dropout and first shift sandwich artist at Subway. An hour earlier, he had stopped by the supermarket to grab a couple of blueberry cake donuts and an energy drink before reporting to work. With one hand in the donut bin, a loud argument had broken out at the deli counter, only twenty feet away. The cursing isn't what made him step closer, but the voice of the customer. Combined with the curly hair and the suit jacket, Lyczek couldn't have been surer of anything.

The man's name escaped his memory. It remained foggy from last night's round of Drunk Jenga with his roommates and sweetheart. But the appearance and loud shrill had taken him back two months. To the night when they ripped him off and sent him and his lame partners crying back to the big city. And even more recent times when the militia members cursed the man to high heaven by all, when those same MREs brought half the Penn Forest Patriots to their knees. A few kneeling in front of and the rest seated on the outdoor latrines.

Lyczek wondered what would bring the man back to town. *Imagine the balls on this guy. What's so important that he'd show his face again on the streets of Grindsville? Either way, the bosses will want to know what he's up to.* Lyczek had abandoned his donuts and followed the man out of the store and down Scalp Avenue to the WinGate Motel.

"Imma need that back now. A guest clogged the shitter in 204. Mr. Patel wants me to prioritize it."

Lyczek jumped at the sound of the voice behind him. The cleaning woman stood, hands on hips and head cocked to the side, waiting for him to return the borrowed cart. Her uniform slightly more dirty than the angry expression on her face.

"My apologies, ma'am. Here ya go." Lyczek stepped out from behind it and stood in back of a cement pillar until the Taurus pulled away. There was no need to follow it, as he had garnered a peek inside when the man first entered the room. A Comfort Inn parking pass lay on the dash. Lyczek had snapped a picture and, along with the others he surreptitiously had taken. They would support his story when he spoke to the Colonel. *Maybe there's a promotion in it for me. Speaking of which...* Lyczek checked the time. His shift started ten minutes ago. *Fuck Jared, I need to find out all I can before asking for an audience. Anyway, Jersey Mikes is always hiring.*

Lyczek nodded at the cleaning woman as she walked away. He hung a right and headed across the parking lot toward the door that led to the front desk to see what he could learn.

* * * * * * * * *

This unseasonably warm Wednesday afternoon found Rockfish and Jawnie out on the back deck, overlooking the inlet. Large pine trees lined the far end of the property. The sun's rays bounced off the water and gave it a bluer hue than its actual color. Jawnie had stopped at Rockfish's house to enjoy the weather and catch up before it got cooler.

"I don't think I've ever seen you out here without a can or glass in your hand," Jawnie said.

"Sometimes you have to drink mixers. Straight. Honestly, I don't know how most of you do it. Not to mention I need to drive Mack this evening, over to the VFW for his monthly poker game. Then swing by later and bring his broke ass home."

"Speaking of dinner, what's he whipping up in there?" Jawnie took a sip from her Coke Zero and placed the can down on the small table between the chairs.

"Egg roll in a bowl, but I'm subbing tofu for the ground turkey since I knew you'd be dropping by," Mack said. His voice carried through the sliding screen door out onto the deck.

Jesus Christ. Another night of moving food around my plate and picking up takeout once I drop him off. Rockfish searched his brain for restaurants along the way.

"Sounds great, Mack," Jawnie said before lowering her voice. "How the heck can he hear us out here, over the volume of the television? Also, can I let Zippy out? Check out his poor face."

Rockfish let out a laugh and set down his own can. Mack's black Labrador, Zippy, sat, nose pressed against the screen, almost willing his body to pass through. "Sure thing. You closed the side gate, right?"

"Absolutely. I learned my lesson the last time having to chase that pup halfway down the street," Jawnie said. "And if I know my stuff, and I do, that's the History Channel bleeding through the screen. I thought Mack was purely Murder Channel?"

"Nothing he likes more than murder in a small town with Joe Kenda, but he's been on a history binge lately. Boat-load of World War II stuff, but today's the 19th and they're running Waco and Oklahoma City marathons. You want me to shut the slider or ask him to lower it?" Rockfish stood up and let Zippy out. The puppy pounded out onto the deck and directly into Jawnie's lap.

"Leave it open," Jawnie said, while giving Zippy all the lovings. "We'll never hear the bell for supper if you do. But back to everyone's favorite, Raffi..."

"I know. You've told me for the past week and a half. He and Decker are allegedly in Grindsville trying to steal back those godawful MREs. Or so you've concluded."

"Convinced. You're not worried about them?" Jawnie said. Zippy gave her a kiss on the cheek and then raced off the deck in search of a squirrel.

"Lynn said it best. Not my circus, not my monkeys. They're grown men. One was a highly decorated police officer, if I recall correctly. The other, not so much. Whatever they've teamed up their Wonder Twins powers for, I'm sure there's no need to worry. With a little luck, at the worst, someone will run them out of town. Decker will come back swearing off Raffi for all eternity and the other will move on to his next sure-thing money-making venture. Time heals all wounds. Except for him and Lynn. That's taking longer than expected."

"Amen, but that's not exactly what I meant. He's back in town. Raffi, that is. Back at all of his old haunts. Or so my sources tell me. Have you heard from Dan or Rosie?"

"Nada. Nothing," Rockfish said. "She's back to ignoring my comms and double for him. The Rockfish signal has remained dark."

Jawnie took a long sip from her water bottle and returned it to the chair's cup holder. "And not a thing from Raffi? That's not normal operating procedure, if you know what I mean."

"He owes me money. Not to mention the infamous face plant of Grindsville. His outreach to us will be far and few between. Unless he needs a favor. Then you can count on him."

"If Dan is up there snooping around, it doesn't make sense for Raffi to be out and about town," Jawnie said. "As if nothing is out of the ordinary. And people have seen the back of his head a few times over the course of the last week."

"Unless he's thrown Dan to the wolves or needs cash. Six of one and half a dozen of the other. None of which pays my bills. And I should care because? Like I said, the signals have all gone dark. For my sake, stop worrying about it."

Before Jawnie answered, they looked at each other and then at the sliding screen door. The sounds emanating had changed in voice, tone, and volume.

...We interrupt our regularly scheduled programming and go live to our ABC News local correspondent Marianela Moreno from WJAC. She's covering the breaking story of an alleged mass poisoning in the small town of Grindsville, Pennsylvania...

The partners leapt from their chairs and the more agile Jawnie arrived at the door first. She slid it open and stepped into the kitchen, Rockfish right on her heels.

"Someone remember the dog's outside," Rockfish said. They moved across the tiled floor and crowded around the small television on the kitchen counter. Mack remained by the stove, oblivious to the news report that gripped the attention of the other two.

... The press release from the Governor's Office detailed that as of this early point in the investigation, there have been no indications of ties to international or domestic terrorism. Officials are erring on the side of caution despite calls from community leaders regarding recently relocated illegal immigrants from the southern border by

the Biden Administration. Allegations are these groups have made unsubstantiated threats against the town and its residents...

"Sounds about right, from our short time there," Jawnie said. Her head slowly moved side-to-side with the reporter's words. Rockfish only nodded, not diverting his attention from the screen.

... Local televangelist Erwin Archibald, Elder of the parish at Calvary United's Covenant of King Solomon, has set up revival tents with supplies to help the Red Cross with recovery efforts. He'll be holding a sermon this evening on the steps of City Hall to bring the community closer and to...

A stock photo of the televangelist appeared on the left side of the screen as Moreno continued her report.

Back in the kitchen, two chins simultaneously hit the floor as they each recognized the man standing behind and off to Archibald's left. Rockfish pointed at the small screen.

"Colonel Fat Patton!"

"Jesus Earnhardt Something or Other, if I recall," Jawnie said.

"No way in hell all of this passes the sniff test," Rockfish said. His laissez-faire attitude regarding his friend's predicament came to a sudden stop.

... Members of Calvary United's Covenant of King Solomon are also handing out flyers with a hand-drawn sketch of a suspect. Residents claimed to have seen the man snooping around the water treatment plant the past few days. Police advise that the man is not a subject of their investigation but would like to speak to him as a person of interest. They have handed me a copy of the flyer and I'll hold it up to the camera until we can get a copy to the station and have it posted on WJAC.com...

"It can't be," Jawnie said.

Mack turned to face Jawnie and said, "Okay, Jawnie, I won't add the onions, but you sure as heck don't know what you're missing."

"Dad, my apologies, but fuck dinner and screw those onions," Rockfish said. "We've got bigger problems. Dan's in trouble, and I've ignored every warning sign." He turned to Jawnie. "You tried to tell me, but I'm thick-headed. You were right all along. Raffi never dropped it and roped Dan into--"

The opening notes of Rob Zombie's *Thunder Kiss '65* filled the kitchen. Jawnie reached for the television remote and muted the volume as Rockfish fumbled for his ringing cell phone.

"Rosie... You saw it too?... Sure as hell could be his twin... No need to apologize... I'll have him home before you know it. Promise."

Rockfish placed his phone down on the kitchen island and pulled a chair away from the table. His head hung low. He felt responsible for Dan. For not reaching out earlier and warning him about Raffi's scheme. *I need to make this right. For all.*

Jawnie shook her head slowly from side to side. "What the heck is going on with the world?" She placed the remote next to Rockfish's cell, leaving the television on mute.

"It's the beginning of what those fuckers hope is the end. We've all seen the original. It's that time of the year. Third week of April. Hitler's Birthday, Waco and Oklahoma City. It appears, at least to me, despite the mixed reviews and low box office, a producer green lit a sequel. Insurrection 2: Electric Boogaloo. And you get to play the part of Jawnie-Claude Van Damme."

"Huh?"

Rockfish didn't answer but stood up and tapped his father on the shoulder.

"Dad, I gotta roll. Sorry about dinner, but we have to head out. See if you can snag a ride with your buddy Iggy to the VFW. And don't forget about Zippy outside." Rockfish walked out of the kitchen with Jawnie on his heels. He stopped in front of the interior door which led to the garage.

"So, now is it your circus and your monkeys?"

"Best three rings in town. Friend in need, will travel. Meet you at the office in thirty."

CHAPTER EIGHT

Thirty minutes turned into ninety before each of the partners pulled into the strip mall parking lot that housed their office. Lana's dashboard clock read seven minutes after seven when Rockfish arrived. He carried a Tupperware full of Mack's Tofu Egg Roll in a Bowl for Jawnie, and she the world's largest go-bag.

They fell further behind schedule, reviewing each new tidbit on the poisoning Jawnie had found online. The Grindsville Plague, as the media had christened it, was the lead story across all the news aggregators, be it left, center or right. Erwin Archibald's sermon at City Hall had not ended even an hour ago, but it was he who first mentioned the word plague.

Some stations carried the homily live, tape delayed on others, but ignored by none. Archibald's hate-filled words were clipped and had spread virally across video streaming services and social media platforms. The views and shares were racking up as Rockfish and Jawnie learned additional details regarding what they were about to walk headfirst into. One such nugget of information was the route the swath of sickness had cut through the Grindsville population.

An analysis of those infected by the Pennsylvania Department of Infectious Disease concluded the vector used to introduce the plague to the population was the municipality's water treatment plant. A review of Lee Hospital intake surveys of those admitted supported the hypothesis. The infected were all associated with city buildings and downtown establishments, as well as new housing developments in affluent neighborhoods.

Your average to below average Grindsvilleer couldn't afford the fees charged by the city to hook-up to the new water lines. They remained tied to their own private wells and thus unaffected. Archibald spun that singular finding to lay blame at the feet of the immigrant communities. All the more reason to shine the law enforcement investigation and interrogation spotlights on this small segment of the population.

And no reporting was complete without a mention of the manhunt for the alleged perpetrator, and charcoal sketch model, known to a handful as Dan Decker. As a person of interest, the authorities wished to only speak to the man.

Speak. Right. If my experience with those yahoos tells me anything, Dan's going to be talked to with a taser and a billy club. They'll assign him an incompetent public defender who probably spends his weekends drilling with the Great Value Boys. Rockfish knew time was running out, despite the sunshine and roses fairytale ending he had repeated to Rosie over the phone.

"Hey, you about ready? I can track any updates from the road. Upgrading to unlimited data was one of the smartest decisions you've made," Jawnie said. She had startled Rockfish, leaning in his doorway while his eyes continued to dart across the computer monitor. "I also made the reservations. Open-ended for a single room at the Edlesburg Econo Lodge."

Rockfish logged off his computer and then raised his head. Jawnie had moved the rest of her body into the doorframe, and he noticed she was itching to get on the road.

Rockfish grabbed his keys from the top drawer. "Being a good half an hour from our target location kept us flying under the radar in the Porbeagle case. It should serve us well here, too. Far enough away to guarantee we won't run into anyone. Nice call, kid."

They grabbed travel and laptop bags, backpacks and a few tools of the trade, which they had stacked by the front door. A couple of minutes later, Lana's trunk burst at the seams. Rockfish stepped back to the office door, locked the door, and set the alarm.

"You think we got everything?" Jawnie said as each buckled up.

"If not, that company credit card should come in handy," Rockfish said.

Rockfish backed Lana out of the parking spot and made a left out onto the street. He expected Jawnie's first question before the words left her lips.

"The highway is in the other direction," Jawnie said. "Please tell me you're not doing what I think you are." The light from Lana's instrument panel illuminated the concern on her face.

"By my estimation, we've only got two rings. The best circuses have three."

Twenty minutes later, they pulled up to Raffi's townhouse. The only light came from a small window on the second floor.

Rockfish pushed the button on his seatbelt and reached across the center console to prevent Jawnie from doing the same.

"You stay. This won't take but a minute," Rockfish said as he opened the door. "He's coming one way or another."

"Should be a fun ride. I'll move to the backseat. I hear you two have a lot of catching up to do."

Rockfish leaned back into the car, one hand on the open door and the other on the headrest. "He's coming and can be a wealth of information on exactly what we're walking into. Especially if you were correct that he's recently returned from Grindsville."

Rockfish stood back up, shut the drivers-side door, and at the same moment, he noticed the upstairs light extinguished.

Not gonna make me go away that easily, my friend. You've got a ton to answer for.

Fifteen minutes later, Raffi opened the passenger side door. He wore a ball cap and sunglasses at night, his chin pinned to his chest and a small travel bag on his lap.

Rockfish backed out of the parking space and Lana eventually made her way to the Beltway and then west on I-70, before Raffi opened up in dribs and drabs. At times, he cowered in the passenger seat, if Rockfish made any sudden moves with his right arm. He imagined what Jawnie thought had happened in the townhouse.

"You know, dude, consider yourself lucky. If you had stayed up there, I'm betting there would have been two composite sketches floating around," Rockfish said. "Nailed to every telephone pole and outhouse within ten miles of Grindsville."

Raffi lifted his head off the window and turned a little to the left. "You don't think I know that? It wasn't like I abandoned him up there. He was the one who learned they dumped my Q-Rations in the landfill. And with that, his work for me was done. I didn't fulfill my end of the agreement then, but my inability to pay was the furthest thing from his mind." Raffi's hands moved almost as fast as his lips, and it was by luck. His left palm barely graced Jawnie's face as she leaned in between the two seats to hear better.

"What did he think was going on?" Rockfish said. "What did he know, and when did he know it?"

"Nothing, Steve, I swear," Raffi said.

Rockfish watched Raffi lean to the side again, head against the window, almost in anticipation of the backhand Rockfish was ready to unleash. Especially if he continued to be evasive. *Had I telegraphed it? I gotta remember he's no dumbass. Raffi's been around the block more than most of us.*

"He kept saying something ain't right. Some sort of cop instinct. I dunno."

"Turns out Dan knew exactly what was about to go down," Jawnie said, leaning in. "Even if he couldn't paint the perfect warning picture."

"That's Decker. Will always do the right thing for the right people," Rockfish said. "How many times has he reamed me aloud, pissed me off royally, only to find he had been in the right the entire time? He's one of the good guys and that's why you're cowering in that seat. You know it, I know it. We're going to get him back to Rosie in one piece if it kills either of us."

Raffi remained silent. Jawnie leaned further in and altered course on the Dan Decker Appreciation Hour.

"Steve, it's obvious Jesus Earnhardt knows--"

"Junior. Don't forget that part. He was very adamant that time about Colonel too," Rockfish said. He felt the tension across both rows of seating and wanted to lessen it as much as possible. Better planning came when people weren't afraid to speak their minds.

"That being said, I'll stick with Fat Patton," Jawnie said. Rockfish saw her smile. "The Crayola wanted poster is proof in my book. They know exactly who Dan is and are hoping to pin him as a scapegoat. I'd like to know how they figured out who he was."

"Dan's careful as shit," Rockfish said. "Must have been another person's fuck up." Rockfish turned and glanced squarely at the passenger seat.

"Hey man, I was cautious as shit, too. Learned from the best." Raffi's attempt to suck up and get back on Rockfish's good side fell flat onto Lana's passenger side floor mat.

"Listen, man, I'm not saying you did anything wrong, or on purpose, but think. Where did you last leave him?"

"That shitty motel on the outskirts of town, Room 109. It was on my dime. You know, picking up expenses along with the rate he charged."

"That's a starting point," Jawnie said. "Can you check the billing on your phone? Check to see when the last time they charged the card?"

"Not while we're driving, but I can as soon as we stop and glom onto an unsecured Wi-Fi. Unlimited data doesn't come with my tax bracket."

Rockfish slowed down as he approached the traffic light, signaling the end of I-70. He had two options in continuing west. Either the Pennsylvania turnpike for two exits or rural Route 30. He glanced over at Raffi and knew he wouldn't be reimbursed for the turnpike tolls. Lana made a left onto Route 30 and neither her Hemi nor Rockfish were thrilled with the forty-five mile an hour posted speed limit. But less traffic would allow his brain to keep working with only slight attention paid to the road.

"Okay. Thinking this through," Rockfish said. "If the room was on your dime and anyone with half a brain figured out that was where Dan was staying..."

"Probably pretty easy to go in and weave a tale to the front desk clerk," Jawnie said. "I've seen you do it a couple of times now. Those clerks aren't exactly the gate keepers of personal identifiable information they need to be."

"Exactly. Raffi, did you ever go there and meet with Dan?" Rockfish reached down and hit the switch for the dome light. He needed to see every nook and cranny of Raffi's face when he answered.

"It was the only place we met," Raffi said. Chin firmly resting on his chest.

"Okay. That explains how the Great Value Boys were able to finally put one and one together. Even a blind dog finds a bone every once in a while."

"Do you think they've hurt him?" Jawnie asked.

"I doubt it," Rockfish said. "No reason to put out that sketch if they had. They want law enforcement focused on Dan and obvious not any other shady dealings that might be next on their redneck to-do list."

"Raffi?" Jawnie said, craning her neck a little further to make eye contact. "Is there anything you can tell us about this clergy guy, Erwin Archibald? Steve and I think he might be tied in with the Great Value Boys. Silent partner? The one actually pulling the strings?"

"I don't know a thing. Never heard of the guy till Steve mentioned the name during his tirade in my living room."

"He runs the Calvary United's Covenant of King Solomon," Jawnie said, holding her phone between the seats. "Unlimited AT&T does an investigation good."

"Wait, repeat that again," Rockfish asked.

"Calvary United's Covenant of King Solomon."

"I'll never understand these religious grifters. No one ever seems to workshop an acronym before printing signs and literature. Second time for us."

Raffi didn't stop laughing until Lana's blinker went on for the turn onto Route 56, ten minutes later.

* * * * * * * * * *

The Friday evening Happy Hour at the Edlesburg Econo Lodge was practically nonexistent, much to the surprise of no one, including Rockfish. His flask at the ready, he kept insisting, at check-in, he had heard someone mention Friday Night Endless Appetizers. Jawnie assured him the person in question must have been talking about a local Houlihan's.

"According to Google, it's out by Altoona," She said. "Over by where all the oil workers stay. Fracking remains big business out here."

"I know. Have you seen the flames coming out of the bathroom sink?" Rockfish laughed.

"Funny, Steve. You specifically said no unnecessary social outings," Jawnie replied. "Your rules. Keep our heads down when we're not out chasing leads."

"True, but I can grab a couple of cookies the front desk put out? Better yet, Raffi, go down and grab us a handful or two."

Despite their room being on the second floor and at the far end of the hallway, Rockfish's ability to smell the freshly baked desserts amazed Jawnie. She hoped this was a superhero ability that would develop once she knocked on late middle age's door. She assumed the cookies weren't vegan, but this wasn't her first time out with Steve in a podunk town. Dietary adjustments would have to be made, a bad thing would need to be eaten to survive and a toilet or two would be destroyed.

The plans for the late afternoon of the second full day in Edlesburg called for a strategy meeting. One that would now include fresh baked goods. Raffi nodded at Rockfish, grabbed a key card off the credenza, and headed for the lobby. Jawnie watched him to make sure he only picked up a room key. The keys to the newly rented Dodge Odyssey lie close by, and since they had arrived, Raffi hinted nonstop about leaving on his own, if given the opportunity. She trusted him as far as she could throw him and, to be perfectly honest, the man had gained a few since the last time they worked together.

Rockfish insisted they needed the minivan, as Lana stood out like a sore thumb. She remained at the far end of the parking lot, alongside the trash dumpsters, and not visible from the road. The partners had considered reaching out to Marvin Trotter for a loaner before leaving the office. But Raffi owed for use of the box truck, which meant technically Rockfish owed. Rockfish had wanted a Ford F Series pickup with an extended cab, but Kendig Motors had a practically non-existent inventory to choose from. Beggars couldn't be choosers.

The three of them shared one room and not because of the current balance on the company card. But under the guise of the lesser their footprint, the less the chances of being found out. Once discovered, the plan to find Decker and return him to Rosie would become nearly impossible. Jawnie's other purchase after renting the van? A stop at a pharmacy to pick up ear plugs in anticipation of the two grizzly bears sharing the other queen bed.

Next on their agenda had been the WinGate Motel. Rockfish could discern from the tweeker behind the front desk that Decker had checked out the morning after Raffi had driven back to Maryland. Raffi noticed no members of the Patel family, who had been extremely friendly during his previous visit, were anywhere to be seen. He filed the observation away and brought it up to Rockfish and Jawnie on the ride back. Not long after, Rockfish pulled the passenger side visor down, and swore aloud they had been made.

With Jawnie behind the wheel, he had spotted Officer Sobotka on the side of the four-lane road, radar gun in hand. All three slid down in their seats, pulling their respective hats down at the same time. The patrol car didn't move off the shoulder and Jawnie let out a tremendous sigh. Despite the relief in her mind, the ticking clock sped up slightly.

Back at the hotel, she glanced up from her bed when she heard the cylinders of the lock. Raffi walked in with a plastic plate, overflowing with fresh oatmeal raisin cookies.

"Did you leave any for the other guests?"

"Have you not seen the parking lot?" Raffi said with a tilt of his head. "You don't have to worry about anyone dinging that rental of yours."

"Don't listen to her, you done good," Rockfish said, grabbing two cookies.

Jawnie noticed the smile on Raffi's face from Steve's attaboy. It was the first she had witnessed on the trip.

"Okay, let's go over tomorrow," Rockfish said with a mouthful of cookie. Small crumbs shot across the narrow passage between beds but fell short and settled into the carpet. He swallowed and picked up his plastic cup of Jameson to help wash it down. "First, nice find, Jawnie. The flyer you noticed at the motel about Archibald's rally in Grindsville Central Park tomorrow is very useful. A decent opportunity for us to gather new intelligence. Might lead someplace."

The stack of flyers had laid on a side table inside the WinGate's lobby door. The red paper, with white and blue comic sans print announced The Take Back Our City Then Country Rally. Hosted by Calvary United's Covenant of King Solomon congregation, with special orator Elder Erwin Archibald, and security provided by the

Penn Forest Patriots. Archibald would address the crowd from the gazebo in the center of the park downtown.

"CUCKS," Rockfish said with a hearty laugh. "Never gonna get old." He reached with both hands for refills on substance and drink.

The vote was unanimous for Jawnie to attend the rally. She had been the only one to pack flannel and hiking boots. And despite her outward appearance, she felt she wouldn't have trouble blending in with the rest of the future insurrectionists. She'd walk amongst them and hopefully be able to gather a clue or two regarding the organization's next step. One of which the trio had crossed fingers would eventually lead them to Decker.

"Observing is all fine and good, but you'll need to press," Rockfish said, leaning in. "Be friendly, talkative, and see what answers you get. The sooner we get something actionable, the sooner we can pounce. We need a line on Dan before they choose a dumb local cop to make the arrest of his career."

"I know how much it eats away at you, Steve, sitting here doing nothing," Jawnie said. She scootched back against the headboard and met his glare. "But honestly, and no offense, Raffi, but we don't want a recreation of when Raffi and Lynn busted into the basement office at Allison's. That hidden camera came back to bite us in the ass. Royally. Nothing off the cuff this time." She glanced over at the door, where Raffi sat on a folding chair. *His head was down. Was it from my reference or his not wanting to be here? No idea, but if he doesn't show an ounce of productivity over the next day or two, I'm telling Steve he needs to go.*

"History has a tendency to repeat itself," Rockfish said. "But I won't permit anyone here to let anything like that happen again. We're lucky if these guys' technology ability reaches the Speak-n-Spell level."

"Yeah, but they're armed to the damn teeth."

Raffi's first comment during the planning session surprised Jawnie. For the man who only a few months earlier retold nonstop the story of how he and Steve had taken down half a mob family on a boat at sea, he was suddenly gun shy. *I wonder if Steve picked up on that?*

"Armed doesn't mean shit, if you remember the past two days," Rockfish said. "We've achieved nothing while trying to be proactive. To accomplish anything and get a barrel pointed my way? I'd welcome it." He drained the last of his plastic cup and slammed it on the small bedside end table to emphasize the point. "Kid, you gotta come through with something tomorrow. No pressure, but yeah, tons of pressure."

Jawnie swallowed hard, and her stomach rumbled. *Nerves? I can only hope. We need to find Decker, and soon. If not for his safety, my sanity and having to share a bathroom with these two.*

* * * * * * * * * *

Later that same evening, as a DoorDash driver approached the Edlesburg EconoLodge, a separate set of headlights illuminated an old hunting cabin. The building currently served as the Penn Forest Patriots' base of operations.

Earnhardt Jr. sat up in his chair and moved his right hand to his sidearm. *You can never be too careful now that things are finally progressing.* He expected a guest, but was this *the* guest?

As the lights drew closer, all Earnhardt Jr. heard was the sound of tires on the forest floor. Leaves crackled and sticks snapped. This was no party crasher. Archibald had arrived in his new Tesla Model X. *Explains the surprise.*

Earnhardt Jr.'s face flushed with anger. A batch of his men still suffered from the expired MREs and survived minimum-wage paycheck to paycheck. While their so-called benefactor tooled around town in his new hundred-thousand-dollar plus car. *We are not the same, no matter how much bull you feed me. I need you for now, but there will come a time. Much like Michael, I will then settle all family business.*

The car came to a stop and the rear gull wing doors flew open. *So much for coming alone. He might feel the need for protection on the way over, but there's not a chance in hell those others will set foot inside.* Earnhardt Jr. walked over and stood at the top of the rickety stairwell; his ample frame illuminated by the propane lamp on the railing. His arms crossed and rested atop his gut. Archibald stepped out of the passenger side rear of the car.

"Not enough chairs inside for your supporting cast, Elder," Earnhardt Jr. said and watched as Archibald leaned back into the car. He didn't hear what they said, but the man moved his hand animatedly. After a minute, he straightened up and walked toward the half-rotted steps. Alone.

The men met at the top of the stairs and said their greetings. Each patting the other's shoulders, arms and back as if they had expected the other to be wired for sound.

"This must really be important if you came all the way out here and did not summon me to your compound," Earnhardt Jr. said. He didn't wait for an answer and instead grabbed the lantern's handle and led the way inside.

The lantern light bounced off the newly installed tongue & groove flooring and walls of the small one-room cabin. Stairs on the far side led up to a loft which extended over half the first floor. The space above served as the Penn Forest Patriots storage and ammunition locker. The first floor was bare, excluding a card table in the center and half-a-dozen stackable chairs next to the stairwell. Earnhardt Jr. put the lantern down on the table and moved toward the stairs. He returned with two chairs and slid them on opposite sides of the table.

"Love what you've done to the place. From the outside, it appears abandoned. You better be careful, or a half-assed community college film major might snoop around to make a horror movie." Archibald sat with his back to the door.

"Owe it all to your generosity, Elder," Earnhardt Jr. said. It pained him to reply to the compliment. *Yeah, if you had settled on a low-end model Lexus, we might have been able to afford proper furniture.*

"I also see enough chairs stacked in the corner for my men. The April night is fraught with chill and dampness."

"I'm sure you've got a full charge on that luxury yacht of yours. They're big boys. They'll be okay. But the sooner we get to business, the sooner you can stop at Eat'n Park and pick them up one of them smiley face cookies on the way home."

Archibald smirked and shook his head slightly from side to side. The men knew each was vital to the other's plan, but it didn't stop the contempt they held for each other from slipping out from time to time. There would come a moment when the battle for supremacy would begin. Earnhardt Jr. was sure of it.

"I need to give recognition where it is definitely deserved, Jesus. Your man at the Tribune Republic is knocking it out of the park with the Op-Eds and hard-right reporting. I should commend his support for the movement."

"He's due for a promotion and it wouldn't hurt if you threw a little tribute his way, too."

"I agree. My man, Hammond, will drop off an envelope," Archibald said. "I assume he also has a line of stories to run when the police apprehend the alleged mastermind behind the poisoning?"

"At the ready," Earnhardt Jr. said. He reached out and moved the lantern to the right a smidge. He wanted to have an unobstructed view of Archibald's face. "The newspaper will spin a story of radicalization by the Patels. Their secret meetings at the WinGate and well thought out plans to turn Grindsville into a socialist third world country."

"That's laying it on pretty thick. I'm not sure many of our faithful actually read past the headline or opening paragraph."

Earnhardt Jr. laughed and slapped his thigh. Despite his occasional contempt for his companion, both men thought along the same lines. Grand plans for their own individual futures, built on the blood, sweat and meth scars of the working man. *I love the poorly educated. A great man once said those exact words.*

"But we need to talk about the fallout from Easy Acres," Earnhardt Jr. added. The smile had vanished from his face. "While the print news has pushed the story below the fold, the same can't be said for the damn television."

Easy Acres was an elderly care facility that, within the last year, had finally raised enough money, along with matching funds from a state grant to upgrade the building's infrastructure. One project included hooking up to the city's water and sewage lines. No one planning the revolution had bothered to think of older adults. Octogenarian immune systems were not compatible with alpacas and the one middle-aged Caucasian test case. Five residents succumbed to dehydration and fever. The unexpected deaths were the only snag in the entire operation, to date.

"The cost of doing business, Jesus," Archibald said. For the second time this evening, he rested his elbows on the table and leaned in. "I know it bothers you. I can see it in your face. But we both knew, coming in, sacrifices would need to be made. Not everyone is going to be around to see the result of our work." Archibald pursed his lips and shook his head.

"But how did we not realize? Not one of us was aware they had upgraded to the city's lines?"

Archibald shrugged his shoulders. "It was not even a thought, as far out of town as the facility is. I don't work for the city. None of my people do either. Who knew they ran lines all the way out there?"

"Public opinion might turn against us," Earnhardt Jr. said. "Your show is on that same channel. Can't you talk to the people there? Get 'em to tone it down?"

"Look, Jesus, I can't wave a hand and have God fix everything. Adversity. It makes a man, and it will make our movement. This whole county is filled with old people dying every day. Have you seen the obits in the Sunday paper? Over the last couple of years, the section has grown to three pages long. Plus, when the police make their arrest, the public will be that much more satisfied." Archibald nodded his head in approval.

"And speaking of the scapegoat, I don't agree with your men keeping watch over him. He would have been more secure here in the cabin. Especially until the time comes for Sobotka to stumble upon him and make headlines." Earnhardt Jr. put down his air quote. He had one more question. "Have you made any progress in determining who he is? Or why he was snooping around?"

"He's safe," Archibald said. He lowered his voice, despite no one else being within earshot. "Don't worry. To think, my wife laughed at me when I had the panic room installed. He's going nowhere soon. And no, we don't have a clue who he is. No ID on him or in that room. The card on file with the motel came back to your Q-Ration friend. So they were associates. But does it really matter? His identity will come out when the police ID him. I'd give a shit if it's through a relative, fingerprints or DNA. We can spin whoever he is to best suit our benefit."

"Anyway, I've got Sobotka ready to go. You say the word." Earnhardt Jr. was proud of the inroads he had made with the local PD. And while those connections weren't at the highest level yet, he was sure the brass would jump on board with the movement once the shit hit the fan.

Archibald held up both his palms. "Pump the brakes, son. I need the base salivating, at a level greater than now, and hanging on my every word before we play that card. They aren't quite where I want them. Yet."

"I'm letting you know. My men are at the ready. Engines revving."

"And go, they will. Don't rush the future. Now speaking of your men..." Archibald leaned away from the table. The flickering light from the lantern bounced off the concern on his face. "They know their assignments for my rally tomorrow?"

"Your security detail will be in place, and I'll have others spread out across the park, keeping an eye out for any troublemakers. According to Sobotka, the police haven't come across any intel regarding counter-protesters. All quiet on the western front. If a problem pops up, he's under orders to report to me first, prior to 'officially' calling it in. It will be written the Penn Forest Patriots were the first true responders."

"Wait. Is he sure?" Archibald said. "I don't think it would hurt us to have somewhat of a disturbance." He tilted his head in anticipation of the answer. "Maybe plan for our benefit. A little extra for the headlines."

"I strongly disagree," Earnhardt Jr. said and slid his chair away from the table. His tone grew serious. "Let's get this first rally off without a hitch. But as the movement grows, we'll need to have measures in place to deal with the drag queens, hippies and eventual Antifa infiltrators. In a perfect world, I'd like to lead and leave the security duties to our own private BlackWater-type group."

"Private armies cost money, Jesus. Which reminds me. A few of your men will need to carry offering baskets as they move through the crowd. Please have them see my wife when y'all arrive. She's overseeing the tithing portion of tomorrow's festivities."

Earnhardt Jr. couldn't believe what he had heard. He stood and slammed an open palm on the table. "We're supposed to be security. Make sure you and your family are safe. Quiet any rabble-rousers. Not assist in the grift. My men are not yours to do with what you please."

"Well, my family and I will be in the gazebo. I'm all for line of sight, but not pressing the flesh with those in attendance." Archibald visibly wrinkled his nose. "Your security will be for show only. But right now, and you need to come to grips with this, revolutions need to be funded. The sheep need to be committed, behind us, and willing to give until it hurts. And then some. We're off to a good start here. Have faith brother..."

Earnhardt Jr. let the man continue. *He'll speak till he's blue in the face, but I've reached my limit for the evening. Let him get it all out and then leave.* His mind moved to a place in the future where the Elder would be answering to him. One where military might set the tone and the Ten Commandments were used to keep the followers in line. Not vice versa.

"... whether it be on tape, still pictures or video on social media. That reminds me, I have to check with Hammond that we've selected the hashtags for the event. Anyway, all will be glorious..."

* * * * * * * * * *

Jawnie stepped off the sidewalk, which ran between Locust Street and the official entrance into Central Park. The green space lie in the middle of Grindsville, a full city block in size. Four cross streets surrounded the area, each lined with boutiques, vacant storefronts and a Subway sandwich shop. She walked under an enormous banner, strung ten feet high, between two lampposts. The Take Back Our City Then Country Rally, hosted by Calvary United's Covenant of King Solomon. She noticed the red background was familiar, along with the same comic sans print from the flyer. *The Windows 95 edition of Printshop only has so many options.*

She gazed at the banner above and then out across the park. To her, the commonality was clear. The banner and she were the only signs of color this morning. *I stand out like a sore thumb, but easier for Steve to keep an eye on you. I can blend in, I know I can.*

Jawnie wondered if he was watching her at the moment. He had dropped her off a few blocks from the park and then took up shop, along with a reluctant Raffi, somewhere in the adjacent five-story parking garage. From the vantage point overlooking the park, Jawnie knew she'd have the proverbial guardian angel on her shoulder. *CUCKS better watch out.* Deep down, she hoped she appeared as confident on the outside.

A peek at her phone showed an hour and five minutes remained until Archibald took the mic. She scanned the park and didn't know what to make of the crowd. *What exactly did you expect? More? Less? I guess I'm surprised anyone would buy into this line of bull.* Men, women, and the occasional child milled around, moving from vendor to vendor. Plastic collapsible tables lined the perimeter of the park. Handwritten pieces of paper taped to the front of each showed the cause supported or local establishment represented. Trump/Archibald 2024 flags waved, many types of baked goods sat covered in cling wrap. Vendors had slapped second amendment slogans on everything from T-shirts to lunch pails. Members of the Great Value Boys patrolled the crowd, visible in their camouflage. Each member was armed as if they expected Antifa's airborne paratrooper division to drop in.

Jawnie waded into the crowd and the morning dew. The too high grass clung to her sneakers. It would be another couple of steps before the moisture soaked through to her socks. She cursed not wearing her Doc Martens, but the aim was to blend in with flannel but avoid the jackbooted thug look. Not to mention she had forgotten to change out the pink laces before the unexpected trip. She tugged her hat down lower.

She noticed not all the Great Value Boys carried weapons. Instead, many carried Longaberger baskets in front of them as they moved about. Jawnie spotted one nearby and changed her path in order to pass as close as possible. When one was within reach, she craned her neck and saw the basket filled with loose bills. *Makeshift collection baskets? I guess Steve was right. No more assuming. The CUCKS and the Great Value Boys are in an unholy alliance. Holy shit, that cop is handing out flyers with Decker's sketch on it. At least they haven't turned him in. Yet. Or is he actually hiding out on his own? No way. He'd have figured out a way to call home. Or us.*

Jawnie continued her walk through the park. She neared the large white wooden bandstand at the center of the space. The outside of the structure had seen better days. The warped wood and paint chips caught her attention. Not seeing where she was headed, Jawnie almost walked straight into the velvet rope, stretched across the steps leading up to what she assumed was the VIP section. She nonchalantly pulled out her phone and snapped a few pictures of the visible faces and moved on.

Opposite the gazebo, along the Main Street side of the park, was a row of bake sale tables. Three women stood behind the first table, selling small round chocolate cakes. *Cake sandwiches? Is that frosting in the middle?* Wrapped in the ever-popular cling wrap, the small confections intrigued Jawnie. As did the sign taped to the front of the table.

'Gobs = $1 - Penn Forest Ladies Volunteer Auxiliary'

The Great Value Bakers? Jawnie giggled on the inside and snapped a picture. In the same motion, she texted it along with the new moniker to Rockfish. She hoped he'd find it as hilarious as she did.

"Excuse me, I'd say take a picture. It will last longer, but it seems you already have."

Jawnie shoved her phone in her pants pocket. All three sets of eyes behind the table stared straight through her. The women, dressed identical, had the same pear-shaped figures, but only differentiated in age. *Apparently, the Great Value Bakers appeal to three generations.* Camo pants, black boots and white, long-sleeve T-shirts. Spelled out across the front, in the familiar comic sans font, *Grab 'em by the Gob*.

Jawnie smiled outwards while her mind spun to plan an apology to the youngest woman who had fired the zinger. "I'm sorry. I just really liked your shirts. A friend of mine would get a kick out of them. Too bad I don't see them for sale." She reached down and picked up two gobs with her left hand while the right dug deep in her front pocket and pulled out a five. "Can you make change or is it too early?" She felt the notification vibration in her back pocket and wondered what Steve thought of her joke. Inside, she smiled again.

The woman scrunched her nose and sighed. "Take 'em. You touched 'em. Hard to sell contaminated product to hard working Patriots. We don't want your money. Take 'em and keep walking. Back to Pittsburgh, Philly, wherever."

Jawnie felt her eyes grow big. *Don't let 'em see you sweat, kid.* Rockfish's voice filled her subconscious. She wouldn't, but tit needed tat. The blatant racism wouldn't go unrecognized. The smile vanished from both inside and out.

"It would be a real shame if I scooped up an armful and you couldn't afford that replica Mike Pence guillotine kit you all have your eyes on." Jawnie turned and took a few steps away from the table, not waiting for the next expected racist slur to drop. Instead, she spun back, cocked her arm, and all three women flinched. Jawnie's high heater sailed through the air and took out a pyramid of gobs on the left side of the table as if she stood on the midway of some bigot carnival.

She knew it was the wrong thing to do as soon as the gob left her grip. But she also knew the satisfaction that currently washed over her was totally worth it. She didn't make out the nonsense shouted behind her as she moved back towards the center of the park, where she hoped to get lost in the growing crowd. Or blend in the best she could. *Not gonna happen. I can count the number of people of color I've run across this morning on one finger. Yup, that would be me.*

Her phone vibrated again. *Steve had to have seen that play out. Probably telling me to abort, but if I don't read the message, then I can claim innocence.* She waded further in, towards the outward facing side of the gazebo and stage.

An announcement blared over the gazebo speakers. The countdown for Archibald's sermon had started. They advised vendors to not peddle any wares until after the guest speaker had concluded. Jawnie watched as the crowd surged in unison towards the stage. Personal space soon became scarce as bodies pressed together. Jawnie wished she was a little taller and could see over the others. *Is there really this many people? Did they all come last minute? Or are the Great Value Boys standing on the outside, slowly walking in, pressing all of us together like cattle into a chute?* A cigarette haze hung over the crowd and Jawnie imagined the grief she'd have caught if she had remembered to bring a mask. *Burn her. She's a witch.* She heard the crowd turn against her in her head.

Erwin Archibald soon appeared at the front of the stage with his wife and children. He and his son wore matching white suits and the ladies peach floral dresses. The crowd erupted in cheers and chants. Jawnie spotted the small red lights on each side of the stage and assumed the hate was being live streamed. At a minimum, the not-so-dark web.

The sermon lasted half an hour, if that, minus the stop and starts between hoots, hollers, and clapping. *The man's ego must be busting at the seams.* Archibald had said nothing Jawnie or most of the audience hadn't already heard on various right wing 'news' channels and Sunday morning clip shows. Archibald expressed sympathy for the victims and criticized those he held accountable for the poisoning. *Or those he specifically wanted the finger pointed at.* But those in attendance hung on every hate-filled word. She felt the fever build as the venom flowed across those in attendance.

She watched as Archibald took the crowd in. He stood, toes hanging over the edge of the stage, arms raised above his head, finger-formed Vs on both hands. *Nixon-like?* Jawnie wasn't sure which was the bigger piece of human waste. He remained there, taking in the last of the dying applause. At the same moment, Jawnie thought about making her way through the crowd to meet the minivan at the pre-determined pickup spot. She cursed herself for having gathered no actionable information. Rockfish's voice was wafting through her head again. *Come on kid, time's wasting. Start pushing your way--*

Crack

Crack

Jawnie hit the ground with the sound of the second shot. Her face buried in the overgrown grass. Other individuals fell alongside her, yet more drove their boots into her back in an attempt to flee. Shouts filled the air. Screams. And more gunshots. *Active shooter. Emphasis on the active. Trigger-happy Great Value Boy? Get up and get moving. Don't be a target. NOW.*

Jawnie pushed herself up to her knees and then onto wobbly legs. Her hands, clenched tight, had pulled clumps of grass from the ground. She let the vegetation and dirt fall with her first step. Her internal guidance system was on the fritz, but Jawnie hoped she stumbled forward toward Locust Street. Her third step resulted in her face down on the ground for the second time. She glanced back to see what tripped her and a gasp escaped from her lungs. Grandma Great Value Baker's outstretched arm reached for her. The old woman's white T-shirt was a spreading crimson mess. *Hers? Another's? Don't care. Sometimes it sucks to be a caring human being.*

Jawnie spun around and helped the woman to her knees. She draped the woman's flabby left arm across her shoulders and half-drug the woman forward.

"Come on, old timer, we need to get you up and out of here," Jawnie said. The woman's mouth moved, but the sound never made it to Jawnie's ears. The two women three-legged-raced the rest of the way across the open space. They trudged over and around those too stunned to move. She willed the old woman forward, with words and silent prayers.

A horn sounded as her feet hit the sidewalk, and Jawnie smiled. The Dodge minivan had come to a stop in the middle of the street, the side door open, as if driven by B. A. Baracus.

"Come with me if you want to live," Rockfish shouted from the drivers seat. It was a line said between the partners many times and with the words came a wave of calm over Jawnie.

"We're going to be okay," Jawnie whispered in the old woman's ear as Raffi reached out.

CHAPTER NINE

The morning sunlight ripped through Room 207's threadbare curtains. But those who had observed from afar the mass shooting event the previous day were already awake. Raffi sat up in bed, arms folded across his chest and disdain on his face. If he were eight, Rockfish would think the tantrum was part of a plan to let him go home early, despite being spread out across the mattress and enjoying the additional space vacated earlier by Rockfish. He had stopped being Raffi's big spoon and thrown back the blankets well before sunrise.

Rockfish had taken up residence at the small table by the door from where he watched the news accounts of yesterday's shooting. He plugged his headphones into his phone, so as not to wake their third wheel. Jawnie lay on her own queen mattress, buried deep under a comforter and crocheted blanket brought from home. She was exhausted, deep in REM sleep.

Yesterday's festivities in the park had continued well into the afternoon at Lee Hospital. Rockfish had wondered from the moment she climbed back in the van if the old Jawnie would manifest. Devastated at the events, overwhelmed and in desperate need of a place to hide. A spot to be alone and to wish it all away. But what he got was unexpected. Jawnie emerged from the van, confident and shouting orders. He and Raffi did as told, the best they could amongst the mad rush for the ER. Chaos and confusion reigned, but Jawnie plowed forward, exhausted and no matter the barrier. He'd never be a father, at least in this lifetime, but damn, his chest welled with pride.

The elderly Baker woman, to be identified within the hour by hospital workers, as Edith Grabowski, had laid across the van's second row seating. Raffi shouted directions from his phone to Rockfish, and Lee Hospital soon came within eyesight. Rockfish had street parked in the first available space he saw. Idling cars lined the stretch of street leading into the ER parking lot. He didn't know exactly how hurt the woman behind his seat was. He and Raffi had carried her down the street and into the ER. Jawnie lagged and upon entry, the nursing staff confronted her, solely because of the amount of blood on her shirt.

Havoc and confusion filled the ill-equipped ER waiting room. The flow of victims, both from gunshots and broken bones, concerned family members and Grindsville police officers seemed to never ebb. Men in uniform moved throughout the crowd and took statements from anyone not in shock and able to speak. Fear of being recognized kept Rockfish moving from one end of the small room to the other. Their good deed for the day was done. He was finally in agreement with Raffi. The motel called their names, but Jawnie felt the need to stay until an update on Edith was available. The wait would be near impossible once the head nurse informed her that the staff would only provide medical updates to family members.

"You're a Grabowski? Honey, you expect me to believe that?"

"By marriage, obviously."

"I'm going to need you to step aside and stop wasting my time."

Jawnie had taken defeat gracefully but not given up hope of obtaining any information on the woman she saved. She had returned to the waiting room when the younger two Grabowskis, nee Great Value Bakers, stormed through the automatic sliding doors. Rockfish had heard the incoming noise long before the door chimed and the two women stormed in.

The Grabowski Tornado started with admissions and then whirled back across the ER, leaving in its wake a smattering of ripped and torn scrubs. No one was safe from their white-trash fury and, with a turn of the head, the youngest locked a set of cold eyes on Jawnie. Her screams were unintelligible, but her index finger pointed. Jawnie looked down.

The sweater. Edith's sweater, previously tied around her waist, was now draped across Jawnie's lap. It had fallen to the floor when the first nurse rushed to their aid. Jawnie had picked it up, not thinking twice, and planned to return it once she figured a way to finagle her way into the back. *Jawnie's intentions aren't going to mean jack shit to either of these two.* Rockfish braced for impact as the youngest, with the middle-aged one right on her heels, sped across the room. Shrieking.

A second later, the youngest Grabowski ripped the sweater from her hands and cocked a balled fist. Jawnie stood, knowing she would have to defend herself, despite not wanting to add to the chaos.

"Don't make me deploy this, ladies. I don't want to turn my body cam on."

A police officer, taser firmly in hand and pointed between the two adversaries, emerged from the shadows. With a wave of the device, he ushered the Grabowski woman through the locked automatic door and out of sight.

Rockfish had watched and wondered if the two wailing banshees had gotten separated from Edith. Or what was more likely, in his opinion, had abandoned her once the free-for-all started. It wasn't until they were safely back in their '89 Monte Carlo SS had one of them noticed grandma was missing.

He hadn't drawn a conclusion by the following morning, as he watched the recounts of the previous day across several media streaming platforms. The Thoughts and Prayers Tour by local, state and Federal Government Officials was well underway. Knowns and unknowns filled the airways between the benedictions. Two audience members were shot dead and yet another trampled to death. The gunfire also wounded one elderly woman, who reports said was expected to pull through. Thirty-seven others suffered a wide variety of injuries from the chaotic rush to flee the scene or were reporting emotional damage. The shooter remained unidentified and at large, almost twenty-four-hours afterwards. Lee Hospital had reached capacity by mid-afternoon, and those with non-life-threatening injuries were transported to Somerset County Hospital. This group included most of those hurt in the aftermath.

The national media had left Grindsville not long after the poisoning news cycle had run its course. They now caught red-eye flights back to the small town after yesterday's shooting. But until the networks had boots on the ground, they used and abused Marianela Moreno for the past eighteen-hours. She conducted live remotes, saying practically the same things over and over. She tweaked her words only because of the network in question's political leaning.

To Rockfish, Moreno seemed she hadn't caught a wink of sleep since Friday night. *Duh, that's exactly the case. Probably only stopped to use the Subway bathroom and change her outfit. You know, if she plays her cards right, the small time WJAC local field reporter might parlay this into a huge jump up the broadcasting ladder. Maybe land herself a desk job in a larger market. Or a new online streaming channel.*

Movement beneath the crocheted blanket to his right caught Rockfish's attention. He closed the browser window, popped out the headphones, and returned them to their case.

"Morning, sunshine. Nice of you to join the living again," Rockfish said. He turned his chair away from the table and faced the bed. Jawnie mumbled an inaudible sentence. Rockfish reached to his left and opened the curtain. The sunlight hit the side of Jawnie's face, and she rolled over, her back now to the window.

"Gimme five to clear the cobwebs. And then the question-and-answer period can begin."

Rockfish gave her five and an additional forty. By the time Jawnie opened the bathroom door, a wall of steam poured out. She followed, puffed, powdered, and dressed for the inquisition.

"... and I chucked that damn cake-thing right back at 'em."

"That's my partner. Not taking any shit and then playing savior to the playground bully," Rockfish said. "In all honesty, better you than me. Maybe a well-placed foot on the wound had she tripped me up."

Jawnie shook her head and directed one of her own questions at Raffi to make him feel part of the conversation.

"So, the gunman remains on the loose?"

"Affirmative, according to the news," Raffi said. His eyes never moved from his phone.

"You'll have to excuse Mr. Candy Crush over there," Rockfish said. "He's cranked up the I wanna go home chants since we got back from the hospital."

"Do you blame me? It's bad enough I'm here with you, searching for a guy who doesn't even work for me any longer. Now people are firing assault rifles off, all willy-nilly. Not exactly where I thought *Patriot Meals on American Made Wheels* would have taken me."

"Raffi--"

"No, don't even let him go there, Steve," Jawnie said, turning back to Rockfish. She had no issue butting her way between the two friends. "We're here for the second damn time because of you. Decker is here, somewhere, unharmed. I sincerely hope, thanks to you and your scam of the day."

"Jawnie--"

She walked toward Raff and pointed her finger at his chest. "No. I need to unload. Shit that should have been said long ago. You handle him with kid gloves. But I didn't play marbles with him on the middle school playground." She turned back to the other bed before continuing. "Either sit there and constructively try to help us right all your wrongs or get to walking. Put out a thumb. Doesn't matter to me how the fuck you go. There's the door." Jawnie walked to the door and pulled it open.

Jawnie's mic drop didn't surprise Rockfish. He saw it as more of a continuation of her leading from the front, exhibited yesterday. Long gone were the days where, after a statement like that, she would look to Rockfish for his reaction and support. Instead, he glanced at Raffi for any reaction. His friend had simply buried his head back into his phone and didn't say another word. The second thing he noticed was the man had not moved. Had not picked up his bindle. Had not exited through the door. She turned away from the two men and ground her teeth over Raffi's ignoring her.

The silence hung over the room for a few minutes before Jawnie picked the mic back up and addressed the tidbits from yesterday that stuck in her craw. "I'm not sure you heard Archibald, word for word, from where you stood, but something about that entire Central Park cluster doesn't sit right."

"The speech or Lee Harvey part?"

"Both," Jawnie said.

"I think he was lucky. Not a scratch and now he's part of the lead story on every major network and a few of the partisan streaming ones." Rockfish shrugged his shoulders. He didn't want to admit he hadn't listened as intently as he should have.

"I dunno. Seems fishy since a few innocent bystanders caught bullets, but the prime target, allegedly, suffered only good press. But I'm also thinking about what he said."

"Go on."

"There were a couple of lines. Something..." Jawnie's hand cradled her chin as if she was caressing a non-existent beard.

"Out with it, McGee." Rockfish wasn't into twenty questions. *Get to the damn point. I'm not getting any younger, and this damn room seems suddenly claustrophobic.*

"Gimme, a sec... here it is... *Be vigilant. The devil is here in Grindsville. If you think he arrived yesterday, I have news for you. He's been here. Watching. 'Bidening' his time. In disguise, he walks amongst us, removing it only to rally his filthy immigrant soldiers. But do not fear, it will only be a matter of time before I bring him before you for trial. By FIRE!* I found it online. There's a transcript on his website. Portions of the speech are available on a ton of outrageously priced inspirational merchandise."

"The grift never ends," Rockfish said. "And you interpret this how?"

"Decker. Archibald has him and is waiting for the right moment to reveal the devil, so to speak. I mean, it's plausible and we have no other leads." Jawnie said. "We can have Lynn run public database checks and see what properties, the more remote the better, the guy owns. Check them all out."

"Good thinking," Rockfish said with a nod. "Let's toss in Earnhardt Jr. too. No telling what properties they might co-own or have in the other's name. Rednecks know the shell game as well as any other."

"I've got nothing on the calendar today. Won't hurt to check out."

"Yeah, yeah it could. Ask that old Great Value Baker broad," Raffi said.

* * * * * * * * *

While Rockfish and Jawnie waited on the results from Lynn's Sunday overtime research project, Clyde had assembled a small team of Penn Forest Patriots on Earnhardt Jr.'s orders. The men were to undertake a special project and earn a few hours of overtime themselves, minus, of course, the time and a half pay.

Earnhardt Jr. had met again with Archibald after the Sunday service at the rented and converted for-the-day elementary school cafeteria. He instructed his men to wait outside this time as the meeting went on long past the lunch hour. When the instructions finally came down, Clyde handpicked his men and set out.

They sat three across the bench seat of an old Ford F-150. Amos behind the wheel, with Clyde pressed against the passenger door and their star recruit, Wilbur John Lyczek, wedged in the middle. Wilbur had provided the cap for the bed of Amos' pickup, where the pawn would be hidden during transportation, and thus, invited along for the ride. Amos wasn't sold on the kid, but the Colonel thought of him as having potential within the organization. *Just because he found that spic from Baltimore and his friend holed up in the WinGate, doesn't mean he should get added responsibilities. Nothing more than dumb luck if you ask me.* Not to mention Amos was more familiar with the Lyczek clan than Earnhardt Jr. *Comes from a long familial line of pooch screwing and half-assing things. Not to mention addictions to anything sold in an alleyway or from an abandoned building in the Dukesville section of town.*

"The Colonel wants us to move the package. Seems the preacher is concerned that after the melee on Saturday, he needs to create distance, in case something goes sideways," Clyde said.

"Always comes back to us when he needs a problem fixed," Amos said. "Which reminds me, nothing said here in this truck goes an inch outside that front fender. You got me, Wilbur?" Amos locked eyes with Clyde first and then both men turned and glared at the bench seat sandwich filling.

"Not a word," Wilbur said. He laid his hands on his thighs, kept his eyes forward, and nodded.

"We're to pick him up and relocate to the cabin. I'll take responsibility for the first babysitting shift. You two work out the rest. Call in Trevor if needed," Clyde said. "Colonel said it shouldn't be much longer. Sobotka will then show up and we wash our hands of it. Prepare for the next stage."

It was Amos' turn to nod in agreement. "The cabin is a smart move. A better location and one not associated with the Calvary United's Covenant of King Solomon."

A chortle escaped from Wilbur's lungs.

"Why the fuck do you kids always find that so funny?" Amos said.

Wilbur dropped his chin to his chest and didn't answer.

"Don't try to figure these new recruits out, Amos," Clyde said. "Concentrate on the mission."

"Yeah, I get it. Focus. But not sure why a group of holy warriors is so gosh darn hysterical. Enlighten me, boy." Amos took his eyes off the road for a second. Wilbur's head remained hung low, as if he wanted to disappear into the seat's fabric. "Any other marching orders, or did you sit around and shoot the shit after church?"

"Nothing more than the Westmoreland job I told you about earlier," Clyde said. "Then other shit that needed to be discussed at the executive level."

"Spill it. I can see the concern in your face from the dash lights. Remember, nothing outside the front fender." Amos shifted his eyes from the road to the passenger door and back to the road. He wasn't sure Clyde would break whatever confidentiality agreement he had with the Colonel. But he wasn't a big fan of moving forward on a mission of this size in the dark. No matter how good for the order it was.

"Yesterday... no, not random at all." Clyde stared out the window as the words spilled from his mouth.

"To be honest witcha, not surprising. Can't say the thought didn't cross my mind." Amos had thought long and hard last night about the possibility of a PR stunt gone wrong. He didn't believe that the Colonel had anything to do with it but wouldn't put it past the Elder. That man was full speed ahead. Damn the torpedoes. And the collateral damage.

"Maybe I shouldn't be here," Wilbur said, finally lifting his head up. "This convo seems way above me."

"Day late and a dollar short for that, bub," Amos said. He made a left turn onto the long road that led back to the Archibald compound.

"I agree," Clyde said. The man continued to gaze out the window. "If the Colonel is going to trust you with more shit, this Westmoreland gig included, then I guess we should follow suit."

"Yeah, like good little soldiers." Amos said with a dash of dripping sarcasm.

There was a moment of silence in the truck cab that seemed to bond the men to the secret.

Clyde reached across his body and tapped Wilbur's thigh. "Elder told the Colonel something to the effect of, much like the unexpected outcome at Shady Acres. There are times you gotta bust a few eggs. The omelet's supposed to be that good."

"But they're our eggs. Both times," Wilbur said with a passion neither of the older men expected. "Not his. Ours. I'm damn near family to the Grabowski's. For Christ's sake, they could have killed a child."

"Wouldn't put it past him," Amos said. His voice strained. His hands, a death grip on the wheel.

"I agree. Not like I don't know where ya both are coming from. If it means a damn thing, ain't none of us happy with someone else calling the shots, either. No matter how fast that money faucet spills. We are rapidly approaching a point--"

"All I can think about is that fat fuck, with his holier than thou attitude, walking the halls of Lee Hospital. An entourage of flunkies around him and the media on his heels." Wilbur said. "Cheyenne's granny..." He punched the dash for emphasis and Amos reached out and grabbed his arm before a second landed.

"Easy boy, this ain't yours," Amos said. His voice was stern. The opposite of concern. "We all knew what we signed up for. Might not have known exactly where it was headed, but we all kinda had an idea. Or else we wouldn't have been training all those Saturday mornings."

"I'm more akin to the beer drinking Saturday nights, if I say so myself," Clyde said. This time, three chuckles filled the cab. "But to put a fork in this sumbitch as soon as we can secure an additional revenue stream... that egomaniac gets kicked to the side. Out of all this shit that's going on now, we need to make friends in higher places, if you understand what I mean."

Amos and Wilbur nodded in agreement. He killed the headlights as the truck rolled to a stop at the guard shack next to the compound's front gate. He reached down and manually rolled down the window. The guard acknowledged the men with a nod and tilt of the head towards the gate.

"You're expected. The barn around back."

Amos took his foot off the brake and let the truck coast down the driveway and around the side of the McMansion. The barn sat fifty yards behind the main house and seemed to have seen better days. *Maybe it doesn't show so bad in the daylight? One pissed off wolf with a set of lungs on him would bring that entire thing crumbling down.*

The truck stopped before the large sliding front doors. Clyde threw open the passenger side door, stepped out, and then poked his head back in the cab. "You two sit tight. Lemme go in and assess."

Amos watched him walk down the short path to the front of the barn. One half of the doors slid open, and Clyde stepped inside. Someone on the inside immediately closed it.

When the last light from inside vanished, Amos turned to Wilbur and grabbed the kid by the bicep.

"Look, I know how you're feeling. Trust me. I do. But don't do nothing stupid."

"I ain't."

"You won't," Amos said and tapped the side of his nose with his free hand. "I know you. What hole you like to crawl into when things don't go the way you want. The Colonel is trusting you with this Westmoreland run. Can't have you fucking it up because you're pissed and used to score there."

Wilbur stared back with a blank expression.

"Oh yeah, I know all about that. Do as you're told. Drive up there and do the pickup. A simple exchange. Your envelope for a small box. Nothing more. Nothing less. He likes you. Don't fuck it up."

Wilbur bit his bottom lip and appeared suddenly nervous to Amos.

"Kid, this will make or--"

The barn doors slid open again, stealing away the attention of both men. Clyde exited and approached the drivers side. He leaned through the already open window.

"Pull in. They'll do the heavy lifting."

* * * * * * * * * *

Thursday morning was day four of the gang's surveillance on all Archibald's associated properties. The list, methodically researched and curated by Lynn back at the home office, lay printed on the seat next to Rockfish. They all agreed it wasn't much to go on, but it was all they had. The hunch that Decker had, in fact, fallen into the wrong hands soon after Raffi had left Grindsville was, in Rockfish's words, a soup sandwich. He prayed for a more solid lead but would take what he could at this point. Anything to get them out of that damn hotel room, where tension and temperature were on the constant rise, he thought. *Praying for some actionable intelligence while staking out a preacher man. A man of God. Classic Steve. Get out of my head, Dad.*

Jawnie drove the van, snacks piled high on the passenger seat and a cooler of water bottles on the floor. Rockfish sat directly behind her, and Raffi was squirreled away in the third row. Out of sight, out of mind, were Jawnie's words, as they had initially loaded into the van back on Monday.

"Where to next, Siri?"

Rockfish checked out Lynn's list and crossed off the vacant lot they had driven past.

"Next up is Cool Rick's Self-Storage. It's going to be back up on Bedford Street, a traffic light past the Giant Eagle. It's one of those jointly owned properties Lynn identified, but only after digging a little under the surface."

Jawnie reached down and punched the name into the GPS and hit go.

"Not that I'm playing along but sounds like a great place to hide a body, er, I mean a person," Raffi added from the peanut gallery.

Rockfish let the man's faux pas slide, but he noticed Jawnie did not. Her furrowed brow and the worry lines above it, in the rearview mirror, stood out. He hoped she wouldn't stoke the flames and was pleasantly surprised she had kept her thoughts to herself and eyes on the road. For that instant.

The squeal of tires and brakes filled the minivan. The seatbelt across Rockfish's chest dug in hard, and his head snapped forward and then back into his headrest. Raffi soon joined him in the second row, tumbling ass over elbows. *Someone wasn't belted in.*

"Whoops. Squirrel in the road." Jawnie's evil grin replaced the concern on her face in the rearview.

Okay, she didn't ignore it and also didn't let him get away with that crack. I'll give you that one, McGee. Rockfish gave Raffi's ass a push as he toppled back into the third row of seating. He then reached down on the floor by his feet and picked up the trouble makers phone.

"Here ya go and keep those comments to yourself. Not all of us let shit slide as easy as me."

Rockfish heard the click of Raffi's seatbelt. *Lesson learned.* He didn't exactly disagree with Raffi, but more the messaging. A self-storage locker would be one hell of a place to hide a person, especially if you owned it and made sure the other lockers were empty. Ensuring no nosey nellys would wander by. *We need a sort of positive outcome after three days of going down on strikes looking. But Christ, did the man own a lot of property. Or should I say, his various LLCs did. Not one property, to include the primary residence, was registered under Erwin Archibald. The man had graduated from the Jim and Tammy University of Asset Concealment with whatever degree outranked a doctorate.*

Jawnie brought the van to a stop across the street from Cool Rick's 24-Hour Self-Storage. The donut shop's parking lot was half-full. She shifted the van into park and reached under Rockfish's open bag of Combos on the front seat for the small binoculars.

"Appears to be legit as can be," Jawnie said. "Not a lot of overhead in these places. Electricity and a warm body to handle problems at the front desk. Maybe even sound proofing on the inside of the units."

"Play it safe," Rockfish said as Jawnie opened the drivers side door. "Head back down the street, hang a left at the second left and then work your way back."

A few minutes later, Jawnie serpentined her way down the street. Rockfish watched as she eventually approached Rick's front door. She spoke with the old man behind the front desk. *More like Old Rick's, if you know what I'm talking about. I gotta remember that one for when she comes back out.*

Rockfish observed Jawnie, hand on hip, standing in front of the counter, deep in conversation with the clerk. The small office area was white and barren except for a single chair to the left of the door. A stack of brochures sat on the counter, to the right of where Jawnie rested her elbows.

Rockfish continued to watch, eyes only leaving the binoculars to check the time. Jawnie shifted her weight from one foot to the other as she listened to the old man's sales pitch. Eventually, papers were pulled out, reviewed and signed before being handed back to the old man. He then spun around to a small Xerox machine before providing the copies back to his customer. Rockfish stewed as the clock continued to click. He neared his breaking point as Jawnie and the old man then shuffled out a back door and out of sight.

What the fuck? Has she not learned a damn thing from me? Get in, get out. No small talk and definitely don't sign a freakin' rental agreement. Rockfish slid to the passenger side of the van to see if he had a better point of view. Nothing. *Christ. I'm going to have to get out and walk along the fence line to glimpse where they went. And that's IF he's only giving her a tour of an empty unit. Yes, Ms. McGee, as you can see, the ten by twelve is exquisite. Cinderblock walls with a high ceiling. All the units are climate controlled, so don't you worry. That old blanket from your grandma? Fresh as a daisy when you come back to retrieve it. Same goes for a drugged beyond belief victim.*

Rockfish's biggest fear was the old man would push Jawnie into the same unit as Decker and slam the door behind her. He moved back to his original seat, contemplated throwing as much caution to the wind as his partner and storm his way into the back lot. After last Saturday, there was a chance Jawnie was as recognizable to someone out and about as he and Raffi. Rockfish bit his bottom lip. He needed to stop with the negative thoughts. He'd give her a little more time before throwing open the van's side door.

"Hey Raffi, if she's not out in a hot minute, throw your hoodie on and--"

The office door swung open before Rockfish finished his request and Jawnie soon made her way back and slid into the drivers seat. She reversed out of the parking lot and didn't say a word until they were at the next stoplight.

"Let me find a spot to pull over and fill you in." She found the space needed at the far end of the Giant Eagle Supermarket parking lot and killed the engine.

"It was nice of you to come back," Rockfish said. "I got worried and wondered where you and Grandpa Munster would be registered at for the engagement party."

"Around here? Five Below," Jawnie said and spun around in her seat. "I can't stand looking through the rearview at you two."

"Whatcha got?"

"I rented a locker," Jawnie said and passed the rental agreement back to Rockfish.

"I volunteer to stay there until you let me go home," Raffi said. The sarcasm in his voice was thick and not by mistake.

"I thought we'd come back after hours and snoop around?" Jawnie ignored Raffi's comment and continued. "Can't get in through that front gate without a code and..."

"Only customers get it. That's using the old noggin."

"Exactly, and by the way, I had to use my personal card. I'll need to be reimbursed."

"The points aren't enough?"

"Not a chance."

"I'll call Lynn right now and tell her to expect the paperwork."

Jawnie spun back around and added the storage locker key to the minivan's key ring. She put the van into reverse and then shifted right back into park. This time she spoke without using the mirror or turning around.

"Do you really think Decker's tied up inside one of those units? I get it. We've seen crazier. Not to mention, the brochure clearly states a ten percent discount on the monthly rental fee if you are church-affiliated."

"Imagine the CUCK parties that are held in the empty units," Rockfish laughed aloud. A chuckle even came from the back row. "I think it's worth our time. It's that or keep burning through tanks of gas, making no progress, by my account."

"I know it's a long shot, but I can hang around here," Jawnie said. "Especially if you want to check on any of the other addresses. I can see how much foot or car traffic the place gets. The fewer people, I think, the greater the odds he's there."

"I like it. Sounds like a plan. What I don't want to do is reach out to the Grindsville Police, if you see anything," Rockfish said. They were an entity he felt needed to be addressed. "They're only to be trusted as a last resort. Hope and pray at that point they believe the man in the drawing isn't our missing friend and there is no way a recently retired cop is responsible for all of this. To include the shooting. You know someone's already floating that theory."

"I don't know what to think," Jawnie said. "Things have taken a strange turn since our first visit here. The authorities might be the trump card we've discounted."

"Unless they find us first," Raffi said. He tapped loudly on the minivan's back window.

Rockfish spun around. Red and blue lights filled the glass.

"Play it cool, do what he says and hope we get back on the road with no setback."

The patrolman rapped his knuckles on the glass, inches from Rockfish's head. Jawnie reached across to the glove box for the rental agreement and her insurance card. Her window was down, but the knocking continued next to Rockfish's ear. He reached for the button and lowered his window. The first thing that came into view was the double chin. Next, the name tag. It was clear as day. *Sobotka. GODDAMNIT!* Rockfish swallowed hard, glanced up, and forced a smile. *The day keeps on getting better. Well, at least we don't have to worry anymore about being seen. The jig is clearly up. Fuck, we're trying Dan!*

"Good morning, Officer Sobotka. Beautiful day, ain't it? Do you recommend the donut shop across the street?"

"Rockfish. Can't say I'm surprised. Your kind never listen." Sobotka smiled revealing yellow, cigarette stained teeth. "I received a loitering complaint from the store's management--"

"We've been here less than ten minutes, officer," Jawnie said, half turned around in her seat. Sobotka hadn't moved from beside Rockfish. "I was getting ready to run in and get a few of those world-famous gobs I hear so much about. I had one Saturday, but the damnedest thing. Some fool shot it right out of my hand. Speaking of the fool, you hot on the trail?"

"When your friend here drove by, I thought to myself, no way they're that stupid. But then I remembered your greasy friend in the back there had come back before. So there's a pattern of not listening." Sobotka pointed at Jawnie. "I'd prefer you all leave town for good this time. Do I make myself clear, Mr. Rockfish? Or is it Taggart today? And if the girl in front opens her mouth one more time, I'm running the lot of you in." He slid his right hand down onto his service weapon.

Rockfish closed his eyes and took a deep breath. *Time to roll the dice and come clean. At a minimum, let them know I know. We know. And won't go away quietly.*

"Officer, we're not here to cause any trouble. We are trying to locate a missing friend. A recently retired officer, much like you one day, whose family is worried and wants him home. Safe and sound. I'm sure you understand."

Rockfish gazed up. The large mirrored sunglasses hid any reaction.

"I think you and your associates have a problem keeping their noses out of other people's business. You sure your squirrelly friend in the back doesn't know more than he's letting on? That would be my guess."

"What the--"

"Consider this an unwritten warning. I don't want to come across you on my streets again." Sobotka abruptly stepped away from the open window and walked back to his cruiser.

What the fuck was that all about? Rockfish turned and stared at Raffi. *Was that a little game to see if the man could drive a wedge between us? Or had he identified a crack in the alliance and chose this instant to take advantage?*

"Get us out of here, Jawnie. I may have screwed the pooch on this one."

* * * * * * * * *

Jesus Earnhardt Jr. placed the receiver back on the cradle. The payphone on the front porch of the Hog Sweat Diner had become a makeshift office the more the plan progressed, and paranoia banged on his front door. After the news Sobotka had dropped, Earnhardt Jr. felt his newfound nemesis making progress. He walked over to the row of wooden rocking chairs and picked one close enough to hear the phone should it ring.

A fucking cop! Can it get any worse? He jabbed and uppercut the imaginary opponent in front of him. His feet kicked out and pumped back and forth. To anyone walking up to the diner, it appeared as if an old man was throwing a tantrum any toddler would be proud of. *Fuck! This entire thing is close to circling the bowl. Archibald's ego is out of control. What the fuck made him think he could kill a few innocent people, our people, to move his agenda forward? I sure as hell never remember hearing bout this minor detour, let alone signed off on it.*

Now he's trying to wrap it all up in a nice bow and blame who we now think is a friggin' retired cop? Highly decorated too, if Sobotka's done his homework. That private dick up here again. Searching for the guy. It can only be the ignition of a ton of serious heat coming down on us. The shooting was bad, man. Bad. Scared away all the damn people we want amped up and rallying to our side.

The cool breeze from the open air and rocking felt good on his flushed face. With each movement, the chair creaked. The fatigued wood struggled with its maximum weight capacity. Three rounds in and Earnhardt Jr.'s punch count had come close to triple digits. The back-and-forth pace increased, and the sweat started. He noticed a middle-aged couple approaching the diner's front steps. *Excuse me, Sir, how much have you had to drink tonight? Is there someone we might call for you?*

Earnhardt Jr. closed his eyes and ignored the gawkers. He tried to enjoy the cool air across his face. The feeling was all he had at the moment. For the first time since well before Daniel Sparks' ill-fated trip to Grindsville, the man had doubts. Not on his beliefs, but on the express lane that Archibald had turned the runaway bus on to, sans blinker. *He's starting to plan and direct based on potential news coverage. I don't give a flying fuck about his self-serving media cycles or how they'd help give us the push needed.*

Earnhardt Jr. understood press is good press, too much is like a magnifying glass on everything he hoped to accomplish. And now? Trying to lay the entire blame on an ex-cop who's somehow sympathetic to the illegals and their plight? Earnhardt Jr. heard the man as if he was preaching in the next rocker over. *See how poisonous their agenda is? Even a patriotic former law enforcement officer isn't immune to it. Like a cancerous earwig, it will burrow its way into your brain.*

A far reach? Yup, at least in Earnhardt Jr. and his men's feeble minds. *Whatever progress we've made gearing up for the run at the march at the state capital will be for nothing.* In his mind, there was an increasing chance the war wouldn't be won, let alone the first battle. He increased the speed at which he threw his weight forward and back onto the wooden rocker. The faster the synapses fired in his mind, the quicker the chair rocked. *Marty, how close to 1.21 gigawatts are we? Almost there, Doc.* He threw open his eyes again. The couple from before had moved inside the building, but a glance to his right showed Darlene behind the register, staring through the front window. Earnhardt Jr. put the brakes on the chair, nodded in her direction, and gave a quick wave. *No use putting off the inevitable.* He stood up, pulled a couple of quarters from his front pants pocket and moved within reach of the receiver.

"Please hold for Elder Archibald."

"Jesus, and before you ask, no, this isn't a good time."

"Alright then," Earnhardt Jr. said. "I've got vital information. For your ears only." He hoped Archibald understood the urgency.

"No siree Bob. Time is of the essence and all mine is reserved today. And probably tomorrow. I have video interviews with OAN and NewsMax. Fox is flying out Maria Bartiromo for a sit-down tomorrow. If it's as important as you say, spill it now or forever hold your peace."

Earnhardt Jr. imagined himself smashing the receiver against the chrome handset cradle. A reaction to bad news he had seen in many old television shows and movies. Instead, he stepped back as far as the receiver's cord would allow and surveyed the area. The front porch was empty, and Darlene had gone back to helping the over-tasked servers. He moved closer and draped his free arm over the physical phone box.

"Sobotka caught that private dick from Baltimore and his greasy haired partner snooping around Cool Rick's this morning. I'm guessing the spic ran home and brought reinforcements. No way this can be about the piece of shit MREs we ripped."

"If you and your men could tie our fall guy to Pérez, you are safe to assume the PI is associated with him also," Archibald said. "I must congratulate you on overruling my decision to move the man to the storage facility. Turns out, the cabin was a much better decision."

"Yeah, about that guy," Earnhart Jr. said. He felt a bead of sweat begin the long trek down his cheek. "Are you sitting down?"

He relayed the information Sobotka had provided twenty-minutes earlier over the same landline. Even with the second playback, it didn't sound any better or less problematic. The man was former law enforcement, according to Rockfish. Truth be told, he originally thought Rockfish had made the entire thing up solely to get a reaction from Sobotka.

"It sounds as if his plan is working," Archibald said.

"If it's true, and I agree, it might be a big IF," Earnhardt Jr. said. "Either way, we need to rule it out. Because if he ain't shitting us—"

"You. If he's not shitting you."

"Erwin, you are trying my ever loving patience." Earnhardt Jr. didn't care about the blasphemy, using Archibald's first name, or how the other end of the line took it. He quickly looked around before continuing. "Line of bull or not, it needs to be verified. If the man was a cop, then all our jobs got one hell of a lot harder. Sobotka can only find out so much with his computer and a few inquisitive phone calls."

"Calm down. Nothing the Lord and I can't handle. Give the man water. I believe your men are keeping him well hydrated?"

"Of course. Fed too, but not too much. When he's brought before the cameras, I'm wanting that starving, lived off the land until captured gaunt face for his big reveal."

"Give the man a water bottle and simply retrieve it," Archibald said. His voice had a condescending tone to it and raised Earnhardt Jr.'s blood pressure. "Give it to your contacts with the department and have one of the crime scene techs run the prints. We don't have the time for DNA, nor does Grindsville the facilities. If he balks, let him know the order came directly from me, and I will intervene with his superiors if he pushes back. Problem solved."

"At least for the moment."

"Brother, you worry too much," Archibald said. "Faith. It's what I preach on the constant and the backbone of this movement. Our movement."

"My faith balloon sprung a leak when you fessed to being behind Saturday's clusterfuck."

"I do not know what you refer to and I concede this is not best done over an open line. A line of thought you should have considered first."

"I tried, but *60 Minutes* has your attention. Not to mention, all your time."

"Touché. You have your orders. When the prints come back, inform me immediately. Now, I need to go prepare for the next interview."

"Okay." Earnhardt Jr. nodded to no one and hesitated before hanging up the phone. There was one more item he had planned to discuss. But realizing how the current conversation had gone, he put that issue back in his pocket. *Nothing I can't handle on my own.* He kept the receiver in his hand and used the index finger to tap down the hook switch, while his free hand dug for more change. Clyde picked up on the first ring.

"I told him. About the cop. Not Wilbur's fuck up."

Despite Amos's words of caution and trust, Wilbur John Lyczek had, in fact, detoured on his way back from Westmoreland. No one said battling addiction was easy. The blue lights had slid in behind him on Route 271, minutes after passing through the town of Linertown. The police processed him and then released him into the custody of his girlfriend, Cheyenne. Earnhardt Jr. and his lieutenants had met for a few late-night conversations. The topics being the man's arrest, interview, and subsequent release.

"None of Archibald's business, as far as I'm concerned," Clyde said.

"Agreed. He's a good kid, but we need to determine what, if anything, he might have said in that interview. There's a lot of shit going on here. I can't believe they wouldn't ask him about any of it."

"Good kid or not, junkies lie."

"To us or them?" Earnhardt Jr. said. The silence on both ends of the phone line spoke volumes. He had pushed for the kid. More responsibility and kudos up the wazoo for locating that spic and the ex-cop. He had gone with his gut instead of listening to those he had trusted from the start of this thing. "Let's hope they directed the questions towards gathering intelligence on his dealer. Shit, that's all they do on the show Cops. Try to work their way up the supply ladder."

"If they didn't figure out his affiliation to us, or he didn't readily offer it up, I think we're good. Someone needs to rein him in a little better. No more responsibility without backup."

"Agreed. Where's he at now?"

"He's on cabin watch," Clyde said. "Out of sight, out of mind, I guess? At least he can't get to his dealer from there. I paired him with Trevor. So yeah, Trevor's monitoring two people."

Earnhardt Jr. then passed along the information regarding Archibald's scheme to identify their mystery man.

"... I don't care if it's a water bottle or a juice box. Get me anything to pass to Sobotka... Don't worry, we'll get past this. Somehow... and keep Wilbur up there, away from trouble. Tie him to a tree for all I care."

The men wrapped up the call and Earnhardt Jr. instinctively dug into the coin slot to see if any of his quarters had fallen through. Coming up empty, his right hand moved to his chest. *Agita.* It had become a constant since the incident in Central Park. *Wonder if Darlene's got a bottle of antacid behind the counter?*

Earnhardt Jr. reached for the diner's front door and walked in. A greasy meal was the opposite of what his stomach needed, but his mind? Earnhardt Jr. would use it to fuel his planning session for the enviable divorce he and Archibald were headed for. He was absolutely sure he wouldn't need any highfalutin egomaniac to make sure he came out on top. Good old American firepower would do the job.

* * * * * * * * *

The plan came to Jawnie the minute she had pulled the minivan out of the supermarket parking lot. Rockfish reminded her to take the road heading out of town, in case Sobotka followed from a distance. And they knew he, or another patrol car, would.

"Listen guys, I'm going to pull into the gas station up on the right. We'll need a full tank if we're headed home. Or for returning the rental." Jawnie winked at Rockfish and spilled the rest of her plan.

When the van came to a stop in front of pump number six, Raffi jumped out the side door with Rockfish's credit card and started pumping.

"Be careful and keep that head of yours on a swivel," Rockfish said. His fist shot out and Jawnie bumped it.

"Make sure you come back for me," Jawnie said with a smile. With that, she jumped out of the drivers side and entered the mini-mart. Whoever was watching would assume she needed to use the bathroom before the long drive up the mountain. *Not to mention snacks. We girls can always use snacks on a trip.*

Jawnie glanced at the clerk behind the hanging plexiglass. The middle-aged woman didn't lift her head from the open magazine on the counter. A smoldering cigarette hung from between her lips. Jawnie surveyed the inside of the small store. Signs for the bathroom hung on the back wall and pointed to the left. A door marked Employees lay straight ahead. She went left and entered the ladies' room. She counted to ten before opening the bathroom door and hustled toward the other door. Jawnie didn't glance at the register. Her left hand found the employee's knob. Effortlessly, it turned. *Exactly like I knew it would.*

She snuck into the small back-office area. Small was an understatement. It contained a desk, a chair, and a video monitor. There was barely enough room for Jawnie's slight frame. *Closet is more like it.* On the screen, Raffi was pumping gas. Rockfish had already slid into the drivers seat. *All good so far.* Another door faced her on the far wall. *Freedom! Or at least, I hope.* A second later, she stood behind the store in front of an overflowing dumpster. Flies buzzed around, but they were the only sound she heard. The clerk appeared to be enthralled with the current issue of the Globe Examiner.

Here the partners went their separate ways. Raffi returned the nozzle to the pump and climbed back into the van. Rockfish shifted into Drive and slowly pulled back onto the road leading out of town, wearing Jawnie's cap to play the role. Jawnie moved behind the dumpster and through a couple of backyards. Once she was a few blocks off the main drag, a circuitous route took her closer to Cool Rick's.

The men left Grindsville and when Rockfish was ninety-seven percent sure no one followed them, he swung the minivan east, with plans to swap it out for a set of wheels not on Sobotka's radar. As for Jawnie, she approached the small parking lot of an abandoned thrift shop. Here, she set up her surveillance shop for the day and began monitoring the traffic in and out of Cool Rick's.

By the time the men returned to Grindsville in the early evening, with a new set of wheels, Jawnie had drawn two conclusions. First, Cool Rick's was a front for shadiness. Not one customer had entered the front door or come through the gate. *Maybe no one had junk to store or retrieve today? Right, or it's a way to launder all the money the town throws at Archibald each Sunday. Not to mention the dollars in those hand-carried baskets in the park.*

Second, she was damn sure Sobotka had bought their rouse, hook, line, and sinker. Not one patrol car passed by, nor had any foot patrol snuck up from behind. *Maybe they're watching me from a distance? Sure, but don't focus on the negatives. I think Steve's doing that enough for both of us right now.*

Rockfish and Raffi caught up with Jawnie on the tail end of the surveillance shift. They left the newly rented green Dodge Durango a few storefronts down and hoofed it the rest of the way. The reunited team hung back until the sun went down. The clerk turned off the lights and locked the door. Three sets of eyes watched him get in his car and leave.

"Let's go. We can drive through and see what we can find," Jawnie said.

Rockfish bit his bottom lip and shook his head. She saw the wheels turning, and he was ready to offer an alternative.

"You have the code, right?" Rockfish said.

"Sure do, he wrote it on the rental agreement."

"Nothing on that document says we need to drive through the gate. If anyone's watching, no need to burn the new car."

"Nobody's watching," Jawnie said. "I'm not a rookie anymore."

"Never said you were. Only erring on the side of caution. Let's get moving before someone shows up and proves us wrong."

They crossed the side street and Jawnie stepped up to the small, waist-high push-pad. She entered the code, and with a loud buzz, the gate slid to the left. "We're in."

Rockfish approached the first row of storage lockers and waved the other two over. They congregated under a burned-out light. He pointed skyward with an index finger and Jawnie's eyes followed. A camera was attached to the light pole below the burned-out bulb. It did not surprise her a place like this would have video surveillance. *Especially if it's a front.*

The camera was the size of a loaf of bread and pointed at the front row of lockers. *By the size of that thing, it records on VHS tapes. I'll bet there's one pointing down the other two rows. What's the over/under on any of them actually works? Maybe a family of squirrels has set up home inside?* Jawnie looked down from the camera, back to Rockfish, and shrugged.

"Right. Who cares?" Rockfish whispered. The cameras didn't seem to cause any major worry on his part. "Be careful. Don't set off any alarms, and the old man will have no reason to watch the footage in the morning. Hopefully, a day or two later, the tape, if there is one, will be overwritten, and the point is moot."

"Unless Sobotka stops by in the morning or next and asks to see the tape," Jawnie said.

"Well, let's not give him any reason to. Everyone take a row, try not to make a scene if you find something and we'll rendezvous back at this spot."

Jawnie took the middle row of lockers and Raffi the last. With a quick walk down the row, she estimated only two of the ten units were in use. Eight were secured with the same gold padlock she had seen earlier in a box on the office floor. The other two had cheap combination locks with different colored faces. One blue, one green. She made her way back to the beginning of the row and stepped to each door. She knocked and listened. Rinsed and repeated. The only sound returned was Rockfish and Raffi's knuckles doing the same.

It didn't take long for each to finish their assignment, come up empty and reconvene under the light pole.

"What if not only are his arms and legs secured, but maybe a solid strip of duct tape covers Dan's mouth?" Raffi offered. "It's expected, right? If you're hiding someone in town? Not like this is out in the middle of nowhere, which is where I would assume he's being held."

That's the second positive input from him since we made the trip back here, almost ten days ago. I wonder if Steve picked up on it? Jawnie glanced across both men's faces. Each shone differently. Raffi's had a "what are we doing here glow" and Steve appeared to be at his wit's end. *Can't blame him. We're flailing and barely staying afloat. I can only imagine what Rosie expects of us.*

"Makes sense, Raffi, but this is all we got to go on," Rockfish said. "Soup fucking sandwich. Nothing to grasp at." He took a few steps away from where they stood, turned his back and threw up his hands in disgust.

Jawnie had seen the frustration before. *When you are used to coming out on top, it's hard to admit you're failing. Especially with saving a friend. Think. Get him back on track. Get the investigative DNA moving forward. Not stalled.*

It was Raffi who spoke first, before Jawnie came up with an angle to turn Rockfish's frown upside down.

"What if we head over to our newly rented unit, and pop the drop ceiling and see if we can peer down into the others? Jawnie, you're the tiniest. I bet you'd be able to traverse through the beams and not come crashing down."

What's up with him? Offering unsolicited for a second time within half-an-hour. While it was encouraging, Jawnie had to step lightly with her rebuttal. Both men didn't have a history of taking bad news well on this trip.

"No can do. The unit, the old man showed me, had a drywall ceiling. A bulb and a fire sprinkler were the only things sticking out of it. None of us have a saw handy."

And just like that, the dejected trio filed out of Cool Rick's single file. They crossed the street and walked down to the Durango.

Rockfish said little on the drive home, but what he did spoke volumes. His sentences were non sequiturs. She didn't get a read on Raffi, who had laid down across the third-row seating.

"Less than a handful of hours with this piece of shit. No pick up, horrible handling."

"Would it kill this damn borough to use tax money for street lights?"

"Turn that radio off. If I hear one more talk radio nimrod reference Archibald..."

Rockfish's overall frustration was apparent with every non sequitur. Lashing out at anything, none of it making sense. Except he avoided the chief topic, the focus on everyone's mind. *Dan was, er, is his friend. Rosie is home counting on Steve to save the day, no matter how much the two of them knocked heads before.* She watched his face, illuminated by the dash lights. The sarcastic Steve, everything's gonna work out because we're the good guys, expression had faded. If she stared hard, it remained slightly below the surface, but it wouldn't be long until the last of it slid out of sight. The losses were mounting and wearing him down. *He's not the only one.*

Jawnie stared out over the hood. The dashed yellow lane markers flew by at a hypnotic rate. Her mind traveled back to the last time Rockfish had practically given up. The same three were bound aboard Annetta Provolone's consigliere, Giovanni Bianchi's boat. Rockfish's head hung down to his chest and Jawnie knew she had to act in order to save them. This evening was no different, but there was no goon sitting before her to surprise with a shoulder to the ribs.

You can allow him to drive us around in circles for a few more days. Sink deeper. Or you can, again, actually show your worth to this team. Solidify you're the partner he needs and get us back on track.

Jawnie leaned to the side and pulled her phone from her back pocket. *Sometimes signing up for the unlimited data plan pays for itself.* She typed her first search term into Google and put on her invisible research hat. It was time to shovel.

* * * * * * * * * *

Friday morning, day two of ignoring Sobotka's verbal eviction notice, found Jawnie seated outside of Room 207. She continued her all night research session and had drug the wobbly room chair outside the minute both men started snoring. She then moved her mobile office down to the lobby for the continental breakfast. But it wasn't long before she wandered back to the small concrete patio outside the room. Nothing in the lobby struck her fancy.

Her laptop had died at a little after 4am and the power cord now ran back into the room, propping the door open and focused the morning rays on the spoons in the far bed. Anger had fueled the all-nighter. She grew pissed with herself because *this* was her thing. The specialty she had always brought to the team. Except on this trip. Indignation that she had sat back to this point and let Rockfish drive the investigation filled her head. It mirrored too much when they first met, and he relied on his investigative instincts and fists. That was, until she pulled out her laptop, and charted out Annetta Provolone's entire Paycheck Protection Plan fraud scheme. It gave their old school investigation a much needed swift twenty-first century kick in the ass.

"Umm, I know Raffi has the worst farts when he sleeps, but did you really need to drag half the room out here?"

Jawnie glanced up from her laptop and smiled. Then stretched it even larger. Joker-like. "No more checking out stupid property today. We should take initiative. I've got a lead that might put us on the road to Dan. Or at least one that we haven't beaten to death already."

"Hold that thought," Rockfish said. He pushed open the door and pulled the other chair out onto the narrow cement walkway. "Okay, dazzle this old fuck."

"Clyde Hayseed. Second in command of the Penn Forest, oh sorry, the Great Value Boys. That, according to this intelligence bulletin, disseminated by the Pennsylvania State Police's Fusion Center. It's from a year ago, but still posted on their unclassified intelligence portal. I'm sure he's high ranking. And if Decker's out there, Hayseed knows where."

"First, I've heard the name."

"Me too. I started searching Penn Forest Patriots and a link six pages deep led me to an abandoned white supremacist forum. While the site is no longer active, Archive.org allowed me to review the thread and find the link to the State Police report."

"Damn, kid, where were you a few days ago?"

"I admit I was slacking, brains taking a backseat to brawn, but gave myself a kick in the ass. Better late than never?" Jawnie shrugged and Rockfish replied with a fist bump.

"The report also mentions your buddy, Jesus Earnhardt Jr., although there is no mention of the hate mongering preacher. Bottom line is, at least a year ago, the State Police believed Hayseed ran the groups' day-to-day operations."

"Could have fooled me," Rockfish said. He pursed his lips. "Earnhardt Jr. seemed pretty in charge when he ripped those Q-Rations and left us to freeze."

"Some heads of state prefer to remain out of the limelight. You know, pull strings from behind the curtain. Heck, you were the one that made me watch *The Sopranos*. Remember, Tony let Uncle Junior think he was the Boss, running everything, to keep the heat off himself. Like Junior, Earnhardt Jr. might not be aware."

"Excellent theory. Worth checking out. Might also explain why we've come up empty on the preacher and Fat Patton. Clyde Hayseed, it is."

"Hold up. Who did you say?" Raffi said. He had cracked open the door further and stuck his head, afro first, outside.

"Clyde. Hayseed." Jawnie said. She turned and stared at the bedhead.

"Sounds very familiar. Dan mentioned something along those lines the last time we met. He wasn't sure if it was a name or not. But it had to do with the bad feeling eating at his gut regarding this entire thing."

"Oh, you mean the poisoning or mass shooting?" Rockfish said. Sarcasm and disappointment hung in the air.

Raffi frowned and closed his eyes for a second. "Nobody knew a thing back then. I didn't. He didn't."

Rockfish ignored Raffi and stood up. He stepped behind Jawnie and placed both hands on her shoulders. A quick squeeze brought a smile to her face. It was his subtle way of giving her an attaboy, and she relished it. *We're back!*

"Let's go find this guy and accidentally cross paths. You got an address?"

Two hours later, with the Durango hidden behind an abandoned roadside farm stand, the partners stood inside the dilapidated building. Rockfish had left Raffi behind. The thought being fewer bodies, the lesser the chance someone might spot them before the team wished to make their presence known. Raffi didn't resist, and that was expected.

Each held their own binoculars and focused in on the intended target. Jawnie leaned out from behind a wooden beam to stay out of sight. Rockfish, as usual, stood directly in front of a cracked window, disregarding caution. Every so often, he would glance back at the pelican case on the floor and then to Jawnie.

"One day, Steve, but not today," she said. There wasn't an investigation they worked where he didn't offer to use the drone. Wanted to use the drone. Needed to use the drone. Rockfish had grown tired of playing with the new toy in his backyard and felt it was time to put the aerial surveillance in furtherance of actual work. Not spying on his neighbors. "The noise from that thing alone will cause a person to step outside and look up."

Jawnie assumed Clyde, if not others, were home. *A Ford family. Good Americans.* A red F-150 pickup and a four-door Fiesta sat in the gravel driveway. From there a flagstone walkway led past a flagpole, flying the American and Gadsden flags. Then it was up three wooden steps to the doublewide trailer. A rusted satellite dish, the size of a small child's inflatable pool, bolted to the roof.

"You know, I think this half-rotted roadside stand would be an upgrade for old Clyde," Rockfish said. "You're right about the drone. The breeze from the rotors would send that whole trailer crashing down around him. Then the jig would be up, and we'd be liable for his injuries."

"You think?" Jawnie said. She noticed the trailer's front windows lacked any type of covering. "If we had something a little more powerful, we peer right in and see if anyone's home or awake. Add those to the shopping list." She had already thought about jogging out and seeing how close, if not right up to the window she could get. However, the fields surrounding the trailer had recently been planted and the six-inch high corn provided little cover.

"Want to try your census worker deal? Knock and see who answers? It worked well in the Porbeagle case," Rockfish said. During that case, Jawnie had impersonated a regional US Census supervisor and knocked on the front door of a cabin in the search of their subject. The ruse had worked well, and Jawnie could tell Rockfish saw it as a viable option. She did not.

"I'd wing it, but I'd rather not. Besides, what census worker shows up packing? Now that I've got my concealed carry, I'm not walking up to a suspect's door, only holding my clipboard. Ever again."

"Newsflash, kid, that permit is good for your home state. No concealed carry reciprocity for Marylanders by Pennsylvania."

"At least you did homework before we hit the road. Good thing it's in a bag under the passenger seat. What about--"

"Shhh, he's on the move."

Jawnie stepped out from behind the pillar, stood alongside Rockfish and focused on their target.

Clyde Hayseed, resembling the booking photo included in the State Police report, headed down the walkway toward the F-150, fishing rod in hand. Rockfish waited until the man laid the rod in the bed, climbed into the drivers seat, and shut the door before ushering Jawnie towards the Durango. They struggled to quickly gather their gear and chuck it into the hatch before losing sight of Hayseed.

"He ain't going fishing," Rockfish said.

"How do you know?"

"You see a tackle box in his hand?" Rockfish pressed down on the accelerator and Jawnie lurched back in her seat, the belt dug in across her chest. It wasn't long before the pickup came back into view.

"And to think, last night you were maligning the acceleration and handling of this baby."

The chase was uneventful and at most times came in ten miles-an-hour under the speed limit. They had covered a little over five miles before Hayseed slowed and turned left onto a dirt road. Rockfish had no other choice but to continue past and continue his ruse.

"He's out of the truck and opening a large wrought-iron gate," Jawnie said. She practically turned around in her seat to catch all of Clyde's actions. She watched until the truck was out of sight and un-corkscrewed herself back into the passenger seat.

"He'll close it behind him, maybe even lock it, but we'll verify once I get turned around up here. Not sure we want to follow, even if it's unsecured. Trail cams are cheap, and it wouldn't surprise me if they had the road lined with them."

"Do you think that's where Decker is?" Jawnie said, not bothering to hide the unsettledness in her voice. "A hunting or fishing cabin?"

"That's a solid thought," Rockfish said and rubbed the scruff on his chin. "Or maybe the rest of his fishing gear was already stowed in the truck bed. Either way, we need to figure out what's up there. Better to cross it off the list."

"I can't tell ya anything. AT&T service is lacking. We'd need to get closer to civilization to pull up Google Maps."

"You brought your hiking boots, right?"

"What kind of LGBTQ+ role model would I be if I didn't bring hiking boots to the country? But also, don't stereotype." She watched as Rockfish shook his head and stared out over the steering wheel for a place ahead to turn around.

"Probably should then head back and get Raffi if we're thinking of doing recon on that trail. Even if it turns out to be a pond or a little trout stream, it would be nice to have the numbers in our favor. What if we stumble across the Third Annual Great Value Boys' Bass Masters Classic?"

Jawnie agreed. Steve's words sounded as if he didn't take this dirt road serious, but he was a methodical investigator, if anything. *Well, at least I've got that going for me. And if it doesn't pan out, it may be time to put the full court press on and have him or Rosie contact an old co-worker back at Dan's precinct. Bring in the big guns. It's close to a time where we have no choice but to ask for help.*

Jawnie kept her thoughts to herself on the ride back to the Econo Lodge. *No need to cast doubt on the man's ego. Yet. But we're running out of time and ideas here.* By the time they were halfway home, the AT&T network kicked in and Jawnie tapped on the Google Maps app. She followed the road from the farm stand to where Hayseed turned off. A thick canopy of trees hid where she had expected to see the dirt road. She slid her finger along the map, anticipating the road went straight, deeper into the woods. She moved the map up, right, and then left. *Nothing but trees. Not a clearing, fishing pond, or any kind of structure visible. I'll show him on the iPad when we get back. DAMN IT.*

By the time Rockfish pulled into the motel's parking lot, Jawnie had put away her phone and stared out the window.

What the hell?

She noticed the small table and chairs she and Rockfish had held court with earlier remained out on the walkway. But it wasn't Raffi's laziness and failure to comply with the simplest of orders that caused her eyebrows to shoot up, close to the start of her hairline.

Who the hell is that? Raffi wasn't alone. A woman sat across from him, her back to the Durango as it approached an open parking spot under the cement walkway.

Raffi looked down over the railing and waved when he recognized the car. His lunch date, with long blonde hair to the middle of her back, turned and Jawnie's jaw dropped. The youngest Great Value Baker girl glanced over but didn't wave or show any emotion.

What the FUCK?

CHAPTER TEN

The unexpected visitor didn't surprise or worry Rockfish as much as Jawnie. But he was aware a large reunion, out in the open, wasn't the best laid plan. A quick glance at each woman's facial expressions disclosed that things between the two might go sideways at a moment's notice. He played the part of a rodeo clown and quickly hustled everyone back into the tiny motel room and shut the door.

Shit, the two chairs are hanging out there, with no one sitting in them, begging for a person to come around and ask stupid questions. Not like Raffi bothered to drag them in while we were gone, either. A quick motion to Raffi with his hand had him drag the furniture back inside. Rockfish turned the deadbolt and then thought better. He added the chain for good measure, knowing it wouldn't hold back anyone that really wanted to get inside.

"Cheyenne, this is Steve, and you've already met Jawnie. Cheyenne says she can help," Raffi said, addressing the elephant in the room. He sat down next to the woman on the far bed. Cheyenne had arrived dressed in her most formal black Stars and Bars long-sleeve T-shirt and white leggings. She'd been crying. Rockfish hadn't seen hair teased that high since his senior prom, when a little-known band at the time called Bon Jovi played. *There are a lot of parts of this county that haven't moved on since 1984. The Grindsville War Memorial Coliseum probably scheduled Molly Hatchet to play this summer.*

"Based on Jawnie's reaction, I'm not sure any of us are glad to see you, Cheyenne," Rockfish said. He crossed his arms slightly shook his head. "Something about you showing up here unannounced stinks on ice. But since you're already here, I need to know how and why you tracked us down. Edlesburg ain't exactly around the corner from Grindsville."

"The why is because I need your help. I know this one over here and I didn't get off on the best of terms at the park," Cheyenne said. She glanced at Jawnie and then lowered her head. She wiped the loose snot from her nose with the help of her sleeve. Rockfish contemplated how long she had cried while talking to Raffi? *Or is this performance worthy of an Oscar? A little bird tells me not to put anything past this one.*

"That's an understatement. Racist hate speech and intimidation is more the way anyone with a brain would define what happened," Jawnie said. "Speaking of, great choice of apparel. Not a lot of thought went into getting dressed before you came to ask us for help? Dress to impress, as they say." Jawnie closed her eyes and her head moved side-to-side with purpose. "What makes you think we would believe one word you have to say? The Penn Forest Patriots finally figured out we didn't leave town and sent you up here to what? Confirm it? How long until they barge in, or are the cops on their way to do the dirty work?" Jawnie took a deep breath and contemplated her next line of questioning.

Rockfish never once thought of cutting his partner off. *Let her get it off her chest. The sooner she does, the sooner we can figure out exactly what the fuck Davidia Duke is doing here. She says she can help and I'm pretty sure Raffi's run out of lies to pander on this trip. Let's see how she all plays out.* When Jawnie finished with her side of the interrogation, Rockfish locked eyes with Cheyenne, gave a curt nod and mouthed *your turn.*

"The shirt? I didn't think. That prolly don't surprise you smart Northerners."

Rockfish and Jawnie stared at each other in amazement. They had the same question, but Rockfish was quicker on the draw.

"You're from Grindsville?"

"Born and raised. Gonna die here too."

"You know that Pennsylvania--"

"Let her go, Jawnie."

Cheyenne looked around as the partner's conversation sailed over her head. Rockfish gave her a nod, and she continued.

"I ain't got an extensive wardrobe. I don't give a fuck about my shirt. My grandmother is still in the hospital. She was supposed to be discharged two days ago, but she's caught an infection that's taking each floor by storm. And now? Who knows when she'll get out," Cheyenne said. She sniffled and used the makeshift tissue sleeve again.

Rockfish walked between the two beds and handed Cheyenne the room's entire box of tissues from the bathroom alcove. The story had taken a quick left turn, and he needed to let her relax and get back on track.

"I'm not proud of what I said to you. But the last couple of days have opened my eyes. People can change. It takes a while to overcome how you were raised. Plus, my boyfriend is in danger by these same men and I, *we*, need your help."

Jawnie jumped at the low hanging fruit. "Ah, and now we know the reason for the alleged defection. It benefits your needs..."

"Easy does it over there," Rockfish said and shot a glance at her. He then turned his attention back to the other bed. "I don't know you from a can of paint, Cheyenne. But magically you believe we're on the same side now? The Great Value Boys are now after you and your boyfriend?"

"Yeah. The Penn Forest Patriots," Cheyenne said. Confusion filled her face with Rockfish's reference to the group. "My boyfriend said there's a lot of talk between the men that one of them was behind the shooting. My grandmother is in the hospital.

She was collateral damage. Yet no one seems to give a flying fuck. Other than me and mom."

"Huh?" Rockfish was confused. *This kid's all over the place with this shit.*

"Cannon fodder to help move their agenda forward," Raffi said. "Give what she has to say a listen. Some serious thought, Steve. You too," Raffi said, pointing at Jawnie. "She needs our help, and we can use hers."

"Oh, it's ours now?" Jawnie said and sighed. "Recently, you were half out the door. Amazing what a mid-day boner does for one's outlook."

"Jawnie, cut the shit." Rockfish said. He walked over to the small alcove and motioned for his partner. "One Team. One Fight. Need I repeat? Lose the attitude. I need you to do you. Listen. Assess. Then we can discuss. You know how we work. Don't let what she said before cloud your mind." His words were direct, quiet and for her ears only. She nodded and slunk back into her chair.

Cheyenne used the break in the conversation to blow her nose again and push a few wild strands of hair out of her face. Rockfish watched as Raffi leaned in and whispered a few words to her. He wasn't sure what Raffi said, but the girl's back straightened and she grabbed another tissue to wipe her eyes. An awkward moment fell over the room before she continued the long and winding story.

Cheyenne talked about the outrage and pain her family experienced within a short period. Support from friends and family, the Penn Forest Community, the day of the shooting. The halls of the hospital overwhelmed the Grabowskis. But it didn't take long for the rumors and accusations to fly. The old middle school game of telephone was up and running before the first staph microbe wandered into Edith Grabowski's blood stream. Innuendo spread like wildfire and fingers pointed.

"It was an inside job, then? Not Antifa, shipped in and smuggled out by Soros without being captured, let alone identified?"

Rockfish had simply tossed out one theory, making the media rounds to judge Cheyenne's reaction.

"More like an individual close to the cause, but no one has elaborated any farther," Cheyenne said. "Every time the topic comes up, the urgency to understand what happened suddenly evaporates. It's like the top guys want to pretend it never even happened."

Cheyenne's family soon noticed the number of daily supporters shrank. Those who continued to take up residency outside the hospital room were more interested in becoming part of the story. Those who remained and claimed they wanted to help did not share the devastation and emotional pain suffered by the family. Their so-called words of encouragement and hope were self-serving. 'The cost of doing business' was how one put it. Don't worry, the ends will justify the means. She'll be fine and think about how far she progressed the movement. Edith might even become our very own martyr, said yet another. There was even the occasional absurd cry of why couldn't it have been my grandmother?

"Can you believe that? Jealously because it is my gram lying in a hospital bed with tubes and IVs. Then the Elder even had the nerve to hold court in her room. Spouting off about one day, they'll teach a history lesson about Gram's sacrifice. Made us all hold hands, like a fucking church ceremony." Cheyenne stopped and blew her nose again. The small pile of used tissues on the bed had grown. "I really think he didn't care if she pulled through or not. He has his story to sell now."

Jawnie stood up and stepped closer to the far bed, where Raffi and Cheyenne sat. She locked eyes with Raffi and gave her head a quick tilt toward the alcove. Raffi stood and moved out of the way so Jawnie would take his spot on the bed. She turned to Cheyenne and laid her left hand on the woman's forearm.

"It all sounds horrible. I wouldn't want to be in your shoes, nor were these events something I would wish on my worst enemy, but again, see, this is where you're losing me. We could sit here and psychoanalyze motive until the cows come home. Yet I can't see how it pertains to any quid pro quo on our part. We need to fast-forward to how you'll scratch our backs. And then get into exactly what is it you want from us." She leaned in towards Cheyenne and raised her eyebrows.

"Psychowhatalize? And what's... squid pro bowl? It doesn't matter. I know where your friend is. All I ask is that when you leave, you take me and my boyfriend with ya."

And just like that, there it was. Magic to Rockfish's ears. The way forward, but with a couple of hitchhikers.

* * * * * * * * * *

"What have you said a million times about coming out of a pigpen, smelling like a rose?" Jawnie had whispered into Rockfish's ear while they both took in what exactly Cheyenne had promised.

"Better to be lucky," was the only reply he managed. His mind continued processing the girl's last sentence and with that, he had one foot out the door, keys in hand, and a fist cocked. *Slow down, Steve.* Rockfish recognized the voice of reason. His father, Mack, had entered his consciousness. *Don't be going off all half-assed like you're prone to do. Squeeze her for every drop of information. Then go bring Dan home to Rosie. I'll start shopping for the reunion dinner.*

Rockfish stepped between the two beds, squatted, and made a point of being at eye level with Cheyenne. She needed to understand how vital the rest of her story was to him and the others.

"And in exchange for the information on my friend Dan. Dan Decker is his name. He's got a worried wife at home. You and whoever want to pile into my backseat and go where?" He reached out and took her right hand in his. He needed a connection for her to understand the friend, his friend, had a name and a worried family too. Same as hers.

"You need to take Wilbur and I witcha. That's his name. I'm his girl. Since Mrs. McCurdy's eighth grade English class. He's in danger and not only from me telling you all of this. I can lead you to him. Then guarantee our safety."

"I ain't guaranteeing anything until Dan's safe in my car. And we're putting serious asphalt between my twenty-twos and this forsaken town. Now tell me about this Wilbur."

Cheyenne bit her bottom lip and didn't speak right away. He'd give her a minute to gather her thoughts before prodding her. *But honey, time is ticking.*

Cheyenne gathered herself and filled in the gaps on her relationship with Wilbur and the demons he continued to face. Her story included his most recent relapse, arrest, and how it affected his standing with his militia buddies.

"Right after he bonded out, they were on his ass. What did you tell the cops? Why should we trust you or anything you say? They claimed no one gets released on bond that quick without providing something useful to the cops. He's no rat! I've known him all my life," Cheyenne said. She sucked the loose snot in her nose, deep down into the back of her throat. "But they didn't believe him, and Wilbur got the feeling right quick he was going to be expendable no matter what he said or did. All the good he's done for them in the past, out the damn window." She stopped again and pulled another tissue from the box.

"They sent him with another guy to this remote cabin in the woods. It's where they're keeping your guy. Wilbur thinks the Patriot with him is actually charged with watching two prisoners, if you know what I mean. Two birds, one stone kinda thing. I think. Maybe. Could be wrong, but Wilbur says he sleeps with one eye open."

Rockfish sat back on the edge of his own bed. "Now we're making progress. Why not tell the cops that arrested him what they wanted to hear? Make an exchange of information for his safety? He should have added the stipulation for them to pick you up and move you both. I think even the state police have a version of witness protection."

"Yeah, cops are always offering to make a deal in order to move up the supply chain," Raffi said. "I've played that game more times than I'd like to admit. That might be your safest route."

"My man is loyal. To a fault, and it may get him killed this time. Say what you will about that group. They've done so much for him over the years. Been there for him too many times to remember, especially when his family's been out of the picture. Non-supportive fucks. Wilbur feels the need to return the favor by not talking."

"But his recent arrest. Did the police there know of his affiliation?" Rockfish said.

"His what?" Cheyenne said.

"That he was a member of the Penn Forest Patriots," Jawnie said.

"Yeah, in a big way. From that point on, the questions weren't about who he scored the meth from. The detectives focused on the water problem and the park shooting."

Rockfish watched as she lowered her head and rubbed the bridge of her nose with the hand that held a wadded-up tissue. *I'm pretty sure this girl ain't acting. And I've been reading people for longer than I'd care to admit. She's gonna get us to Dan and the least we can do is help her and this Wilbur escape from Hillbilly Mountain.*

"Like I said, he ain't told them nuttin'. Not a damn thing. Wilbur thinks the Colonel and his men are searching for proof he's a rat and once they find or make it up, they'll come for him."

"Sounds like being loyal might get him in a whole heap of trouble," Rockfish said.

"He's a good man. Not very bright, but I love him. He won't snitch, no matter how bad it gets. He swore to me if anything he said got out, or if the Colonel believes he ratted, my gram wouldn't be the only martyr for the cause in the family."

"They'd come for you?" Jawnie said. "Your family?"

"In a heartbeat. That's why we're a package deal. I'll lead you to this Dean guy but take us with you afterwards."

"Dan," Jawnie said.

"Forget it, she's rolling," Rockfish said with a grin he knew went right over her head. "Dan and Wilbur. Where are they?" He wanted the conversation to move on from the emotional heartstring tugging of the last fifteen minutes and move on to the planning stage. Actual preparation for the thing they had come all this way for. The three, now four, had made no progress for far too long.

"They're at an old hunting cabin, deep in the Penn Forest. The group uses it as a base of operations, but now it's more like a prison camp. But light on guards, which should benefit you."

"Us," Rockfish said. He leaned forward and squeezed her hand. He then took a shot in the dark to validate his recent investigative findings.

"Let me guess. Dirt road. Big-ass metal gate? A few miles past where Clyde Hayseed lives?"

"You know it?"

"Yeah, but only since earlier today," Rockfish said and brought a heavy fist down on the mattress. The others in the room jumped. *I should have acted. Thrown damn caution to the fucking wind and headed home with Dan an hour ago. Dumbass.*

"Steve, there was no way you knew," Jawnie said, anticipating Rockfish's self-deprecating mood.

"Yet I did. We should have been balls to the wall and back home with our feet up by this time."

"Still can," Jawnie said. She stood and put her hand on his shoulder. For a second, Rockfish imagined he felt the Wonder Twins' power flow through her to him.

"Wilbur's waiting on my signal," Cheyenne added. "But we have to act fast. He's sure there's a meeting scheduled at the cabin for tomorrow. The whole reason behind him sending me here today. He thinks something bad might happen to him and your guy after that."

"And if we wait for afterwards? Allow time to plan properly?" Jawnie said. "Then we might have a larger window to work in?"

"Wilbur doesn't think he or your guy will be in any shape to be rescued by then."

"Then we need to get moving," Rockfish said. "Gear up people. We've got a hike and a half in front of us." He stood and moved away from the bed. "Jawnie, dig out those hiking boots--"

"My family has a four-wheeler that will get us close," Cheyenne said. "It's fast on the trails but won't fit all of us. A couple will have to stay back with the cars. Ready to floor it as soon as the rescue party comes back."

Jawnie turned and put her arm across Cheyenne's shoulders. She wanted to make sure there were no hard feelings, at least until they were safely away. Not to mention a little more information to convince herself this woman wasn't there to walk them into a backwoods trap.

"Cheyenne, I have to ask, how are you in communication with Wilbur? When Steve and I were driving past this morning, I had no cell service. Google Maps wouldn't even load."

Cheyenne reached into the side pocket of her leggings, from behind the bulge of her phone, and pulled out a folded scrap of paper.

"Scribbled notes. Like in high school. I hide them in a half-hollowed out tree behind the cabin. He gets or leaves one of his own when he goes out to pee or have a smoke. I got the idea from an old *Hogan's Heroes* episode. Works for us."

"Dead drops?" Rockfish hoped she didn't notice the bewilderment in his voice. "Aren't you a little young for World War II Nazi-centric sitcoms?"

"We ain't got no cable, just an antenna. It's what the UHF channel 48 played after school. That and *Far Out Space Nuts*."

Explains the mindset of the current residents. Get 'em indoctrinated early and sign-ups for the Great Value Boys will pay off in the long run. But good for her, she might not be as dumb and racist as she appears on the outside.

Despite the argument he knew was around the corner, Rockfish had already made the decision that Cheyenne and Jawnie would wait by the cars. Engines revved and foot on the gas, ready to go at a moment's notice. The small size of the vehicle and two rescues left little room for anyone else. Raffi would be his wingman. Someone he's fought with, back-to-back, in the past. Didn't matter how negative his attitude's been for the trip, Rockfish knew he'd be there when needed. *Fuck, I saw how he handled himself with that last go round with the Provolones.*

Rockfish made sure he had everyone's attention before laying out his plan. He made sure his tone and volume inferred there would be no questions. No alternate plans. No audibles. No cry of we need to go back for Gram.

"... and you two wait where Cheyenne feels is the best spot for the cars. From there, we'll load everyone in, and it will be a straight shot home. No looking back." He aimed the last bit at Cheyenne. She understood and gave a quick nod of her head.

Rockfish opened the credenza and grabbed his small tactical backpack. He packed a few essentials for the mission when Jawnie grabbed his bicep and tugged him back toward the alcove.

"Steve, I really think this plan is pressing our luck. We need to reach out to someone. Decker's old superiors? Agent Thomas? Bring in professionals to hit that cabin and handle the extraction. It's what they do."

"Kid, we are the professionals. You have the same certificate on the wall of your office as I do." Rockfish shoved his binoculars atop everything else and zipped it up. "Plus, there ain't no time."

* * * * * * * * * *

The afternoon sun shone through the trees and Rockfish glanced down at the crude hand-drawn map. Cheyenne had handed it to him as he slid behind the wheel of the four-wheeler. The vehicle lurched forward, and he kept one eye on the path and the other on the map. His hands steered through the dense hardwoods and eventually out across a small clearing near the Great Value Boy's cabin. Here, he backed it up until he was satisfied no one walking about would come across their only means of escape. *No fucking way I would have thought these directions, scribbled on the back of a damn super-sized Kit Kat wrapper, would have gotten us here. Girl knows her backwoods shit. Without it, we would've been walking and driving around somewhere back there, in circles, for the next hour or two.*

"The Gods are shining upon us, Raffi," Rockfish said with a pat on his friend's back. "We've made good time and have close to five hours of daylight left to handle our business."

"Not sure daylight is a good thing here, Steve. Looking out, there isn't a lot of cover between the tree line and the cabin's steps. Although with this wind, they might not hear us if I drove the damn four-wheeler right up to the door."

"We already put a pin in that idea. Surprised by the one nudnik is all we need in the grand scheme of things."

"I'll drink to that," Raffi said. The two clinked imaginary rocks glasses and then turned their attention back to the cabin.

Rockfish lifted the binoculars that hung from his neck and focused again on the small clearing. The cabin didn't seem like something out of a horror movie, as described by Cheyenne. Functional was more how he would describe it. The rear, which was all they saw from their vantage point, had a back door which led out to a tiny wooden landing. From there, it was three steps down to the pine needle covered ground. The one window was set to the far right of the stairs. Neither the panes in the door nor window had any kind of covering. *And that my friends would cause us serious shit if Wilbur's partner stared out back when the time came. Like running across this small clearing with only our dicks in our hands. Well, that would put Wilbur in quite the dilemma. And we already know he's riding the loyalty fence.*

At the edge of the so-called backyard, the dead tree Cheyenne had spoken of was easy to locate. The old hemlock was a good fifty yards away. Raffi had already made his way down, on a sort of test run, and around to the dead drop. He had deposited a note from Cheyenne, detailing exactly how everything was to go down. From this point forward, all Wilbur had to do was to come out, unzip and read with his free hand. The go signal was to be a lit cigarette for confirmation. The light would begin a five-minute countdown once Wilbur stepped back inside. Rockfish and Raffi would then swoop down and execute a rescue that every character played by Liam Neeson would be envious of.

The plan was rock solid in Rockfish's mind. But all came down to how much truth Cheyenne's story held. She stuck to her words on the drive over to the eventual rendezvous spot. She had chosen the location behind a large roadside billboard off of Route 56, where apparently Hulk Hogan still shilled for Rent-A-Center. Well hidden, both Lana and the Durango were gassed, packed and ready to go at a moment's notice. *How much of her tale of woe had I actually believed? Had total faith in? Jawnie's doubt remained, and that was good. Why don't I? Is there an angle I've overlooked? A story told so well that I missed the obvious flaw? Too late now.*

All Rockfish knew for sure was that three men loitered within the cabin's walls. Two of which Cheyenne swore were on Team America. *Well, supposedly one solid and one, depending on the time of day, teetering on the line. And who only knows the physical and mental shape Dan's in.* But in the end, he couldn't expect his friend to be more than deadweight and planned accordingly. *Like that damn log the Navy Seal candidates carry in the surf during Hell Week.*

"Raffi, how quick do you think we can get down off these damn boulders and get across to that door?" They had climbed a small rock formation ten yards from the parked vehicle for a better view of the drop zone.

"Depends. Are you rolling an ankle when you hit the ground?" Raffi laughed aloud and quickly moved on when he noticed the frown on Rockfish's face. "When we see the signal, we might want to make our way down. Get into a better position while he's dragging on that butt. This way, once he's back inside, it's a hop, skip and a jump. Don't have to rush it."

"Speaking of butt," Rockfish said. He felt the need to go over his firm's lethal force policy one more time before Raffi pulled a John Wick. He had already pictured his rescue partner diving through the rear window, gun blazing. Rockfish's handy Glock 23 remained stuffed in the small of his back and he sincerely hoped with every bone in his body that was where it would remain. Raffi fought the urge to wave Jawnie's Hello Kitty Glock 19 in the face of any and everyone. The hot pink grip stuck out of his front pants pocket.

"If Mr. Murphy doesn't pay us a visit, Wilbur would have already taken the other guy by surprise. At the minimum, have him on the ground. We'll need to secure him, grab Dan, and go. No fucking about and waving that thing around. You know the deal. I'm repeating it for my benefit and any future depositions."

"I gotcha, Steve. If Murph is floating around, then I'll aim to scare or wing. Can't promise which. Heat of the moment and all. You grab Dan. He might go kicking and screaming when he glances up and sees it's me trying to wrap my arms around him."

"Don't give me that shit," Rockfish said. At this late hour in the plan, any differences between the two had to be pushed. *Plenty of time to argue dumb shit another day.* "As soon as the Great Value Boy is down and out, we find Dan and get him out. I don't care who lays eyes on him first, or his preference. Then we get him back here and secure him in the four-wheeler's passenger seat. I'm driving and you and what's-his-name can hang on for dear life in the back."

Earlier, Cheyenne had her father remove the side doors on the dark gray, two-man Polaris for speed loading. The short bed would double as a make-shift rumble seat. Rockfish turned to where he had left the vehicle parked, a choice that continued to cause consternation between him and Raffi.

Raffi pushed again to move the vehicle closer once Wilbur returned inside. The closer to the back steps, the less energy they would expel with whatever shape Decker was in. Rockfish understood the easier loading side of the argument, but felt the exhaust and engine noise, no matter the wind, would easily be heard. And losing that tiny element of surprise would make Wilbur's job harder than it already would be.

"We've been over this. Ad nauseam. Cut the shit. We can have an after action-report, after the action."

Agreeing to disagree on half-a-dozen issues, but in concurrence that Rockfish held the power of veto, the men sat. And waited. And watched.

It wasn't long before they got their first glimpse of the Great Value Boy not named Wilbur. The man exited the back door twice over the course of an hour. He marked his territory far from the corner Wilbur used. On the first trip out, Rockfish thanked his lucky stars the man hadn't chosen the corner with the Hemlock. He did not thank those same stars once he got a good look at the man. Rockfish never watched *Game of Thrones*, but he was familiar with the character *The Mountain*, from listening to Jawnie and Lynn. Apart from his size, an AR-15 hung across his chest and what Rockfish guessed were Asian throwing knives clipped to a separate strap across his middle. *Did we bring enough duct tape? Check out the BMI on that motherfucker. Wilbur better know what the fuck he's doing because there is no way the three of us will hold him down if it comes to old-fashioned wrestling.*

"We might have to rethink our plan of attack," Rockfish turned and whispered.

"That's a big boy," was all Raffi replied with.

"We'll turtle him. Somehow get him on his back, then watch him flail. Shouldn't be over ten minutes before he's all tuckered out."

Raffi let out a quiet laugh, but then the seriousness returned to his face. "Tell me, Steve, are you worried we ain't seen hide nor hair of our boy yet?"

Rockfish knew the question was coming. Unlike himself, Raffi would say it aloud and not let it spin around his head, going unanswered.

"Speak of the devil. I guess they take turns while the other watches over Dan."

The two men, dressed alike in fatigues, passed through the doorway, headed in opposite directions.

"You'd need four Wilburs to almost equal one of that other dude," Raffi said. The concern in his voice trumped the sarcasm-dipped words.

Wilbur was meth thin, which didn't surprise Rockfish after Cheyenne's tale. His clothes hung off his frame, and a simple sidearm was strapped to his side. Compared to his partner, Wilbur was not loaded for bear. And Rockfish immediately realized that monkey wrench might come into play.

Both men watched in anticipation as Wilbur pulled the paper from the tree and read while he soaked the ground. A minute later, a lighter flickered to life and Rockfish smiled at Raffi.

"Go time!"

* * * * * * * * * *

The countdown clock in Rockfish's mind had clicked past two hundred and forty seconds when Raffi overtook him and headed up the cabin's back stairs. *What's his rush? We're a good minute earlier than Wilbur would expect us. Shit, is that kid even keeping count inside?* He caught up as Raffi reached for the doorknob with his left hand. The pink Glock in his right pointed skyward.

Rockfish's hand shot out also, coming to rest on Raffi's shoulder. He gave a short tug and Raffi's head whipped around. Rockfish let go and his index finger pointed back to himself. With a silent nod, the men traded places. *If we're walking into a fucked up situation, I should at least be the one that picks the order. Although he appears gung-ho to finally get revenge for those MREs.*

Rockfish reached for the rusted doorknob and half expected it not to move. Instead, it easily turned. He pushed the door open a foot. *Not today, Mr. Murphy.* He gritted his teeth and half expected the hinges to cry out as it swung inward. Silence answered back, and he pushed a little more, enough for each man to slip through. *So far, so good.* The men stepped into the small back room; weapons drawn. A simple storage room was Rockfish's first thought. Boxes and black garbage bags littered the floor. Only a small, well-traversed pathway led to the cabin's main room. The doorway separating the two areas was nothing more than a blanket nailed above the doorframe. It hung to within four inches of the wood floor. Each man stepped back and to opposite sides of the blanket.

Rockfish took a deep breath. He was surprised no one had stuck their head through the blanket, as loud and fast as his heartbeat was. He understood the time spent in the back area was the calm before the storm. A phrase he always hated, but odds were bullets were about to fly since they had heard nothing and encountered no resistance to this point. *Something's bound to go FUBAR. Wilbur can't be this competent, can he?* He said a silent prayer for the boy he had never met. Rockfish pulled the right edge of the blanket out an inch and tried to get a lay of the room. His eyes met a second blanket, hung from the other side of the door frame. *FUCK! Nothing getting accomplished standing here.*

Rockfish looked over at Raffi, opened his eyes wide, and nodded. With the return nod received, Rockfish raised three fingers. The countdown started. When his index finger curled back into his fist, the free hand moved the barriers to the side and his gun hand led the charge.

Late afternoon sunlight streamed in through the front windows. The beams made the large empty room the complete opposite of the space they had emerged from. A folding table and stacked chairs were to Rockfish's left, and a stairway led up, over their heads from the right. His first thought was that the Great Value Boys had done a marvelous job renovating the inside. Leaving the outside run down, it wouldn't draw a second glance. They stepped from under the stairs and, heads on a swivel, searched the large room. In the middle stood Wilbur and at his feet, the Mountain had fallen.

The man lay stomach down, spread eagle, in the middle of the floor. An inflatable twin mattress and an AR-15 were off to the side, slightly out of reach. Wilbur forced a smile and kept his sidearm trained on his former compatriot.

"Your guy is upstairs. I yelled for him not to come down until we get this one secured," Wilbur said without moving his eyes or head.

Rockfish exhaled. He moved closer to the man on the ground, his own gun at the ready.

"Wilbur, you piece of shit turncoat. You'll never stop staring over your shoulder, no matter where the fuck you run. Coward. You'll hang with the rest--"

Raffi stepped in front of Rockfish and bent down. A strip of duct tape put an end to the man's rant. He then added a second for good measure. "No telling how long it will take him to eat through that, but it should give us a couple minutes of silence to work with." He stepped back towards the front door. "Well shit, this couldn't have gone any smoother. Piece of fucking cake, Stevie!"

Raffi hadn't finished the second sentence when Rockfish felt the icy breath of Mr. Murphy. Hairs rose on the back of his neck in anticipation, but he was too slow at putting one and one together. Like the others, he had exhaled again, with Raffi's emphasis on the word smoother. Not one of the three of them noticed the man on the floor bring his left hand up and under his chest. A second later, Wilbur screamed as the throwing knife entered his calf. He dropped to a knee and gripped the knife. The apparently very agile fat man had rolled to his side as the saviors prematurely celebrated. Rockfish and Wilbur had glanced at Raffi, and it cost them.

That could have been me! Rockfish cursed himself for exhaling and glancing over at Raffi. That thought caused him to pause. He was watching again. Raffi leapt forward and placed the pink barrel to the side of the man's head.

"Not today, Fat man. Down. I won't say it a second time. How many of my Q-Rations did you eat? Steve, a little help over here."

Rockfish shook the cobwebs from his head and ignored Wilbur's screams off to his left. He moved to help Raffi up before the Great Value Boy did anything further to inflict pain or call attention to the rescue mission gone off the rails.

"I knew this would not be uneventful," Rockfish said. He moved his gun hand in line with the man, now face down on the floor for the second time and surveyed the rest of the room.

"Old Raffi's got everything under control," Raffi said, before turning his attention to Wilbur. "Leave that knife in. Don't touch it until we get something to wrap it up all proper, like."

Wilbur's screams had decreased in volume from a solid eleven to a five, but neither man knew if he had comprehended Raffi's order. Instead, Wilbur pointed toward the air mattress.

Rockfish followed the tip of the man's finger and remembered the AR. "Don't worry, he's not getting to that rifle. It's coming with us. Speaking of which, we need to get moving."

"No," was all Wilbur said. He pointed again, and this time his agitation caused the tip of his finger to shake.

Rockfish stepped over to the mattress and looked again. He reached down, pulled the thin blanket to the side, and a small walkie talkie slid off onto the floor. He raised his boot above it.

"Wait, we can use that to listen for intel. Depending on the range," Raffi said.

Rockfish turned, surprised by the on-point thought.

"I got one, too," Wilbur sputtered and pointed to his own belt. "Only good for up to two miles, though."

Rockfish brought the boot down. Pieces of cheap Chinese plastic skittered in all directions. He picked up and draped the AR-15 across his back. *Never know when she might come in handy. They outgunned us the last time we dealt with these chucklefucks.*

"At a point when neither of you answer, they'll know the jig is up," Rockfish said. "We need to be long gone by then. Enough fucking around. Secure this clown. Then I'm coming up for you, Dan. Hang tight." Rockfish glanced up as his voice echoed upward and off the ceiling.

Wilbur regained his composure, aimed his gun, and made sure the prisoner didn't move again. Rockfish and Raffi used close to an entire roll of duct tape to secure the man.

"I told you we should have brought two rolls," Raffi said as they stepped aside and admired their work.

"He's not going anywhere. At least until one of them wanders up to check on the radio silence and finds him. You help Wilbur out onto the ride. I'm going up for Dan."

"There's a backpack filled with important stuff in the back," Wilbur said as Raffi helped the man back to his feet. "You'll want that." Raffi draped Wilbur's left arm across the back of his shoulders. The two men began a three-legged race towards the back room and eventually across the clearing. "I bet it's important to y'all or someone."

Rockfish was halfway up the stairs when he stopped to listen. Raffi assured Wilbur, if he pointed it out on the way past, he'd come back for it. "But I've got my hands full on this trip."

"Get him out of here, Raffi. I'll keep an eye on Fattie McGoo from the loft. Even from that range, he'd be hard to miss."

Rockfish waited a couple of minutes as Raffi helped Wilbur towards the back room and out the door before climbing the last few stairs. The loft area was not as well lit as the main level, but there wasn't much for Rockfish to see, either. Dan Decker sat upright on a blanket in the center of the space. A metal bed pan was within reach and when Rockfish stepped closer, he saw it was stamped *Property of Lee Hospital.*

He doesn't seem half bad, if I say so. Decker was dressed in dirty jeans, sans shoes and socks, and a long sleeve T-shirt. Filthy, but healthy was the best description Rockfish produced. Dan held his hands out. They, like his ankles, were secured by zip ties.

"Figured I'd keep my mouth shut and let you do your thing down there," Dan said with an enormous smile. It was clear he was thrilled to see his savior.

"We're not out of this yet," Rockfish said. He stepped back and stared over the railing to make sure the prisoner hadn't moved. "Let me cut those. Can you walk?"

"That's why I'm restrained. I had a tendency to wander off."

Rockfish pulled a Spyderco knife from his front pants pocket and slid the blade between the plastic and Dan's skin.

"Careful with that, will ya?"

Rockfish let the plastic cords fall to the floor and helped Decker to his feet.

"No idea where my shoes and socks got off to, but I'm guessing we don't have the time to send out a search party?"

"Stop flappin' your gums and lean on me. Can't afford to lose you to these stairs after all this shit. Raffi should be back shortly to help." Rockfish saw the change in emotions on Decker's face when he mentioned Raffi. *It's not like his ears were covered up there. He heard us down below. Shouldn't be a surprise.* "Slow and steady wins the race."

Rockfish kept one eye on Decker and the other on the man on the floor as they made their way down. The man, wearing a solid two pounds of duct tape, had rolled closer to the front door.

Rockfish knew there was no way he was in any position to sit up and open the door, let alone complete the escape.

"Wait here. I'll roll him back into the center of the room."

"What good will that do if we're leaving?" Decker said as he followed Rockfish.

They stood on either side of the man. Decker surprised Rockfish when, without warning, he curb-stomped the man with a bare foot. Rockfish, taken aback, fought the instinct to join in.

"For good measure. I owe that piece of shit. A lot. But that will do for now."

They made their way to the back room, where they met Raffi, sprinting up the steps. Each non-disabled man took up position on either side of Decker and made sure he kept moving. Raffi slung one strap of the backpack Wilbur had pointed out over his shoulder. From there it was out the door, down the steps and across the forest.

They approached the idling vehicle and Rockfish gave Raffi a thumbs up for starting the four-wheeler. Wilbur sat on the drivers side of the small rear bed. Blood soaked through the bottom half of his pant leg. He held the throwing knife steady with one free hand while the other held on to an overhead bar.

"Raffi, help me get Dan buckled in."

"You say that like I can't hear you," Decker said. "I can get in on my own."

Both men let off of Decker and he immediately dropped to his knees.

"Dan, you're in worse shape than you're letting yourself believe," Rockfish said. He and Raffi reached down and hoisted Decker back to his feet. "Put a sock in it and go with the program."

Raffi dropped the backpack to the ground as they maneuvered Dan into the seat and secured him. He then picked up the bag and placed it on Dan's lap, all the while oblivious to Rockfish's inquisitive look.

"What are you stealing now?" Rockfish said.

"The kid said it's incriminating."

The backpack intrigued Rockfish, but again, time was at a premium. He jumped into the drivers seat and Raffi in the back next to Wilbur.

"Hold on, everybody."

The ride through the forest trail was uneventful and on the second time through, Rockfish only referred to Cheyenne's hand-drawn map twice.

Twenty minutes later, the main road and the giant billboard came into view. He maneuvered the Polaris across the field and brought it to a sudden stop behind where the cars waited. Jawnie gave a thumbs up from the open drivers-side window and revved Lana's engine.

"Music to my damn ears." Rockfish said to no one in particular.

CHAPTER ELEVEN

Earnhardt Jr. pulled his Ram pickup off the dirt road and brought it to a stop alongside three other similar trucks. His men had heeded the call and arrived with numbers this early Saturday morning. Dew covered most surfaces and what little sunlight made its way through the trees had yet to burn any of it off. Men milled around the outside of the cabin, looking. *Searching. Presumably to find a clue or two. Not that any of them would know what the hell they hoped to find if they tripped over it. Those fucks are long gone and smart enough to not leave anything behind. Best we figure what they got away with and begin planning for the worst-case scenario.* He gazed out his window and spotted Clyde and Amos. His top two men leaned against the railing to the small porch, not-so-patiently waiting for his arrival.

The news of the turncoat and the great escape had awoken Earnhardt Jr. an hour prior to sunrise. He had informed Archibald before even getting out of bed. This wasn't an issue he figured to quickly resolve and then report back. Archibald actually beat him to Clyde's trailer where the Elder remained inside. The man needed a little plausible deniability with knowledge of the situation, but he also insisted on being on scene to micromanage. That was where the walkie talkie, handed to Archibald by Clyde's wife, came into play.

As if on cue, the device in Earnhardt Jr.'s jacket pocket chirped. He pulled it out and swallowed. *The last thing I want to spend my time up here doing is giving that man a constant play-by-play on the absolute nothing that is going on. Best he go home and prepare for the shit-storm that's a coming.* In Earnhardt Jr.'s mind, it was only a matter of time before Rockfish and that cop showed up on another cop's doorstep. A department far from either of their influence. Earnhardt Jr. was ready to start his plan if anyone came a-knocking. His plan was simple. *A tactical retreat and wait 'em out. If they wanted to force their way in, then God bless the Penn Forest Patriot arsenal. We'll jump-start this second revolution.*

For a split second, he considered ignoring the handheld device, dropping it back into his pocket, and heading to where his men waited. They needed him to lead in this dark time. And he couldn't lead if he had to hand-hold Archibald. The radio squawked a second time.

"Rover One to Rover Two. Over."

"Elder, I just got here. Ain't even turned off the truck yet. Hold your damn britches."

Radio silence. It didn't surprise Earnhardt Jr. the man wanted him to know who was in charge. *Him and his damn radio signal names. Bush league, if you ask me.* But he'd not say it aloud. He knew the last thing he wanted to do now was create further waves between the two men. Since the shooting at the park, Archibald had become a tremendous pain in the ass. Acting more like the leader of the movement, instead of writing checks. *I'm running the friggin show, especially since the true battle for our very souls is coming fast over the horizon. Know your role, preacher man.*

Earnhardt Jr. looked up and caught his men's attention. He held up a single finger and hoped they understood what he was dealing with on the management side.

"If you're still there, do me a favor. Take a deep breath and stop shouting orders. Let me talk to my guys. I'll fill you in when we find something. I'm out."

Earnhardt Jr. climbed the front steps and was out of breath by the third step.

"Guys, give us space, will ya? Go help those in the back," he said to the underlings milling around the porch and within the cabin's front door. He stepped closer to Clyde and Amos and tried to get his breathing under control. *Don't rip them a new asshole, yet. Maybe we come out of this without the FBI running an armored vehicle through this front door. Right. And maybe monkeys will fly out of my ass too.*

"Tell me what we got. I already know what we ain't got. I need a positive to report back up the chain. If not, then I might let one of you deal with him."

"Come on inside. No need for any of these guys to overhear more than they've already heard," Amos said. "Plus, Trevor's inside."

The three men walked through the front door and before the door slammed behind them, Earnhardt Jr. spotted Trevor's enormous frame. On the floor. Bound.

"What the fuck? You haven't even cut him loose?"

"Now how's he gonna learn that way?" Amos said. He took a step closer to the man on the floor and the other two followed. "I'll let him go when we're done. Plus, I'm not sure we're getting all the right answers. The ones we need in order to put the damn cork back in the bottle."

Earnhardt Jr. peered around the cabin's floor. To his eyes, nothing had changed since the last time he was up here. Other than the failure on the floor. That previous meeting with Archibald, who now knew better than to come within two miles of the cabin, was the first sign of cracks in the alliance. *He's been looking out for number one this whole time and damn, you need to do the same.*

"Other than Rerun here stretched out on the floor, what am I missing?" Earnhardt Jr. said. Despite being at the cabin on a fact-finding mission, the biting words came, and he chose not to stop them. "I mean, not including the prisoner. You know, the one thing your men were supposed to keep safe. The cop. The Deep State actor that's done all this horrendous shit, only to pin it on the poor patriot front. Get that line to our newspaper man, stat. It'll make one hell of a headline. We need to get out in front of this. Gentlemen, we're to follow the leader here. It's the Trump game plan all the way. Never go backwards. Deny, deny, deny."

"I get it, Colonel, but--"

Earnhardt Jr. crossed his arms and a sour look spread across his face. "No buts, Amos. Move forward. Now, before you cut this man free, I want to hear exactly what happened. In his own words."

Amos grabbed Trevor's feet and spun him, so he faced Earnhardt Jr. The Colonel then ordered Clyde to grab a folding chair from under the stairwell. He sat and leaned forward; the plastic groaned under his weight. He stared down at the terrified man.

"Spill it, son. Don't leave out the smallest detail. Contrary to what Amos has said, you ain't in trouble. Yet."

Trevor recounted the same story he had earlier told, first to Clyde, then Amos. His voice peaked with the stabbing of Wilbur. And bottomed out when he spoke of being bound, losing his weapon and forced to lie on the floor for close to twelve hours in his own piss, replaying his failure in his head.

Earnhardt Jr. went over the story. He knew he was on the hook for the meth kid. It had been his idea to keep Wilbur close by, give him more chances than anyone else would have deserved. He'd have to answer for the cog that started this entire clusterfuck. But it was one thing to think about it, another to admit it aloud to his men. *There's a time for accountability, but now ain't it. I need to lead. Lead with--*

"Come in Rover Two, this is Rover One. Requesting an immediate status update."

Earnhardt Jr. closed his eyes and bit down on the inside of his cheek. He pulled the walkie talkie from his pocket and pushed the send button on the side. "Said I'd give you one when I had one."

"How close are we to retrieving the goods? Exactly, no estimations."

"For the tenth time, we've got nothing here. Still assessing the situation," Earnhardt Jr. said. Spittle covered the face of the device.

"Assess Faster. Get back down here and report in. You're breaking up and I can't spend another second in this trailer--"

Earnhardt Jr. smiled and side-armed the device across the room. It shattered against the wall and joined the pieces of Trevor's all over the floor.

"Clyde, take the cost of that out of petty cash. I've about had it with that clown. Now give me your side. I thought these little handheld things were supposed to keep you in touch with the men and prevent anything like this from sneaking up on us."

"That was the plan. We didn't account for the insider threat." Clyde shrugged and his head dropped.

"When was the last time you had heard from Wilbur or this one?" Earnhardt Jr. gave Trevor a swift kick to the thigh with his boot.

He watched Clyde shift his weight from one foot to the other. The man searched for the right words and Earnhardt Jr. would have settled for any.

"Around five last night," Clyde finally said. "Wilbur reported in. The connection was choppy, but he said everything was normal. Boring as shit was the phrase he used."

"Nothing out of the ordinary that you didn't speak to this one?" Earnhardt said with another kick. This time harder, and Trevor muffled a yelp.

"No, but I figure that must have been right around the time of the great escape," Clyde said. He spit on the floor and stepped on it as if putting out a cigarette.

Earnhardt Jr. saw the frustration on Clyde's face. His eyes moved to Amos' blank face and then out the window to the men who combed the ground for anything the previous sweep missed.

"Amos, give us a sec, will ya?" Earnhardt Jr. said.

Amos stepped around Trevor and walked towards the stairwell and the hanging blankets in the back of the room. Earnhardt Jr.

tilted his head toward the front and Clyde followed him out to the front porch, where they talked freely as most of their men had moved around back.

"With the preacher man getting static, how long till he orders my wife to drive his fat ass up here?" Clyde said, after none of the other patriots were within earshot.

"He's not coming," Earnhardt Jr. said with a shake of his head. "The man is all for plans when they unfold perfectly. Throw in a few curveballs and he cowers with even the slightest hint of a drop in donations."

"You think we need to regroup, Colonel?" Clyde shook his head in frustration.

"Our ace in the hole is gone. Dead or alive, that cop was only good to us when we could reveal him as the covert agent of the weaponized left. Now? He gets to tell his story and we're in no position to lead the narrative. Setback? Yes. Regroup? No."

"But what if the Elder gets in front of a camera and goes off script? Tell you the truth, Colonel, I think he done fucked us sideways with the thing in the park."

"Agreed." Earnhardt Jr. had wondered how many of his troops felt he had some sort of advanced notice and had signed off on the audible. "Leave him to me. His threats are harmless and if he cuts off the gravy train, so be it. We've suckled on that tit long enough. Everything ends."

"I agree. We've got more important shit," Clyde said. He stepped closer to Earnhardt Jr. and leaned his head in. "Those two, hell, six, are long gone. Drove through the night. I know I would have. Probably back home by now." He kicked at a loose board on the porch. "Fuck, all these problems!"

"You think him and that dipshit cunt of his are around here? Maybe Trevor's lying about wounding him?" Earnhardt Jr. said, pointing over his shoulder and through the cabin window with his thumb.

"Blood on the floor. But yeah, too many questions."

"I know. But here's what you need to do. I'll deal with the Elder. Might be time to serve him those separation papers. Best to surprise him on that front."

Clyde nodded and waited for his orders.

"I also don't think that kid and his crackhead girlfriend are smart enough to leave the area. Apron strings don't stretch all the way down to Baltimore. If they're around, I want 'em found."

"Copy that. I'm on it."

"I ain't done. Keep a few men up here. Empty this place out. Spic and span clean. No prints, hairs or fibers. It's no longer viable or safe. The shit-ton of boxes and bags stacked in the back? Move them off site and do a complete inventory. I want to know if anything is missing." Earnhardt Jr. paused. *Where can I store this shit for the time being? Cool Rick's? The storage place. Perfect. And let him know how serious you are so he can have a quote to keep the men in line and inspired.*

"Put it all in an empty unit down at Cool Rick's. Tell Jethro the order came from me. He'll open a unit for y'all. It will buy us time if they serve a warrant on this location. And believe you me, they will. We need to prepare. Let all the men know our Lexington and Concord moment is close at hand."

* * * * * * * * *

Rockfish put down the half-eaten bacon, egg and cheese on a Kaiser roll onto his desk and reached for the remote. He shut off the office television, crumpled up the rest of breakfast in the greasy wrapper, and dropped it into the garbage. *This is the life. I know Sally, kids are starving, but I can't mail this to help them.*

How he had missed kicking back, watching the previous night's highlights on SportsCenter while enjoying the peace and quiet. Once the sound faded from the wall-mounted big screen, he heard Jawnie and Lynn down the hall. The rest of the firm was hard at work, at the conference table, going through the contents of the backpack Wilbur was so insistent they take.

Jawnie felt the team needed a firmer grasp on the motivation and actual evidence to tie the Great Value Boys and the preacher to the poisoning and mass shooting. Rockfish wasn't so sure. With the current political situation and limited law enforcement resources, would anyone pay attention? Let alone take action from their accusations. And with no proof, that was all they were. Solid evidence would direct the cavalry and enable them to spot and extinguish the spark. Groups like the Great Value Boys were so desperate to ignite.

Four days had passed since the evening drive straight outta Grindsville, and Rockfish still had questions. Some would be answered by his document exploitation team and the remainder by a well-rested Dan Decker. The man had slept the entire drive home. From time to time, Rockfish had Raffi turn around and poke him from the front seat, if only to make sure he was breathing. *I'm not sure bears hibernate that deeply*, he remembered thinking. They even had trouble waking him once they pulled into his driveway and Lana's engine died. Turned out, all the man needed was to hear Rosie's voice. Not three syllables into her weepy first couple of words, Decker snapped back to attention.

Jawnie had to convince Rockfish to let the man go. She had parked in the street, leaving Wilbur and Cheyenne in the rented Durango. Jawnie then arrived in time to tug on the back of Rockfish's jacket, so he didn't follow the reunited couple up the steps and into their house. She reminded him Rosie was the wife, not him. He had done all he promised, and it was now time to let her take over. There would be time soon to figure out exactly what happened and what information Dan might remember. Give him space, she had recommended, to regain his strength, both mental and physical.

Jawnie then returned to the rental and started the last part of the evening's plan. She and Rockfish had agreed to monitor the couple until it was clear to all parties that no one was coming after them. On the trip back, a stop at a chain pharmacy resulted in bandages and cream to help prevent amputation until they had a professional examine Wilbur's wound. Cheyenne sat in the back with Wilbur's leg draped across her lap and she applied pressure the entire drive. After dropping off Decker, Jawnie's job was to find that professional, get Wilbur all *antibiotic'd up*, as Rockfish had put it, and then deposit them at his house. His was the only place with space for them and a caring paternal figure that would watch over them in the short term.

Rockfish glanced around the office and grabbed his keys from the desk drawer. He picked up the Styrofoam coffee cup and made a mental note to top it off before getting into the car. He closed the office door behind him and stopped at the conference table at the end of the short hallway. Jawnie and Lynn had piles of paper spread out, practically covering every square inch. Jawnie had started the day before, categorizing each item in a spreadsheet to make sense of what they brought back. Her work should also help save the police time when they turn over what Jawnie now referred to as the Walmart document exploitation project.

"I'll be on my cell if anything comes up," Rockfish said over his shoulder as he stopped, only to refill his cup. The new Keurig fired up and the rush of compressed air drowned out the first few words of Jawnie's reply.

"... letting you come over to see him?"

"Rosie? Yeah."

"You really can't blame her, Steve, for being protective," Lynn said. "After all, he went through and her not knowing if he'd return in one or seventeen pieces."

"Oh, I get it. For a hot minute, I thought she had returned to the Ice Queen, and we'd have to sneak around like star-crossed teenage lovers."

"Romeo and Juliet," Jawnie said.

"I was thinking more like Lloyd and Diane."

"Huh?" the ladies said in unison.

"Say Anything," Rockfish said.

"Say What?" Lynn said. Confusion settled across the faces at the table. But both women had been on the losing end of Rockfish movie trivia way too many times to be very concerned about yet another missed Gen-X culture reference.

"Before your time. But enough Siskel and Ebert for one day. I gotta get moving before she changes her mind."

"Before you head out, Mom always said never show up empty-handed," Lynn said and nodded her head for emphasis.

"Liquor store doesn't open for another two hours."

"Dude. Something for her," Lynn said.

"Yeah, food, a gift certificate for a cleaning service," Jawnie said with a nod of her own. "Think of a gift to make her life a little easier in the short term."

"Topless maid services are all the rage these days," Rockfish said. He backpedaled out the door before the ladies threw anything from the table in his general direction.

* * * * * * * * * *

Rockfish backed Lana into Decker's driveway. On the off-hand chance he needed to make a fast exit and then turned off the engine. *You never know when she'll flip the switch, take anything the wrong way and I'll be headed out the door followed by a shoe, vase or the closest kitchen utensil.*

He had not taken the advice lightly provided by the ladies back at the office. Rockfish stopped at Fanucci's Flowers and wedged the largest arrangement he found into the passenger seat. The seatbelt fit perfectly around the base and kept the flowers from flying forward with each sudden braking. In addition, to ensure the good vibes kept flowing between the two former combatants, Rockfish followed Jawnie's advice. Sort of. He left Mamma Zu's, a local gourmet caterer, after signing the Decker's up for two weeks' worth of handmade and delivered meals. Last, he dug into his own personal reserve and brought a bottle of Red Spot Irish Whiskey for Dan. Secretly, Rockfish hoped his host would offer to open the bottle on the spot. This way, not to totally lose out one of the more expensive purchases he had made for himself.

Rockfish rang the video doorbell with his elbow. The gigantic bouquet was in his right hand and a gift bag with the whiskey and catered meals, information packet in the other.

"Steve!"

Rosie's enthusiasm continued to surprise him. But he also knew it might disappear as quickly. He smiled to himself and walked through the foyer as she held the door. Rockfish didn't stop until he put the flowers down on the kitchen island.

"And this is for you. Something to help ease the household pressures over the next week." He handed her the folder from Mamma Zu's that detailed each meal option and delivery instructions. Rosie's face glowed as she quickly perused the options available for each meal.

"Thank you, Steve. And tell your team the same. Even that one guy that aggravates Dan to no end when his name comes up. But you're not here to hear me babble. He's through the door on the porch."

Rockfish pulled the bottle of Red Spot from the bag and headed for the screen door. He turned before grasping the handle. "If you don't mind, we'll need a couple of rocks--"

"Glasses," Rosie said, finishing his sentence. "He knew you were coming. They're already out there, along with a bucket of ice."

"Mixers?"

"You wouldn't be able to fit into one of my skirts if you tried."

Rockfish gave Rosie a hearty smile and stepped out into the Florida room. *Dan has spoken well of me in front of her. And she thinks Raffi works for me. I'm sure Dan will clear that up with her the next time it's mentioned.*

Dan sat on the rattan rocker and Rockfish made a point of speed-walking toward it, so he wouldn't have to get up. From there, ice rattled, and whiskey poured. The men made small talk before Rockfish steered Dan to his story. The one that began with Raffi storming out of the WinGate parking lot and abandoning him.

"... it wasn't a few hours later after Raffi ran away, as I sat there contemplating what was I even doing staying up there, no matter what my gut was telling me. Then the next moment, the door flew off the hinges..."

Rockfish noticed the disgust that usually filled Dan's face when Raffi's name came up, was absent on this occasion. *Strange, but I'll chalk it up to all he's been through. Or keep an eye out for any other Dan expressions that don't meet the smell test.*

"... four of 'em came rushing in. I don't care how much training you have, when it's that many and you don't expect it... well, you can probably tell how it went. Especially in my weakened condition."

"Nobody expects the Spanish Inquisition!" Rockfish slammed his open palm on the table's surface. Decker didn't jump. He did laugh, though.

"Nice Steve jokes to keep the patient's outlook up. I get it. Now let me tell it."

Decker continued on about the men ransacking the room, leaving everything of his behind. The bad guys led him nonchalantly out of the room, with a gun to his back. They didn't bother to secure him until he fell across the back seat of an old Lincoln Continental.

"Roomy enough for me to lay and have one of those halfwits sit watch over me. First, it was a house. A safe room, I think. A cushy gig, if you ask me. Then, for no reason mentioned aloud, they packed me up and took me to the cabin. Pushed to the top of the loft and left to my own thoughts. The babysitters rotated often, even in the number of 'em."

"It wasn't Wilbur and the fat one the entire time?"

"No, only towards the end of my stay in the cabin. When I was at the house, in the beginning, different ones questioned me. Suit-types. They wanted to know what I knew. How I knew Raffi? What was I doing trying to infiltrate their so-called organization?" Decker stopped and shifted his weight in the rocker before continuing. "I've seen new patrol officers perform better in the box than these amateurs. No rhyme or reason to their flow of questioning. They harped one hell of a lot on who I was. Fake name, rank and serial number were all I gave. Hell, after a couple of days of the same shit, I finally said I was here to help Raffi find his damn MREs, thinking that would satisfy them. They didn't believe a word of it. Fucking morons, so I went back to shrugging my shoulders to their questions."

"I'm surprised they didn't beat it out of you only to get their hands on Raffi," Rockfish said. "They had to have been pissed he sent a guy up to recover that trash."

"The physical shit never came. Not that I'm complaining, but at some point, you'd expect a gun butt to the side of the head, at a minimum."

"Horrible hosts."

"I should have known. Anyway, they relied on threats, but even that changed when the fat fuck, the one you had the joy of meeting, arrived. He liked to fuck with me mentally and try other dumb shit. Leaving me to piss myself or making a point of bringing cold pierogies for multiple days straight. You ain't ever had constipation like that."

"Color me shocked the guy didn't bring a salad."

"Long story short, they held me hostage, with no actual idea why except with overhearing the constant talk of bigger things to come. Did they come? I do not know. But it's nice to get back on the home throne. Almost got my routine back."

"Did they come?" Rockfish said. His eyebrows lurched up, and he lost his smile. "Oh yeah, and then some. Let me fill you in."

Rockfish reached for the bottle of Red Spot. He freshened each glass before he told Decker of the water poisoning and subsequent active shooter in Grindsville's Central Park. Decker shook his head in disbelief and Rockfish didn't blame him. *Couldn't make this shit up if I tried.*

"... and to think, they figured you to be the fall guy. I'm not sure how they planned that one. You were going to be the Antifa spy that instigated the second civil war. All kinds of famous, in a Gavrilo Princip kinda way."

"At least in their minds."

"True. I mean, I don't think they had reserved any buses to drive to D.C. The United States Capitol was never in any kind of danger."

"Speaking of transportation," Decker said. "In all your adventures up there, did you see my car? I should have mentioned it before you dumped me in that souped-up golf cart, but I was too happy to be leaving the premises."

"My guess? I mean, at a minimum, one of them moved it from the WinGate parking lot. Had it towed, who knows where."

"I figured as much but had to ask. I'll need to get on the phone with the insurance company. More pain in the ass shit to do."

"I can lend you Lynn to help with the administrative bullshit. She's good at it."

"Nah, we're good here. But I've got a few more questions. But what about that kid and the girl? I mean, I noticed from the first day he arrived at the cabin he didn't want to be there. Something about that one. The fat one constantly rode his ass. Made him do most of the grunt work around the place. Those two were definitely not friends. Makes me think they might come after him? Do you think he's smart enough to know anything of value?"

"The two of them are probably on my back deck at the moment, with Mack and Zippy watching over them. Really didn't know anywhere else to stick 'em. I mean, I've got the room. And the kid has information. He pointed out a box full of paper and a backpack for us to take. Said it could help our case. I have to keep reminding people, I have no paying client, hence no case. Don't worry, bud," Rockfish said and leaned over to shake Decker's shoulder. "I told Rosie this one was on the house."

"My pension thanks you for your generosity. So, what did you do with the shit you took from the cabin? Anything worthwhile?"

Rockfish detailed Jawnie's document exploitation project she had undertaken the previous day.

"She's not sure what all the paper is about, but the backpack appeared to belong to a student. Notebooks, travel accessories and a phone. Her and Lynn dove into it before I headed over here. I've washed my hands of the whole mess. Or at least I will once those kids move on from Chez Rockfish. You're home safe and so are we. I don't care about those Q-Rations." Rockfish rubbed the palms of his hands.

"Good, because the one thing I learned was they were thrown away. A bunch of those Great Value Boys got sick eating them and the rest went straight to the dump."

"Something good finally came out of this whole clusterfuck," Rockfish said. "Nice!" He drained the rest of his glass and contemplated another.

"Enough," Dan said, and Rockfish's hand retracted from the bottle. "Let's get moving. I've got a ton of experience with making heads or tails from seized documents. Sooner we find a promising nugget, sooner we can have someone in power hang those rednecks."

Makes sense. He wants to help. How much was experience and how much revenge? I'm tiring of this revenge angle with everything and everyone these past couple of months. Let it go, people.

"Sounds like a man planning revenge, Dan."

"No. That was your buddy's mission. I'm offering to lead this one. Ten times the leader he is. Was. If there's anything on your conference table worth a damn, you'll need my contacts and reputation to get anyone to take you seriously."

"People died from the poisoning. An unknown person shot into a public space in order to jumpstart a cultural war that would be fought with more than memes. It's serious as all fuck." Rockfish stared long and hard at his friend.

"All the more reason to get this information in the right person's hands. I'm not downplaying any of it, Steve. Only reminding you of how the system works. Plus, I overheard those nudniks talking on more than one occasion. Nothing that I understood, but maybe the stuff back at your office will ring a bell or give me a different perspective than your ladies?"

Rockfish stared. Hard. But he couldn't find a soft spot in the man's argument. *How many times has he pulled me from the fire? And me him? We make a damn good team.*

"Dan, that makes all the sense in the world. But Rosie will pitch a fit if you leave with me. I'm finally on her good side. Let's not press our luck. Maybe we can FaceTime or Zoom you in? Some shit like that?"

"You let me handle the blowback. Out this back door and through the side gate. You know the old adage, better to ask for forgiveness than permission."

"Fuck, I live by those words," Rockfish said. He filled his mouth with the ice from his glass for the road.

* * * * * * * * *

Lynn thanked the Uber Eats driver and pressed a ten-dollar bill into his palm before shutting the door. She placed the bag of food down on the table in their small waiting area. The sun arched high across the sky and light poured in through the front windows. She closed the blinds to prevent any lookie-loos, who ignored the *Closed* sign on the door from checking out what was going on.

"Lunch is served," Lynn called out after moving the bag to her desk.

Jawnie gazed up from the mess in front of her on the conference table and sighed. Not understanding what to hope for, made their effort equivalent to working on a four-thousand-piece puzzle without the box cover to help.

"Be there in a sec," Jawnie said. Her eyes dropped to the table and then to the inventory list to her immediate right. Not a damn thing stood out the first time through and the same for the third.

You remember the definition of insanity. I'm smarter than this. Find an item you can exploit. Make progress and the rest will fall in line. Jawnie kept her disappointment from Lynn. Her partner was working just as hard, reading each piece of paper, taking copious notes, and trying her damnedest. *Each of us wanting to have something of value in hand by the time Steve staggered in from day-drinking with Dan.*

Jawnie stood up and brought her tofu salad with gluten-free Italian dressing back to her work area. She removed the top of the plastic container and added the dressing. Three minutes into lunch, she shifted her focus. Despite her success in uncovering the Provolone fraud scheme, she would move away from the forensic accountant angle. *The very first case Steve and I worked. The reason behind the show. But it doesn't mean I'm the expert. People think I am. Change it up, McGee, if you're in a rut. Work the problem from a different angle.*

Jawnie put on her internal blinker and moved into the research lane. Research was her expertise and the next exit. She pushed the half-eaten salad to her right and grabbed a new pair of purple nitrile exam gloves from the box on the end of the table, then cleared off a swath of table and moved down one chair, having room to work. She reached for the backpack and made sure her iPad was within reach. The contents spilled out in front of her and told a story, albeit most likely not one with a happy ending.

One of those newfangled front pocket wallets. Inside, there was a driver's license, Wells Fargo cards, and a Topeka Pharmaceutical

Labs ID. All in the name of Daniel L. Sparks. Plenty of information here to jumpstart a Google deep dive.

Jawnie ignored the wad of bills clipped to the backside of the wallet. Next was a small yellow pelican box, roughly the size of a small portable hard drive. She opened the clips and threw back the lid. The box was empty except for the cushioned lining which used to protect an item. *What? Something worth dying for?* A blood splattered knit hat was next on the agenda. *This did not end well.* The last item was an iPhone with a shattered screen, as if someone had put the blunt side of an axe through it. *No one called for help on this thing. We'd need FBI-type forensic tools, if it were to even power up.*

The thought of the nation's premier law enforcement organization brought to mind Rhonda Thomas. The Baltimore Division Special Agent was one of the good guys, despite being mostly a thorn in the firm's side. A stack of the woman's business cards sat in the top right drawer of Jawnie's desk from all their dealings over the past two plus years. *Had things gotten to that point? We might be there, but Steve would go apeshit if I brought his arch nemesis into this mess. Wait. The organization or person? Both. There might be a time, soon, where his feelings get trumped. Remember that.*

"Lynn, can you grab the box of various chargers in my office next to the filing cabinet? See if you can get this monstrosity to turn on. It's a long shot but might as well cross it off the list that we tried."

"No problem, J," Lynn said with a wink. She took the phone and moved it to her end of the table before continuing down the short hallway to locate the matching cord.

As Lynn disappeared from view, Jawnie pulled off her gloves. She dropped them onto the vacant chair next to her and reached for the iPad. A simple search for Daniel Sparks Topeka Pharmaceutical Labs pulled up more information than she had time to sift through. *Sometimes the simplest things are the most productive. Remind me again why I listened to Steve and took a couple days of much needed R&R before I started down this path?*

The first result was from Google News, an Associated Press story from January 23 of this year. *Missing Boston bio scientist left behind pregnant fiancé; family says he left them in the dark. Thirty-year-old Daniel Sparks of Bunker Hill left work the afternoon of January 18th and was never heard from again... last seen on video at Pittsburgh International Airport...*

The notification from her phone jerked Jawnie back from the information superhighway and she looked up from the iPad. She had lost track of time and the number of online stories and blogs she had read regarding Daniel Sparks. But the five pages of handwritten notes to her right told her it was close to an hour. The alert let her know an individual approached the office door. A second later, before her phone connected to the live feed, Rockfish and Dan Decker strolled through the doorway.

"Steve, I didn't expect--"

"Hey, if Rosie calls, you didn't see us."

"That doesn't sound very good," Jawnie said and emphasized the concern in her tone. "And you know I'm not the best liar in the firm."

"Who's calling?" Lynn said as she emerged from the back-office area.

"My wife," Decker said. "Tell her you haven't seen Steve or me. I'll smooth things over when I get home." He grinned suspiciously.

"You got it," Lynn said. She turned to Jawnie, who had stood up and pushed her chair back from the table. "We taking a break?"

"Yup. I need to catch these two up. Take five."

"Aye aye Captain, I'll retreat to my desk and wait on the angry, yet inquisitive Mrs. Decker."

Jawnie walked out from the other side of the conference table and stepped into the bullpen area where the two men now stood.

"Catch us up?" Rockfish said. "That means you've found the goods?" He tilted his head on the last word and Jawnie smiled.

"Your timing couldn't be more perfect. The soup thickened a bit this morning."

Jawnie turned back and picked up her iPad and notes from the table before taking up her normal spot on the couch. Rockfish collapsed into his recliner and Decker found the other, but not before each poured themselves a drink from the bottle they carried in. Jawnie from two years ago would have worried about an alcohol-fueled audience, but now? *Now, I'm pretty sure he'll hang on to every word I say. Even provide value-added clarity to the entire situation.*

Jawnie held court from the couch, her vegan peach iced tea from Wawa on the coffee table. She detailed points uncovered since typing the initial Google search and her own thoughts.

"... and with that, I think we might have identified our poisoner. It's not a far leap as far as scenarios go. I'm lacking a motive. Although, to be honest, none of the articles mentioned anything missing from Spark's lab."

"That's standard operating procedure, Jawnie," Decker said. "Why start a panic? I'm sure the lab and the police are aware of exactly what went missing but chose not to publicize the information."

Everyone nodded in agreement and Rockfish leaned forward. He held a hand up.

"Back to your point, Jawnie. Maybe not the actual poisoner, based on when he went missing and when the action happened, but instead Great Value Boys' supplier," Rockfish said. "Maybe he was all *I'm on the side of these men, creating false flags to get people riled up*? You mentioned Sparks was engaged. Or maybe his wife-to-be was running up the wedding bills. You know, he made a quick buck and got out of debt quick. Motives are a plenty."

"Greed. The oldest one, Steve," Decker said. He shifted in his chair before continuing. "If the guy needed money and found a buyer for whatever he smuggled out of the lab... people do stranger shit for less. And based on all my years on the force, if the bad guys want something and don't want to pay for it, well, there was no good outcome for Mr. Sparks. My professional opinion? That beanie is the trophy. One of those sick fucks kept it and the other stuff around to get their rocks off."

"Well, my professional opinion tells me the same idiot was told to get rid of this shit and they dumped it in the back room," Rockfish said. "Out of sight, out of mind. Again, not the smartest or most active lot."

All three sat in silence. Jawnie realized the people they'd dealt with since the original Q-Rations caper weren't the dumb, somewhat harmless, good old boys Rockfish implied.

"I haven't even really dug into all the papers in that box," Jawnie said, breaking the silence. "There's a lot of handwritten stuff. I might be wrong, but they might have tested what Daniel brought out on farm animals first. I know, it makes little sense, but it seems they were working toward figuring out the right amount or dosage."

"Right dose? Dump a shit load in and watch the bodies fall. They wanted to make a point, right?" Rockfish said. He stood up and walked back to the bar to freshen his drink. "You want another, Dan?"

"I'm good for now."

"Suit yourself. But back to the dose thing. What if they didn't want people to die? Stick with me, here. Maybe get a small population sick and blame it on an African American smarty pants from the liberal northeast? Exactly the picture of an Antifa operative they wanted to draw. Something happened and Dan became the back-up plan," Rockfish said. He poured himself another two fingers. He maneuvered his way back to his recliner while Jawnie and Decker debated the scenario he had presented.

"I don't know, Steve," Jawnie said. "Why wait? The gap between Sparks going missing and Dan being grabbed is wide as hell. Why not snatch one of us the night they ripped us off? I mean, I fit the bill."

"Jawnie, I've spent time with these men," Decker said. "Although not by choice. We're going to burn out in a short time if we sit around and try to figure out how their minds work. Don't sweat the whys. Ours is not to wonder, ours is to get this information to the hands of those who can act."

"Yeah, crush insurrectionist skulls," Rockfish added and raised his glass.

"Again, someone who can act on the info, not necessarily do something that would make them TikTok famous. I didn't lose my contacts with the FBI's Joint Terrorism Task Force."

"Don't they handle terrorists?" Jawnie said.

"Both kinds. International and Domestic."

"Like, country and western," Rockfish said under this breath and laughed.

Decker and Jawnie looked over, and Rockfish's smile diminished. "A joke, sorry."

"*The Blues Brothers.* I'm old enough to get that one, Steve," Decker said with a brief shake of his head. "The JTTF are going to be very interested in all of this."

"Maybe they've got additional information on Sparks and what he may have removed from a lab? Two separate investigations not talking to each other? Wouldn't be the first time the Feds kept their information stove-piped. Has anyone even considered putting these two pieces together?" Jawnie said.

"I'll make a few calls. They should have answers by now."

"Well, what are you waiting for?" Rockfish said with a smile, "My office is your office."

* * * * * * * * *

On an afternoon five days after Decker pulled a weathered business card from his wallet and placed a well-received call, an aggravated Earnhardt Jr. stopped at Cool Rick's. His fingers shook and finally found the correct sequence of numbers on the keypad. He tried to will the gate to move faster as it slowly slid to the right. His eyes followed it and glimpsed the small duffle bag on the passenger seat. The bag contained his Plan B, and underneath? What remained of the cabin's incriminating evidence tying Archibald to the Penn Forest Patriots? *Maybe he'll have a decent idea about what to do with this crap. Probably not, but it's worth a try. Should've burned it in the fire pit out back, so it doesn't come back to haunt me like that damn backpack. I told fucking Amos to get rid of it, not to hide it. Fucking out of sight, out of mind shit.*

Earnhardt Jr. parked his wife's rusted-out Chevy Cobalt in the handicapped spot nearest the entrance, hung her placard from the rearview and fake limped to the front door. After letting himself inside, he made his way to the office area and dropped the small duffle bag on the ground. He pulled out the chair from behind the desk and waited.

Fucking Amos. If I had any idea he had kept that damn backpack, I would have chained him to it before tossing them both overboard. The backpack had his mind spinning since he learned someone hadn't properly disposed of it. Not to mention Clyde's admission that he had kept his notes on the test trials stuffed inside it. It made up the trifecta of missing stuff, once you added in the retired cop fall-guy, that had kept him awake the past five nights. His mind spun with scenarios of his twilight years spent in twenty-three hours a day of solitary, as opposed to going down in the history books as the leader of the glorious cause. Worry had replaced delusions of grandeur.

No way that guy just returned home and put his feet up. Shit storm's a comin'. And neither one of us is prepared. Me because of piss poor planning and Erwin because he can't see shit anymore over the haze of media stories and the flood of donations.

Earnhardt Jr. got up and paced in front of the windows overlooking Bedford Street. *Big surprise, the preacher man is late. Again.* He glanced across the parking lot, to the street, and then to the supermarket on the far side. The self-service storage facility was an unlikely meeting place. Especially after another long three-hour sermon by Archibald at the converted elementary school cafeteria. But Earnhardt Jr. knew he had every right to be more than slightly paranoid. Archibald didn't see, or wouldn't admit to seeing, the storm clouds forming on the horizon. Cool Rick's would be the last place anyone would check for either of them. Exactly why the Dodge Ram 1500 remained in his driveway. *Dumbass, if they're watching, they noticed you leave the house, no matter if you walked here. I'd kill for a thought that wasn't negative.* Earnhardt Jr. pounded the plexiglass window with his fist in frustration.

His phone vibrated, and he struggled with the holder clipped to his belt. The text was from Archibald. Not a surprise. Neither was the message. *change of plans my place when you can*

Earnhardt Jr. squeezed the sides of his phone with pressure and imagined the device exploding into a million pieces. *Damn that man. He says jump and expects me to text back, how high? No sense of urgency whatsoever.* Earnhardt Jr. didn't answer the text. Instead, he walked over and picked up the duffle bag. A minute later, he backed the Cobalt out of the parking spot and again waited for the gate to roll open. It would take him twenty minutes to reach the preacher's place on the outskirts of town.

He made it in a little over sixteen and continued past the house, eventually turning off the engine behind the old barn. Having the car out of sight was important with his current paranoia. A backdoor exit plan, always at the ready, would be a necessity from this point on. *Now if only Archibald would view shit the same way.* He picked up the bag from the front seat and walked around to the front of the house. One of Archibald's men met him at the door and led him to the large office down the hall, past the family room.

Archibald sat behind a large wooden desk. He had decorated the rest of the room with gold fixtures at every turn. Gold picture frames, desk accessories and furniture. The eggshell walls were the only other color. An unpleasant odor wafted across the room as Earnhardt Jr. pulled up a chair. He noticed the preacher had not changed from the sweat-soaked clothes he had sermonized in earlier. *Had something important kept him here, let alone meeting me at where we had agreed upon? Counting the donations? I wouldn't put it past him.* Archibald always had put the count before his so-called partner. A fact of which Earnhardt Jr. was finally sorely aware of.

"Sorry about that, Jesus. I didn't have the energy to get back up once I sat down. Us big boys don't have the piss and vinegar we had years ago," Archibald said. "But I don't have to tell you that. And Paul, you can leave us alone," He waved off his man and the double doors closed behind him.

Earnhardt Jr. caught another whiff across the desk. He wanted out of the enclosed space and thought of the small porch area behind Archibald, on the other side of a sliding glass door.

"Any chance we can talk out on the porch?"

"No, I don't have a lot of time for whatever you need. Out with it now. I've got a Zoom interview with the 700 Club coming up. Seems old Pat's not doing so hot. And they're open to other options." Archibald shuffled papers on his desk without looking up.

Earnhardt Jr. felt the blood pumping through his veins. His ears pounded, and the needle on the imaginary cuff approached redline status.

"I think we should have solid contingency plans in case, well not in case, but when--"

"You find those redneck kids yet? Need to make an example of each of 'em." Archibald's eyes still had yet to move on from those important desk items. Earnhardt Jr. gritted his teeth and stood up.

"No luck on that front. Either with my men or Sobotka's. If the family knows anything, they ain't saying." Earnhardt Jr. wasn't happy with his answer, or the progress made to date, but he wanted to be upfront. He paced back and forth behind his chair.

"It's damn obvious where they went. Don't take a brainiac to figure this out. Send a team of your so-called best to Maryland and retrieve. Lord knows what they've already spilled to who knows who. Why do I have to come up with all the solutions? I don't want to hear anything until you have them ready to answer for their sins. Next. Again. I'm short on time." Archibald picked up a pencil and started making notes on the legal pad to his right.

Earnhardt Jr.'s fingers curled into tight fists, and he stopped behind the chair he had sat in. The high back hid his diamond makers as the pressure increased.

"I've got men already on it. Wilbur doesn't know much about the ex-cop, anyway," Earnhardt Jr. said.

"Jesus, you'd be surprised at what even the dimmest bulbs pick up on, standing around and listening. What if he gets jammed up? Again. Rat to save his own ass. That is our primary concern right now. Your plan, once perfect, has turned to shit. Do I really have to sit here and repeat my previous order? I don't think we're in any position to let him remain in the catch and release program." Archibald's voice rose, and the pencil tip tore into the paper before snapping off.

"I'll admit, our plan ain't what it used to be because someone's lost sight of the prize and is focused too damn much on personal gains." Earnhardt brought a fist down on the top of the chair and shot a glance at the bag on the floor. With the preacher's eyes avoiding him, he bent slightly and placed the bag on the chair. He methodically moved to the right side of the chair.

"Elder. I'm here because of these costs. Everything I need my men to do, ain't free. And it's been a few weeks since your coffers spilled over to further the cause."

"Money? Is that what this entire thing is about? Hands out again, huh? Expect me to scoop a bunch of cash out of the new church fund? We're breaking ground on the new facility in two weeks. It's going to be a monumental event for Grindsville..."

Earnhardt Jr. didn't believe what he was hearing. He also felt his face flush. The color and emotion raced to see who'd get to the finish line first.

"... and I'm going to need to see tangible results before I can give you an advance..."

The pounding in Earnhardt's head increased. His fists clenched tighter and dropped to his side. They tapped against the sides of his legs. A second later, the phone in his pocket vibrated. He reached for it while Archibald continued to ramble. He glanced down at the text.

Feds on scene, 2 execute search warrants not sure where, but make yourself scarce

Good old Sobotka. At least one of his men was at attention and on the ball. Earnhardt Jr. knew there wasn't any time left.

"... the amount of cash I've provided for weapons alone, weapons that you and your men have failed to even pull the trigger once on, is not my best ROI--"

Earnhardt's hand was in the duffle bag before he knew it. The Taurus handgun felt like an extension of his arm, and the suppressor did its job. The shots, one in the head and one in the heart, threw the preacher back against the chair and then forward, face first, on the desk. *Don't need you or your money anymore, preacher man.*

"I really should thank you for the silencers, as I don't think I ever really did," Earnhardt Jr. said. The gun slipped back into the bag, and he pulled out a half-empty water bottle. He removed the cloth that it was wrapped in and placed it on the desk. He used the same cloth to unscrew the lid and left both.

One last shot at letting that ex-cop take the fall. At the very least, the attempted frame up will buy me time.

Earnhardt Jr. wiped down the chair with the cloth and grabbed his bag. He used the cloth again to open and close the sliding glass door behind him before dropping it into his pocket. He then made his way around the barn to where he parked the Cobalt. The car lunged forward, and he started a voice text group message to Amos, Clyde and Sobotka.

It's done. See you next Tuesday.

He dropped the phone into the center console and pressed harder on the gas. The small tires battled to gain traction on the dirt road, but he was in the clear. He hoped.

Whew. Started the first try. You watch too many movies. Now keep moving. Are those sirens? Can't be this quick. Not that I can risk it. For a second, Earnhardt Jr. questioned everything around him, before slowing the car to handle a sharp right turn. He followed the dirt road across the open field and towards the woods. The paths leading deep into the Penn Forest would test the Cobalt, but it was the last time he'd need to call upon it to perform.

CHAPTER TWELVE

Stay with CNN for further coverage of the execution of the Federal search and arrest warrants in Grindsville, Pennsylvania, later in the hour with our correspondent in the field, Marianela Moreno...

Rockfish picked up the remote and muted the incoming run of commercials.

"Two days of this dominating the news cycle and not a mention of the backstory and us saving Dan's bacon," Raffi said.

"Newsflash, Liam Neeson. Meal Team Six is the actual story," Decker said. "Nipping a second insurrection in the bud before the folks who don't know better are further exploited."

Rockfish glanced over at Decker and then to Raffi. The two had played verbal tennis most of the late morning while he made the occasional out-of-bounds call. *I'm rethinking my idea of asking them over to watch the festivities. I had hoped for a live shot of some Branch Davidian shit. Is it too much to ask for a 4K shot of the Great Value Boys running out of that cabin, playing human torch? Would have been a nice ending. Roll credits.*

The three men sat around the office conference table. Coffee cups, cell phones and empty breakfast wrappers littered the table. Rockfish had the news projected on the large pull-down screen Jawnie used for presentations. The initial good vibes which had filled the trio when Decker's sources provided a heads up of the impending raids had soon soured. Rockfish's current mood teetered on the edge of anger as the first reports trickled in. The leadership of the Great Value Boys had scattered to the wind. With only second in command, Clyde Hayseed apprehended and taken into custody.

Rockfish was happy the Feds had acted as quickly as they did, based on the information his team provided. But knowing Earnhardt Jr. and the thin man from the Steel Museum had slipped through the dragnet was disheartening. He assumed they'd retreated deep into the far reaches of a forest playing *Naked and Afraid: On the Run,* for the foreseeable future.

"Dan, you hear anything else about that other call you got?" Rockfish said.

"Not a word."

"Alibi checked out, though," Rockfish said, already knowing the answer.

"Rock-fucking-solid. Piss poor attempt to throw off the scent as they ran for the hills." The Task Force had reached out to Decker a second time, in as many days, and the voice on the phone wasn't as cheerful as the first. The call came not long after someone discovered Archibald's body but had not yet reported it to the press. "All I know is the prints are a match, and the DNA is out for analysis."

"If it's one of yours from the loft in the cabin..." Raffi said.

"Let's not pretend it's not," Rockfish said with a quick shake of his head. "Red herring. At least they're keeping you in the loop and not reading you your Miranda Rights."

Raffi smirked. "Steve, let's try to be serious here. They tried to set up your friend and my former employee for murder. No telling what their next move will be. With only Clyde in custody and not talking--"

"Yet," Rockfish said. It wasn't the only correction to Raffi he wanted to make but made a mental note to pull him aside later.

"Yeah, only a matter of time," Decker said with a nod before he drained the rest of his coffee. "Same old story with this type. A brave front, but a few days eating green bologna and fending off the horny bunkee, tend to break 'em down real fast. And when he does, Earnhardt Jr. and Amos won't have anywhere to hide."

"I think we're missing the point here, fellas," Raffi said. He stood up and moved closer to the head of the table. "I mean, we're all gathered here to watch the demise of these fucks and feel good about the part we played in it." He raised his coffee mug.

"He's right," Rockfish said.

"And that's not very often," Decker said with a laugh. "But I digress. With a few on the run, it's not the ending we wanted, but..."

"Give 'em time," Rockfish said and raised his own cup. "He'll break and they'll track 'em down. You said it."

"If that's the vibe, then we sure as shit should celebrate," Raffi said. "And, Steve, I didn't want to bring this up earlier, but these aren't Irish coffees. It reflects negatively and my Google review of this establishment will attest to such."

Rockfish let out an audible chuckle and stood up. "I'll grab a bottle then. You don't have to twist my arm." He turned towards the bar behind him, back in the office's bullpen area, but the sudden flashes of light off to his right caught his attention. He shifted his stance, picked up the remote and unmuted the broadcast.

We go live to Marianela Moreno, live at Grindsville City Hall, where a crowd of people have gathered to protest the actions taken the past two days by Federal Law Enforcement.

That's right Trisha, the crowd continues to grow, and tensions rise as the Federal Task Force, now including the United States Marshals continue to search for the two fugitives and a disgraced Grindsville former police officer reported to be persons of interest in the recent mass poisoning and shooting that...

Rockfish muted the sound for a second time.

"Natives are getting restless," Raffi said. He looked back to toward the bar and then back to Rockfish, realizing the news had distracted the man from his task.

"Yeah, I'm sure Earnhardt Jr. is sending out instructions from deep within whatever bunker he's hiding in," Rockfish said and turned back toward the table. "The puppeteer has no plans of stopping. He wanted violence all along and won't stop now."

"Pulling strings from afar or not, the Feds better not let it turn into mass riots," Decker added.

Rockfish pursed his lips and gave a slight nod. *The country's been a cunt hair close to a lit powder keg since before the pandemic. Christ, can I even remember a time when half the country was remotely civil to the other half? Late '80s or early '90s, at a minimum. Had to be.* He turned away from the screen and noticed an empty chair. Raffi had moved from the conference table to the couch and had put it upon himself to add the last building block to his coffee.

"Let's hope not, Dan. Your associates had to have learned from past experiences. Nip that violence in the bud."

"We hope. But with Sobotka also on the Fed's radar, don't expect the other Grindsville officers to be fully engaged. Most are probably wondering what the Government has on them and how long until they can expect a knock on the door."

Both men walked back to where Raffi had made himself comfortable. Rockfish had his fill of doom and gloom reporting for the day.

"Hey Steve, how much time do I have before you kick me out?" Raffi said.

At least he remembered. That's a good thing. He didn't think Raffi and Lynn would ever make amends. For the sanity of his employee, it was best Raffi was only around when duty called, or circumstances prevented either from leaving.

"Jawnie should pick her up and be back here after lunch. She's out with Cheyenne and Wilbur, helping them find a temporary place of their own. At least until the JTTF finishes with their debriefs. Then they're on their own."

"Wore out their welcome with you already?" Raffi said with a grin.

"Mack."

"Shut up. Who the hell can't get along with your old man?" Dan moved to the recliner opposite Rockfish and laughed aloud.

"Yeah, turns out Cheyenne is a little demanding princess and Wilbur kinda takes it. Who would have thought?"

"Sounds plausible, Steve. Need I remind you?"

"Huh? What are you talking about, Raffi?"

"Calvary United's Covenant of King Solomon."

Rockfish got the joke but didn't give Raffi the satisfaction of an audible laugh. *Can't let him get too full of himself.*

"She was part of the problem. The other half is that with each year older, my old man loses more and more of that filter that keeps you from saying dumb shit. Tensions were reaching Chernobyl levels. Eventually, I think when the Task Force is done with them, they'll do something boneheaded like move back to Grindsville."

"Agreed. It's all either of them know," Decker said. "Shit, I'd bet on it. Let's hope they're thinking straight and wait until a few more of the Great Value Boys are behind bars. Neither one of those kids seems like the kind to accept any type of witness protection."

All agreed, and Rockfish reached for the remote again. He turned the channel to the replay of last evening's Orioles and Rays game. He already knew the outcome, but the announcers would serve as background noise while the three men continued to cover a myriad of topics. Each moving farther from the happenings in Grindsville than the previous. *Old times, and good ones, might have finally returned.*

An hour later, Raffi excused himself for a reason Rockfish couldn't remember until he heard the glass door swing shut. *Crisis averted. No worries of him saying anything or Lynn pulling out the bear spray.* He and Decker continued with their conversation.

"... you gotta be able to spin this experience into a post-retirement gig. Make serious bank with a security company, with all your experience and exposure."

"I'm reaching out, updating LinkedIn and keeping my fingers in the..."

The buzzing in his pocket caused Rockfish to miss the last few words from Decker. He reached in and pulled out his phone. Jawnie's text comprised one word.

Recognize?

A picture came through a second later and Rockfish inhaled deeply.

"Everything kosher?"

He turned the screen so Decker could see.

"That's the fat fuck from the cabin."

* * * * * * * * * *

Rockfish and Decker scaled the last wooden waist-high fence, this one separating the neighbor's backyard from his own. They had left Lana in the HOA's clubhouse parking lot. Then made their way through a serpentine of backyards, waving at the occasional curious neighbor, until Rockfish's back deck finally came into view. Lynn stood at the top of the stairs and audibly laughed as the two men struggled to overcome the last obstacle.

Decker had come up to arrive through the back, instead of making a scene out front, in case the house remained under surveillance by the time they arrived. Rockfish wanted to come in via the inlet to his dock, but time was of the essence, and he'd never find someone to loan him a skiff on such short notice.

"Not funny, Lynn. I'd like to see you hurdle half a dozen of these damn things."

"Damn, Steve, that was quick," Lynn said and smiled at Decker. "The gang's inside."

Rockfish saw through the sliding glass door Jawnie, Cheyenne and Wilbur sat around the kitchen's small dinette.

"Bad guys?" Decker said.

"They parked the truck out on Jarvis Court, facing the house."

Jarvis ran perpendicular to Rockfish's street, albeit the intersection was three houses down.

"Not bad," Decker said. "Tubby might have learned a few things recently. If I had to scope out this house, it's exactly where I would set up. Easy exit, if spotted."

"Okay, last question," Rockfish said. "Where's Dad?"

"Jawnie sent him away," Lynn said and reached for the slider's handle. "She had one of his friends come pick him up. That was her idea. He didn't drive his truck out of the garage and have those idiots follow him. What if they had a harebrained scheme thinking Mack was smuggling Cheyenne and Wilbur out of the house under a tarp?"

Rockfish and Decker glanced at each other and gave slight nods. *Couldn't have thought of a better plan myself.* They followed Lynn through the doorway into the kitchen. Three sets of eyes moved from the table and Decker reached behind to slide the door shut.

"It's about time. I thought you said we'd be safe here," Cheyenne said, arms folded across her chest, disgust on her face. "They've been following us around all day."

"Lynn, can you escort our guests downstairs?" Rockfish said. He ignored Cheyenne's whining, and this normally would be the point in the conversation where he would appeal to the man. In this case, Wilbur, to keep the obnoxious other half in check. Except the man at the table had a thousand-yard stare. *Dreaming of slipping away to score? Gotta keep the kid under someone's thumb and clean if he's to be believable in a future courtroom.* "Play air hockey or watch Honey Boo Boo. I don't give a shit. Keep them out of sight until I figure out what's going on."

Lynn nodded and moved toward the basement door. Wilbur was quick to push back his chair and was on her heels. Cheyenne hadn't moved, elbows now resting firmly on the table.

"I'm going out there to confront them with you," Cheyenne said. Her face grew red, and her fists were tight. "I ain't afraid."

"I'm not headed anywhere, and no one mentioned being scared," Decker said as he walked past the dinette towards the front window. "Taking a peek, Steve."

"My house, my rules," Rockfish said. "You don't have to listen, but then you and milquetoast can march right out the front door and the rest of us can finally wash our hands of this."

Cheyenne pursed her lips and slowly pushed her chair away from the table. She walked over to the basement door, shaking her head, where Lynn patiently waited. Wilbur had already headed down the stairs and Rockfish pictured him on the couch, Xbox controller in hand. Lynn was the last down the stairs and shut the door.

Rockfish pulled out a chair, and a second later, Decker walked back in from the living room.

"Black F-150 has a direct sightline. Nice looking truck," Decker said.

"Okay, someone's continuing to finance this expedition, with the golden goose dead. But that's a question for later," Rockfish said. He turned to his partner. "Short and sweet, how'd you come across the tail?"

"Lynn spotted it, err them," Jawnie said and recounted the events of the late morning.

She had arrived at a client's office to drop off a final case summary and expense report when a panicked Lynn called. The three of them had walked out of a second leasing office and she noticed the same black pickup truck parked on the opposite side of the street.

"She had noticed it earlier too but said nothing to frighten Cheyenne or Wilbur. When she let me know, I cut my meeting short and met them at the next apartment complex. I set up where I could get a few shots of the truck and its occupants with my Nikon, sent them to you and here we are," Jawnie said. She showed Rockfish the pictures she had transferred to her phone. "The truck then followed Lynn back here. You recognized the large one, but how about the passenger?"

"I don't," Rockfish said.

"Me neither," Decker added. "But that answer will come in time. We need to turn the tables on 'em before we can start being the ones asking questions."

"Everyone else has had a peek, let me check 'em out," Rockfish said and stood up.

Jawnie and Decker followed, and the three gathered in front of the living room's windows. The blinds were closed, but Rockfish stuck his fingers through the blades and leaned in.

"Still there."

"I could've told you that," Decker said. "And did."

"I've got an idea," Jawnie said. "Dan, you said we need to flip the script before we can start demanding answers. Let's make them aware of a little counter surveillance. I see you, type of deal."

Rockfish pulled his fingers back, looked over at his partner, and raised his eyebrows.

"I like it. But instead of one of us circling up behind them and risking some sort of confrontation that we don't know how they'll react to; I have a different tack. Any chance, Dan, you can call in a favor and have a patrol car roust 'em?"

"I can make the call. Heck, I probably have a marker or two to cash in, but whether it gets done is another story. Understaffed and not to mention the crap shoot of who's on duty. And if a patrol car did light them up, what's stopping them from returning in an hour or two and setting up shop again?"

"Can't hurt to try," Rockfish said. "And who cares if they come back? I plan to be on their ass as soon as your man sends them on their merry way." He hoped each followed his plan. "I'll go back out the way I came, retrieve the car and set up further down the road."

"I gotcha," Dan said. "Have the patrol car run them off and fall in line to see where they go. Puts the element of surprise back on our side."

Jawnie's eyes went wide, and she nodded in agreement. Rockfish grabbed his keys and headed for the back door while Decker pulled out his phone.

"Hey Sergeant Baker, Dan Decker here. Long time no see..."

Twenty-five minutes later, Lana crept down Philip Court. She came to a stop where Rockfish had a diagonal view, one street over, through a backyard to the black truck. He waited and hoped Decker could find anyone on duty who he hadn't pissed off on his way out the door. Rockfish pressed the lenses of the small handheld tactical binoculars against the tinted window. From this vantage point, he made out the two men. *Trevor is driving, I see. The passenger resembles a young Tom Petty.*

What he hadn't seen was the patrol car as it rolled up behind the truck until the red and blue lights reflected off the aluminum siding of a house. From his angle, he didn't see where the cruiser had stopped and held his breath until the officer came into view. He followed with the binoculars as the cop moved slow and methodical. The officer touched the rear bumper and surveyed the contents of the truck's bed before moving on. Rockfish shut off the radio and put down his window. He risked being seen but hoped at even this distance to catch a few words of the conversation. *My kingdom for one of those parabolic microphones like they used to sell in the back of comic books.* He added that to a mental list of tech-toys for Jawnie to research. *Maybe Dan can make a second call and get a copy of the traffic stop report? Find out exactly what line of bull they're slinging.*

Rockfish watched as the patrolman accepted the driver's paperwork, thrust out the drivers-side window. He spoke to the occupants of the truck for a solid five minutes before walking back to his car. The minutes felt like hours until Rockfish heard a door shut and the cop re-emerge at the rear of the truck. This time, he stopped at the wheel well and leaned over. *Something caught his attention.*

He watched the cop hand back the documents through the window. The back and forth continued for a few more minutes before the patrolman ripped what Rockfish presumed was a ticket from a pad. Five stubby fingers reached through the open window and snatched the citation. The driver's hands grew animated and from where Rockfish sat, the patrolman remained calm. A few minutes later, the cop turned and retreated toward his car while Trevor's arms flailed. Then the flashing lights stopped, and the truck pulled away with the patrol car on its rear bumper.

Rockfish placed the binoculars down on the passenger seat and slipped the car into drive. The truck's occupants, too focused on the patrolman on their bumper, would not notice the very familiar Dodge Challenger a few cars back. He thought about texting Jawnie that he was on the move, but knew she'd be watching his every move with the Find My iPhone app. It wouldn't be long before she and Decker in the Subaru fell in line as the caboose.

Ah, you Great Value pieces of shit, how the tables have turned. The element of surprise was back with the good guys. Take care of you two and then we can sit back and finally have that celebratory drink. Rockfish turned to the passenger seat and smiled. *What say you, Mr. Murphy?*

* * * * * * * * *

Rockfish pulled Lana's wheel slightly to the left and drifted over the center line. His head leaned out the window and tried to gaze past two SUVs and the patrol car. The pickup had turned on its left blinker, a good hundred yards prior, but continued straight down the road. He waited for a brake light to hint of a direction. *Any day now, it's not like you don't have a cop behind you that is more than willing to write a second ticket. Maybe that's why the blinker is on with PLENTY of notice.* The slow speed chase had entered its twentieth minute and the trio of autos had entered familiar territory. Jamocha Jubblies passed by on the left, half-a-mile back. Another Rockfish investigative landmark would come up soon if they remained southbound on Braddock Road.

Allison's Adult Superstore. Christ, I haven't been past it in a good solid year. But he didn't expect to be greeted with the familiar large pink neon sign atop the roof. Building ownership had changed hands twice as the real estate market slowed, but as far as he knew, the storefront remained vacant. Linthicum Heights residents had found other online avenues to buy their much-needed fleshlights, personal massagers, and other party favors.

Rockfish's eyes moved from the truck's blinker back to the upcoming building. He made out an unfamiliar large white sign on the front facade. No sooner had his eyes strained to make out the lettering from an acute angle, the pickup turned left into one of the few spots available in the building's front. He knew from experience, most of the building's parking spots were in the rear. *Rimshot.*

Lana followed past the building, behind the patrol car, so as not to raise any suspicions. But the sign, finally within eyesight, raised more questions. Large red letters on a white background spelled out *MG's Army/Navy Surplus Outlet. Hmm, the new owners had changed focus from dildos and not-so-novelty butt plugs to military surplus items.* Rockfish kept Lana on Braddock for another block before putting on his own blinker. He made a quick right into BMK Dojo and parked facing the street. Rockfish grabbed the binoculars off the passenger seat and put the window down. The store front was to his left at ten o'clock. He turned the focus knob until the cab of the pickup came in clear. *Empty. Not a stretch to assume they've gone inside.* He laid the binoculars on his lap and caught sight of the patrol car headed back in the opposite direction. The drivers-side window was down, and the man acknowledged Rockfish with a two-finger salute and kept going.

Nice job, Dan. This guy knew the assignment. Now for the waiting game. What's first? Jawnie and Dan get here ready to storm the castle or Heckle and Jeckle walk out with bags filled from the big J6th Everything Must Go Sale! If they take off again, I've got no buffer between them and me. Stay a couple of car lengths back, Chief, this ain't your first time--

A rapping sound on Lana's roof cut off the daydream and Rockfish swung his head out the open window. Decker stood alongside the door; his right arm draped across the roof.

"Scared me for a sec," Rockfish said. "They parked over there." He pointed at the military surplus store.

"Ah, resupplying on the Insurrectionist Underground Railroad."

"I gotta remember that one." Rockfish laughed aloud.

"Seriously, though, Steve, we got here as fast as possible. Had a slight problem getting out the door." Decker threw a thumb over his left shoulder.

Rockfish leaned further out. Jawnie and Cheyenne stood ten-feet back. Jawnie's facial expression screamed *Don't shoot the messenger.* She shrugged and tilted her head at Cheyenne for emphasis.

"What the?"

"It was the only way. If we continued to fight her, we would have never gotten here and who the hell knows what she might have done. Better to keep an eye on her." Decker smirked and Rockfish knew his friend did what he could with what he had.

"Yeah, I'm not afraid of Trevor and Scotty," Cheyenne said. She moved closer to the car, arms flailing as if she was walking across the stage at Maury Povich, easily spotted from many storefronts. "If they don't have the others to back 'em up, they ain't shit."

"Now we've got both names," Rockfish said. "I needed that information a couple of hours ago. But I really wish you would have stayed back with Wilbur. I'm assuming he's not hiding in the back of the Subaru?"

Jawnie frowned and Rockfish knew it was a topic best dropped or risk Cheyenne going full Maury meltdown.

"What's the plan, Rockfish?" Cheyenne said. She had hip-checked Decker away from the car door and stared down through the open window. "We gonna sit here and do a whole lot of nothing?"

"Well, something like that. Your schoolmates walked into the surplus store across the street and haven't come out. Yet. We can either wait 'em out or flush 'em out. I'm waiting on the idea fairy to tell me which."

"Flush 'em, giant fucking turds." Cheyenne hawked up a surprisingly large loogie and spit across an open parking space.

This girl's growing on me. No fairy wings sprouting out of her back, but I'll take the enthusiasm. Rockfish glanced from side-to-side and pointed back towards where Jawnie had parked. "Okay, if we're going to congregate, let's not do it in the open. And one of us needs to watch that front door."

Rockfish opened the car door and stepped out. He held the door open and the binoculars out to Cheyenne.

"Make yourself less noticeable and holler if you see Frick and Frack. And for the love of God, touch nothing."

"But..."

"No buts. You want to play; you listen to the ref." Rockfish didn't wait for a response and instead shut the door. He motioned for the other two to huddle up. *Not you Mr. Murphy. You stay over there.*

Rockfish leaned on the trunk of Jawnie's car while Decker and she stared over his shoulders at Cheyenne and further on to the storefront.

"Like I told Cher back there--"

"Cheyenne," Jawnie said softly. She chuckled when Rockfish closed his eyes for a second and shook his head.

"Doesn't matter. She was right. We sit and wait or force the issue. What says our resident expert?"

"A lot of variables at play here," Decker said. Rockfish watched him shift his weight from one foot to the other. "You said it best. We've got surprise on our side. Let's shake a tree. Take the fight to them or any other rah rah motivational poster you want to quote. It's the middle of the day. What's the worst that can happen?"

"Yeah, show these two they aren't moving around here all stealth like," Rockfish said. "We see you. Now get the fuck out. Maybe leave one of your old business cards on the counter for emphasis?"

"We send these two packing with their tails between their legs, and go home, crack open a cold one. Then tune back into the game of cat and mouse between the Feds and Earnhardt Jr."

"I'm all about being a spectator," Rockfish said. "Have been for quite a while now." He held out his fist and Decker bumped it.

"I hate to break up the bromance," Jawnie said and stepped closer to the two men. "And I don't have the experience you two have, but I don't see this ending with them turning tail. All I can picture is the bank job gone wrong scene in *Heat*. And neither one of you has body armor."

"Kid's got a point, Steve. Maybe we were a slight bit ahead of ourselves?" Decker kicked at loose gravel on the ground. "Loose cannons and such."

All agreed on the passive approach. Jawnie would throw on a pair of glasses and the ball cap from her backseat. She'd walk into the store, check out the lay of the land, and maybe do a little eavesdropping if the scenario permitted.

"Better to have worthwhile intel on our side if we end up crashing the party," Rockfish said.

"Agreed, Steve. I don't expect them to be out on the store floor, shopping, but what if they are and get spooked? They bolt. We're going to have to regroup, and play catch up."

"Hold up, a sec," Jawnie said. "I got just the thing." She popped the trunk with her key fob, causing Rockfish to leap from the back of her car. Jawnie reached in and unzipped her bag of goodies. She then softly shut the trunk and handed Rockfish what he mistook for a USB drive. "If they leave for good, then we'll know it. Follow or pass along the information. Totally up to you. Those two might even lead the Feds to where the others are hiding."

"When did we get these?" Rockfish said, inspecting the small device in his hand. The black piece of plastic was no larger than a Bic lighter but had a thin magnetic strip down one side. "Our old ones were clunky."

"Yup, new, smaller and with a stronger GPS signal," Jawnie said, taking the device back from Rockfish. "I can slip it in one of the truck's stake pocket holes, or if the bed has a ton of junk in it, bury it underneath something."

Damn, I love having a young, tech savvy partner. Rockfish turned to Decker and smiled. "We don't have the big brother police budget, but we make do. Now Jawnie, don't spend a lot of time checking for the perfect spot, especially since that place has giant plate-glass windows in the front. Drop it in and move on."

"Aye Aye Captain."

"We need serious-Jawnie," Decker said.

"He's right. Seems simple, but you know how quickly things can go south," Rockfish said. His voice was stern, his demeanor straight-faced. "I need you to bolt outta there if anything smells fishy. Phone in hand, ready to hit the call button. My shit rings, I'm running in. Matter of fact, I'll follow you over and stand outside the liquor store..."

"Home away from home." Jawnie couldn't resist.

"... hopefully out of the way of any cameras the surplus store might have out front," Rockfish said, staring daggers at his partner.

Jawnie didn't wait for Rockfish to follow. She headed off between parked cars towards the street, eventually the pickup and the surplus store's front door.

Play it safe, kid. Last thing I need is you taking any kind of risk. I've got a feeling no one's gonna be wrapping this one up in a nice bow today.

Rockfish glanced in Decker's direction before he took off. "Keep an eye on that," he said, pointing toward where Cheyenne sat. "You brought her. You watch her."

Rockfish didn't wait for an answer. He turned and jogged across the parking lot.

* * * * * * * * *

Rockfish reached the median as Jawnie moved with a dash of stealth along the passenger side of the pickup truck. He looked right and noticed heavy westbound traffic headed his way. A small convoy of box trucks barreled along and soon obstructed his view. By the time the last lift gate passed, Jawnie had vanished from sight. *Through the door and into the mouth of the beast. I need to get my ass in gear.*

He stepped off the cement and onto the asphalt, his right palm up and facing oncoming traffic as if he were a poorly dressed traffic cop. Brakes squealed and horns blared. *So much for the element of surprise.* Rockfish hustled across the two lanes and cut diagonally towards the front of the liquor store. He glanced over his shoulder and attempted to see through the surplus store's front windows. The only image he caught in the reflective glass was Decker waving his arms wildly in what appeared to be an animated conversation with Cheyenne. *I hope things go smoother on this side of the road. Seems like he's got his hands full.*

Rockfish took up his sentry position under the window advertisement for Popov's new dragon fruit infused jalapeño vodka. He winced. The liquor store was a good half an hour from the office, but based on the sale items listed behind him, it might as well have been another country. *Whiskey on the rocks people, what's wrong with you?*

Two minutes into guard duty, Mr. Murphy made his much expected appearance. He came in hard and well above the speed limit. Rockfish tasted a flush of copper in his mouth as the gang's not-so well thought out plan turned on its side.

The screech of rubber on asphalt had diverted his attention from reading the rest of the liquor store's sale signs. Rockfish's neck snapped back to the front of the surplus store.

A familiar orange Ford Taurus had slammed on its brakes, fishtailed into the parking lot, and came to a sudden stop alongside the pickup. *Raffi. Handicapped spot. Go Figure.* Rockfish watched as Raffi slammed the drivers-side door and power walked toward the entrance. Rockfish heard his friend's voice and a few choice curse words before the door closed behind Raffi.

Oh Fuck.

* * * * * * * * * *

A few minutes prior to the impending Raffi bomb, Jawnie tugged at the bill of her cap. A bell above her head sounded as she stepped in, and the door closed. She lifted her head and surveyed the inside of the store. The main entrance aisle was narrow and crowded with merchandise. To her right, shelves stacked high with mess kits, small shovels, and boots. She would need to stand on her tiptoes to see over to the next aisle. A sea of camouflage filled round clothing racks, crowded the store's left side. *A hoarder's paradise, not to mention a fire hazard. Dang, that would have been an excellent cover. Hi, I'm with the Anne Arundel County Fire Marshal's office. Stopped by for a mandatory inspection of the premises...*

Jawnie had worked her way towards the middle of the store when an older man approached from between the clothing racks. She initially didn't see him and jerked away when his hand settled on her shoulder.

"Can I help you, Miss?"

She looked down at the old man, the only thing not painted various shades of olive green within the four walls. He dressed in pants cinched a couple of inches below his man boobs and only the top half of his T-shirt's Ravens logo was visible above the belt line. She wouldn't ask about the Vietnam-era helmet perched atop his white hair. Nor would she allow his hand to throw her. Jawnie knew better than to deviate from her rehearsed story.

"I need a couple of durable ammo boxes? All weather like. I want to use them to hide geocaches out at Weichmann's Farm." Technically, it wasn't a lie. She and Pilar had picked up on the hide and seek hobby earlier in the spring. "I'm thinking of--"

They both turned at the sound of the bell and the rapid-fire verbal diarrhea that followed.

"... Moreland, you magnificent bastard. A fucking little bird told me you were expanding this shit hole. Thinking of moving into the prepper grocery lane. First Jim Baker and now you. But lemme tell ya, I can stock those shelves of yours on the cheap..."

Raffi locked eyes with Jawnie and his voice trailed off. She gave the shortest, hardest implied head shake of her life. *He's back on his Q-Ration shit. Of all the days to play door-to-door salesperson.*

"You two know each other?" Moreland said.

"Moreland Godsped, proprietor of MG's Army/Navy Surplus Outlet. Meet a friend of mine, Jawnie McGee."

She forced a smile in Moreland's direction, but again, the sound of the bell above the door caused her head to swivel. Rockfish had bulled his way into the China shop.

"... and that's Steve Rockfish. Card-carrying member of the Hollywood elite. But don't hold that liberalism against him. But I digress. What brings you two to Moreland's fine establishment? Need gear for an overnight stakeout or a quick trip down memory lane? I can't be the only one who misses Allison's?"

Jawnie stepped back into a rack of rain ponchos and watched as Rockfish approached from behind. He smiled and draped an arm across Raffi's shoulder. They stood in the middle of the aisle, Raffi pressed tight against a shelf of silver mess kits.

"We're definitely not here to sell expired MREs as a patriot protein bar, if that's what you're asking. I wouldn't think of honing in on your grift. But, yeah, we're checking out a couple of things."

If looks could kill. I knew Steve wouldn't be able to hold back. She turned and saw the confusion on Moreland's face. *Why hasn't he called for those two goons that are hiding?* Jawnie's eyes darted across the layout of the store. *Maybe he's not put one and one together? If they're anywhere, a back office is the only place out of sight.* She glanced back at the show in the aisle.

"... wait, if you and Jawnie are here, something must be up," Raffi said. His eyes moved from the partners to Moreland and back again. "I'm wondering if it's better I come back when you're not busy, Morey." Raffi tried to pull away from Rockfish, but the arm across his shoulders held tight.

He's a little late to the party, but finally gets the situation. But three on two benefits us, albeit if Morey and his helmet stay out of the fray.

The expected commotion from the area behind the register finally came and Jawnie's head turned around. A door hung open behind the counter and she spotted them. Trevor and Scotty stood off to the side, having knocked over the 5-Hour ENERGY and Moose jerky displays next to the checkout aisle. Neither cleaned up the mess and began their way down the center aisle with a purpose.

"Don't even think about moving!" Rockfish said. He pulled Raffi in tighter and assumed a defensive stance.

Jawnie's mind raced on how to help. Or hide. There wasn't much to the potential squared circle, with the aisle being narrow. She noticed Morey hadn't moved an inch. *Should I step closer to help? Exactly how? I do not know but put up a brave front. You are part of this team.*

Jawnie stepped out from in-between the ponchos and moved to a spot a few feet behind Rockfish and Raffi. The gruesome twosome did not heed Rockfish's warning and picked up speed. A second later, Morey was thrown to the side and a small table of hand crank radios collapsed. *So much for partners in crime.* Only three things stood between the Great Value Boys and the door. *Maybe two and a half.* Jawnie closed her eyes and braced for impact while the others prepared for fisticuffs. Truth be told, she squinted out of one eye, not wanting to be surprised by a rogue punch that either Raffi or Rockfish ducked.

Trevor, the obese guard from the cabin, moved to the front and Scotty fell in line behind as the aisle narrowed. Jawnie thought neither one seemed to itch for a fight but was more concerned about approaching ramming speed. *The door. They're making a mad dash for the truck!* She turned to see if the door had an accessible locking latch when Raffi plowed into the back of her legs. Jawnie went down hard and knew the human bowling ball had made contact. The boots that shuffled past her open eyes told her the two men were not slowing down.

Raffi rolled off her legs, and Jawnie crawled toward the front of the store. She watched the pickup doors slam shut. The sound of rubber desperately searching for traction filled the air as she cracked open the door. Jawnie watched the truck perform a tight, reverse J-turn before the tailgate slammed into the back of Raffi's Taurus. Shouts from the outside caught her attention as the truck's engine screamed in desperation to pry apart the locked bumpers. Two individuals froggered across the street, hands waving.

Cheyenne and Dan! She was in full sprint and him, two strides behind. They reached the parking lot as the bumpers broke their kiss and the pickup lurched forward. The front left fender of the truck caught Cheyenne's hip and down she went. Trevor didn't stop to exchange insurance information. Dan knelt by her side when Jawnie, now back on her feet, reached the edge of the parking lot. The black pickup, long gone and out of sight, left Cheyenne's screams of pain behind.

"What the fuck happened in there?" Decker said. "Don't move, Cheyenne. We'll get help here."

"We've got to move her away from the shoulder, Dan." Jawnie's eyes were wide and pleading.

"Can't risk moving her, call 9-1-1 for Christ's sake. Where the fuck are the other two dolts?"

As if on cue, Rockfish and Raffi emerged from Morey's as she stepped away to call.

"Keep that door open. I don't want that midget to lock us out. I got questions," Rockfish said, and Raffi slid a foot back in the doorway.

A second later, Jawnie hung up and moved back to where Rockfish and Decker now knelt.

"Ambulance is on the way," Jawnie said. "Maybe you should give her a little breathing room?"

"Okay, Nurse Ratched. You handle the patient," Rockfish said. "Raffi, help over here. Do whatever Jawnie tells you to. Dan and I need to go inside and talk to helmet head."

"What about those two clowns?" Raffi said.

"What are you going to do, run after them?"

"They fucked up my car!" Raffi ran his fingers through his hair and kicked at the ground.

"Let 'em go. We'll know soon enough where they're headed," Rockfish said. "Call the talking lizard from television on your own time. Get over here and do what she says. Now!"

Rockfish moved to the door and traded places with Raffi.

"Come on, Dan, let's get answers or test out the durability of this guy's helmet. Wait till you see it. Is it up to Army regulations? Let's go, before the cops show up and ruin our fun."

The door shut behind them and the two made their way toward the now closed office door behind the checkout counter. Morey had retreated to his office and most likely locked the door. Rockfish stopped and wondered aloud what were the odds if the office had a window that overlooked the back parking lot? One the man might wiggle out of. Off in the distance, the sirens of an ambulance emerged, and he caught up to Dan, already banging on the door.

CHAPTER THIRTEEN

Ten days had passed since the Battle of MG's Army/Navy Surplus Outlet. The office door was stronger than it appeared, and Morey had hidden from his inquisitors until the police arrived on scene. He denied knowing who Trevor and Scotty were, despite inviting him into the office and serving tea and crumpets. A somewhat promising lead went nowhere.

Saturday morning found Rockfish and Jawnie at Decker's house. All three sat around the Florida room small table. The television in the corner was muted, but all three sets of eyes watched the continued, larger, and now violent, protests at Grindsville City Hall. Rockfish considered the recreational space an adjunct office with the time he had spent here recently.

"Not gonna lie," Rockfish said and put down his coffee cup. "Kind of glad to be rid of this whole mess. Stop me if you've heard me say this a few times already."

"Not me. Being a spectator has never really sat well," Decker said. He frowned and gave his head a quick shake.

"With the bad guys on the run, we've done our job. Damn good for a pro bono case, if you ask me," Rockfish said. He noticed by Dan's expression, despite being retired and the mess of the last three months, he missed the job. Especially the closure brought when the perpetrators end up in handcuffs.

"I see where both of you are coming from," Jawnie said. "But with Earnhardt Jr., Amos and Sobotka on the run, I'll be scoping out over my shoulder for a while." She picked up her self-brought chai latte and raised her eyebrows. "We all should."

Shortly after Trevor and Scotty escaped and Cheyenne went to the hospital with a broken hip, the team shared the GPS tracking information with the Feds.

"I wouldn't worry about it, kid," Rockfish said. "Those clowns are hightailing it somewhere. No time to think about retaliatory measures for little old us. They've got the weight of the US Government bearing down on them."

The Task Force had tracked the F-150 to a campground halfway between Grindsville and Erie, Pennsylvania. There the device stopped beaconing. When law enforcement arrived on scene, they located the burned-out hulk of what remained of the black pickup. There were no signs of Trevor or Scotty, nor any immediate sign in which direction they fled. Decker's sources informed him they had received new intelligence. The source believed the pair had continued west. Their plan was to meet up with the small remaining portion of the Janus Sixth Nationalist Militia that weren't already behind bars.

As for what was left of the leadership of the Great Value Boys, the Task Force had no solid leads on where they were headed or holed up. A rumor flew that the trio headed to the western part of the state, too. But this account came from a single source and was uncorroborated. Those running the investigation waited on the results from search warrants served on all three of the fugitives' phones and email accounts. The hope was that a review of this data would reveal the clues needed to get these men behind bars and cause Jawnie to finally exhale.

"Only a matter of time until the Feds get 'em. Soon, Earnhardt Jr. will raise that big old head to see if the coast is clear and a sniper will be there to knock that fucking goofy hat off." Rockfish took another sip of his coffee.

"From your mouth to God's ear, Steve." Decker reached across the table and took a McDonald's breakfast burrito from the pile

Rockfish had brought. "But honestly, I don't think my source is giving me the 4K version of what's going on."

"What gives you that idea, Dan?"

"Well, Jawnie, for one, in a case like this, it shouldn't take the phone companies and internet service providers this long to respond to the search warrants. The investigators want that shit expedited and gone through like yesterday. If I had to make an educated guess, they already have the results and teams of analysts are pulling all-nighters culling through the returns. But no one's found the smoking gun yet. That's only my thoughts based on thirty-plus years of having been on the job. Then again, might be a holdup at the companies served, but what do I know?"

"You make it sound like it's a simple locate and apprehension mission," Jawnie said. She shook her head at Rockfish, who waved a burrito in her direction. "But your tone is different. I agree, sounds like there's way more to it than your source is letting on. Bigger than finding the three."

"Exactly why the whole mess is stuck in my craw," Decker said. He leaned back and took a sip of coffee. "Without a drop of proof, I feel the Feds are expecting one last hurrah from these guys on the way out. Might be something on the grand scale of the domestic terrorism we last saw in the years running up to the millennium. Picking up these three might not resolve the endgame. They might have sleeper cells already out in the wild. Waiting for orders. Either way, I'd be wary of any claims of a soft ending."

"Sorry to interrupt you harbingers of doom and gloom, but we cashed out the minute those guys took off. You remember the EMTs loading Cheyenne onto the stretcher," Rockfish said. "The Feds will handle this the rest of the way. That's why they're paid the big bucks, government shutdowns aside. I'm ready to cheer on the FBI, HSI and all the other three letter agencies. If Earnhardt Jr. wants to go out with a bang, let them put out the fuse before anything goes boom."

"Speaking of Cheyenne, how's she doing?"

"The pain has subsided, but you'd never know if from her mouth," Rockfish said.

"Knock it off, Steve," Jawnie said and faked a punch to his shoulder. "She's worried. I've helped her with the paperwork, as she has no real insurance to speak of. Only a little coverage from her parents' plan. The hip replacement operation went off with no complications. If I recall correctly, she has a couple of days in recovery. Then she's scheduled to be moved to a rehab facility to work on strength and mobility. The doctor said she'd be there anywhere from four to six weeks, depending on her progress and willpower."

"That's six more weeks of that annoying fuck Wilbur at my house," Rockfish added. "Now, Dan, pass that bottle of Jameson over. Your ritzy Ethiopian coffee ain't cutting it and I'm getting aggravated. I find it easier to deal with Wilbur with a slight buzz when he's not at the hospital during visiting hours. I mean, seriously, she should have taken one for the team only after they had settled on a place of their own." He poured a healthy shot of whiskey into his coffee mug and smiled.

"So what's on the horizon for Rockfish & McGee now?" Decker held out his hand and took the bottle back. He dropped a smaller amount into his own and stirred with a half-eaten McDonald's breakfast burrito.

"We've never had a shortage of clients, and right now is no different," Jawnie said. "Business is picking back up. Divorce, insurance fraud and a couple of missing person cases should keep us busy in the meantime. Not exactly thriller caliber, but the checks cash all the same."

"I'll drink to that," Rockfish said and raised his cup. The two ceramic mugs and Jawnie's polyethylene cup met over the burrito pyramid. "But it will get old fast."

"I know, Steve. I've gotten used to you whining the past couple of years, when the action doesn't live up to your expectations."

"Jawnie, sometimes it pays not to get complacent. Keeps you on your toes. But right this second, I'll take a couple weeks on easy street and no Raffi before I welcome trouble again."

"Speaking of--"

"Don't want to hear it, Dan. Don't care. The man lives to ride on my last nerve, but this time he's gnawed it for too long. That stunt of trying to breathe life into his Q-Rations scam at absolutely the wrong time will take me a while to move past."

"Raffi's doing Raffi. Seriously, would you expect any different? Man has to make a buck. He owes me, you and probably Marvin, too."

"Dan, I think Steve's complaint is Cheyenne's injury could be pinned on Raffi, walking into the store at the most inopportune time. First domino to fall, so to speak."

"Agreed, but if she had listened to me and stayed with the cars... we can play the blame game forever."

"Enough with the Raffi talk," Rockfish said. "You logging back on LinkedIn, Dan? Making any progress lining up the retirement job now that the job with *Patriot Meals on American Made Wheels* has left you battered and bruised? Although you heal well."

"I've got irons in the fire. Not sure if any will pan out, but we'll see," Decker said.

"Always room for part-time side work for us, Dan," Jawnie added. "Never know what type of opportunities that could lead to."

"But don't expect your name on the marquee soon," Rockfish said. He smiled widely.

"Never say never, old friend," Decker said with his own laugh. "And by the way, who buys all these damn burritos for three people, one of which wouldn't touch them with a ten-foot pole, yet forgets to pick up any hash browns?"

* * * * * * * * *

Earnhardt Jr. glanced to his left, right, and once more behind him, before squeezing his gigantic frame through the rocks and jagged slate of the entrance to the mine. The sun had disappeared over the horizon a little over an hour ago, but he couldn't be too cautious. They might position anyone up on the mountain crest to observe. *The only people who know we're here are those that are here. Ain't no leak. But I can't overlook some dumb shit lost in the woods and trying to flag me down to ask for help.* He turned on his headlamp and a flashlight. The abandoned coal mine's main shaft illuminated. The florescent light bounced off the rocky walls and low ceiling before dissolving into the darkness ahead.

From the outside, the hideout's entrance was well hidden from plain view. Vegetation, mountain laurel thickets and large rock formations created a natural barrier. Most hikers wouldn't think to wade through it. *Hopefully to include any lost hiker that stumbled into the area.* Very few residents of Grindsville remembered or knew of the abandoned mine. Most had died and not passed on the information. The younger generations hadn't the urge to explore. Or the imagination to do so. Video games, then computers and handheld devices made sure of that.

Earnhardt Jr.'s flashlight was a bonus. For as the years passed, his memory of the place he had spent a ton of time exploring as a kid had faded. Despite his parents' warnings, the one-time Haynicz Brothers Mining Company's most productive vein had served him well. As a childhood fort and then the first place he put his hand on a set of real-life titties. And now? A combination hideaway and command post. He stumbled forward over a rock and cursed. *I used to run barefoot through this shaft in the pitch black without an issue. Well, now that we're squatting here, maybe that muscle memory will return.* He hoped to get to the point again where he'd be able to close his eyes and make his way, unscathed, down to the large open area nicknamed The Vault.

He, Amos and Sobotka had hid out under cover of darkness and rock since that glorious evening The Lord called Archibald home. Trevor and Scotty had arrived soon after their trip to Linthicum Heights turned to shit, and they ditched the truck. Although if Earnhardt Jr. had his way, those boys' mining tenure would soon draw to a quick close. *They will be the distraction I need to launch the last offensive. Sacrificed for the good of the order. Their story was to be written and toasts made by future Patriots. As long as they don't fuck up in drawing Johnny Law's attention away from my primary objective.* The revised endgame. One that he and his top men believed, would change the tide in the culture war for what was left of America's soul. It would be his Hail Mary. All he waited on now was the snap count.

Earnhardt Jr. navigated the last fifty yards where the narrow passage gradually sloped down and then angled to the left. He inhaled deeply. A damp stale earthy smell filled his lungs. He stepped through the stone arch and into The Vault. The cavern's ceiling was high, and the occasional moon beam found its way through the rock formation and down to the open area. Propane lanterns lit the enormous cavern, stacked on milk crates and makeshift tables. Beams of light from four other headlamps crisscrossed the space. Earnhardt Jr.'s light joined the party as he approached. Amos and Sobotka sat in fairly new canvas folding camping chairs around a small card table. Trevor and Scotty sat on the rocky floor, backs against the far wall. *Seems like those boys are missing their video games more than expected. Need to put 'em to work.*

"Okay, boys, your turn to stand watch," Earnhardt Jr. said. He aimed the flashlight towards the back wall. "You know the routine. One slightly inside the entrance and the other behind the large rocks off to the left. Switch it up every hour and one of us will be out in a few to relieve ya. Don't forget the walkies this time." The small group continued to use walkie talkies because of unreliable cell service in the valley and not an inkling below the surface. The nine-volt powered, handheld devices provided direct lines of communication between those on watch duty and the others back in The Vault. Not to mention they all believed the Government had Title III intercepts on all of their devices.

Earnhardt Jr. had hidden a burner cell in the woods, not too far off, but in a location only known to him. He used it daily to keep in contact with those Patriots remaining in town, undercover, and fighting the good fight out on the front lines. He coordinated supply deliveries with those same loyal men and women. *Had they been found out yet and their phones tapped?* The question hung heavy each time he punched send.

"Is there anything we need to know?" Trevor said as he struggled to his feet.

"Nothing pressing," Earnhardt Jr. said. He continued to walk towards the center of the vault. "You guys will realize your purpose soon enough. Don't dwell on Maryland. Don't continue to carry around that negative energy. When the time is right and you're called upon, I have total faith. You're essential to the movement." *Technically, you're pretty much all I have left. Those in town already have full plates.*

Trevor and Scotty didn't reply but simply nodded as they passed the table and picked up a set of walkie talkies. Earnhardt Jr. stepped closer to the card table but didn't say a word until a few minutes after Trevor and Scotty disappeared from sight. He pulled up an old Coleman cooler and sat down.

"What's the word?" Amos said.

"The natives outside City Hall are getting restless."

"No shit," Sobotka said. The light atop his head moved back and forth. "Probably tiring of the peaceful protest with only a small sprinkling of riot. Waiting for the genuine spark."

"Some have begun to lash out. I have instructed them to turn it up a half-dozen notches."

"Finally," Amos said.

"You don't think I know that time's running out?" Earnhardt Jr. said. He heard his men's frustration. "I don't plan living out my golden years on this damn dirt floor." He placed the flashlight on the table and doused the light. "With our original plan out the window, we're running out of time. We can't continue to hope what's happening back home will grow organically across the country, let alone the state. That shit died on the vine--"

"When you felt threatened and took out the golden goose," Sobotka said.

Earnhardt Jr. focused the beam from his headlamp on Sobotka's face. The man stared back; stone faced. The light moved to Amos and the old man's eyes were wide in disbelief at the words of insubordination.

"Improvise, adapt, and overcome. It's been our mantra since day one. If you don't have faith or believe in the mission anymore, you're free to walk out of here and put that uniform back on. All bets are off when we come face-to-face after that." Earnhardt Jr. stared back, hard.

"Not questioning you, Colonel, more like wondering how things might have been."

"We will have our time. Well-funded with the tithing of supporters or not. Time draws closer and our Harrisburg moment, while not as glorious as first expected, will be remembered alongside the first battles of other revolutions. Believe you me."

The men on either side of the table nodded in agreement but didn't speak.

I get it. No one's thrilled with how this is turning out, but we've got one last play. I need these men fully committed if we're to pull it off. If Harrisburg is to serve as our coup de grâce, then it needs to be as glorious as my dreams. He paused before continuing with the rally speech, lost in his thoughts. The original plan wasn't what it once was, thanks to Rockfish and the former cop. Earnhardt Jr. kept hope alive that his on-the-fly audible would be the spark the large base needed to finally pick up arms and start the necessary change. He pictured he and his men lining up in victory formation.

The Fantabulous Commonwealth Furries, Harrisburg Chapter, was planning a March For Equality. The expected date of the rally, rain or shine, was fifteen days away. Earnhardt Jr.'s window for planning and operational coordination was shrinking. Picturing defenseless woke perverts parading down Main Street spreading their depraved message made his stomach ache with pain and his fingers twitch with anticipation. *How fast can they actually move in those costumes? Easy pickings for a sharpshooter and a few strategically placed homemade IEDs.*

"It won't be long now," Earnhardt Jr. finally said. "The end is in sight. It never really mattered if Archibald were here to lead. All I ask is that you hold on. Keep our heads down and count on those on the outside to provide our much-needed supplies and logistics."

"We're with you. The three of us. From the start to the upcoming glory days. You know that," Sobotka said. He stood up and paced back and forth in front of the card table.

"What about Heckle and Fat Jeckle out there?" Amos said. He, too, stood but remained still.

"They'll depart for Ohio in a few days prior to us going east. What's left of the Janus Sixers are waiting and knows the deal. Sobotka's reliable men, on the force, have leaked parts of the diversion plan to the Feds. Hell, I wouldn't be surprised if the jackbooted thugs are waiting for them when they pull up and shut off the engine. And if not, our associates will make sure the diversion will go boom, allowing us to slip into Harrisburg unnoticed."

"I just want a nice steak, not coated in dirt. Even that fuckwit spic's expired MREs were better than the shit we've been eating," Sobotka said as he walked away from the table.

"Valhalla is within sight. You'll dine there soon enough."

* * * * * * * * *

The wheels on Jawnie's chair squeaked as her legs pushed back. Her hands methodically shuffled the papers lying on the desk in front of her. She glanced across her workspace at the two men sitting on the far side of the small office. Her eyes and thoughts moved over their heads and through the open doorway. Rockfish's closed door stared back from the opposite end of the short hallway. He was out, somewhere between here and Columbia, Maryland, working another case. Deep down she wished him on the other side of the thin interior door, eavesdropping. *Sure could use his guidance and words of wisdom right about now.*

Dan Decker leaned forward in one of the visitor chairs, fingers interlocked and resting on the edge of her desk. Three days had passed since the informal meeting at his house. He had called earlier today with information he wanted to run by the team, received earlier from his source within the Earnhardt Jr. Task Force. Rockfish wasn't giving him the time of day for wanting to dig into things further. Dan was relentless on the matter and pushed back on Rockfish's claim of having moved strictly to a spectator role. *I thought, what's the big deal hearing him out? Keep the lines of communication open and information flowing both ways. I didn't think Steve would get that pissed off and storm out before Dan pulled up.*

Wilbur, fresh off from getting Cheyenne registered with a rehabilitation facility, slouched in the other chair. His posture screamed an uncomfortable, disinterested teenager. She had called and asked Mack to drop him off. Based on what Dan had preliminarily said, she wanted Wilbur's two cents. Rockfish had made a joke regarding Wilbur not even having Monopoly money, let alone a couple of pennies, as the front door shut behind him. *This kid's history or experience, no matter how short, with the Penn Forest Patriots, might prove valuable. At some point. Hopefully real soon.* Both Dan and Jawnie agreed that any context Wilbur had might help serve as a force multiplier. Context, in this situation, was undefined and exactly why Rockfish wanted nothing to do with it.

"Steve's out chasing white collar guys for a change?"

"The Andrist case calls, or so this morning's excuse was," Jawnie said. She made sure Decker noticed her eye roll. "He's using it to stay as far away from this mess as possible. Continues to say he's over anything that has the stink of Grindsville on it. His comment last night was now that you and Raffi are safe, no one's parked outside his house, and since we have no paying client, he's done. Packed up his toys and gone home. Cleaning up any mistakes or messes the Feds make aren't in his job description."

"I get him. He keeps busting my balls," Decker said. He leaned back and crossed his legs. "Berated me the other day. Said the only reason I'm sticking with it is to turn the experience into my next job. He keeps beating that drum. Truth be told, my time on Raffi's payroll pretty much put the kibosh on anyone proactively reaching out to interview me. Hindsight tells me I probably should have left it off my resume."

Two of the three let out loud laughs. Jawnie spotted Wilbur rolling his eyes. *At least he's listening. After all, it's the reason he's here. Mission accomplished, I guess?*

"Enough about the grumpy old man across the hall. Your guy on the Task Force leaking anything worthwhile? I guess he did or else we all wouldn't be sitting here boring young Wilbur here to tears."

"He has," Decker said with a cheshire grin.

"Please tell me they're close to rounding up the rest of these not-so-well-regulated militia men."

"Meal Team Six was how Steve referred to them," Decker said.

"Gravy Seals, too," Wilbur added.

"Yeah, he's got a ton of nicknames for everyone we seem to find ourselves at odds with. But it seems the Walmart brand has staying power on Rockfish's top 40."

"Ah yes, the Great Value Boys. The man has a way of crowning people with the best fitting nicknames. But as I was saying, Jawnie, close is a relative term," Decker said. He leaned back and crossed his legs. "If you're asking if they know the whereabouts, then no."

"Then what?"

"Cricket Wireless finally provided the contents of Earnhardt Jr.'s text messages. I can't harp enough on how strange I find it took so long for them to comply with the orders of a Federal search warrant. But my guy thinks one of their data analysts found a possible game changer, in the last message sent. If they can only figure out what it translates to."

"Some sort of code?" Jawnie said. She, too, leaned in. She was always interested in cryptanalysis and knew one day it might benefit the work she and Rockfish did. "Out with it, Dan."

"He sent a short group message. To his underlings Clyde and Amos and that dirty cop."

"Sobotka."

"Yeah, Steve's favorite. That's the one. But Clyde Hayseed is currently in Federal lockup, so only two are acting on this coded order."

"Three, if you include the sender, who obviously isn't in custody. Don't make me ask a second time, Dan."

"Okay, okay. Shit or get off the pot. I got it," Dan said with a wide grin. "According to the coroner and this analyst, Earnhardt Jr. sent a brief message moments after Archibald's estimated time of death. *It's done. See you next Tuesday."*

Jawnie's eyes grew wide at the mention of the double entendre. It wasn't the first time that phrase had come up in one of their investigations. But she was pretty darn sure this occurrence had nothing to do with Earl Porbeagle, Lilith Hightower, and the Church of the Universal Nurturing II. She also noticed she wasn't the only one who perked up at the mention. *I knew I forced Wilbur to sit here for a reason.* Decker continued on before Jawnie addressed Wilbur's sudden rise to attention.

"... they think he's planning something big, memorable, for an upcoming Tuesday. The Task Force has those same data analysts searching for any kind of liberal, left-leaning event planned for a Tuesday in the near future. It's not much, but all they have to go on right now. My guy says they're singularly focused on identifying the event. Pretty sure they can stop whatever's planned and round up the rest of The Great Value Boys."

"Well, Dan, the phrase doesn't mean much to me in context to the insurrectionists, but I think it might to someone," Jawnie said. She swiveled her chair and stared daggers at a now posture-positive Wilbur.

"Did you say, see you next Tuesday?" Wilbur said.

"Yes, I did," Decker said and turned to join Jawnie's gaze. "Does it mean anything to you? Anything? Doesn't matter how inconsequential you might think."

Eyes remaining wide, Wilbur gave his head a quick shake.

Jawnie didn't believe it for a second. She saw in Decker's face that the ex-cop didn't either. *What's he contemplating or hiding? Maybe he's trying to figure out what happens to him, down the line. If it gets out, he told us what he knows? The Task Force has already debriefed him on two occasions. What's the harm in divulging a little more?* She stared at him. His posture returned to partially slouched. *He's swallowed the canary for damn sure. Now to figure out how much he's willing to regurgitate.*

"I can see you're torn, Wilbur," Jawnie said. Allegiances he once thought severed might hang on by a thread, despite Cheyenne's continued recovery and his fear of the same happening to him. *There's no hiding those emotions in his face. I have a feeling the boy's never played serious poker.*

Wilbur didn't say a word with either his lips or facial muscles. Jawnie looked over to Decker and tilted her head toward the doorway.

"Excuse us for a second, will you?"

Jawnie stood up and walked around the desk. Decker slid his chair out of the way and the two reconvened in the hallway, but not before he shut the office door behind him.

"What do you make of him?" Jawnie said in a barely audible tone.

"Knows a lot more than he's letting on regarding this Tuesday message. But I can't tell if he's got a nugget he's hiding or isn't sure what part of him thinks he does."

"Time for you to shine the light in his face and make him break?" Jawnie said and took a step back toward the door. "Too bad Steve's not here. He's perfect playing the part of the bad cop. He doesn't think twice before letting a slap or two fly."

"I'll take a shot with him. And now that I'm retired, I'm not covered by the same code of ethics," Decker said with a wink, and reached for the doorknob.

"What the--"

"Get your ass back in here," Decker demand. Wilbur stopped dead in his tracks. The upper portion of his body hung outside the small window behind Jawnie's desk. The screen, twisted and bent, lay on the floor under his flailing feet. Decker didn't wait for Wilbur to acknowledge the order. He stepped behind the desk and forcefully pulled the escapee by his belt, back into the office. "You're going to tell us exactly what you know."

Decker slammed Wilbur back into the chair and Jawnie's phone chimed. She picked it up from the desk. The front door camera alarm had triggered. When the app opened, the screen filled with video of Rockfish walking into the office.

"Perfect timing. The bad cop has entered the arena."

* * * * * * * * * *

Decker drug Wilbur by his collar out of the chair, down the hallway and to the office's bullpen. The partner offices were too small for four bodies and the dance that was about to start. The shirt stitching gave way and Wilbur landed with a thud on the couch. Decker plopped down right next to him, hand grasping the back of the man's neck.

"Well, this doesn't seem good," Rockfish said as he stepped past Lynn's desk. She shrugged and kept her eyes on her monitor. "The less you know, the easier it will be for you to deny any involvement if this person sues," he said as he walked over to Jawnie and placed his bag on the recliner.

"Let me catch you up to speed," Jawnie said. "Dan's got things under control here." She turned around and stopped at the end of the short hallway between their respective office doors.

"Dan, try to keep our guest in a talkative mood and preferably in one piece. I'll be right back," Rockfish said. He patted Decker on the shoulder and caught up with Jawnie.

The partners emerged a few minutes later, Jawnie with her laptop under her arm and eyebrows raised. Rockfish followed a step behind, sleeves rolled up with a look of determination on his face. Jawnie searched for a safe space to watch the show from and settled on standing behind the small bar, laptop open.

"I thought you didn't give a shit anymore?" Decker glanced at Rockfish and stood up from the couch. The two men were now side-by-side, staring down at Wilbur. Their prisoner did not know what was about to happen.

"Still don't, Dan. But contrary to popular belief, I love my country. I ain't talking about the Chinese-stitched red hat, cover your car with goofy fucking flags jingoism. My blood pressure skyrockets when morons choose violence. Especially when those, like our friend here, have information of value, but can't exactly figure out where his loyalties lie."

"You come up with that all on your own, or did Jawnie have you memorize it in the back?" Decker smirked.

Rockfish pursed his lips and shook his head. Decker sat back on the couch and turned to face Wilbur. Rockfish followed suit from the other side but changed his mind. He pushed the coffee table back a bit and sat on the edge of the glass.

"I'm going to cut straight to the chase," Rockfish said. "If you don't mind, Dan."

"Not at all. I think I pulled something in my rotator cuff, hauling this sack of shit back into the building."

"And that affects your interrogation skills, how? Don't answer that. Jawnie, bend down and grab Dan one of my hangover ice packs from the small fridge behind the bar."

"Coming in hot," Jawnie said after standing back up. The ice pack sailed across the room and hit Wilbur on the side of the head.

Rockfish scootched his ass closer to the edge of the coffee table and leaned forward. His nose was inches from Wilbur's face and echoes of his morning breakfast burrito hung in the air. Wilbur's eyes grew wide and a drop of sweat slid down the side of his face. Rockfish pressed his hands against the glass, elbows locked out and arms rigid.

"I'll be honest with you, Wilbur. One shot is all you get at this. Tell us what you know, or I'll beat your ass across this strip mall. I've got three witnesses here who will provide very official statements that it was totally in self-defense. Trust me, I'll take the zip ties off your wrists before the EMTs arrive." Rockfish leaned back and his mouth formed a sinister grin. He released the tension in his arms and rubbed his hands together in anticipation. He watched Wilbur's eyes dart from him to Jawnie and then to Decker.

"Yo! We've got a runner," Dan said. Wilbur had shot to his feet and taken Dan's hold on the back of his neck with him. The two now stood in front of the couch, and Rockfish knew Wilbur had put little thought into his fight-or-flight instinct.

"Ouch! damn it, kid, I'm already hurting over here," Decker said. He used his weight to pull Wilbur back down onto the leather cushions.

"Lynn, a couple of Advil for Dan, please," Rockfish shouted before continuing. "Old Dan here, once he recovers and after I beat your ass, might pull a few strings and set you up in the same rehab facility as your sweetie. Maybe put you in the room across the hall. Then slip a few Benjamins to a nurse to leave your door open. A front-row seat to the train of orderlies coming in hot, if you get my drift."

"Steve!" Jawnie said.

"Open and honest, isn't that the road you're always preaching?" Rockfish said. He glanced at Wilbur and watched as the color drained from the man's face. He reached out and grabbed the front of Wilbur's T-shirt and pulled him in close. Dan winced in pain as his arm shot forward as well.

"Out with it, son. I don't plan shit ending well if you continue to keep quiet."

"The Vault," Wilbur said. He had lifted his head, and the words were barely audible.

"I don't doubt the corruption running rampant in Grindsville. But I highly doubt the Great Value Boys are hiding out at the First National Bank of Hicksville." Rockfish shook his head. "Try again."

"Can y'all let go of me? I'll tell you want you want."

Rockfish and Decker released their grips and Wilbur fell back against the couch.

"See you next Tuesday," Wilbur said. The man's voice, slightly louder. "It's slang for a woman's private parts."

"No shit Sherlock. I think we're all familiar with the secret meaning of the phrase. The more crude four letter version," Rockfish said with a wide grin.

"They're hiding out in an old, abandoned coal mine. It hasn't been operational for over a century. The Colonel and the other leaders planned to use it as a cold site, should the cabin ever be compromised. The large stones jutting out from the mountain dovetail perfectly into each other, with a small opening towards the bottom. And with all the moss, well, you get the picture."

"You know this for a fact," Decker said and returned his hand to the back of Wilbur's neck.

"I mean, I've not been there or seen it. Heard of it like, fifth hand from the other guys. But it's the only place I can think of that is practically one hundred percent safe, in the Colonel's eyes."

"Could be a wild goose trip," Rockfish said.

"Agreed."

"Disinformation, possibly," Jawnie said from behind the bar. "Get the Feds searching an area while they're hiding or doing who knows what in the opposite direction. Stick with me, I'm Googling. See what I can come up with to corroborate. Wilbur, do you have a name for this mountain?"

"Lord help you if you open that mouth and come out with another acronym of cunt," Decker said. He tightened his grip.

"Aaahhh! Okay, okay. The place is in Gallitzin State Forest. Near the horseshoe curve on Route 56. Cheyenne might know more; her kin are planted all around that part of the forest."

Rockfish stood up and gave serious thought to what Wilbur had divulged. *The Feds won't listen to another half-assed lead from us. Dan's buddy made that abundantly clear. Do we go run all this past Cheyenne? Where can we stow this clown, so he doesn't escape or worse, question his loyalties and try to report back? I trust him as much as I trust Dan to leave me out of this mess.*

"Who's up for a drive out to LifeCare Center of Halethorpe? Cheyenne's probably up for company."

"No need to bother her, Steve," Jawnie said, spinning the laptop around for Rockfish and Decker to see. "X marks the spot. Or somewhat close."

* * * * * * * * *

Everyone, except for Lynn, made their way to the conference table at the center of the office's open area. Here, Jawnie grabbed a couple of cables and connected her laptop to the projector. Rockfish grabbed the remote and pushed the button. The retractable screen hummed to life and inched its way down the wall.

"Lynn, hate to bother you again, but can you grab a roll of duct tape? Dan and I need to pay close attention to Jawnie's presentation and can't chance Wilbur suddenly thinking he needs to train for the Barkley Marathons. Nothing personal, Wilbur." Rockfish smiled as Wilbur rolled his eyes.

When Wilbur was secured to the chair, Jawnie stepped in front of the screen.

"Hold on a second," Rockfish said. He reached for the tape on the table and ripped off a short piece. "One more for good measure." He placed the six-inch piece firmly over Wilbur's mouth. "Lynn, pull the shade and lock the door. Can't have a potential client walk in and see Harry Houdini here struggling to escape."

"Who?"

"David Blaine."

"On it, Boss."

Rockfish nodded and gave Jawnie the thumbs up to start.

"As you can see, Pennsylvania's Department of Environmental Protection has this nifty tool on the state website. Most use it to determine if they built your house on top of an abandoned mine, but I've worked backwards to find Wilbur's stone vagina."

Rockfish patted Wilbur on the shoulder and turned his attention back to the map on the wall.

"The tool is quite handy. You can search by address, municipality or latitude and longitude. The captive member of our audience mentioned a horseshoe curve on a particular road. I located that spot on the map, then determined the coordinates. A simple cut and paste later, we're within a hundred yards of the supposed big V. The website listed a few locales for an entrance, but Wilbur's description doesn't sound like a man-made one. More Mother Nature," Jawnie said. She paused for an expected laugh over her Mother Nature mention. It didn't come, and she continued.

"Sadly, that's as close as we can get with help from the Pennsylvania state government. Three years ago, in a recent round of budget cuts, the Pennsylvania General Assembly cut funding for the mapping project." The audible sigh from those around the table was loud and deep. "The cuts affected a good portion of Cambria County. And if any legislative committee has re-funded the initiative, no one's updated the website. In closing, I can get you close. It's up to the Ranger Rick inside you to finish the job."

"Goddamn Jawnie. You don't know how happy I am to have you as a partner. The definition of work smarter and not harder,"

Rockfish said with another hard slap of Wilbur's shoulder. "Saves me from tedious shit and having to get my knuckles dirty."

"Don't get ahead of yourself, Steve," Decker said. "We might want to follow up on this in case I get laughed out of the building when I report back with our findings."

"Dan, I keep drawing a line in the sand and you have no qualms stepping over it. You're killing me."

"No, Steve, I know you're always on the side of right. Maybe hugging the line, but with a pleasant breeze, you always fall on the side of good."

Rockfish shrugged.

Decker waved Rockfish away from the conference table and lowered his voice. "Can we retreat to your office for a few, Steve?" Decker said. "I want to give you my thoughts, but taping over Wilbur's ears seems a bit too much."

"Jawnie, watch him. We'll talk afterwards." Rockfish didn't wait for a response before he turned and walked down the hallway.

Rockfish slid into the familiar seat behind his desk, and Decker closed the door behind him. He pulled up the chair opposite and reached for the television remote on the corner of the desk. Decker pushed the power button and raised the volume.

"In case these walls are paper thin. Maybe I should have covered his ears?"

Rockfish nodded in agreement and leaned back. "Okay. Tell me where you're headed with this."

"I can see this thing shaking out two ways. I can relate every bit of nonsense that kid said to my guy on the Task Force. He'll listen and after the GPS tracking failure, he'll pat me on the head, maybe give me a candy bar and send me on my way."

"They ain't buying a stone pussy hideout story."

"Exactly. Did you?"

Rockfish leaned forward in his chair and rolled his shoulders. "I mean, I've heard crazier. But I also don't think the kid has a creative bone in his body. Crazy enough to be true."

"Agreed. I've worked on cases like this where the investigator had tunnel vision," Decker said. His left hand raised up and rubbed the three days of growth on his face. "Focused and hard charging to identify a political event taking place on an upcoming Tuesday. One that's ripe for a bunch of rednecks, armed to the teeth, to crash."

"First, we gave them all the GPS information we had, as soon as we verified the tracker was operational. We provided actionable intel. No crime in that. Also, not my problem. They took their sweet time following up on it." Rockfish ran his hand through his hair. The Government's slow call to action still bothered him. *Can't expect anything different this time when the legend of the stone vagina comes across some bureaucrat's desk. Just toss it on the pile over there, Jenkins, with the Phoenix Memo. Christ. If they would only listen to the little people, so much death and destruction would be avoided.*

"That look on your face tells me you and I might agree," Decker said.

"Yeah. You pass this intel on, and it doesn't make it very far up the chain. Especially if Wilbur's never been there or even seen the location on a map. Hearsay. And we all know how the Feds love to jump on shit like that."

"Let's give them a little corroboration."

"Gonna need more than a little," Rockfish said. "Corroboration out the yin-yang is more like it."

"Glad we're in agreement, buddy. Verify and then call in an artillery strike."

"Pin-point that motherfucker, because I swear, this is the last time."

"Don't worry, Steve. We're going to win this one. Be on the right side of history and not twiddling our thumbs watching Rome burn."

"No offense, Dan, but you're giving these men way too much credit," Rockfish said and stood up from his chair. "Any attempt on a second January 6th by Earnhardt Jr. and his stooges will rival the Bay of Pigs in utter failure."

"I think I've seen that movie. Insurrection 2: Electric Boogaloo," Decker said and stood up.

Rockfish held out his fist, Decker leaned across, and bumped it. He then picked up the phone on his desk and dialed zero.

"Lynn, grab a razor knife. I gotta cut that doofus loose. He's gonna need a signed permission slip before heading out on our field trip."

CHAPTER FOURTEEN

The small campfire crackled, and bits of embers floated into the evening sky. Rockfish stared at the empty collapsible chair on the other side of the flames and the small two-man tent pitched behind it. Despite being late May, he shivered and held his hands out, closer to the fire. *Am I an idiot for allowing Dan to talk me into this goat rodeo? There's no way this goes as smooth and uneventful as he claims. But how many times have you asked for a favor when he was on the job?* The markers owed weighed heavily in his friend's favor.

The trek north had taken two days after hearing and discussing Wilbur's baffling theory. After strategizing, a credit card-taxing trip to REI was in order before Lana hit the road on Thursday, a few minutes before noon. They had set up camp on a small bluff, where Decker assured Rockfish no one would see them. The spot also allowed for a climb a little further up and to be positioned to scout the valley floor for any militia maneuvers. He had sold the idea to Rockfish. In a perfect world, they'd spot someone walking back towards the entrance and get a pin dropped on the location. Then scoot down and get closer to document what they could. *Right, you wanna bet on it?*

Rockfish would have felt slightly better if Wilbur wasn't torn between his allegiances and his willingness to help guide them. The kid might not have ever been to the abandoned mine, but he was way more familiar with the terrain. Instead, Wilbur sat in a nondescript, no-tell motel in Ferndale, Maryland. Decker had called in a couple of his own markers and two off-duty patrolmen now moonlighted as babysitters. In the end, neither Rockfish nor Decker felt as if they fully trusted Wilbur if he were to accompany them. Put in a tough situation, Rockfish wouldn't depend on him to do the right thing on the right side. As soon as the team returned with the information, they hoped the Feds would act upon, they'd dump Wilbur on the steps of the US Attorney's office. *From that point forward, he's their problem and you can finally wash your hands of the mess,* was how Decker kept putting it. *Promises, promises.*

Despite Decker's constant sunshine and roses vibes, Rockfish's time on watch had come up empty. He had pulled the first shift, four to eight, with Decker scheduled to relieve him as the late-May sun disappeared over the horizon. Decker would keep watch until midnight before both men grabbed a few winks and started all over again around eight a.m.

Jawnie had splurged and purchased new binoculars for the trip. She claimed the normal ones in the supply cabinet were good for peeking through bedroom windows from a parked car but would woefully underperform in the environment to where Rockfish and Decker were headed. The set, one for the day and the other equipped with night vision, contained multimedia capabilities and cost more than Rockfish would ever be willing to pay.

Decker had taken the Cadillac of high-tech toys when he had left camp for his shift. The lightweight night vision model saved pictures and video clips on an SD card and contained built in GPS. The only downside was the zoom wasn't as powerful as the daylight model. *I'm always for working smarter, but Jawnie didn't have to lug the damn portable solar generator up the side of the mountain needed to charge all this fancy shit.* The instruction manual detailed a charge on each set of binoculars would last six hours and Rockfish didn't believe it for a second. When Decker swore, with Jawnie's map, they'd need not recharge them. *No way we're glimpsing these fuckers right off the bat, then dropping a pin on the map and hike our way down to get closer for a few confirming pictures. I've got a bridge over the Patapsco river I'd like to sell him and Rosie.*

On Rockfish's earlier shift, an eight-point buck was his only visual. Sounds were also few. When he heard something close by, it startled him, but didn't take long to find the source. He had rolled to his side and realized the noise was nothing more than his stomach growling. Rockfish cursed not bringing a snack, but what he really needed was a drink. He pictured the flask back at camp in his sleeping bag and lost count at the number of times he had considered climbing back down to retrieve it. *Good things come to those who wait. Remember that.* The saying also fit with Decker's plan, but Rockfish's patience had arrived at camp already paper thin.

An hour before the designated break time both men had agreed on, Decker hiked back down to camp.

"You're early," Rockfish said. "It's only nine, p.m. Good news to report?"

"No, your buck hasn't wandered back. But my stomach's talking to me. You put the thought of sweet venison steaks in my head, and I've felt the rumbling ever since. I need a snack or a sandwich."

Rockfish nodded. "I'll join ya."

The men ate in silence. Each devoured a turkey and Swiss wrap before Decker gathered himself to head back and finish his shift. Rockfish waved his flask.

Decker laughed. "My shift doesn't end for another three hours."

"Unless your plan has us rappelling down the side of that cliff in the next hour, I think you'll be okay," Rockfish said. He took a long swig and then a second for good measure. "I'll leave her here on your chair in case you want a little warmth in your belly. Gonna get cold here in a few."

Decker shook his head and picked up his gear bag. Rockfish stood up and dropped the flask on the empty chair. *Can't win 'em all, Dan. I'm not questioning you about that three-quarters gone box of Girl Scout cookies on your sleeping bag.*

"You sure this ain't no wild goose trip? The big stone pussy. Right." Rockfish moved back to his chair. He stood behind it. "I know I'm beating a dead horse, but seem's like old Wilbur might laugh his ass off right about now, while we're freezing ours off."

"Maybe, Steve. But there's a feeling inside that tells me I've seen this movie. Things will come out in our favor."

"So have I. The treasure was buried under the Big W instead of inside a mossy rock vag. That didn't turn out so well."

"Wait, you're comparing this to *It's a Mad, Mad, Mad, Mad World?* Who are we, Buddy Hackett and Phil Silvers?"

"First thing that came to mind," Rockfish said with a smile. "Yet I've always pictured you as a young Ethel Merman. Anyway, head back up and wake me when you come back at midnight. That late night sandwich might put me to sleep," Rockfish said as he sat back down. He pulled his chair closer to the fire and added a small log to the flames once Decker disappeared from view.

Shit. Are those flames too high? Can someone spot them from a distance? Dan swears not, but I should knock it off. Put another layer on if you're cold or drag the sleeping bag out to drape over you. He moved the rest of the firewood gathered earlier, further away, so he wouldn't be tempted. Instead, he found a long stick and used it to poke at the coals. He poked and prodded as his mind moved on to his proper partner. It did not thrill Jawnie when they left her home to coordinate logistics and mother Cheyenne, since Wilbur was temporarily indisposed. He then moved on from her disappointment to the beginning of the entire ordeal. Another Raffi get rich scheme and how it turned into a domestic terrorism event which the Feds seemed tepid to dive into head first. *Can't blame them, can you? Yeah, I can. When an entire community is besieged and then whipped up into a riot frenzy, forgive me if I feel something should have been done a lot sooner.*

Rockfish heard a rustle from behind the tent. Decker emerged a minute later, and Rockfish glanced at his watch. Midnight. He had been lost in thought for a little under three hours. *How the hell did that happen? Strange events and a ton of unanswered questions. That's how.*

"Your face tells me you had more luck than I did. Can we go home now?" Rockfish hoped for some good news.

"Shit, I'm surprised you're upright. But I have good news. It's more knowing what to keep an eye out for with these jokers," Decker said. He maneuvered around the crude stone fire pit to his seat. "They teach 'em young here to enjoy their cigarettes. I spotted two red cherries down there. On the outskirts of that clearing to the left. Piece of cake picking them out with these." Decker said and pulled the night vision binoculars from his bag. "I gotta thank Jawnie for knowing exactly what we needed and paying for the overnight shipping. If she had left it up to you..."

"Yeah, point made. Next."

"Anyway, the fat fuck is pacing around smoking," Decker said. "I'm pretty sure it's the same two from the pickup truck. They pace around and then disappear back into the brush. Pin dropped."

"Could be Earnhardt Jr., he reeked of unfiltered Pall Malls and it's not like he's exactly svelte."

"Outline of a different hat, if that means anything. It's as good a place as any to start tomorrow. Pack up, hike down, get lucky and hit the road."

"Can't wait, just don't tell my calves," Rockfish said with a shrug.

Decker didn't respond. He put the night vision binoculars back in his bag and zipped the top. "Need to find a place like this down there and then see how close we can creep to get a better view. Grab a couple of pictures, hike out. We'll definitely need a place with a better signal or Wi-Fi to upload all this for Jawnie to move forward."

Rockfish dreaded the mention of a better signal. Since their arrival, his phone alternated between a single bar and SOS. Despite those times when he assumed the single bar meant AT&T was working on his behalf, every text failed to send. His attention returned to Decker.

"Pictures only. From a distance. Not a chance we're stepping inside, right?" Rockfish said.

"Neither one of us is sufficiently prepared or armed to take that on."

"Or stupid enough," Rockfish said with a laugh. "And that damn artillery strike better not be late."

"We need sleep, buddy. Tomorrow's a long ass hike, round trip."

"Outstanding. I can already feel my legs cramping."

* * * * * * * * *

Rockfish stretched his legs within his sleeping bag and stared at the top of the flimsy tent. It surprised him how much body heat the material kept. But sleep escaped him as Decker had been hard at work sawing down a mighty redwood for the past two hours. He wished they had any kind of cell service and could share with Jawnie the good news of a possible quick end of the trip. She'd then inform the powers that be to expect their newfound evidence. *If they were expecting it, then they damn well better act on it in a timely manner before things go screwy. Right, Mr. Murphy?*

Rockfish's nighttime day dreaming came to an abrupt stop. Something rustled the brush far behind the tent. *What was that? Camping imagination, an animal, or worse? Don't you dare think of a bear.* He held his breath and listened. A hand on his abdomen let him know the sound wasn't the same as earlier. The crackle of dead leaves and twigs came again. Rockfish was positive the commotion wasn't coming from anywhere within their camp.

"Dan. Dan, get up. There's shit stirring outside. Did you bother to pack bear spray or any wild animal deterrent?"

"Huh? What?" Decker said. He struggled to sit up and instead turned his head to Rockfish. "It's nothing but your buddy the buck or maybe a fox. Go back to sleep, Steve. We can't react to every cricket chirp or animal howl."

This time the rustle came louder, and Rockfish swore it had grown closer. He unzipped his sleeping bag and reached for his handgun, conveniently placed next to his pillow for quick access.

"Now do you think we should get the jump on it before it does us?"

Decker agreed and followed suit by the light of a phone screen. He motioned for Rockfish to come around from the right side of the tent and he to the left. A pincer maneuver would send whatever it was, scampering back to its own den. The screen faded and Rockfish reached for the front of the tent. The movement was the slowest unzipping of his life. They exited the tent in single file and swung around on their respective sides.

Despite the moonlight, Rockfish couldn't make out Decker's silhouette as he blended into the dark and brush. He held the gun in his left hand and a tactical flashlight in the right. His thumb pressed lightly against the button on the end, waiting for the exact moment to blind their prey. Rockfish bent at the knees and took small steps, trying to continue forward while not making noise to announce their arrival. Behind the tent, he lost all visual and continued on, taking the occasional tree branch to the face. Rockfish hadn't heard the particular sound since exiting the tent and wondered if it was his imagination working after all. *Dan will never let me live it down.*

As if on cue, his ears caught the sound of it again. *Is it behind me now? How the fuck did it circle around and get the advantage?*

The rustling again. *Definitely behind now. Fuck me.*

Rockfish spun and pressed down with his thumb. Light shot from the handheld device and lit the surrounding area.

"Raffi!" Rockfish was confused. There in the light, his friend stood, a backpack in one hand and a deli sandwich in the other. "What the fuck are you doing here?"

The voices and bright light brought Decker at a full sprint, and he slammed into the back of Rockfish. Both men picked themselves up off the ground and didn't believe their eyes.

"How dare you come up here on your own revenge tour when you took a giant shit on mine? Cried over and over, it wasn't worth it. The time and energy you spent trying to convince me what not to do, and then this." Raffi shook his head in disgust and spit. "Am I ever disappointed in you two."

"That's not what this is," Decker said. "This isn't about violence. Can we figure this all out around the fire? I doubt any of us are going back to sleep tonight."

Rockfish nodded, and Raffi didn't say a word. Rockfish swept the flashlight from Raffi and towards the vicinity of the campsite. He noticed the crimson color on the man's face. *Raffi will get over it and play nice. He always does.* The three men hiked through the brush back to camp. Decker added twigs and sticks to the embers, and it wasn't long before the fire came back to life. Then all eyes were on Raffi for answers.

"There was no way in hell I was going to let you two come up here to kick ass and take names without me. Steve, I gotta say, your partner was less than helpful when I asked her where the hell you had gotten off to."

"That's her job. I'll give her a gold star sticker when I get back," Rockfish said. "But in the meantime, you need to get over it. Now, how about you tell me how you came across us out here in the middle of nowhere?"

"Remember our time lounging at the scenic Grindsville Holiday Inn?" Raffi said with raised eyebrows and a tilt of his head. "Well, you left your phone on the table at breakfast, unlocked, and I made a point of sharing your location with me."

"What the fuck?"

"Listen, no harm meant. I needed to make sure I knew where you were if our original plan with the Q-Ration exchange went to shit. If we got separated. You know, it was for the good of the order. If you and Jawnie happened to zig when I zagged. An assurance you wouldn't head back without me. And if you did, well, I'd know and try to catch up."

"We wouldn't have done that. And then you coincidentally forgot to tell me about it, or ask me to turn it off when we finally schlepped back to the hotel that night?"

"Something like that. But then I used it to drive up here. Not the greatest signal, but it did the job. Shit, it went out from time to time, and I had to guess the direction. But I stayed the course until I heard your big ass crunching around. Technically, I didn't know it was you, so I swung around behind in case it was an apex predator hoping for an after-dinner snack. But enough about me. Why didn't you tell me? I've got a bone to pick with these hick motherfuckers as much as you two. One would even say I have dibs."

"You don't listen at all," Rockfish said. He raised his fist and slammed it down on the canvas arm of the chair. "This isn't about getting even and even less about you."

"Well, it kinda is," Dan said. "But we're the facilitators for the long arm of the law. Not the appendage itself."

"We're trying to get proof of the exact location of where these mopes are hiding," Rockfish said. "We turn that information over and watch the Feds cover this place like white on rice. That's our plan. You still want to help, or I can point you in the hideout's general direction if you want to go all John Rambo."

"Yeah, but don't expect either of us to play Colonel Trautman and try to save your ass," Decker added.

"Wait. A surveillance mission? And for your information, Trautman didn't save Rambo. He was more about antagonizing the locals and Brian Dennehy."

"Calm and cool, Raffi," Rockfish said and leaned in, hands on knees, to emphasize the point.

"I'm in. Whatever you guys need. Level-headed. That's me. I can pivot with the best of 'em."

Rockfish pursed his lips and closed his eyes. *I can only hope this is the first time he's not bullshitting me, but you know damn sure he's lying through his teeth.* Rockfish looked over at Decker, head in hand, and was already rubbing his temples.

"Trust me, man," Raffi said. "Whatever I can do to see these yokels end up in pound-me-in-the-ass federal prison. I guess I won't be needing these." He unzipped the top of his backpack and pulled out several handguns, wrapped in dish towels. Rockfish noticed the after-market silencers on more than one.

"You know those are illegal," Decker said with a shade of authority in his voice.

"And you know you're retired and at most would call 9-1-1 and report me. IF you had a decent signal."

"Lighten up, you two. Raffi came strapped, full of obtuse movie trivia, but not a sleeping bag or proper pair of hiking boots." Rockfish's hand moved to his own temples.

"Maybe I'll be your little spoon, amigo?"

* * * * * * * * * *

The spoons, big and little, and solitary butter knife, awoke mid-morning and milled around the extinguished fire. Rockfish and Decker had no thoughts of energizing morning coffee as they packed and planned. The three men stood around the circle of rocks and ash as Decker laid out his initial thoughts for the day.

They would leave most of their gear in the tent and make their way down into the valley. Each carried only what they needed to protect themselves and document what they found. When Decker declared the mission a success, they would work their way back up to camp. Depending on the time of day, they would either pack up and make haste for the cars or spend the night and hike out at daybreak.

The plan, to Rockfish, seemed simple enough. He glanced over at Raffi, who started down the path between him and Decker. He hoped the wildcard was onboard with every one of Decker's instructions. *If there was ever a time, I need you to listen and do what you're told, without some harebrained action coming out of left field.* Raffi seemed to sense Rockfish's thoughts and turned his head and smirked. *Well, that doesn't give me the warm and fuzzies.*

Decker had picked out another outcropping, one a hundred yards west of the small clearing where he had spotted the cigarette silhouettes. This space would serve as their base of operations for the day. From there, it would be his job to creep closer to the clearing and hopefully spot the sentries before they saw him. With luck and good police training, he'd capture the photographic evidence needed and return to the base camp.

Raffi's sudden appearance had thrown a wrench into Decker's plans, and he made a point of pulling Rockfish aside. He reemphasized he would be the one taking all the risks.

"I'm gonna need you to monitor this one and make sure he does nothing to draw attention to us. Aloud, I'll say we'll take turns scouting, but in reality, I'll go first and not come back until I've secured what we need."

Rockfish was on board before Decker had finished spelling it out, but with one major edit. He would take the first scout mission. Decker would sit with Raffi until Rockfish came back, either with what they needed or empty-handed.

"If you want him to play along and not cause a scene," Rockfish said. "My way shouldn't raise any red flags in that half-cocked brain of his. Yours might give him reason to doubt and maybe even act. Trust me on this one."

"You know him best."

"Yeah, not a day goes by I don't regret it."

The hike took three hours and descended the party in a serpentine fashion, almost two thousand feet. When they finally arrived at the day's base of operations, Decker grinned widely. His estimated location, one which he had hoped to have cover by the rock formations, was actually better than he imagined. After a climb back up of less than five feet, the ground leveled out. Fortunately for them, chin-high mountain laurel was abundant. The plant's branches, leaves and small flowers formed a natural tight boma.

Once Decker and Raffi had settled inside the plant fort, Rockfish slid down the rocks and walked around. Between the flowers and branches, one would have to have a damn good reason to climb up and then get on their hands and knees in order to peer in. None of which were traits associated with the Great Value Boys.

"Good call, Dan. Those hillbillies could walk within three feet of this place and not have a clue. You two stay all bundled up and keep your traps shut. You never know, those cigarettes might move in wider circles. I'll take the first hack at finding the prize."

"My ex-wife used to call it the prize, too."

"Go get 'em, Steve. We'll be here waiting to help in any way you need," Raffi said.

Rockfish brought his index finger to his lips and turned around. His other hand felt for the handgun in the small of his back and then reached for the daytime binoculars. Between them and his phone, he'd be able to document findings from near and far.

"Ah, clearing's that way," Dan whispered. "Not off to a good start."

Rockfish ignored the sarcasm but spun around and walked off in the opposite direction. A few minutes later, he came across the clearing. It was not larger than a backyard aboveground swimming pool. He didn't want to risk walking across it in the open and instead stuck to the outskirts, lined with pine and oak trees. The mountain laurel was plentiful here too, easing his mind if he had to drop to the ground quickly in order to seek cover.

By the time he reached the clearing's far side, Rockfish wondered if he was being too cautious and needed to pick up the pace. Wanting to get this done and over with was competing in his mind with not getting caught. He stepped it up and tripped over an exposed root. By the time Rockfish caught his balance, he stared back at the trail of disturbed leaves left behind. *Fuck. If that's not a telltale sign of someone being here, I--hold on, what do we have here?*

Rockfish took two steps backwards and noticed a cigarette butt. *Mom always said everything happens for a reason. Better document that, especially if it leads to another clue.*

Click

It wasn't long before he found another and above it, at eye level, a yellow disposable Bic lighter wedged between a tree trunk and a branch.

Click

Rockfish had dropped to one knee to take another picture of the ground litter when the sound of a twig snapping echoed through the forest. The sound had come from in front of him and Rockfish's first thought was to make himself smaller, without having to lie face down on the forest floor. *Fuck it.* He laid prone on the ground, but kept his head up, in case the need to flee became apparent or simply overtook him.

A minute passed and then a second. He hadn't heard another sound and thought about getting back to his feet. But then he saw it. Not twenty feet in front of him, a wide swath of orange came into view and moved across his field of vision. Hunter orange. *Trevor by the size of it. The man's camo must be in the dirty hamper. How dirty must something be for him to actually change clothes?* Rockfish lifted his phone and snapped off a string of photos before dropping a pin for good measure.

He remained statuesque and didn't move until the orange did. *Should I hang here and wait for his return trip? Shit! What if he's already on the return trip and I missed the first part of the lap?* Rockfish didn't have a choice. He'd have to trail Trevor at a safe distance and say a brief prayer if he wanted to find the exact location of the mine entrance. He moved into a crouch position and moved parallel. The bright color helped with Rockfish's less than

Daniel Boone tracking skills. He stopped and started when his target did and tried to avoid any roots or sticks on the ground. And before Rockfish patted himself on the back for a job well done, his target vanished.

What the hell? Rockfish continued forward but slowed his pace to a crawl. He moved his head left, right, and straight ahead with each baby step. Two large Douglas Fir trees stood directly ahead, and that was the point where he had lost sight of Trevor. He reached into the small of his back and pulled his weapon, before using it and his free hand to brush aside the tree branches. Another clearing, the size of a kiddie pool, appeared, and Rockfish suppressed a shout.

FUCK YEAH! He struggled to hold it in while reaching for his camera. His gun hand held a large branch at bay.

Click Click Click Click Click

He dropped yet another pin before putting the phone back in his pocket. He paused and admired the scenery before him. Moss covered the top and sides of the narrow stone opening. *Yup. The rock dovetails perfectly. Exactly as advertised. A solid Miss January 1979, if memory serves.*

Rockfish was less cautious as he retraced his steps back to the boma. As he approached the area, he did not see Decker or Raffi and momentarily swallowed hard. He then remembered how dense the brush was and stepped up the slight incline and found both men sitting in silence. Their eyes grew wide when they recognized Rockfish and put their weapons aside.

"That expression on your face says success," Raffi said, barely above a whisper.

Rockfish nodded, and Decker pointed back towards the trail that brought them down the mountain. The three men began the ascent, and no one talked until an hour had passed. At that point, Raffi was bursting, and truth be told, Rockfish wanted to brag a little. He recounted the pure luck of coming across Trevor after finding the butts and lighter. He passed his phone back and forth between the others, each marveling at the wonders of nature.

"Definitely Candy Loving," Decker said with a laugh. "I remember that issue like no other."

The men continued the long climb back to their original camp. By the time they arrived, the sun had started its downward trek, and the men were tired. Thrilled to death, but exhausted. They sat around the long-extinguished fire and the next set of steps moving forward was at the forefront of the agenda.

Decker wanted to press on. Pack up and hike back to the cars. Get to the first available place with reliable Wi-Fi and upload the evidence. Raffi preached from the other side of the congregation. A setting sun and fatigue, both mental and physical, caused him to rally for one last night in the tent.

"The odds of one of us taking a nasty fall in the dark, lugging all this shit? Then who's carrying the cripple, while the other suffocates under the weight of our gear? Let's pack everything but the sleeping gear and be ready to head out at dawn."

Rockfish didn't favor one course of action over the other. He rode the high of success. Doing old-fashioned PI work. Choosing to get hands on rather than relying on a computer to do the work. How long had it been since he had physically trailed a suspect, found the secret location, and made it out undetected? *Too damn long.*

Not that Raffi's argument was more interesting. It was more like neither Rockfish nor Decker had the energy to debate him with a better option.

"Excellent," Raffi said. "Let's get this fire going again. Steve, you got that flask? 'Cause I know you do."

Rockfish reached into the tent and pulled out his small bag. There wasn't much left in the flask, but enough for all three men to have a celebratory swig and say a few words of congratulations. Decker and Rockfish kept it short, but there was no denying Raffi when handed the mic.

"Thanks, you guys. And I mean that sincerely. I tend to go half-cocked off the rails and throughout this entire ordeal, you've kept me on the straight and narrow. I owe you more than I can ever repay. To see these clowns go before the judge to be sentenced? I'll never be able to make that up to you. But I'm going to try my damnedest. Cheers!"

CHAPTER FIFTEEN

Sunlight streamed through the thin fabric of the tent, and Rockfish's eyes shot open. He turned onto his side and two realizations immediately hit. One, his alarm hadn't gone off as set and two, his little spoon had already risen and shined. Across from him, Decker continued to snore nary a care.

At least Raffi had the common sense to get up and start preparing for the march out. Now where the fuck did I put my phone? Two draws from the flask ain't near enough to cause me to lose my shit. Probably on the chair by the fire, dumbass.

"Hey Dan, get up. Seems we've overslept. Who knew six hours of hiking and major altitude differences would have such an effect on our old ass bones. Raffi's getting ready to go without us."

Decker grumbled a few words Rockfish didn't make out but sat up. His hands reached into his sleeping bag, under his pillow, and into the back corner of the tent. They had started out calmly but shifted to frantic in no time. His arm shot out and under the blanket Raffi had slept under.

No. No. No. Rockfish's eyes met Decker's, and both knew exactly what the other was thinking. Both men hustled out of the tent and scanned the landscape. Raffi's backpack wasn't inside or out.

Without saying a word, Rockfish searched behind the tent, and Decker moved toward the trail that led down.

Maybe he's taking a dump in the bushes? Come on buddy, don't regress to being that guy. I had such high hopes for you this time.

Both met back at the ashes of last night's campfire and shook their heads.

"Maybe he got restless and headed down to wherever he parked. You know, left a note on our windshield."

Decker rolled his eyes. And then again. "Steve, I know you like the guy, but with our phones? Come the fuck on!"

Rockfish knew Decker was right. A quick check of his own bag confirmed the night vision binoculars were also among the missing. *My stuff and his bag o' guns. None of which were stolen from camp by a curious bear or den of foxes. Motherfucker. Tiger. Stripes. Never changes.*

"That confirms it. He's gone rogue. Out for Justice or pick another bad Steven Seagal movie title." Rockfish kicked at the ground and cursed under his breath. "I'm sorry, Dan. I thought I submitted the cancellation orders for Raffi's Revenge Tour. Swore he had signed 'em with a nod and a handshake. But in actuality, all we did was drive him to the venue and give him an all access lanyard." Rockfish inhaled deeply and exhaled his embarrassment.

"He knows exactly where he's going thanks to us being so damn accepting when he showed up," Dan said. Rockfish saw the man's face flush with half-a-dozen shades of crimson. "He left us with no freakin' way of alerting a soul."

"Yeah, it wasn't by accident. No calls to the cavalry or for the artillery strike."

Decker pursed his lips and tilted his head. Rockfish knew the man was close to the edge and stepped back. He didn't need to make the situation worse. They needed to rely on each other to resolve whatever the hell this was.

Neither man spoke. Each deep in their own thoughts. Ideas for moving forward or straight up torturing the man who seemed to be the source of their problems on almost every occasion. Both subjects overlapped. After a few minutes, a frown and head shake met a slow shoulder shrug.

Rockfish double-checked the daylight binoculars remained in his sling bag. His hand reached in and pulled them out. He let out a small sigh of relief before tossing them back in, along with a handful of energy bars and two bottles of water.

"We're going to need to get moving." Decker's straightforwardness with a rescue mission caught Rockfish by surprise.

"Agreed. No telling what they've done with him or plan to." They both were sure Raffi's plan hadn't gone off without a hitch.

"You don't think they'd actually kill him, do you?" Dan said. He moved towards his own overnight bag and grabbed his gun and two magazines. "Because they're not going to."

This time, it was Rockfish's turn to tilt his head in confusion while he grabbed his own extraction supplies.

"Steve, they can't hide in there forever. The Feds won't stop searching. It's only a matter of time before one of them comes out and tries to blend back into society. Somewhere. Somehow."

"I think the camo BLM shirts would be a dead giveaway. You know, 'A' for effort, type of deal."

"Dude. I'm serious. Raffi's their ticket to safe passage. I mean, he's not, but that's how the cornered rat thinks. Always have, always will. Trust me, you learn a few things about the criminal mind after way too many years on the job."

"Sweet, but we need to get moving. Again."

"Can you retrace your steps from yesterday a second time? Those dropped pins aren't here to help anymore."

"Yeah, you ain't the only one with work experience. But I gotta say, I wouldn't mind rappelling down this time."

* * * * * * * * * *

The hike down the mountain took half the time as the previous day, as both men threw caution to the wind and rolled ankles all the way down.

"Flat from here out," Decker said. He had stopped and bent at the waist to catch his breath.

"But not without unexpected curves ahead. Or did you miss the warning sign a half-mile back?"

Decker laughed aloud, and Rockfish followed. A moment of levity was long overdue and almost a necessity before the men continued on. Both were drenched in sweat before the thermometer crested seventy.

They stopped next at the boma to down energy bars and take a much-needed rest break. The seclusion made the location a perfect for refueling and respite. The rustle of small animals across the forest floor filled the air. *My apologies guys. Squirrels, rabbits and who knows what, we'll be out of your way shortly.*

"After that hike, we can't slide into that vagina out of breath. Not sure about you, buddy, but I need a refresh on the stamina bar, and I've left all my generic Cialis back in the office."

"Always with the jokes, Steve. And I appreciate it in times like this. I may not seem or look it, but I do."

Each man made a fist, and they bumped before getting back to their feet.

Rockfish crouched and tried to replicate his movement from the previous afternoon. He missed the first butt, but the yellow Bic lighter was the breadcrumb that kept on giving. He turned back to Decker and mouthed *close*. Decker said nothing in return. Instead, his eyes widened, and he pointed violently with his index finger to Rockfish's right. Rockfish followed the straight line from Decker's fingertip to the body that lie face down at two o'clock.

How the fuck did I practically walk up on that and miss it? 'Cause you were checking for bodies walking towards you, not taking dirt nap, dummy.

The size of the body told Rockfish the napper had to be Scotty or another Great Value Boy. *Who knows exactly how many are down in the hole?* Decker slowly approached and dropped to one knee.

After a second, he held up two fingers and pointed to the back of his own head.

When? How? Rockfish mouthed in return.

Decker shrugged his shoulders at the first question and mouthed the word *silencer* for the second.

Rockfish wanted to smack himself upside the head for not remembering the big dish towel reveal from the night Raffi crashed camp. *Had he gotten the jump on Scotty or had there been a tussle before shots fired? Raffi, the Ninja. One part Call of Duty, one part Assassins Creed. Never thought he had it in him.*

Rockfish no longer questioned his friend's commitment to the bit. Honestly, he had hoped to find Raffi, somewhere along the way, sitting deep in second thoughts. Contemplating all his rash decisions up until this time. At that point, Rockfish would have been more than happy to drape an arm across Raffi's shoulder and help him forgive and forget. But today would not end like that. He was sure of it and Scotty, if he could talk, would confirm.

The image of his arm around Raffi hadn't left his mind when Decker's hand on his shoulder brought Rockfish back to the present. They needed to keep moving. There would be plenty of time to reminisce and second guess every decision when they were all home safe. Beer in hand. Game on the tube.

"Gimme a sec, need to get my bearings." Rockfish said. He pulled out the binoculars and scanned everywhere but the direction they had come from.

Now which way to the two Douglas Firs? That was the question atop Rockfish's mind for the next fifteen minutes as he and Decker roamed in what each thought were endless circles. Every so often, Rockfish would pull out the binoculars, glance around and make an educated guess in which direction to proceed. Nothing seemed familiar. No discarded trash or dead bodies let them know they were on the right path. But Scotty let them know, from time to time, no progress was being made.

On one such trek, Decker reached out and Rockfish came to an abrupt stop. He turned around, and the men leaned in toward each other.

"I'm not sure we're getting any closer. Progress has been scarce since we left Scotty back there."

"Which time?"

"Anything familiar?" Rockfish barely heard Decker's words.

"All looks the same. But a couple of big ass Douglas Firs would sure help shine a light on the right way."

Decker stepped back and gave the surroundings an intense three-hundred-and-sixty-degree review. He spun a second time but stopped short and pointed at eleven o'clock.

Bingo! For Christ's sake, how many times have we walked right past 'em? Also, are they THE firs? Only one way...

Rockfish raised his hand and Decker met his high five and stopped short by half an inch. Silence was on their side and hence the element of surprise. Both men agreed. They needed to keep it that way.

With the trees in sight, the men split up and approached from opposite sides. Rockfish wondered if another sentry lingered. One missed by Raffi, or placed back outside the entrance after Raffi was quickly overwhelmed. The men moved closer. Their heads moved from side-to-side and up and around, hoping to spot anyone.

Rockfish dipped under the large fir's lower branches and stepped into the tiny, yet familiar, clearing. Decker was already there, standing to the left of the opening. His back was against the rock. Rockfish crossed in front of the opening and moved to Dan's right.

"Fuck, anyone could've seen you," Dan said. His lips were practically against Rockfish's ear.

"Sorry. I wasn't thinking."

"Start."

The men waited and Rockfish even longer for Decker's signal. The roles had reversed now that they had arrived on site. Rockfish

314 THE BALLAD OF THE GREAT VALUE BOYS

had no problem giving up the lead. After all, breaching and hostage rescue were Decker's forte. *Times like this, I don't mind being in a support role. Follow his lead, get Raffi out, if he's even in there, and get the fuck home. In one piece.* Rockfish took in the mine's entrance and let out a soft chuckle.

"Raffi's gotta be in there. Deep in the back."

Decker turned toward Rockfish with a concerned look of what was coming next. He squinted.

"Well, with us two headed in the front..."

"And?" The aggravation in Decker's face became clear, but Rockfish trudged on, committed to the bit.

"Two in the pink and one in the stink."

Decker's eyes closed for a couple of seconds and then he leaned in. "I know what I said before about appreciating the levity, but seriously cut the shit."

Rockfish gave a brief nod and switched his internal control knob to *All Business.*

"Leave the bag. It won't be of any use to us from this point forward," Decker said. "In a couple of minutes, we're gonna need all the free hands we can get."

Rockfish did as instructed and made a mental note to pick it up on the way out. Or order Raffi to do it. His hand then pulled the handgun from the small of his back. He waited on edge, for Decker's go sign.

"Just follow me, keep your eyes on the right side, and I'll manage the left. It's going to get dark as shit as soon as the sunlight can't reach any further. Hopefully, wherever they are, and Raffi is, is lit."

Rockfish nodded and swallowed hard.

"Stay on my back. Once we're inside, full stop until our eyes adjust. Unless we encounter hostiles."

Rockfish held up his fist, and Decker awkwardly raised his own.

"And, Steve, be careful where you aim. If it comes to lethal force. Ricochets are going to be a motherfucker in that confined space."

The next couple of minutes felt like hours. *I don't know what he's waiting for. It's not like we can wait out here for all of them to exit one by one and handle this--*

Before Rockfish finished his thought, Decker stepped out, turned sideways, and slipped between the stone labia majora.

* * * * * * * * * *

Rockfish didn't make it two full steps into the main shaft before he slammed into Decker's back. He glanced over Decker's left shoulder and then to his assigned right flank. The passage was narrow, only six feet from where they stood. With what little light made it through the opening, Rockfish did not know if the birth canal grew wider the deeper they would go. He only hoped. *Think big baby coming through. The less claustrophobic, the better.* He stepped to the side and reached out to the wall. The surface was rough. Jagged stone stuck out at different angles and Rockfish's eyes followed the wall up to where it met the ceiling. He noticed a lack of timber support on the sides and above. *I've seen this movie, too. There's a case of dynamite hidden somewhere to bring the whole shebang down.*

Decker took a step forward, and Rockfish followed. Rockfish held his gun in his left hand and kept his eyes peeled to the right for any openings or crevices where a Great Value Boy could hide. He tried his best to be attentive, but with each step, the natural light faded. Rockfish cursed himself the second time he reached for his phone. He thought the backlit screen could help guide their journey undetected. *Fucking Raffi. I'm not sure why he made it so hard for us to come get him. Maybe that was it, dummy. He's not expecting anyone to come, let alone him walking out under his own power. He ain't ever gotten over the deal the Great Value Boys played him for. Solo Suicide Squad?* Rockfish shook his head. Raffi had put on one hell of a cooperative show the past couple of days. *It was his plan all along.*

He had the tactical flashlight in the side pocket of his pants. But that was the same as blaring *As the Saints Go Marching In* on a Bluetooth speaker. *Might as well shout out and announce, ready or not, here we come.*

Decker slowed his pace to a near stop and Rockfish followed suit. The floor angled downward, and each man stepped to their respective side. With arms stretched, they touched shoulders and couldn't get separated, while their opposite arms felt their way forward against the wall. This lasted only ten yards, when Rockfish tugged on Decker's sleeve. Forward progress stopped. He leaned in.

"It's going to take us forever to get wherever we're headed."

"The darkness also means they can't see us," Decker said. Rockfish couldn't read his face, and it also meant Decker didn't see him grimace. "We need to keep moving forward. No matter how slow. Soon, we'll come across light. It's not like they're sitting down in the dark."

"If they're still here."

"You gotta trust me, Steve."

Rockfish felt Decker move forward again. The sideways conga line lasted another ten feet before Rockfish caught his foot on something and fell forward. He landed hard on his knees. His arms, out front, prevented a face plant into who knew what. He said a brief prayer that the gun didn't go off and got back to his knees. Rockfish imagined Decker standing above him, an outstretched arm offering help. He stood up on his own, then reached out and felt for Decker.

"Dan, we've got to use this tactical light. One of us is going to split our heads open before long. That ain't gonna do the other or Raffi any good."

He waited, but Decker said nothing. Rockfish pondered the matter.

"I can cover most of the beam with my palm," Rockfish said. "It won't be much, maybe a sliver, but better than playing Helen Keller the rest of the way."

Silence. Rockfish pictured Decker giving him the cut sign. Then two quick tugs followed on his sleeve. *Doesn't matter how you meant it buddy, I'm taking it as a yes.* Rockfish re-holstered the gun in the small of his back and pulled out the small flashlight. He covered the head with the palm of his right hand before pushing the power button with his left thumb. To their dilated eyes, the small amount of light was the equivalent of a solar flare. He made out Decker's face and the cautious nod of approval. In order to block their exposure, Rockfish stepped behind Decker, and they proceeded forward, single file, down the incline.

Once the ground leveled out again, Rockfish made out an almost ninety-degree turn to the left. They approached the turn with caution. Decker raised a fist, and the line came to a stop. He peeked around the corner and raised his hand again. This time, his thumb raised. Rockfish moved around Decker to get a look for himself. The passage ahead was straight, but there was light at the end of the proverbial tunnel. Soft voices too, if his ears or the cavern's echoes weren't playing tricks. Rockfish killed the light, and his handgun replaced it. He glanced up and had a brief conversation with a man he doubted was listening. *Let him be back there and in one piece, will ya?*

They continued forward, each hugging their respective walls. The shaft widened, the light grew, and the sounds increased with each step. Rockfish didn't make out a word of what they said. But a party was about to be crashed. They had separated enough, so Decker's face was no longer visible, but at the moment, Rockfish was more concerned with who might spot them. He hugged his side of the passageway harder, trying to blend in with the stone as much as possible.

Less than three minutes later, each man stood on opposite sides of what appeared to be a crude stone doorway. On the other side?

A large cavern. Wilbur's Vault. The space was enormous and from his angle, Rockfish couldn't see the back wall or ceiling. The voices were distinguishable now, four in total, each man wearing a headlamp, with most of the light coming from a few Coleman lanterns. A hiss from each took Rockfish back momentarily to camping trips with Mack, which was supposed to take his mind off the death of his mother.

A card table, a handful of chairs and rectangle objects, coolers, Rockfish assumed, took up the rest of the space. Each headlamp illuminated a recognizable face. Earnhardt Jr., Amos - the scarecrow from the Steel Museum, Fat Trevor and one other. *Sobotka. That fucking dirty cop. I know you can't hear me, Dan, but he's mine.*

The observation minutes ticked away as he waited for Decker to lead the charge. *What's he waiting for? Step in, disarm, and maybe pop a kneecap or two, in order to show we mean business.* Rockfish worried about the odds. The size of Earnhardt Jr. and Trevor made them equal to two people apiece. Six on two by his count. He didn't like the odds, even if Amos seemed like a stiff wind would blow him over. Equally eating at his stomach was what he didn't see. No sign of Raffi. He'd have to deal with this small platoon of Great Value Boys before continuing on with the search. If they had anything, it was the element of surprise. *Fuck 'em, and Mr. Murphy. Leeeeeeeeroy Jenkins!*

Rockfish stepped through the opening and a surprised Decker had no other option but to follow.

"Hands up, Fuckwads! Drop your shit."

Four headlamps turned simultaneously. The surprise had worked and none of the Great Value Boys had time to reach for their equalizers. Mouths dropped and so did weapons. Decker moved quickly and piled the surrendered firepower pile outside the Vault's opening.

"Raffi!" Rockfish called out, to no answer.

"I told you Colonel. That fucking Pérez said his friends would come," Amos said. The man angrily spit on the ground. "Someone should have been outside waiting."

"Shut the fuck up, Amos. They're here. So what? Neither one got the balls to shoot. Ricochets and a cave-in are the worst-case scenarios running through their brains. Look at 'em. Scared shitless."

"Then why did we drop ours?"

"Shut the fuck up, Amos," Sobotka said.

Rockfish noticed Decker had moved to his left. All four of the Great Value Boys had slowly spread out, testing their leader's theory while chatting aloud amongst themselves. A flanking maneuver was well underway and without a word, Rockfish and Decker took a few steps away from each other to expand their perimeter. If they allowed themselves to be surrounded, their weapons would be their only savior.

Rockfish felt the sweat on his trigger finger. The thought of taking all four men out with one magazine streamed through his brain, but he held steadfast with Decker's instructions.

"Raffi?" Rockfish tried again, hoping his friend would magically unbound, and come up from behind the approaching mini-army and lend a hand or two.

"Your friend can't come to the phone right now," Sobotka said. The cop turned his head, and the headlamp illuminated a body slumped against the far back wall. Rockfish didn't spot any movement.

"He better be alive or you'll all be joining Scotty out there at the great Ruby Ridge in the sky," Rockfish said.

"Oh, he's all tuckered out, that's all. Chloroform will do that to a man," Earnhardt Jr. said. "He's our ticket out of here and now, so are you." He laughed and held his grin.

Sobotka had continued forward during the exchange, and Rockfish was surprised to see how close the man had actually gotten while he was fraught with concern for Raffi. Anger flooded in, overtaking concern, and Rockfish gripped the pistol tighter. He stepped forward, raised his left arm and met Sobotka halfway. The pistol crashed down on the side of the man's head and the cop collapsed to the ground.

Rockfish didn't waste a second. He pounced on the man's chest, reigning down blows.

"Steve!" Decker said. Instincts kicked in and Decker moved back and to the side. But Earnhardt Jr. and Trevor used the opportunity to pick up the pace. Rockfish's flailing gun hand had caught Decker's attention for a split second too long.

Rockfish alternated wild overhand rights with pistol whips until a weight hit his back and grabbed his left arm. He stood up and Amos held on for dear life. Rockfish ran backwards and smashed Amos into the nearest wall. The jagged rock caught the old man square in his spine and he crumbled to the ground in a heap.

Rockfish turned his attention back to his partner. The large frames of the two Great Value Boys eclipsed his view. "DAN!"

"Stay back, I said!" But Decker's warning had no effect on the men. They had closed the gap and their headlamps blinded him. A shot rang out. The echo and a man's scream reached Rockfish's ears at the same time.

He got one! Another shot ran out and ricocheted off the wall. Rockfish watched in horror as Decker disappeared under the weight of one of the men. *A scene straight out of a zombie movie.* But with Dan's previously stated Rules of Engagement broken, Rockfish raised his weapon. *I got this.*

He closed one eye and aimed. Sudden and immense pain flashed across his skull from the back and Rockfish dropped to his knees. The gun fell from his grasp and landed on the floor to his left. An extinguished Coleman lantern then landed to the right. Amos then limped on in Decker's direction past a prone Rockfish. Rockfish's right hand went straight to the back of his head while the other searched frantically for his weapon.

Rockfish frantically felt for the gun but came up empty. Instead, he stumbled to his feet, solely on adrenaline. The room spun and his head thumped. He reached for the only thing he saw. The thin steel handle to the lantern. It felt good in his hand. Two steps later, he returned the favor with all of his might to an unsuspecting Amos. The man collapsed for a second time. Rockfish knew with the force he had exerted; Amos wouldn't be getting up.

He stepped around Amos and squinted. He made out Trevor standing above a prone body, swinging something that resembled a stick down on presumably Decker's lower half. Screams came from both Decker and Earnhardt Jr. who was off to the side. Earnhardt Jr. held his own leg. *Decker's first shot? No time to debate.*

Rockfish stumbled forward, head throbbing and vision blurred. He honed in on Decker's cries. He made it three steps before a blast slammed into him from the front. Rockfish skipped dropping to his knees and was blown backwards. His head bounced off the rocky ground and his eyes watered.

No getting up from this one kid. Here comes the darkness. Welcome, my old friend.

* * * * * * * * *

Rockfish's chest lurched and filled with stale air. Pain raced from his head to his feet. He exhaled and gulped in air a second time. He had regained consciousness right where he had left off, gasping for air. His eyes remained shut. He remembered the feeling of the sting and tears. But the consistent throbbing, emanating from the back of his head, took the cake. He mentally tried to stuff the gray matter back in, recalling the shock wave that had knocked him down. Rockfish willed his left arm to move, to no avail. He tried the right. Nothing.

What the fuck? Paralyzed wasn't one option I agreed to in order to save your sorry ass, Raffi.

Rockfish struggled to keep his head above the proverbial water. His other senses slowly came around. Noise. Chatter, but not loud, filled his ears. He tried to turn his head toward where the sound emanated. No luck. He felt the panic beginning to set in. The worry and impending doom dropped anchor as soon as he realized his legs also refused to obey an order.

"Steve, stop struggling. You're going to be all right."

The voice. Familiar, but not possible. I'm dreaming. Or worse. Rockfish concentrated all he had on opening his eyes. He felt the dirt and gunk coating the lids and lashes. Some fell into the whites and pupil. He already knew the answer as to attempting to rub them clean.

Two giant heads floated above. Lips moved, and he tried to concentrate on the words. Between the pain in his head and the noise making it only worse, he wanted to close his eyes and go back to sleep. But the faces were familiar.

"Jawnie? Raffi? Is... this... heaven?" The pain only increased as he forced his jaw to move.

"If it is, the church sure relaxed the rules for us, Steve. And especially for this one," Raffi said, nudging Jawnie with an elbow.

Jawnie forced a smile and laughed. Rockfish tried to understand what was so funny. He squinted again, trying hard to bring the heads into focus, but the throbbing from behind his eyes and ears didn't allow it. Resigned, he closed his crusted eyelids.

".... water," was all he managed.

"No can do, Steve. The medics said nothing until they can get you out of this hole and stabilized."

"Raffi's right," Jawnie said. "Try to stay as still as possible. They've got you strapped to a spine board. You need to stay immobile. They have to carry you out then to a hospital. It's all precautionary. An air flight is coming for you and Dan."

"... we're alive? Not... dreaming?"

"No, Steve, I'm here," Jawnie said. "Try not to talk. We've only got a few minutes before the men who carried Dan come back for you. I'll fill you in the best I can."

"... Dan?"

"He's going to be okay."

"Eventually."

"Knock if off, Raffi."

Despite his eyes closed and feeling as if he was on a life raft in the middle of an ocean storm, Rockfish imagined the anger on Jawnie's face.

"The FBI's Hostage Rescue Team got here in time. They tossed in a couple of flash bangs. The field commander explained it was the only way, with the enclosed space, they could guarantee entry while keeping the element of surprise. Not to mention increase the odds for minimal casualties. They flooded the chamber with operators and these tough revolutionaries gave up without a fight. I know, not shocked. Once they secured the area and a few of us civilians were permitted down. You should have seen it. I watched the body cam footage from one of their laptops. Incredible."

"... but... Dan?"

"They busted his leg up pretty good," Jawnie said. "Multiple fractures and major bleeding. Trevor went to town on him with a stainless-steel expandable baton. The entry team took him out quickly with a beanbag bazooka thingamabob right off the bat."

"Bam, bam, bam, bam. All subdued, although Amos was already out and Earnhardt Jr was crying like a bitch in the corner," Raffi said. "Appears Dan nailed him before Trevor got the upper hand. And the FBI did it all without firing a lethal shot. They really want all four pieces of shit to stand trial. No martyrdom for you!"

Rockfish tried to smile at Raffi's nod to the Soup Nazi. A few days later, he hoped to have the energy to ask if Jawnie had gotten the reference.

"I know you're going to be shocked at this," Jawnie said. "But Raffi is in the best shape of the three of you. The flash bangs woke him from his chloroform nap."

Rockfish wanted to shake his head in disbelief, but the pain was too much, even with it strapped down.

"Can you believe it, buddy? I'm walking out of here with only a few bumps and bruises." Raffi leaned in close as the other side of the chamber drew Jawnie's attention away. "I fucking owe you. This time, it's for real. You get that head screwed back on and we'll talk. Love you, bud."

"... how?"

"Raffi came around asking for you. I played dumb, like you said. But then he went AWOL," Jawnie said. She kept one eye on the men walking across the cavern. She had little time. "By the time I figured out he was probably headed to you, I tried to reach out, but your phone was off. Panic set in, but it was Lynn who remembered my love of inventory control." Jawnie took in a deep breath and squeezed Rockfish's bicep. He felt the calming grip and swore his heart slowed its beat.

"The switch to MirageTrax came in the nick of time. Those trackers are so popular now, devices are being manufactured with their own little storage space for them. Your fancy new recording binoculars? Lynn inventoried and tagged 'em before you tossed them in your bag. Standard procedure. Once I honed in on that signal, and a big thanks for eventually leaving the bag outside the entrance, I called Agent Thomas. She took care of the rest. I was frantic or convincing. Take your pick."

"Sorry to break up the reunion, but we've got to get him topside. His ride is fifteen minutes out." Two men in full SWAT gear stood a few feet to the side, waiting.

Jawnie nodded, and each stepped to opposite ends of the spine board. She bent closer, wiped away a tear, and gave Rockfish a light hug as the men picked him up.

"Get to the choppa!"

"... that was... supposed to be... my line

EPILOGUE

Rockfish pulled Lana into the LifeCare Center of Halethorpe's visitor parking lot. Jawnie rode shotgun and the world's largest Edible Arrangements belted into the back seat. When the engine died, he threw open the door and stepped out. A second step caught the curb and Rockfish stumbled forward.

"Fucking cocksucker!" He caught his balance a split-second before tipping over and slamming his head on the cement walkway. *Maybe then I could add to the never-ending concussion symptoms since I'm here. Might as well toss in my eardrums, sprained collarbone, and sciatica while I'm at it.*

"Careful, Steve," Jawnie said as she struggled to see around the large basket of chocolate-covered fruit. "Your doctor said the balance issues won't go away soon. There's a reason he's prescribed physical therapy. Twice. I'd like for you to actually make one of those appointments."

"I'm fine," Rockfish said and picked up his pace.

Thirty days had passed since the FBI Pittsburgh's Hostage Rescue Team flooded the abandoned mine with two teams of operators and saved the day. An anniversary Rockfish hated to be reminded of. Each news article or special edition of 20/20 re-opened the shame flood gates. His ongoing balance problems only added to the humiliation he could not get a handle on and move past.

Jawnie caught up before he reached the glass door.

"I told you I'd carry that for you."

"I got it. I need to keep shifting it in my arms to see where I'm going. But if you can hold the door, that would be great."

"Already on it," Rockfish said. He pulled and held the door for Jawnie. Three other visitors followed her through the entrance. *Not a thank you from the bunch. People.* Rockfish contemplated saying something but swallowed the insult and searched for his partner. He found her on the other side of the foyer. She pushed the elevator call button with her elbow.

"He's on three, right?" Rockfish wasn't exactly sure where Dan's room was.

"Was. They moved him off the medical floor once the staph infection got under control. He's on two, rehab only."

The elevator door chimed, and they stepped inside. Rockfish pushed two and waited for the door to close.

"Isn't this the same dump Cheyenne was in?"

She shushed him with her elevator button pushing elbow. "Yes, and it's not a dump. There are better, more costly options. But this is where Dan's at. Don't judge."

"You'd think a police pension would have better insurance. Serve and protect. I guess it's only while you're on the job."

"His days here are numbered and you better believe he's counting down. Rosie said he's got it down to the hour. Then it's on to a home plan where a physical therapist would come to the house and work him out."

"That alone should cheer his ornery ass up."

Rockfish couldn't see Jawnie's face from the chocolate-covered strawberries and pineapple. He assumed she had agreed. They walked down the long quiet hall, past the nurses' station and around the corner to a long stretch of patient rooms.

"Do we knock?" Rockfish said. "I mean, if this was a proper hospital, I would."

Jawnie ignored the question and used her multipurpose elbow. The partners heard a noise on the other side of the door but didn't make it out. Rockfish didn't wait and pushed open the wide, heavy door. He held it open for Jawnie and followed her into the room. She put the arrangement down on the small table between the two visitor chairs and quickly moved to Decker's side, where she applied a hug and kiss on the forehead.

"Gang's all here, huh?"

"Only the ones that matter, Dan," Rockfish said. He moved around the end of the bed, to the opposite side. "Mind if I open the curtains a bit? Dark as shit in here."

"It's the way I like it," Decker said, and Rockfish did as instructed.

His face appears better, but the mood hasn't changed since the last time I was here. I'd have sworn Jawnie said he had a better outlook over the past week? We've all got our problems from that day. Put this in perspective. I guess I should thank my lucky stars. At least I'm sleeping in my own bed. Might fall out from time to time, but home is home.

"You're looking good today, Dan," Jawnie said.

"Yeah, nice to also see they've cut down on the number of beeping machines and monitors here. You'll be home watching the O's in no time. I can't believe this place doesn't have MASN on the channel list. They're only a game and a half behind the Sox for the division lead."

"Any word on a trial date yet?" Decker said. He didn't need or want any of Rockfish's small talk. "I want a seat in that gallery for my first stop when I finally get discharged."

Jawnie caught Decker up on the current legal situation of all four surviving Great Value Boys. Unable to secure proper representation, all four remained in Federal holding cells. Two lawyers, known to represent many white nationalists in the days following January 6th, had unexpectedly dropped out. Rumor had it Luke Martindale, creator of the MAGA My Snuggy empire, was sending two of his best men.

"Federal trials take forever to get on the docket and once they do, the motions to delay begin. Just ask this one over here," Rockfish said and pointed to Jawnie.

"Well, whenever it gets there, the case should be a slam dunk for the United States Attorney's Office," Decker said. He turned his eyes from his visitors to the ceiling above. "Glad somebody's gonna close the book on these short bus Proud Boys."

"The two of you are going to drive me to drink," Jawnie said with a large exhale. "If it weren't for your effort, the march in Harrisburg could have turned into one of the greatest tragedies since the Boston Marathon bombing. I'm not the only one with that belief. That domino falls, and a lot of bad follows." She reached out for Decker's arm, and he surprised her by not jerking it away.

"Shit, Dan. Agent Thomas mentioned that you and I might be in line for an award from the Director of Homeland Security. You'll need to press a suit and I'll have to buy one."

"Nice to know, Steve," Decker said and smiled. He had returned his eyes from the ceiling and both visitors took note. "Maybe they'll want to hire an old cripple. Rosie says the pile of medical bills on the dining room table is higher than the mountain of empties in your recycle bin."

Rockfish bit his bottom lip and glanced across the bed at his partner. It was the moment they had planned and waited on for the perfect time. I *couldn't have set it up any better if I had tried.* Rockfish took a deep breath before springing the surprise, but that second cost him.

"Or you can come work alongside us," Jawnie said, taking the wind out of Rockfish's sails. He whipped his head in her direction, and she smiled. "Not for. With."

"We're thinking of expanding," Rockfish said. "The candidate list was long. Tons of men with storied pasts out there desperate to solve cases for us and get a shot at reality star television. But fame and glory are second. Not our primary mission. The phone hasn't stopped ringing. Surprising, with the latest job report and all, but you aced the operational interview. Of course, there is paperwork we'll need filled out in triplicate and a drug test..."

"I thought your buddy that abandoned us was next in line. Or so he kept saying."

"Raffi's got his own issues," Rockfish said. "The whole Scotty thing ain't going away soon. His claims of self-defense, and, granted, there isn't a contradicting story to be told, probably won't get him off scot-free."

"The wounds to the back of the head are going to be hard for his lawyer to overcome," Jawnie added. "But I spoke with Susan Giacchino. She's watching the proceedings with interest. Under the circumstances, she thinks he stands a chance of house arrest with lengthy probation to follow."

"I mean, he has the Government stepping up saying they're not keen on prosecuting the case," Rockfish said.

"I've never seen a dude step in so much shit and constantly come out smelling like a rose," Decker said. The disgust was obvious to all in the room.

"But enough about the black sheep. Dan, you've got a very particular set of skills and we've already got too much flying by the seat of our pants as it is. Of course, you'll have to work out of the bullpen area until we can find a way out of our lease and find more accommodating office space. The good news is Jawnie's got her finger on the buy now button for a new marquee out front."

"Rockfish, McGee & Decker?"

"It doesn't roll off the tongue, but yeah. We'll come up with a catchy ad campaign to announce the re-branding and try to get the firm back to a full caseload of *paying* clients."

"I'm in," Decker said. The enthusiasm in his voice wasn't missed by the other two. "We're like The Three Musketeers."

"More like the Three Stooges," Rockfish said. "But we get shit done."

ACKNOWLEDGEMENTS

Each time I am lucky enough to have a book published, I must start by thanking my awesome and extremely patient wife, Nicolita. From reading printed out scenes and chapters to being handed a three hundred-page plus, three-ring binder, she was there to tell me what worked, what didn't, and when my inside jokes or witty dialogue fell flat.

My editor Ben Eads, who for the fourth straight time showed me how to better my craft and had me realize how good a story this actually was.

Thanks also to my solid critic group - Tim Paul, Jason Little, Susan Niner, and Terry Niner. Your keen eye and input catches all of my screw-ups. Your attention to detail is greatly appreciated. Wouldn't be here without ya!

To my Twitch viewers, followers and even subscribers that tune in each morning to watch paint dry – You keep me motivated to bang these keys and create storylines and characters. You've helped me go from extreme introvert to Twitch streamer. And nothing beats real time, online brainstorming feedback.

To those early readers - Haris Orkin, Patti Liszkay, Rebecca Warner, Val Conrad and TG Wolff – Thank you for your kind words regarding this rollercoaster of a novel.

Lastly, I am grateful to Reagan Rothe and Black Rose Writing team support in allowing me to continue this wild ride.

ABOUT THE AUTHOR

Ken Harris retired from the FBI, after thirty-two years, as a cybersecurity executive. With over three decades writing intelligence products for senior Government officials, Ken provides unique perspectives on the conventional fast-paced crime thriller. He is the author of the "From the Case Files of Steve Rockfish" series. He spends days with his wife Nicolita, and two Labradors, Shady and Chalupa Batman. Evenings are spent playing Walkabout Mini Golf and cheering on Philadelphia sports. Ken firmly believes Pink Floyd, Irish whiskey and a Montecristo cigar are the only muses necessary. He is a native of New Jersey and currently resides in Virginia's Northern Neck.

BOOKS BY
KEN HARRIS

FROM THE CASE FILES OF STEVE ROCKFISH SERIES:

THE PINE BARRENS STRATAGEM

SEE YOU NEXT TUESDAY

A BAD BOUT OF THE YIPS

NOTE FROM KEN HARRIS

Word-of-mouth is crucial for any author to succeed. If you enjoyed *The Ballad of the Great Value Boys*, please leave a review online—anywhere you are able. Even if it's just a sentence or two. It would make all the difference and would be very much appreciated.

Thanks!
Ken Harris

We hope you enjoyed reading this title from:

Subscribe to our mailing list – *The Rosevine* – and receive **FREE** books, daily deals, and stay current with news about upcoming releases and our hottest authors.
Scan the QR code below to sign up.

Already a subscriber? Please accept a sincere thank you for being a fan of Black Rose Writing authors.

View other Black Rose Writing titles at
www.blackrosewriting.com/books and use promo code
PRINT to receive a **20% discount** when purchasing.